NOT JUST A JOB

About the Author

Michael Long is a former Navy quartermaster. He has an English degree from California State University, Long Beach.

Not Just a Job is his first novel.

NOT JUST A JOB

Michael Long

FALLING MARBLES PRESS
Marble Falls, Texas
www.fallingmarbles.com

"Cascading Worth, One Work at a Time"

Officer (O) and Enlisted (E) Navy Ranks

O-9: Admiral	E-9: Master Chief Petty Officer
O-8: Vice Admiral	E-8: Senior Chief Petty Officer
O-7: Rear Admiral	E-7: Chief Petty Officer
O-6: Captain	E-6: Petty Officer First Class
O-5: Commander	E-5: Petty Officer Second Class
O-4: Lieutenant Commander	E-4: Petty Officer Third Class
O-3: Lieutenant	E-3: Seaman
O-2: Lieutenant Junior Grade	E-2: Seaman Apprentice
O-1: Ensign	E-1: Seaman Recruit

Partial List of Navy Rates (Job Descriptions)

Boatswain's Mate (pronounced bosun's mate): in charge of small boats, cargo rigging, mooring lines, anchors, marlinspike seamanship

Boiler Technician: maintains and repairs boilers, pipefitting

Commisaryman: prepares food; operates galley

Electrician's Mate: repairs electrical generators, motors, lighting, telephone circuits

Electronics Technician: installs and repairs electronic equipment

Gunner's Mate: operates and maintains ship's guns

Hospital Corpsman: provides first aid, healthcare, minor surgery

Hull Technician: plumbing, welding, metal fabrication, damage control

Machinist's Mate: operates and maintains engines, compressors, pumps

Master-At-Arms: enforces regulations; maintains order

Operations Specialist: operates and maintains radar

Quartermaster: assists with navigation duties; steers the ship

Radioman: transmits and receives radio messages

Signalman: performs visual communications with blinkers, flags, and semaphore

Storekeeper: procures and maintains supply stores

Yeoman: performs administrative and clerical work

PART ONE

PART TWO

PART ONE

*"The Navy. It's not just a job,
it's an adventure."*

—early 1970s television
recruiting campaign

CHAPTER 1

No Pier One

The December morning sky was filled with black clouds. That would mean rain for sure in most places, but this was northern California. The bus slowed down and stopped next to the sign for Naval Weapons Station Concord. The base looked like a bigger version of the one in Seal Beach. I got off the bus and carried my sea bag toward the main gate. Two marines on guard duty looked at me.

"I'm reporting aboard an ammunition ship," I said to the sergeant, "USS *Okmok*, AE-73."

"Port Chicago Shuttle, over there," he replied, pointing toward a parked gray jeep.

The guy sitting behind the wheel was a yeoman third-class, according to the crow on his sleeve.

"Heading for the *Okmok*," I told him. "AE-73."

He nodded and aimed his thumb toward the seat beside him. I got in, and we took off.

"THEY KEEP THE AEs AT PORT CHICAGO," he yelled over the wind.

"HOW COME THEY DESIGNATE AMMO SHIPS AE?" I yelled back. "SHOULDN'T IT BE AS?"

"STANDS FOR ANOTHER EXPLOSION. THE *OKMOK* HAS GOT TO BE AT PIER TWO, THREE, OR FOUR."

"WHAT ABOUT PIER ONE?"

"THERE IS NO PIER ONE."

"WHY NOT?"

"FUCKIN' AE BLEW UP." He paused and looked at me. "RELAX, THAT WAS DURING WORLD WAR TWO."

He was talking about the Port Chicago disaster. It wasn't an AE that blew up. It was a cargo ship, the SS *E.A. Bryan*. Our instructor in quartermaster school, a first-class named Kelso, enjoyed telling me all about it when he found out I was assigned here. To make sure Kelso wasn't laying it on too thick, I looked it up in the base library.

On the night of July 17, 1944, 320 sailors and civilian dockworkers were killed when the *Bryan*, which they were loading with bombs, exploded. Another cargo ship, the SS *Quinault Victory*, was moored at the pier alongside the *Bryan* after having taken on a load of fuel oil from the nearby Shell refinery in Martinez. The chain reaction created a fireball that lit up the night sky and threw white-hot debris some 12,000 feet in the air. Windows shattered on buildings as far as thirty miles away in San Francisco. The detonation registered at a magnitude of three-point-four on the seismograph at the University of California in Berkeley. The force of the blasts lifted the *Quinault Victory* out of the water. She landed 500 feet away, upside down and facing the opposite direction. The *Bryan* was vaporized. No identifiable remains of her were found. The Port Chicago disaster was the biggest loss of life on U.S. soil during World War II. Far more sailors died at Pearl Harbor, but Hawaii didn't become the 50th state until 1959.

That's why there was no pier one.

We drove past two ammo ships tied up at pier two, the *Pyro* and the *Kilauea*. The driver dropped me at pier three, where the *Okmok* floated at her mooring, her starboard side facing us. She was a haze gray monster almost two football fields long and eighty feet across. The number 73 was painted in white on each side of her bow. Hoses hung from her main deck, dripping rusty water into Suisun Bay. There were four pairs of kingposts on the forward deck and another pair on the after deck, with booms attached for cargo handling. A radio mast stood forward of the stack. Aft of the stack, I could see one of her two twin gun mounts. There was a row of windows at the top of the superstructure where the bridge was located. That's where I would be working.

I hauled my sea bag up the brow to the quarterdeck. Three guys in dress blue uniforms were on watch. The officer of the deck was a chief radioman with four hash marks on his sleeve, one for every four-year hitch he'd served. He was maybe five-and-a-half feet tall, with malicious eyes and a .45 on his hip. I saluted aft toward the flag. Then, I saluted the chief.

"Request permission to come aboard."

"Permission granted," the chief said, returning my salute.

He examined the manila envelope I handed him, with my orders and service record, like he was reading bad news.

"Quartermaster Thorpe, huh?"

"Yes, sir."

"I'm a chief, lad, Radioman Chief Hackburn. Don't call me sir."

"Okay, Chief."

He took off his hat, ran a hand through his patchy red hair, and put his hat back on.

"Your uniform looks pretty sorry, Thorpe. What the fuck did you do, sleep in it?"

"Sorry, Chief."

"Don't be sorry. Just get your shit in one sock. *Koslowski!*"

"Yeah, Chief?" the junior OOD answered. He was a second-class machinist's mate. Like the chief, he wore a .45 on his white duty belt.

"Call the bridge and tell Chief Lasko to send someone down here to get his new quartergasket, Thorpe. But first, call the ship's office and tell them we need a new plan of the day on the quarterdeck. Someone spilled fucking coffee all over this one."

Koslowski picked up the phone, dialed three digits, then said:

"The OOD wants a POD ASAP."

"Estorga, get this man checked in," Chief Hackburn said, handing my envelope to the messenger of the watch, a seaman with a short black beard. Instead of a .45, he carried a billy stick.

Estorga stepped into the quarterdeck shack behind a podium and looked at my orders.

"I need to put your name down in the deck log," he said. "According to this, you're a day early. You're not supposed to be here until tomorrow. The ship's office won't file your records until the day of the arrival date on your orders, or after."

"That doesn't make sense," I said.

"Yeah, well, welcome aboard. Don't worry, man. I work in the ship's office. I'll make sure they get your records filed. Hey, it says here you're from southern Cal."

"Yeah."

"Me, too, man, I'm from Whittier. Raul Estorga."

"Gary Thorpe."

"If you want to help out with gas money, I can give you a ride home on weekends."

Koslowski stuck his head into the shack.

"Somebody's coming to take you up to the bridge," he told me as a food and coffee truck rolled up on the pier.

"Pass the word, Koslowski," Chief Hackburn said, "the rolling gedunk is here."

Koslowski picked up the microphone to the ship's number one main circuit, 1MC, public address system and made an announcement:

"THE MOBILE CANTEEN IS ON THE PIER. THAT IS, THE MOBILE CANTEEN IS ON THE PIER."

Chief Hackburn was busy for the next few minutes returning salutes from sailors as they stepped off the quarterdeck and went down the brow to buy snacks. A tall guy in dungarees approached us. He was at least six foot six, with blond hair. The name STROMSVAG was stenciled above his shirt pocket.

"Hey, Stretch," Estorga said. "The roach coach is on the pier. You fly, I'll buy. Get me a pack of Kools and a Coke and whatever you want, buddy."

"Gotta get back," Stromsvag replied. "Southcott's got a bug up his ass."

"Sounds like a personal problem," Estorga said.

Stromsvag looked at me.

"I'm Eric Stromsvag, but everybody calls me Stretch. Come on, let's get you a rack."

We walked past a couple of guys painting a kingpost. Stretch stepped through an open oval-shaped doorway into the superstructure. The threshold of the door frame was high, and the header was low. I lifted my feet to get over the bottom, but I forgot to duck and hit my head on the top.

"I had that problem when I first got here," Stretch said. "Now, I move real slow."

We climbed up a ladder to the 02 level, walked down a long passageway, and entered a berthing compartment not much bigger than a two-car garage. In the center of the compartment were two tables bolted down to the green tile deck and eight straight-backed chairs below an overhead hatch. A bright red butt-kit overflowing with cigarette butts and ashes sat on one of the tables. Another half dozen butt-kits were attached at various places along the bulkheads. The forward and aft sides of the compartment were lined with four aisles barely two feet wide. Each aisle contained racks stacked three high and six deep on each side.

"Quartermasters bunk over here," Stretch told me. "This upper rack is empty since Thompson got discharged."

There was maybe fourteen inches of space between the thin mattress and the fluorescent reading light on the overhead. The racks opened on hinges, like shallow coffins, to serve double duty as lockers. I took a combination lock out of my sea bag, opened the coffin locker, put my sea bag inside the upper rack, and locked it up.

"Who was that chief on the quarterdeck?" I asked.

"Hackburn," Stretch replied, shaking his head. "He's haze gray all the way. Don't worry about him. He's in our division, so he thinks he's in charge of us, but we have our own chief. Just be glad you're not a radioman."

"Who's our chief?"

"You'll see."

I followed Stretch up the ladders to the 06 level. We went through another low doorway. I ducked this time. We walked past the Combat Information Center (CIC), where two guys sat among radar scopes and transparent plastic status boards. At the end of the passageway, Stretch opened a door, and I followed him through.

The bridge was forty feet across. In the center stood the steering console, which included the ship's wheel or helm, a gyroscope repeater, and the engine order telegraph also known as the lee helm. A brass binnacle with a magnetic compass inside stood just to the right of the console. In front of that was the row of windows I had seen from the pier. Voice tubes ran up the bulkheads, and exposed wiring ran across the overhead. Two watertight doors led to the port and starboard bridge wings. A door on the after bulkhead had a small brass plaque screwed to it that read: CHART HOUSE. Everything was painted the same shade of government green as a post office.

At the chart table to the left of the console stood a potbellied chief quartermaster. He was smoking a cigarette, and his brown eyes needed an alignment job. When he looked at me, I had the feeling he was looking at something behind me at the same time. His short-sleeved khaki uniform revealed faded green tattoos on both his forearms. On his right arm was an anchor with the letters *USN* across it; on his left, a rose over a curling banner that said *Mom*.

"Thorpe," Stretch said. "This is Chief Lasko."

"Glad to have another non-rate aboard, Thorpe," the chief said. "Did you save all your notes from quartermaster school?"

"Sure did, Chief."

"Good. Now, throw 'em all away. *AH HA HA HA HA HA!*"

The chart house door opened, and a guy with a first-class crow on his sleeve came out. He had a quartermaster wheel insignia pinned to the front of his ball cap, a narrow black mustache, and a tattoo on his left hand with the word *Alfonso*.

"Is this our new guy, Stretch?" he asked.

"Yeah, Al," Stretch replied. "Thorpe, this is Al Mendoza, our leading PO."

As Mendoza shook my hand, the door we had come through opened again, and an officer stepped in from the passageway. He was under thirty, with reddish hair. He wore government-issue black horn-rimmed glasses and the single silver bar of a lieutenant junior grade on each of his khaki collar wings. He looked like a man with a lot on his mind, and none of it pleasant.

"This is Mr. Southcott," Stretch said, "our navigator and division officer. Mr. Southcott, this is our new quartermaster, Thorpe."

"I know who he is, Stromsvag," Mr. Southcott replied. "I'm the one who ordered him from BUPERS."

Mr. Southcott pronounced ordered "awdahd" and BUPERS "BUPAHS." With his red hair and glasses, he reminded me of Woody Allen doing an impression of President Kennedy. That idea must have put a smile on my face.

"Is something funny, Thawpe?" he asked.

"No, sir."

"What is yaw EAOS?"

It sounded like a pop quiz.

"My End Active Obligated Service, sir."

Mr. Southcott looked at me in disgust.

"I know what it *means*, Thawpe. When *is* it?"

"July of 1977, sir."

"Well, that's something, at least. The last man we requested only had six months left on his hitch. Mendoza, let's get Thawpe up to speed."

Mendoza put his hand on my shoulder.

"The bridge is a showplace, Thorpe," he said. "Stretch, let's break my man Thorpe in right."

"Let's go," Stretch said.

I followed him through the door to the starboard bridge wing outside. A thin black guy with a sparse mustache was scraping gray paint from a bulkhead.

"Thorpe, meet Cooley," Stretch said. "Truly Cooley. Honest, that's his real name, but we call him Cool. He's got three brothers back home in Baton Rouge, Very, Really, and Damn."

"That ain' funny, man," Cool replied. "Got a smoke?"

Stretch took a pack of Marlboros from his shirt pocket and put one in his mouth.

"Got a light?" he asked.

Cool gave Stretch a light with a Zippo lighter, and Stretch gave him a cigarette. Stretch took two wire brushes from a gear locker and handed me one. We all started scraping the bulkhead.

"Slow down, man," Cool told me. "We jus' gon' be scrapin' it again soon as we paint it."

"The chief pulled that same dumb joke on me about shitcanning my notes from QM school," Stretch said. "He says that to everybody."

"Not me," Cool said. "I never went to no 'A' school."

"You're a non-rate?" I asked.

"We're all non-rates," Stretch replied. "Anyone below E-4 is a non-rate. Cool here is an unrated non-rate."

"I'm a striker," Cool said. "Come up here from deck almos' a year ago."

A striker was like an apprentice, a guy who learned his rate by on-the-job training instead of 'A' school.

"Once we get underway, you'll learn a lot from Al," Stretch said. "Al's a good guy. He's pretty easy to work for. The chief can be a goofball, but he's better than most of the chiefs."

"He an alcoholic," Cool added.

"What about Mr. Southcott?" I asked.

"He comes from some snobby family back east," Stretch replied. "His great-grandfather or somebody was a charter member of the Boston Yacht Club. You don't want to get on his bad side. He's got an Adolf Hitler inferiority complex."

"He a one-way muthafucka," Cool added.

"Aren't quartermasters supposed to correct charts and pubs in port?" I asked.

"Aw, naw, man," Cool replied. "Al do that. We got 350 men aboard this muthafucka. Only take thirty-five or forty to run the ship. Gotta keep them extra hands busy scrapin', paintin', an' scrapin' again."

"Al answers to the chief," Stretch explained. "The chief answers to Mr. Southcott, and we answer to Al. Shit rolls downhill."

"And we at the bottom of the hill," Cool added.

"The first rule is: If it moves, salute it, and if it doesn't move, paint it," Stretch said. "This paint we're scraping off, we just put it on last week."

"Doesn't make sense," I said.

"Welcome aboard."

They never mentioned scraping paint in those Navy recruiting ads.

Mr. Southcott opened the door and leaned outside.

"A little less chattah, and a little maw elbow grease," he said. "Thawpe, yaw to repawt to the XO, Commandah Crookshank, for an orientation speech. His stateroom is in officers' country, on the 05 level. Come back as soon as he's finished with you."

"Yes, sir."

I found the door to officers' country on the 05 level and went in. As I walked down the passageway, a guy in dungarees came toward me from the other direction. He had to be at least my age, but he looked too young to be in the Navy.

"Orientation?" I asked.

He nodded.

"I'm Crimmons."

"Thorpe."

"I just reported aboard today."

"Me, too."

We stood in front of a door with an engraved brass plaque that read: LIEUTENANT COMMANDER CRANSTON CROOKSHANK, EXECUTIVE OFFICER. I knocked.

"Come in," came a voice.

I opened the door. Mr. Crookshank sat behind a small desk. He had iron-gray hair, big ears, bushy eyebrows, and a horse face.

"Welcome aboard, men. Sit down," he said, looking at some paperwork. "Normally, Captain Grant would be here, but we will be getting a new

CO in the next few weeks, and Captain Grant is busy making preparations. Alvin Crimmons?"

"Yes, sir," Crimmons replied.

"Snipe striker from Idaho Falls."

"Yes, sir,"

"Never been there. And you must be Quartermaster Thorpe."

"Yes, sir," I said.

"You look like a troublemaker, Thorpe."

I felt it best to maintain silence. Mr. Crookshank cleared his throat and rattled off a speech that sounded like he'd said it many times.

"The *Okmok* is a Kilauea-class ammunition ship. She was named after a volcano in the Aleutian Islands. Her displacement is 10,417 long tons light and 18,088 long tons fully loaded. Her overall length is 564 feet. Beam: eighty-one feet. Draft: twenty-seven feet. Propulsion: three boilers, three steam turbines, and a single shaft. Maximum speed: twenty-three knots. Our complement is twenty-eight officers with air detachment, twenty without; 375 enlisted men with air detachment, 350 without. Our armament is four twin-mounted three-inch fifty guns and twelve fifty caliber machine guns. We can also carry two CH-46 Sea Knight helicopters, also known as whistling shitcans of death."

Crimmons had his hand up.

"Yes, Crimmons?"

"Sir, what's a three-inch fifty gun? I didn't know we made a three-inch gun."

"The three-inch fifty is not a three-inch gun, Crimmons. It fires a projectile that is three inches in diameter. To get the caliber of a big gun, you divide the barrel length by the bore. A three-inch bore times fifty caliber is a gun 150 inches or twelve and a half feet long. Make sense, Crimmons?"

"Yes, sir."

Mr. Crookshank continued.

"The mission of the *Okmok* is to perform UNREPS, or underway replenishments. During RAS detail—that's replenishment at sea—we steam alongside other line ships, sixty feet apart, and rig up gear to transfer ammunition, supplies, or fuel to the receiving ship. When BUPERS sends us our new CO, we will be going on REFTRA so we can perform SERVOPS during our upcoming WESTPAC deployment in accordance with COMSERVFLEET."

A lot of military jargon comes from taking the first syllable off two or three words and stringing them together to form a new word, like BUPERS for Bureau of Personnel, REFTRA for refresher training, SERVOPS for service operations, WESTPAC for West Pacific, and COMSERVFLEET for commander of the service fleet.

"Any questions?"

"No, sir," Crimmons said.

"Thorpe?"

"No, sir."

"Crimmons, you are assigned to in-port duty section four. Your section leader is Lieutenant Kempton, our first lieutenant and third in command. Thorpe, you are in duty section six. Your section leader is Lieutenant Osterkamp, the gunnery officer. Is that clear?"

"Yes, sir," Crimmons said.

"Yes, sir," I said.

"That will be all."

"Stromsvag," Mr. Southcott said when I got back to the bridge, "take Thawpe down to the paint lockah and get some red lead primah and haze gray paint. And don't get lost."

"Aye aye, sir," Stretch answered.

We walked down six flights of ladders to the main deck. A dozen deck apes were untangling lines. A second-class boatswain's mate with a knife and a fid on his belt was supervising them.

"Hey, Smitty, give Evans and Salazar a hand there," he said. "Hi, Stretch. Who's the new guy?"

"Thorpe," Stretch said, "this is Loophole."

Loophole had the name O'TOOLE stenciled over his shirt pocket. There was a green tattoo on his right forearm of Popeye over the words *Blow Me.*

"No, don't coil it, Smitty. That's how it gets tangled," Loophole said. "Fake it down. Don't you guys know how to fake down lines? Lay it down in long bights. It takes up less space that way, and it runs easier. Gink, you and Thumbs get up here, and let's show 'em how. I might not be the smartest boatswain's mate in the world, but if you guys got questions, and I don't know the answer, I know where to find out."

"I got a question," said a lanky blond guy with his hand up. "Why me?"

"Yeah," said another guy with the hairiest arms I ever saw. "Why Thumbs? He can't hardly tie his own shoes."

"Shut up, Doglike," Thumbs said.

It wasn't hard to see why they called him Doglike. Dark hair sprouted up out of his collar, and the hair on his arms was as thick as a dog's coat.

"He ain't much with a cutting torch, either," said a squatty guy with curly hair and dark sunglasses.

Everybody laughed.

"Knock it off, Bootleg," Loophole said. "Get up here, Thumbs."

"Let's go," Stretch said, and we walked toward the bow.

"What was that guy saying about a cutting torch?" I asked.

"That was Volker," Stretch replied. "They call him Bootleg. He was talking about last week. A door got jammed below decks. Chief Skinner told Thumbs to get an acetylene torch and cut it open, but the drifty motherfucker went to the wrong door. He tried to cut open the door to the master-at-arms' office, but, instead, he welded it shut. Needler was stuck in there for hours."

"Who's Needler?"

"The master-at-arms."

When we got to the forecastle, Stretch grabbed a dogging wrench, a piece of pipe used to lever the long-handled fittings or "dogs" that sealed off watertight doors. He gave a few taps to a steel door with the words PAINT LOCKER stenciled on it. The door opened slowly. A droopy face poked out of the darkness.

"Stringbean," Stretch said, "you're gonna die in there with all those paint fumes."

Stringbean looked like he just woke up. He wore a dirty white hat that was too big for him and paint-spattered dungarees. He was as bony as an x-ray.

"What d'ya want?" Stringbean asked. Behind him were shelves filled with paint buckets and square cans of thinner.

"We need some red lead and some haze gray."

"Got a chit?"

"No, but I'll go get one if you want. I'm in no big hurry to get started."

Stringbean smiled, but his eyes stayed gloomy.

"Here ya go," he said, handing us two buckets of each.

Stretch took two, and I took two, and then we headed back across the main deck to the bridge.

"Stringbean's from somewheres in Nebraska," Stretch told me. "Needler had guys following him around to find out where he was getting his drugs. It took them two weeks to figure out that Stringbean is just like that all the time."

This was not what I signed up for. I was beginning to suspect my Navy recruiter had not been completely honest. I liked boats. I could sail before I could drive. I wanted to travel. Those had been my reasons for joining the Navy. They already seemed ridiculous.

I didn't know it then, but I hadn't seen anything yet.

CHAPTER 2

Hothead

For the next few weeks, Stretch, Cool, and I did more than just scrape and paint bulkheads. We swept and swabbed the decks of the bridge and chart house. We shined the brass. We used foxtail brushes to dust horizontal surfaces, and we scrubbed toilets in the passageway head. It was not the job I had been trained for, but it gave my mind time to wander over the past ten years.

Had I seen this in my future, I might have had a better attitude toward school. By the time I was in the third grade, the school-every-day stuff was already getting old. One day, our teacher, Miss Harris, walked into the classroom after lunch with tears in her eyes.

"President Kennedy has been assassinated in Dallas, Texas," she said. "He was shot and killed."

All the girls started crying. I felt terrible, not for President Kennedy but for Miss Harris. Miss Harris was the most beautiful teacher at Franklin Elementary. She had dark shoulder-length hair. She smelled good. She spoke with a southern accent that sent chills down my spine. When we got under our desks during duck-and-cover drills, I would sneak looks at her legs.

During a softball game at recess, I was still thinking about Miss Harris, and I didn't notice a pop fly coming right at me at second base. It fell on the ground a few feet away. The batter, Kevin Cramer, made it to first base.

"Hey, Thorpe, wake up out there," Greg West, our pitcher, called out. "My grandmother could've caught that."

The other guys were laughing. I felt myself turning red.

"Move him out to right field, Greg," Mickey Walsh said. "I can handle second."

"Good idea," West said. "Thorpe, trade places with Walsh."

The other guys were still laughing.

"What a dorky play, Thorpe," Walsh said as he ran past me.

"Shut up," I said.

"Wanna make me?"

"I don't make trash. I burn it."

"Better light yourself on fire, then."

That was what passed for wit in third grade. He took a swing at me, but he stopped short, and I ducked.

"FLINCH!" he yelled. "ROYAL FLINCH!"

He punched me in the arm—hard. So, I shoved him. He tripped and fell on the dirt.

"What a chop," I said.

The bell rang to go back to class.

"I choose you off, Thorpe," he said. "After school."

When a guy chose you off, you had to show up for the showdown. Otherwise, you were a chicken, and you would never hear the end of it. Those were the rules. Things are different now, but back then, most of our fathers were World War II veterans who taught their sons to stand up for themselves. Their code of honor was: Don't start a fight, but don't run from one. My dad put it a little bit differently. His line was: You can run from a fight, but you can't run from yourself.

The hard part was waiting for hours to get out of school. I had a short fuse, and I hadn't had my butt kicked enough yet to learn to control it. I wanted to get the fight over with right away. Without a word, I attacked Walsh, hitting him as many times as I could.

"FIGHT," the other guys yelled. "FIGHT!"

Walsh was surprised. I was getting the best of him when one of the teachers, Mr. Farber, pulled us apart.

"Who started it?" Mr. Farber asked.

"Gary Thorpe," Walsh replied, pointing at me. West, Cramer, and the rest of the guys backed him up.

"Okay, young man," Mr. Farber said to me, "let's go see Mr. Grimes."

Mr. Grimes was the principal. He had a flattop haircut and always wore a short-sleeved white shirt with a narrow black tie. He told me to sit down in the chair in front of his desk. He didn't say anything for a long time. Then, he cleared his throat.

"Hello again, Gary. You were just here last week for fighting with Tony Lopez."

"He started it."

"Before that, it was Frank Lyle."

"He hit me first."

"What happened this time?"

"Mickey Walsh chose me off."

"So, it's everybody else's fault, is that it? You're developing a bad reputation. Miss Harris says you're ornery. Mr. Farber says you're a hothead."

At the time, I didn't know what ornery meant, but I could tell it was no compliment. Hothead seemed self-explanatory.

"Fighting is no way to solve problems, Gary. We don't allow fighting in school. Do you understand me?"

"Yes, Mr. Grimes."

"I'm going to give you one more warning. I'm also going to telephone your mother. You're getting too big for this—big enough for a swat if this happens again. Is that clear?"

The big wooden paddle that he used on the older boys was hanging on the wall behind his head.

"Yes, Mr. Grimes."

Mr. Grimes must have had a talk with Walsh, too, because he didn't want to fight me after school. That was fine with me. I walked home thinking about Mr. Grimes talking to Mom on the phone. As I approached our front door, someone inside was hitting sour notes on Beethoven's *Moonlight Sonata*.

Mom gave piano lessons in our house. I opened the door slowly and went in.

Cynthia Clark was sitting at Mom's upright piano. Cynthia was a few years older than me. She lived down the block. Cynthia and Mom sat with their backs to me. I closed the door quietly, but not quietly enough. Mom looked at me, and I could tell by her eyes that she had talked to Mr. Grimes. I went to my room.

Luckily for me, Dad was in Kuwait on one of his business trips. My dad was rarely home. He was the international sales manager for the Bespoke Oilwell Rotary Equipment Corporation — known as BORECO.

When the Beatles arrived, all the girls at school were crazy about them. I didn't like them at first, but I liked to watch Ringo play the drums. When I saw Buddy Rich, I asked my parents if I could take drum lessons. Mom was glad I was taking an interest in music. Dad agreed to pay for lessons, but only for as long as I was willing to practice. Mom bought me a pair of sticks and a practice pad, a flat piece of rubberized plastic. She let me have an old aluminum cooking pot to pound on.

Since we lined up alphabetically at school for calisthenics, Nate Stansfield and Chuck Throckmorton stood next to me. Nate was a sports fan. His dad had a subscription to *Sports Illustrated*, and Nate liked to spout off baseball statistics. Chuck loved to talk about cars and racing. His dad was always taking him to Lion's Drag Strip. One day at recess, I got tired of hearing them yap about

Sandy Koufax and Don Garlits. So, I came up with a lie, just to see if they'd bite.

"I have a brother."

"Where is he?" Nate asked.

"He ran away."

"How come we never saw him?" Chuck asked.

Once I had their interest up, I couldn't help myself.

"It was before I knew you guys."

"What's his name?" Nate asked.

"Joe," I said, having recently seen an episode of *Bonanza*.

"Didn't your mom and dad call the police?" Nate asked.

"Yeah, but by that time, Jim was dead. Killed in a train wreck."

I tried to look bored so they wouldn't suspect I was making up answers as fast as they asked questions.

"Who's Jim?" Chuck asked.

"My brother."

"I thought you said it was Joe."

"He's been gone so long that I'm starting to forget his name."

I wanted to see how far I could push it before one of them came out and said I was full of crap, but neither of them did.

"I saw a movie," Chuck said, "*The Great Escape*. These prisoners of war tunnel their way out of a German prison camp."

He told us the whole plot of the movie with machine gun and motorcycle sound effects. We decided to dig our own tunnel next weekend near the construction site where they were extending the freeway. Our "tunnel" turned out more like an underground cave about six feet deep and big enough for all three of us. If it had collapsed, we never would have been found.

In fourth grade, I ran into my first bully, Lonny Bupp. He had red hair, freckles, gaps between his teeth, and ears that didn't match. The girls didn't like him, but the girls didn't like me much, either, and I wasn't picking on everyone, like Lonny. Nobody ever stood up to him. I avoided him until one day when I was in the boys' bathroom. Tad Neff and Freddy Turley were squatted down on the tile floor breathing in and out fast. Tad stood up with a goofy smile on his face.

"What are you guys doing?" I asked.

"You take about twenty deep breaths," Tad replied, spinning around. "Then, you stand up real quick. It makes you feel good."

Freddy stood up, passed out, and fell down, hitting his head on the sink. Tad started laughing. They had discovered hyperventilation. In a few more years, these guys would be doing speed, downers, and acid.

When I came out of the bathroom, a third grader named Jay Phillips was bent over the drinking fountain. Lonny Bupp was waiting behind him. Lonny thought Jay was taking too much time drinking, so he shoved his head into the spigot. Jay spit out a tooth and started bleeding and crying. Our teacher, Mrs. Marshall, heard Jay crying, and she was on her way over. Lonny Bupp whispered to me.

"If you tell her what happened, I'll get you after school."

He didn't have time to say much else because Mrs. Marshall was right there, and she was angry.

"What's going on here?" she asked.

Jay told her that Lonny shoved his head into the fountain. Of course, Lonny denied it. Mrs. Marshall turned to me.

"Gary, did you see what happened?"

I could lie, or tell the truth and antagonize Lonny, so I lied.

"No, Mrs. Marshall," I said. "I was in the boys' room."

Jay Phillips didn't really know if I'd seen anything or not because his head was down. Lonny grinned, but only for a second. Mrs. Marshall had him by the ear.

"Come along, Lonny. We're going to Mr. Grimes' office."

She dragged Lonny away and sent Jay to see the school nurse. It turned out that Jay's tooth wasn't a permanent tooth, and it was loose, anyway, but I still felt ashamed that I didn't have the guts to fink on Lonny Bupp. Lonny got a swat from Mr. Grimes, just like he would have if I'd snitched on him, but I still felt like a coward. Dad was right. You can't run away from yourself.

I hated school.

Fourth grade was the year they started the "new math." The other kids seemed to get it, but not me. I didn't understand the old math, but I knew enough arithmetic to know that I had eight more years of school ahead of me. The thought made me miserable.

Mrs. Marshall made us go to the blackboard to do long division problems in front of the class. When she called on me, I went up there and froze, staring at the blackboard with my back to the class and listening to the other kids snicker until Mrs. Marshall finally told me to sit down. Tad Neff called me a retard. Mickey Walsh called me a spaz. Even some of the girls laughed at me.

Lonny Bupp seemed to think we were buddies. He took lunch money from other guys, but he never took mine. At recess, he would invite me to come out on the playground with him. The other kids started avoiding me because I was hanging around with Lonny. I felt trapped. I was afraid to tell Lonny I didn't want to be his friend, but I couldn't go on like this. One day at recess, Lonny waved at me to come out in the field away from the buildings. He had found a gray kitten.

"Watch this," he said.

He grabbed the kitten by the tail. He swung it around in a circle, and he let it fly over the chain-link fence. He started laughing.

"I hate cats," he said. "Yesterday —"

He never finished telling me what happened yesterday because I punched him in the mouth as hard as I could. It caught him by surprise, and he fell down. I was surprised, too. I had hit him without thinking. Out of fear of what he'd do to me next, I jumped on him and started hammering him with punches. Lonny got ahold of himself. He slowly began to get up, and I couldn't hold him down because he was bigger than me. He would have pounded me if Mr. Farber hadn't come along to break it up. He sent us to see Mr. Grimes, and we each got a swat. Before we went back to class, Lonny leaned toward me and whispered like a hissing snake:

"After school, Thorpe. You're chosen."

I felt sick for the rest of the day. I wished I was as big as my dad, six foot three and built like a cross between a linebacker and a gorilla. Dad could have thrown Lonny Bupp over the fence like that kitten. Of course, if I was as big as Dad, Lonny Bupp wouldn't be picking on me. The word got around that I was going to fight Lonny Bupp. The other guys didn't help build my confidence any.

"He's going to kill you, Thorpe," Tad Neff predicted, and he didn't sound too unhappy about it.

"Boy, I'd hate to be in your shoes," Nate Stansfield said.

Waiting for the fight was the hard part. The clock stopped. Not that I was in a hurry to go to my own funeral. Finally, school was out, and we all started to leave the schoolyard. There was a bunch of guys on old man Ferguson's front lawn. Mr. Ferguson had the best-looking lawn on the block. We always had our after-school fights there because his house was on the corner closest to the school. Lonny was waiting for me. The crowd parted to let me through. In seconds, we were rolling around, tearing up Mr. Ferguson's nice lawn. It was strange how my fear was gone once I was *in* the fight instead of sitting in the classroom thinking about it.

Sometimes, my short temper was an advantage. Once I got riled up, I could throw a lot of punches. My problem was, to reach the right rage level, I had to get hit first. When the other guy was a better fighter, letting him take the first punch was bad strategy. Lonny didn't fight fair. He kicked and pulled my hair, but he also punched hard and fast. I got in a few licks, too.

"IT'S OLD MAN FERGUSON," Chuck Throckmorton yelled. "RUN!"

Mr. Ferguson ran us off, and the fight was over. My nose was bleeding. My shirt was torn and covered with blood and dirt, but I felt better than I did before the fight. I walked home hoping I could get past Mom without her seeing me. Then, I remembered it was Thursday. Mom played bridge with a group of women every Thursday. Luckily for me, it wasn't her turn to have them at our house.

The next day, Lonny had a fat lip, but everyone said I lost the fight, and I guess I did. Lonny Bupp never bothered me again.

CHAPTER 3

Shortcut

Every morning at exactly 0600, the shriek of the boatswain's pipe came over the 1MC, piercing the air throughout the *Okmok*, followed by the metallic reverberating voice of the petty officer of the watch.

"NOW REVEILLE, REVEILLE, REVEILLE. ALL HANDS HEAVE OUT AND TRICE UP. ALL REVEILLE POs MAKE THEIR REPORTS TO THE OOD ON THE QUARTERDECK. THE SMOKING LAMP IS LIT IN ALL AUTHORIZED SPACES. REVEILLE."

The quartermasters' racks were in the center of the 02 berthing compartment, aft of the two card tables. Mendoza had the middle rack across the aisle from me. Cool had the rack below him. Stretch had a top rack on the next aisle with the signalmen. Stretch needed a top rack so his feet could stick out into the compartment.

The duty reveille petty officer came through 02 berthing to ensure that everyone was out of his rack. Anyone still in his rack was put on report. It was Chief Hackburn's turn. He stood in the middle of the compartment, yelling at us with his fists on his hips. His khaki sleeves were rolled up, revealing a faded green tattoo on his left forearm of a topless mermaid.

"Okay, let's get the fuck up, Hankins. Cooley, out of the rack, goddammit, and tuck in your shirt tail. Stromsvag, wake the fuck up. Thorpe, wipe that look off your face. It's another fucking wonderful Navy day."

As we got dressed, shaved, and brushed our teeth, radio central piped a local station over the 1MC.

"And that was the Steve Miller band on KFRC with 'The Joker.' Speaking of jokers, this is Doctor Don Rose, and the time is 6:05, five after six. I'd have been here sooner, but I was looking for a parking space. Say, how about that score last night? Seventy-Sixers 49, Forty-Niners 76. [cowbell] We have a request for some Jim Croce from Janet in Walnut Creek. She wants to hear 'Time in a Bottle.' You know, I was dancing with a girl to that song, and my contact lenses fell down the front of her dress. [slide whistle] I couldn't take my eyes off her."

Hoodwink, Finesse, Alaska, and Billings sat at a table smoking and getting in a few hands of casino before breakfast. They used cigarettes as betting chips. They were plank owners, part of the original commissioning crew who came aboard with Captain Grant.

Gunther Hood, known as Hoodwink, was the senior shellback, a second-class gunner's mate from

Hoboken with a walrus mustache. His dungaree shirt was unbuttoned. He had a sumo-wrestler's gut and a big green tattoo on his chest of King Neptune holding a trident. The Hoodwink handle was not only a play on his last name but a suggestion that he wasn't above cheating at cards if he thought he could get away with it.

Finesse held his cards close to his chest. He was a second-class hospital corpsman named Wendell Fitzgibbon from Akron, Ohio, medium-sized, with sandy hair, glasses, and a pointy nose. He and a hospitalman striker named Garvey ran the sick bay. The *Okmok* didn't rate an MD, so Finesse was the highest medical authority aboard. Supposedly, when some of the guys called him Doc, Finesse told them to knock it off because nobody wants to play cards with a guy named Doc. Hoodwink said it took finesse to see that, and the nickname stuck.

"Wanna play some casino, Thorpe?" Billings asked me.

Billy Billings was a radioman striker from Albuquerque and a source of news. He wore John Lennon spectacles. His brown hair, parted down the middle, was as Navy-regulation short as any of us, but, somehow, he managed to make it look long. Everybody felt sorry for Billings and his fellow radiomen Carlson and Pitt because they had to work under Chief Hackburn.

"I don't smoke," I said. "I got no chips."

"Gambling for real money is against Navy regs," Alaska said. His real name was Virgil Stillwell, a third-class gunner's mate from Skagway, over six feet tall, with black hair, a square jaw, and a big chin. He always looked aggravated, like he was just one minor inconvenience away from giving someone a severe beating.

"Another STUPNAVREG," Billings said.

"The gentry frowns on betting," Finesse said — 'the gentry' was our term for the officers — "but they rarely enforce it."

"My wife's gonna kill me if I lose any more *cigarettes*," Hoodwink said.

"Sounds like an ANGWOMPROB," Finesse replied.

"*Your* wife?" Alaska told Hoodwink. "My wife's divorcing me."

"I don't blame her, ya cheap bastard," Hoodwink said. "The last time you took a dollar out of your wallet, George Washington blinked at the light."

"Your mother," Alaska said.

Their cigarette smoke only partially masked the ungodly stink of Harmon "Swampass" Kroot as he got up from his rack on the other side of the compartment. Swampass was a gunner's mate striker from somewhere in Arkansas. His reluctance to take showers got him his moniker. Stretch and Estorga surrounded his rack one night and emptied two cans of spray deodorant on him, and he still didn't get the hint.

The word idiot gets thrown around a lot, but for sheer stupidity, for a near-complete lack of intelligence, I never knew a better example of a horrible example than Swampass. He had green letters tattooed on his flabby right arm: *US Nayv*. I could believe that some tattoo artist couldn't spell

Navy or that Swampass wasn't smart enough to notice, but I couldn't guess the odds against two guys that dumb getting together.

"BREAKFAST FOR THE CREW," came the word over the 1MC.

Every morning, we stood in line in the passageway outside the mess decks, waiting our turn to single-file past Sweeny, the cook, holding our trays out over the steam tables as he asked the same question again and again:

"What d'ya need?"

"Two over easy, man," Cool said.

"What d'ya need?"

"Two scrambled," Stretch said, "and hold the taste."

"What d'ya need?"

"I believe I'll have eggs Benedict this morning, Sweeny, my man," Mendoza said, "with strawberries and champagne."

Sweeny looked at us through his steamy glasses as he slapped the same runny yellow mass on each tray.

"Are those really eggs?" I asked.

"Grade H," Stretch replied, "just like the meat."

"Close enough for government work," Sweeny said.

"Hey, Sweeny," Estorga said, "You hear about the guy aboard the *Pyro* who got a medal for saving his division? He shot the cook."

After breakfast, another announcement came over the 1MC.

"NOW QUARTERS, QUARTERS. ALL HANDS TO QUARTERS FOR MUSTER, INSPECTION, AND INSTRUCTION. THAT IS ALL."

The crew formed up on the second deck in four departments: operations, engineering, supply, and deck. Quartermasters were in X and N division, part of the operations department under Mr. Sforzando that included signalmen, radiomen, hospital corpsmen, yeomen, operations specialists, and electronic techs. The engineering department under Mr. Barker was made up of electrician's mates, hull techs, boiler techs, and machinist's mates—all known as snipes. The supply department, storekeepers, commisarymen, stewards, worked under Mr. Wheeler, the supply officer. The joke was that, during General Quarters, the supply clerks would put on helmets and gas masks and man the junk food store known as the gedunk. Deck department included first and second divisions, boatswain's mates and deck apes, and third division, the gunner's mates. The deck apes worked under Mr. Kempton and Senior Chief Skinner. The gunner's mates worked under Mr. Osterkamp and Chief Gunner's Mate Strickland. In the pecking order, deck apes were lower than whale shit.

Chief Hackburn and Chief Lasko stood side by side as Skidmore, a second-class signalman, called roll. Skidmore had red hair, a crooked nose, a constant frown, and a green tattoo of a python coiled around his right arm.

"Abernathy?"

"Here."

"Billings?"

"Yeah."

"Carlson?"

"Here."

"Cooley?"

"Here."

"Estorga?"

"Here."

"Fitzgibbon?"

"Here."

"Garvey?"

"Aye."

"Goldberg?"

"Here."

"Hankins?"

"Yo."

"Hayashi?"

"Yep."

"Kettrick?"

"Yes."

"Larkin?"

"Yeah."

"Mendoza?"

"Here."

"Pitt?"

"Here."

"Stromsvag?"

"Aye."

"Thorpe?"

"Here."

"Wilcox?"

"Yo."

The officers, in their starched khakis, stood off in a group by themselves. They reported to Mr. Crookshank. Their group broke up.

"*Attention*," Chief Lasko said as Mr. Southcott and Mr. Sforzando approached us.

We stood at attention until Chief Lasko and Chief Hackburn saluted Mr. Southcott and Mr. Sforzando, and they returned the salutes. Lieutenant Sforzando was the operations officer, in charge of radio and CIC. Some guys had a five o' clock shadow, but Mr. Sforzando had one by 0930. Though he shaved every morning, the dark lines of his beard were always visible below the surface of his skin, high on his cheekbones, just below his eyes. Behind his back, the crew called him Raccoon Face.

"At ease," Mr. Southcott said. "Skidmaw, read the POD."

Skidmore cleared his throat.

"Item one," he said. "The ship's Coke machines will not take foreign coins, slugs, and etcetera. Also, if empty cans are found discarded about the ship, the Coke machines will be secured. Item two. There will be no more basketball games in the hangar bay during working hours."

"NOW TURN TO," said the 1MC, "COMMENCE SHIP'S WORK."

When Stretch and Cool and I got to the bridge, Mendoza said the same thing he said almost every morning.

"OK, wheels, let's get a broom and a swab and a foxtail and some rags and some Brasso, and let's clean up this shithouse up here."

He called us "wheels" because the quartermaster insignia was a ship's wheel.

"Cool, you sweep and swab the deck. Stretch, get a foxtail and dust the wiring and voice tubes along the bulkheads. Thorpe, get a rag and a can of Brasso and start shining the brass. The bridge is a showplace."

Cool was right when he said Navy ships had ten times the crew necessary to run the ship. That was so we could absorb casualties in wartime. In peacetime, there was plenty of deadweight aboard with not much to do. Non-rates spent most days on make-work jobs like the never-ending paint job or the everlasting field day, cleaning things that were already clean. The important thing was to keep moving. It was never smart to be idle in front of the officers, especially Mr. Southcott. Almost every day, they called up one of us, Stretch, Cool, or me, for a "working party" with other non-rates from the other divisions, usually to load food or supplies.

One afternoon, Mendoza had Stretch making ornamental knots on all the weather deck handrails. Stretch could tie decorative knots like Turk's heads and Chinese butterflies. He could even tie a monkey's fist. Cool was priming the bridge wings with red lead while I varnished Stretch's fancy work.

"Hey, Stretch," I said, "where'd you pick up the marlinspike seamanship?"

"Loophole showed me some. Some, I learned from my dad."

"But that's deck stuff. You're a quartermaster."

"Beats scrapin' and paintin'."

He had a point. I was beginning to see what Chief Lasko meant by throwing away my notes from quartermaster school. I wasn't using anything I learned. Stretch wrapped loops of line around the handrails and tied braided Turk's heads at the ends. I brushed a mixture of stain and varnish on the lines to seal them from the weather. I got tired holding the varnish bucket with one hand, so I took one end of the wire bail off the bucket and put it over the rail where Stretch had finished wrapping some line. Then, I reattached the bail to the bucket so it hung from the rail. I dipped my brush into the varnish and let it drip through the wrapped line back into the bucket. When it stopped dripping, I moved the bucket six inches along the rail and did it again. That way, I didn't have to hold the bucket or worry about spilling any varnish. I was getting it done faster and easier.

"What choo doin'?" Cool asked.

"It's a shortcut," I said.

"Looky here, Shortcut. What choo think gon' happen if we work faster? Southcott gon' give us a raise? He jus' gon' find more work for us."

"He's right," Stretch said. "We ain't goin' nowheres. Slow down, man. Don't make us look bad. Nobody needs a fucking shortcut."

I took the bucket off the rail and went back to doing it the long way. After that, they kept calling me Shortcut.

The first time my section—section six—had the duty, I had to stay aboard ship after liberty call.

Mendoza showed me what to do as duty quartermaster. We stood on the bridge beside the 1MC microphone mounted on the after-bulkhead.

"When we're in port, the duty QM announces morning and evening colors," he said, referring to the ceremonial raising and lowering of the flag on the fantail. "Every morning at 0755 and every evening at five minutes before sunset, the duty QM says over the 1MC: 'First call, first call to colors.' Five minutes later, at 0800 and sunset, you say: 'On deck, attention to colors.' Anyone on a weather deck is supposed to stop and salute toward the fantail. You wait a minute to give the duty boatswain's mate time to raise or lower the flag, then you say: 'Carry on.' Got it?"

"Got it, Al."

"Come with me."

We went into the chart house. Mendoza opened the glass top of a narrow box embedded into the chart table. The box held two brass Navy chronometers mounted on gimbals. He wound them up. Then, he wrote the date and time in the chronometer logbook and signed it.

"The duty QM has to wind the chronometers and enter it in the log. Okay?"

"Okay."

"Forgetting to wind chronometers used to be a death penalty offense during wartime," he said, grinning at my shocked look, "but things are lightening up now. Follow me."

We went outside on the port wing and aft to a ladder. We climbed up to the signal bridge, where

Duane Hankins, an E-3 signalman, was smoking a cigarette.

"Sometimes, we take the duty for the signalmen because we don't have enough signalmen in each duty section," Mendoza explained. "Hankins, who's the slickest signalman in port, you or Skidmore?"

"I figure I'm about the slickest," Hankins replied with a smirk. Hankins was almost as tall as Stretch but skinny as a snake, with a bony face, hollow cheeks, sunken eyes, and a green tattoo of the Zig Zag man on his left forearm.

"Good. You can help my man Thorpe to learn semaphore. Quartermasters and signalmen are supposed to be interchangeable."

"Bullshit," Hankins said.

"That's right," Mendoza said with a grin. "I never met a signalman yet who can steer worth a shit. Show Thorpe where we keep the captain's absentee pennant."

Hankins opened a haze gray box filled with signal flags. He held up a pennant with blue and white stripes. Mendoza kept talking.

"If there's no duty signalman, the duty QM is supposed to raise this pennant whenever the captain goes ashore and lower it when he comes back aboard. Sometimes, the old man waits in his car to see if it's raised before he drives off. If it isn't raised, he comes back aboard and puts the duty signalman on report. So, don't forget to do it, or it's BOHICA."

"BOHICA?"

"Bend Over, Here It Comes Again," Hankins said.

Every day after knockoff, the crew went to their berthing compartments to change clothes and get ready for liberty call. Deck, engineering, and supply departments lived below the second deck. The operations department and the gunnery division lived in 02 berthing. Hoodwink, Finesse, Alaska, and Estorga were playing casino.

"Your move, Shortcut," Billings said, nodding at the small magnetic chessboard on the steel bulkhead beside his rack. We were in the middle of our third game. He had won the first two. He had me in a spot where every move was bad for me. I took his bishop with my knight, knowing that he would take my knight, which he did.

"Checkmate."

"*Damn it!* I didn't see that."

"If you win every game, you aren't learning."

"A few more games like this, and I'll be an expert. Aren't you bored playing me?"

"You're the only guy in 02 who knows the game besides Finesse."

"Why not play him?"

"He always beats me."

Delgado's voice came over the 1MC, passing the word to muster the duty in-port fire party. Like many Tagalog-speaking Filipinos, Delgado inverted his Ps and Fs.

"NOW MUSTER THE DUTY IN-FORT PIRE FARTY ON THE MAIN DECK WITH CHIEF SKINNER. THAT IS, MUSTER THE DUTY IN-

FORT PIRE FARTY ON THE MAIN DECK WITH CHIEF SKINNER."

"Listen to that mealy-mouthed motherfucker," Hoodwink said, throwing a card. "I think Skinner puts him on the 1MC on purpose."

"Not the finest military phraseology," Finesse said.

"THE MOBILE CANTEEN IS ON THE PIER," echoed Delgado's voice over the 1MC.

"Get us two Cokes from the gedunk, Alaska," Hoodwink said. "You fly, I'll buy."

"Get it yourself," Alaska replied.

"How about it, Billy?" Hoodwink asked, waving a five-dollar bill. "Take care of my light work."

"Okay," Billings said. "I need more cigarettes, anyway."

He grabbed the five and left as Delgado passed the word:

"NOW, LIBERTY CALL FOR ALL NON-DUTY SECTIONS TO EXPIRE ONBOARD AT 0700 TOMORROW. LIBERTY CALL."

"TWENTY FOR FORTY," Alaska yelled, "ANYBODY, TWENTY FOR FORTY. HOW ABOUT TEN FOR TWENTY?"

Slushing was against Navy regs, but there were slushers in every berthing compartment. Alaska was ours. Known in civilian life as loan sharks, slushers offered cash to broke sailors going on liberty at one hundred percent interest — only, they didn't put it that way. The offer was ten bucks for twenty, or twenty for forty.

Everybody went ashore except for section six. Non-rates were supposed to stand messenger of the quarterdeck watch on their duty days, but my name was not on the watch bill. I didn't think much of it.

Six days later, I had duty again, and again, my name did not appear on the watch bill. It looked like my section leader, Mr. Osterkamp, never got the word that I was in his section. I didn't particularly want to stand quarterdeck watches. If Mr. Osterkamp didn't straighten it out by next time, I would tell him.

Six days later, when it still wasn't straightened out, I kept my mouth shut. This wasn't my doing, so it was easy to kid myself. Things were working in my favor. It wasn't my job to fix this happy accident. Mr. Osterkamp would catch on, sooner or later.

Weeks passed, and Mr. Osterkamp did not catch on. It got harder to tell him that I had slipped through the bureaucratic cracks. On my duty days, I stayed aboard after liberty call. I announced morning and evening colors over the 1MC. I wound the chronometers and signed the log. I raised or lowered the captain's absentee pennant if Skidmore or Hankins weren't around to do it. Otherwise, I was free to read and re-read paperbacks or sit in the TV lounge inhaling cigarette smoke while the other guys in the duty section yelled for channel checks until they finally compromised on some program everybody could dislike. I never stood a quarterdeck watch. Each duty day, I told myself I would come clean with Mr. Osterkamp—next time, just not yet.

Later, I would regret it.

CHAPTER 4

Punchiments

Ross Slagle was a year older than me. He lived on my street. Ross was pretty smart. His parents sent him to private school. His dad was a chemical engineer. In fifth grade, Ross taught me to play chess. He always beat me.

"How come I never win?" I asked.

"You don't play enough," he said. "Chess masters play eighteen hours a day, and they spend the other six hours sleeping, thinking about chess."

One Saturday, Ross's dad had him paint a wooden lawn chair in their front yard.

"All the colors put together make white," Ross said. "They told us at school. If you shine a light through a prism, it breaks down into all the colors of the rainbow."

"It seems like all colors put together would make black," I said. I didn't tell him I didn't know what a prism was.

"What are you talking about?"

"If you take a piece of paper and put blue ink on it and red ink and green ink and every color ink, they won't turn white."

"Look, when the sun shines through rain, you see a rainbow, and, for your information, sunlight isn't black." Sometimes, Ross would make snotty cracks like that.

"I bet if we poured a bunch of different colors of paint together in your garage, it'll look more like black than white."

"I'm not going to mess up my garage."

"You're afraid you're wrong."

"I'm afraid you're stupid," he said, and he shoved me, so I shoved him back.

We got into a fight on his front lawn. I was bigger than Ross, but he was taking boxing lessons. He was the first guy I ever fought who knew what he was doing. When he hit me in the mouth, I didn't see it coming. Then, he hit me again. Before I knew it, I was on the grass on my ass. Mr. Slagle came out of the house and broke it up.

"Let's go to the boxing ring at the YMCA to settle this," he said. "Gary, I'm going to phone your dad to make sure it's okay with him."

Dad thought it was a great idea. At the Y, we put on some boxing gloves and got in the ring.

"Show me how you hit me like that," I said.

"Footwork," Ross replied. "The coach says you can't run fast without using your arms, and you can't punch hard without using your legs."

"How do I use my legs?"

"Don't let your heels touch the ground. Stay on the balls of your feet. Crouch a little, and when you throw a punch, use your back foot to launch yourself and step forward with your front foot."

I tried it. We sparred around for a while. Pretty soon, we weren't angry at each other anymore.

"Now shake hands," Mr. Slagle said, "and find another way to settle your differences."

We shook hands. When we got home, we looked up black and white in the dictionary. We were both half right. White was the absence of pigment, and black was the absence of light.

Mr. Slagle took Ross for boxing lessons every Saturday. I wanted to go, but Dad said either boxing lessons or drum lessons. He wasn't paying for both. I didn't want to give up drums. I was just getting good at double stroke rolls. After his boxing lessons, Ross would show me what he learned that week.

"Coach says you don't have to be real strong to knock a guy out," he told me. "If you catch him just right on the chin, it only takes a few pounds of pressure."

Ross talked about timing. Timing was important in drumming, too. Ross showed me a combination, a left jab followed by a right cross. That reminded me of a drum rudiment called a right flam. To play a flam, one stick hits the drumhead, playing a grace note, just before the other stick hits, creating a loud pop. The sticks aren't supposed to hit at the same time but almost. When we were sparring around in Ross's driveway, I caught him by surprise with a flam to his jaw.

That got me wondering. If flams worked, maybe other drum rudiments would work. I tried a flam tap, a right flam followed by another right. When Ross saw it coming, I changed it and played the grace note with my right hand followed by two lefts. Ross was getting pissed off. I tried a paradiddle on him, left jab, right cross, and two left jabs. That last left jab was harder, so I dropped it, which made it a triplet. With what Ross showed me about footwork combined with drum rudiments, I was outfighting him.

"What are you doing?" he asked.

"Punching rudiments," I said. "Punchiments."

I started to explain, but Ross wasn't interested. Mr. Slagle, who was watching us through the window, wasn't too happy that his son was suddenly being defeated by the guy down the block who wasn't even taking boxing lessons. He took us to the YMCA again and talked to the coach. We put on gloves and got in the ring. Ross smacked me twice, and I felt the old rage kicking in. Then, I had an idea. Nobody knew about punchiments, so nobody was expecting them.

I tried a ratatap, two short left ghost notes to fake him out followed by a quick right-left-right to his ribs with an accent on the final stroke. Ross backed up, and I stepped in with a single ratamacue, ghosting two short rights followed by a left-right-left sixteenth note triplet and a hard eighth note right to the gut. Ross looked wobbly. He left himself open. On Ross's face, I played the first two bars of Exercise One from the Ted Reed

Syncopation book, counting out loud, "*ONE, AND, rest, AND, THREE, FOUR, ONE, TWO…*"

The coach stopped the fight before I could play the last two notes.

My punchiments self-defense method gave me enough variety to surprise a few guys after school in old man Ferguson's yard. Most drum rudiments wouldn't work for fighting—a nine-stroke roll, for instance, or a paradiddle-diddle was never going to happen—but my fist control improved when I started to *visualize* them happening. It even helped my drumming.

The Slagles moved away the year I started seventh grade. Sycamore Junior High was made up of different cliques. There were the cool kids, the jocks, the socials, the hard guys, the stoners, the surfers, the Mexicans, and the dorks. It was possible to be in more than one group. Greg West was a jock and a social. Tad Neff was a surfer and a stoner. Tony Lopez was a Mexican hard guy. I wasn't cool, social, a hard guy, or Mexican. I didn't go out for sports. I didn't surf, and I was too chicken to try drugs. So, I was considered lame but not lame enough to fit into the dork category. Dorks were wimps who kissed up to the teachers. They cared about schoolwork and got good grades. I failed on both counts.

I spent my first week avoiding anybody big or mean-looking, which seemed to be everybody. Some of the ninth graders took cuts in the lunch lines, but no one did anything about it. One day, I bought a pint of milk, opened it, turned around, and dropped it. It splashed up on a ninth grader's leg, a big guy with ugly eyes. His buddies started laughing.

"Let's go, punk," he said to me. "Behind the building."

"Keith Pike is gonna beat up a seventh grader," said one of his pals.

"Hurry up, punk," Keith Pike said, shoving me toward the building.

I started walking. His group followed, eager to witness my death. During the few steps to the other side of the building, I decided I wasn't going to surrender like a trapped rat. When we turned the last corner, I rushed Keith Pike and beat the hell out of him before I realized we were standing in front of an office door with a glass window. A man sitting at a desk inside had seen everything. A sign on the door said: MR. HELLFRICK, VICE PRINCIPAL. He stood up from behind his desk and came outside. He was big, over six feet tall, with a burr haircut and a bright green suit.

"What's going on here?" he said, looking at me. He had seen me pounding on Pike, so I figured he already knew what was going on.

"He threw milk on me, Mr. Hellfrick," Pike said, pointing at his milk-soaked jeans. "I was bringing him to your office."

There was nothing for me to say. To Mr. Hellfrick, it looked like I started it.

"What are you?" Mr. Hellfrick asked me. "Some kind of tough guy? What's your name?"

I told him my name. Mr. Hellfrick led me into his office. He picked up the phone and called the school nurse for Pike. Then, he told me to empty my pockets on his desk and bend over. He gave me three swats with an inch-thick paddle the size of a breadboard. It had holes drilled through it to add speed to his golf-like swing. My butt was on fire.

"I hope you learned something here today, Gary," he said. "If I hear of your involvement in any more fighting, you're suspended."

I didn't fit in anywhere. I was only halfway through school. I felt like a prisoner. I couldn't wait to be an adult. I walked around the campus trying to look scary. I thought I could avoid fights by looking like the last guy anyone would want to mess with. Sometimes, it worked, and sometimes, it didn't. The counselors thought I was a hard guy because I had a few fights. The cool kids thought I was a weirdo because of my bad attitude. The stoners thought I was lame because I didn't take drugs. The teachers thought I was a class clown because I was a smart-ass. Mrs. Pierson, my English teacher, would write big words on the board and ask us if we knew what they meant. She called on me.

"Gary, can you use the word *circumlocution* in a sentence?"

"Yes," I said. "I have no idea what circumlocution means."

I didn't realize it was funny until I heard everyone laughing. My best lines were usually accidental.

I didn't try in school. I liked history and science, but I didn't admit it, even when I knew an answer. For some reason, reading and spelling came easy to me, but I played dumb writing book reports, deliberately using bad grammar and misspelling words so I could salvage decent grades at the end of the semester by my apparent "improvement." With math, I didn't have to pretend to be dumb. Numbers had the perfect name. They made my brain numb. My dad offered his own brand of advice.

"You have to work at it," he said. "Nobody ever got hit in the ass with a magic wand and woke up smart."

One of Mom's bridge cronies, Barbara Pratt, was good with numbers. Mom asked her to tutor me in algebra. Once a week, I went to her house after school.

"Now, Gary, can you name the factors for 231?"

"Mrs. Pratt, when would I use this?"

"When you're factoring," she said, opening my textbook. "Let's try a word problem. Inside a cash register is 227 dollars in bills. There are six more five-dollar bills than tens. The number of one-dollar bills is two more than twenty-four times the number of ten-dollar bills. How many tens, fives, and ones are in the cash register?"

These kinds of questions seemed like practical jokes. How could anyone know in advance that there were 227 dollars, much less six more fives than tens and "two more than twenty-four times" ones than tens? How could anyone know all that without counting how many tens, fives, and ones were there in the first place? A store manager would ask how much is in the register and leave it at that. If he wanted to know how many tens, fives, or ones there were, he wouldn't make some artificial puzzle out of it. He'd count them.

The next day, Mom had her bridge group to our house. While I was in the kitchen, I overheard Mrs. Pratt talking.

"I'm sorry, Regina," Mrs. Pratt told Mom, "I don't think I can help Gary."

At school, they stuck me in Mr. Stratton's bonehead math class. Mr. Stratton was a hard-ass. He had been in the Marine Corps. He still wore a crew cut. He was hard of hearing because a grenade had gone off near him in Korea. He called us by our last names, even the girls. Mr. Stratton used the Vietnam War as a scare tactic to get us guys to do our algebra homework.

"All you guys are gonna come back from Vietnam in a wooden box," he said. "You're getting an opportunity for an education, and you're blowing it. You think school's gonna last forever, but it's gonna be over before you know it. You guys who can't get into college are the ones they put on the front lines IN VIETNAM! YOU GUYS BETTER LISTEN UP, OR YOU'RE GONNA COME BACK IN A WOODEN BOX FROM *VIETNAM*!"

"What a dick," Randy Rydell whispered.

Randy had longish, straight hair. He wore paisley shirts. He ate lunch every day with three girls, a blonde named Sally Parker, a brunette named Sandra Foster, and a redhead, Nancy Turner. They were crazy about Randy. They were as uninterested in me as Randy seemed to be in them. Girls just didn't feel the same pull toward guys that we felt toward them. I didn't understand it. One day at lunch, I decided to watch Randy. I thought I could learn something from him.

"Isn't Jefferson Airplane a bitchin band?" Sally asked.

"Sure," Randy replied.

"Lend me a quarter, Randy," Nancy said.

"Sure," he said, holding out a coin.

"Lend me one, too," Sandra said.

"Okay," he said.

"Thanks, Randy. You're so boss."

"Yeah, Randy," Nancy said. "You're a really bitchin guy."

Maybe that was my problem with girls. I wasn't bitchin enough. Mr. Hellfrick, wearing a light purple suit, was scanning the lunchtime crowd for guys with long hair.

"Shit, here comes Hellfrick," Randy said. "Gotta go."

Randy hid behind the cafeteria.

"Mr. Hellfrick's so lame," Sandra said.

"He's a narc," Sally added.

"YOU THERE, JOHNSON," Mr. Hellfrick yelled, "GET A HAIRCUT! AND YOU, FISHMAN, AND YOU, TOO, LA PAGE!"

Mr. Hellfrick carried a clipboard where he wrote a list of names. I didn't have to worry about Mr. Hellfrick's haircut list since my dad made me keep it short.

"HEY YOU, THORPE!"

"Me?"

"YES, YOU. TUCK IN YOUR SHIRT!"

CHAPTER 5

Cumshaw

"What d'ya need?" Sweeny asked.

"Two sunny side," Estorga replied.

"How's that laundry basket coming?"

"Working on it."

I was standing in the breakfast chow line behind Estorga.

"What's he talking about?" I asked.

"Cumshaw."

"What?"

"Nothing. Part of my job."

"What is your job, anyway? I thought you worked in the ship's office."

"That's just part time. I work in the 3-M office for the XO and Chief Skinner."

"What's the 3-M office?"

"Maintenance and Material Management. It's on the 01 level. Whenever any of the division chiefs need anything built or repaired, they have to submit a two-kilo form to the 3-M office for the XO's approval."

"So, you're a yeoman?"

"Yeah. Well, no. Abernathy, Hayashi, and Wilcox are yeomen. I'm a striker. I never went to 'A' school."

"How did you get the job?"

"I can type."

We saw two empty chairs at a table with Cool and Mendoza. Cool was pouring his coffee over his corn flakes.

"*Qué paso*, Uncle Al," Estorga said, putting his tray down.

Mendoza nodded without taking his eyes off Cool. We were coming in on the middle of their conversation.

"Mr. Southcott shot down my chit for 'A' school," Cool said. "He keep sayin' can't nobody stand watch who didn' go to 'A' school. Then, when I put in for it, he say he got too many strikers already. What I look like? A fool?"

"You don't think an officer would lie, do ya?" Mendoza asked with a grin.

"Ain' they lied to us before? I tell him I'm here longer than anybody. He jus' say pick up a wire brush and turn to."

"I wanted to send you to 'A' school, before they busted me down to second class."

"You got busted, Al?" Estorga asked.

Mendoza sipped his coffee.

"A year ago, I was the lead quartermaster. I was going on two weeks leave, but Mr. Southcott shot down my request chit because I put down my girlfriend's address in Oakland for my leave address instead of my wife's address in El Paso. I figured that was none of his business, but I couldn't do shit about it. But then, the XO had a raffle to raise money for the Red Cross, and I won. First prize was two weeks leave. I wrote out a new request chit with my girlfriend's address, and this time Southcott *had* to sign it, but he got pissed off. While I was gone, he requested a replacement from BUPERS. When I got back, Chief Lasko was here—the *new* lead quartermaster. I went out and got drunk. I forgot it was my duty day, so Southcott wrote me up, and I went to captain's mast. Captain Grant busted me to second class, but I made first again."

Captain's mast is an old Navy tradition. The name is a holdover from the wooden-ship days, when malefactors were lashed to the mast and flogged with a cat o' nine tails. In the modern Navy, captain's mast refers to non-judicial punishment, a mock trial with the ship's captain in the triple role of prosecutor, judge, and interpreter of the UCMJ—Uniform Code of Military Justice. Punishment mostly consists of fines, restrictions, reduction of rank, or combinations of all three, but they haven't completely abandoned the old days. Occasionally, they still hand down a sentence of three days in the brig on bread and water.

"How I'ma get to 'A' school now?" Cool asked. "Won't nobody recommen' me. I axed the chief, but he say put in a chit to Mr. Southcott. Then, Mr. Southcott shoot down my chit, and he requess' strikers from BUPERS. Thass how you got here, Shortcut, and he got two more on the way. But I'ma keep puttin' in a chit every month, anyhow. I know

Southcott jus' gon' shoot 'em down, but I like messin' with him."

"NOW QUARTERS, QUARTERS," said the 1MC, "ALL HANDS TO QUARTERS FOR MUSTER, INSPECTION, AND INSTRUCTION. THAT IS ALL."

"Skidmaw," Mr. Southcott said, "read the POD."

"Item one," Skidmore recited. "The following appliances are not allowed aboard ship due to possible faulty wiring and leakage currents: fans, portable extension cords, electric blankets, heating pads, power tools, high-intensity lamps, heat lamps, sun lamps, hot plates, griddles, electric clocks, microwave ovens, electric heaters, portable refrigerators, portable air conditioners, and immersion water heaters. Item two. Anyone with knowledge of who dropped firecrackers down the voice tubes into officers' country, see the master-at-arms, Petty Officer Needler. Item three. Payday will commence on the mess decks at 0930."

"NOW TURN TO," said the 1MC, "COMMENCE SHIP'S WORK."

"OK, wheels," Mendoza said when we got to the bridge, "the bridge is a showplace. Let's get a broom and a swab and a foxtail and some rags and some Brasso, and let's clean up this shithouse up here. Shortcut, get a bucket of suds and a scrub brush and start scrubbing off all the shoe scuff marks from around the base of the steering console."

I was lying on my side, scrubbing the console with my head an inch above the deck, when Mr. Southcott and Chief Lasko came through the after door. Mr. Southcott was talking.

"Chief, I don't know why anyone in his right mind would make a careeah of the Navy. I'm only heah long enough to get my sea time for the merchant marine. The Southcott family has a military tradition going back to the Revolutionary Wah."

I was dying to ask him which side they were on.

"Chief, did you awdah those new charts from the hydrographic office?" Mr. Southcott asked.

"Yes, sir."

"Did the latest Notice to Mariners come in yet?"

"It's over on the chart table, sir."

"Make a hole, Thawpe," Mr. Southcott said because I was on the deck between him and the chart table, "I said, MOVE IT!"

When I didn't move it fast enough, Mr. Southcott gave me a kick in the ribs. I rolled over on my back and looked up at him. Our eyes locked. I could feel the blood rushing to my head. It was a weak kick. I wasn't hurt, but I was pissed off, and it must have shown because Mr. Southcott's eyes opened wide behind his glasses. I saw a trace of panic, as if he could read my thoughts that, officer or no officer, I just might get up and kick his sorry ass halfway back to Boston. Instead, I got a grip on my temper and kept myself from saying out loud the obscenities that came rushing to mind.

When he saw I wasn't going to do anything, Mr. Southcott's expression returned to his usual cold glare. I doubted that the academy encouraged officers to kick enlisted men, but I didn't expect him to apologize to a lower-than-whale-shit nonrate like me. I think that was the day Mr. Southcott started hating me. I know it was the day I started hating him.

"It's your turn to wind the clocks, Thorpe," Chief Lasko said. "Let's get at it. And stop in at supply. We're almost out of pencils."

Once a week, one of the quartermasters had to wind and set all the clocks in every space on the ship but radio central. You needed a clearance to get in there. I still didn't know my way around the ship very well. First stop was CIC. The two operations specialists, Goldbrick and Coatrack, were doing routine maintenance on a radar scope, taking it apart and putting it back together.

"What d'ya want, Shortcut?" Goldbrick asked. He was a second-class whose real name was Goldberg.

"I'm here to wind the clock."

Coatrack, a third-class whose real name was Kettrick, pointed out the clock on the bulkhead behind a status board. I opened the glass face of the clock, inserted my key, and wound it up. I set the clock and checked it off my list.

I went to officers' country on the 05 level. In the wardroom, two stewards, Lim and Delgado, were setting the long dining table with silverware and blue-and-white china. I wound and set the clock next to a cabinet filled with glassware. The empty chiefs' quarters on the 04 level was a more spacious version of 02 berthing. They had forty racks, though we maybe had twenty-five chiefs aboard, and their own TV set, which was why we never saw anyone above E-6 in the TV lounge. I wound the clock on the bulkhead above the TV.

On the 03 level, Larkin, the postal clerk, let me into the little post office to wind his clock. Garvey was swabbing the deck in sick bay while I wound the clock over Finesse's desk. Hayashi, a third-class yeoman, didn't look up from his typing as I wound the clock in the ship's office. Below the main deck, I stopped in at the ship's storeroom. The head supply clerk, a bald black chief named Bledsoe, watched me wind his clock and yawned.

"The quartermaster gang needs a box of pencils, Chief," I said.

"Gotta fill out a request chit," he said, handing me a form that looked like a tax return.

"For a box of pencils? Are you serious?"

"As a heart attack."

After I filled it out, he took it and disappeared into the storeroom. He came back without the pencils.

"We can't let you have the pencils, Thorpe," he said. "Mr. Wheeler says your division is over budget. You guys owe us from last month."

"You mean we have to *buy* them?"

"That's affirmative."

"But haven't they already been paid for? Aren't they government property?"

"Sure, they're government property. You don't think the government gives things away for free, do ya? You gotta buy 'em, like everybody else."

"But aren't we all in the same boat here, Chief? Don't we both work for the same government? It sounds like we're selling pencils to ourselves."

Mr. Wheeler came out of the storeroom. He was the supply officer, a pudgy lieutenant with hair like steel wool.

"Listen, Thorpe, we don't have time for this," he said. "You tell your division PO to settle up, and you'll get the pencils."

"Aye aye, sir."

Either the government was crazy, or I was.

I made my way down to the engineering spaces where the ship's massive boilers and generators were housed. I edged along the narrow catwalks through a maze of pipes and valves and purple JP5 fuel lines. There were a bunch of snipes in the engine room, where the orders from the lee helm on the bridge were received and answered. Mr. Barker, the engineering officer, was standing over some paperwork with Machinist's Mate Chief Graves. Koslowski, the second-class who was on quarterdeck watch the morning I reported aboard, was drinking coffee with Big Time, a black first-class boiler technician who looked like an overweight Joe Frazier. A red-headed third-class hull technician called Screwball was tightening a valve handle. Crimmons was swabbing the deck. They all looked up when I came in.

"Who are you?" Chief Graves asked me. He had sleepy eyes, a nose like a radish, and a faded green propeller tattooed on his right forearm.

"Thorpe, Chief. I'm here to wind your clocks."

"The new naviguesser, huh? It's on the after bulkhead."

"Chief, do you have any extra pencils you can spare?" I asked.

"Got any cumshaw?" Screwball asked, grinning. "Gotta give something to get something."

"If you want pencils, try supply, Thorpe," Mr. Barker said, "and don't forget to wind the clock in after-steering."

"Yes, sir."

"Crimmons," Chief Graves said, "run up to supply and get us another ration of coffee."

"Okay, Chief," Crimmons replied, and he grabbed the empty can.

"How do I get to after-steering, Chief?" I asked.

"Show him, Koslowski," Chief Graves said.

"Let's go," Koslowski said.

Crimmons and I followed him out of the engine room.

"How do you guys find your way around down here?" I asked. "I can't even find the ladder I came down on."

"Let's take the freight elevator," Crimmons said.

The big freight elevator ran from the main deck down past the engineering spaces to the holds. We could hear it rumbling. Koslowski pointed at a sign that read: PERSONNEL ARE FORBIDDEN TO RIDE THE ELEVATOR.

"I do it all the time," Crimmons said.

The empty elevator was moving up slowly. When it was level with the third deck, Koslowski grabbed Crimmons by his arm.

"About a year ago, we had a new guy named Cross," Koslowski said. "A week after he reported aboard, he thought he'd ride that elevator. He thought it was going up, so he jumped aboard, but it was going down. When he tried to jump off, he slipped and fell. He was halfway in and halfway out. Nobody was there to push the stop button. The elevator came down and cut him in half. So, no riding the freight elevator, or you're on report."

We climbed up out of the engineering spaces. Koslowski pointed me toward after-steering, located at the stern of the ship, right below the fantail and directly over the ship's rudder. In case there was ever a loss of steering control from the bridge, the rudder could be directly operated by cable from after-steering. I found the clock, wound it up, and checked it off my list.

I went up the ladders to the 01 level. I headed aft along the passageway past the TV lounge to the 3-M office and opened the door. It was a quiet little hole with just enough room for a desk and two filing cabinets. Estorga looked up from behind the typewriter.

"Say, Raul, you got any pencils?"

"Got any cumshaw?" he asked.

"What does that mean?"

"Trading stolen goods. A bribe to get around red tape."

"All you guys are in business for yourselves."

"Don't worry about it, man. Check the bottom desk drawer."

Inside the drawer was a stack of porn magazines. I pulled out the top two, *Sappho* and *Apartment Sinners*.

"Wrong drawer," he said.

He opened another drawer and handed me the pencils.

"Is that hot chocolate?" I asked, pointing at a box full of envelopes next to the coffee maker. "Man, I could drink that like these lifers drink Navy coffee."

"Take some."

"Thanks."

When I got back to the bridge and handed Chief Lasko his pencils, he wasn't exactly grateful.

"Grab a wire brush, Thorpe."

At 0930, an announcement came over the 1MC.

"NOW PAYDAY WILL COMMENCE ON THE MESS DECKS WITH THE DISBURSING OFFICER."

Everyone lined up outside the mess decks, waiting to get paid. The disbursing officer, Ensign Benson, paid us in cash. I got 160 dollars twice a month. It was not just a job. You got paid more on a job. I walked out of the mess decks with my cash and headed down the passageway toward Graff, Malolo, and Shilgenkrauser, muscle boys who worked in deck and collected for Kickback, a supply clerk striker who worked in the gedunk. According to the scuttlebutt, Kickback made more from his slushing racket than he did from his regular pay. Since we were paid in cash, payday was the time to settle debts with no excuses. Slushers like Alaska collected debts themselves, but Kickback's operation was big enough for him to hire guys like Graff, Malolo, and Shilgenkrauser to do it. Graff and Malolo took up space in the passageway until Shilgenkrauser shook his head, and they let me through.

That afternoon, after knockoff in 02 berthing, Koslowski's voice came over the 1MC.

"NOW SWEEPERS, SWEEPERS, MAN YOUR BROOMS. GIVE THE SHIP A CLEAN SWEEP DOWN FORE AND AFT. SWEEP DOWN ALL DECKS, LADDERS, AND PASSAGEWAYS. EMPTY ALL TRASH CANS AND BUTT-KITS. SWEEPERS."

Billings grabbed a broom. The duty non-rates had to sweep their compartments and passageways twice a day.

"Come on, Estorga," Stretch said. "Let's take the rookie out for a beer. Bring your laundry, Shortcut."

We took Estorga's green '68 Plymouth Satellite to the enlisted men's club on base where they served anybody with a military ID. Next door to the EM club was the first-class bachelor enlisted quarters. We stopped there first. There were washers and dryers in the head of the BEQ with cardboard signs taped to the bulkheads. The signs read: THESE MACHINES ARE FOR USE OF THE FIRST-CLASS BACHELOR ENLISTED QUARTERS ONLY! OFF-LIMITS TO ALL OTHERS!

"Maybe we should get out of here," I said.

"Nobody's going to look in the machines to see if there's a first-class crow on our sleeves," Stretch said.

We dumped our laundry into three washing machines and walked over to the EM club, a big room with a bar and two pool tables. The place was empty except for a couple of guys at the bar. We sat in a red vinyl booth. Stretch and Estorga lit cigarettes. A waitress old enough to be a grandmother came to the table.

"I'll have a triple zombie," Stretch said.

"A pitcher of beer," Estorga said.

"How come none of the guys from the ship are in here?" I asked.

"They go to the bars in town," Stretch replied. "Chasing WESTPAC widows."

"WESTPAC widows?"

"Wives of guys gone on WESTPAC."

"Hoodwink's wife has a boyfriend aboard the *Pyro*," Estorga said.

"And another one aboard the *Kilauea*," Stretch added.

After we had another round, Estorga went back to the BEQ to put our laundry into dryers. We ordered another pitcher.

"Got a mission for ya, rookie," Stretch told me. "New guy folds."

They sent me back to the laundry room to fold our clothes. When I was almost done, a guy walked in. He looked old enough to be a first class, but I couldn't tell his rank because he was in his underwear. I could guess what he was thinking. I was in civilian clothes, but I looked too young to be a first class doing his laundry in the BEQ. The guy was looking at me like he was coming to some kind of decision.

"You know this laundry room's for first classes only," he said, pointing at the cardboard signs taped over the washing machines. "See those notices?"

"I never noticed those notices," I said.

"What's your name, lad?"

"You about done there, Landry?"

It was Stretch at the door, with Estorga beside him.

"Almost," I replied, putting the last dungaree shirt into my sea bag.

"Hold on a minute," the guy said. "I'm Yeoman First Class Walker. Who are you?"

"Quartermaster First Class Hudson," Stretch replied.

Like me, Stretch didn't look old enough to be a first class, but his height and his civilian clothes left some doubt.

"How am I supposed to know that?" Walker asked, looking at Stretch with suspicion. "You're out of uniform."

"Look who's talking," Stretch replied. "If you're gonna run around in your skivs, Walker, maybe you'd better get your stripes tattooed on."

"Maybe we should tell the XO there's a guy in his boxers hassling people in the head," Estorga said.

"Good idea," Stretch replied.

Yeoman First Class Walker's face flushed bright red.

"Who are you?" he asked Estorga.

"Chief Garcia," Estorga replied.

"You guys stay right here. I'm gonna call the master-at-arms."

Yeoman First Class Walker stepped out through the door. We grabbed our laundry and hurried outside to Estorga's car. By the time Yeoman First Class Walker got his uniform on, we were on our way back to the ship.

CHAPTER 6

Sight Reduction

In eighth grade, I read a *National Geographic* story about Robin Lee Graham, the kid who sailed alone around the world aboard a twenty-six-foot fiberglass sloop called *The Dove*. I kept re-reading it. I couldn't stop thinking about boats and sailing. I made lists of supplies that I would need for an ocean voyage. I mowed lawns and cleaned windows to earn money for the sailboat I intended to buy someday.

I joined the Sea Scouts partly for free sailing lessons and partly because my mom thought it was a good way for me to make new friends, but the group was full of jerks like Frank Lyle and Mickey Walsh. We met on Wednesday nights. The skipper was Mr. Hessler, a tall guy with thin hair and a pointed chin. He was also a little league coach, and he owned an auto dealership called Hessler Chrysler.

Mr. Hessler taught us the points of sail, nautical terminology, and how to tie knots. On Saturdays, we went day-sailing in a thirty-foot sloop from Long Beach to Newport and back. The first time we went out, one guy got seasick and caught a face full of his own vomit, which gave us an important lesson: Never throw up over the windward side. We learned to steer with a tiller and how to trim the main sail and the jib to go in any direction except straight upwind. On our way back in the late afternoons, the wind would get high, blowing spray in our faces. The boat would heel way over, with the fiberglass hull pounding through the swells.

One afternoon, I was coming out of my Spanish class on the second floor of the language building. Tony Lopez was right behind me. We never liked each other since that time in grade school when I tried to kiss a girl named Cristina who turned out to be his little sister. She ran and told him, and we got into a fight.

"This class must be an easy A for you, Lopez," I said. "You already speak Spanish."

He hawked up a loogie, spit at me, and missed. I spit one back at him, but it went over the rail to ground level and landed dead center on the bald head of Mr. Heywood, the chemistry teacher. He looked up, and I pulled back. Mr. Heywood came running up the stairs fast. I hoped he didn't see me. I figured my best plan was to stay still and keep quiet. There were a lot of us on the second floor. If I ran, he'd spot me for sure. He came toward me like a magnet.

"PRINCIPAL'S OFFICE, THORPE," he yelled, pointing at me. "LET'S GO."

"Busted," Lopez said with a happy grin.

"Cram it," I said.

Lopez and some other guys started laughing. Mr. Heywood took me to see the principal, Mr. Granger, a craggy-faced southerner with a nose shaped like a lightbulb. Mr. Heywood had to leave for his next class, and Mr. Granger read the referral form that Mr. Heywood had filled out while I sat on the other side of his desk. Without saying anything, he went to a filing cabinet and took out a folder. He studied it for some time. I was getting nervous with him not saying anything. If I was going to get a swat or a suspension, why not just get it over with?

"Don't you like school, Gary?" he finally said, lifting his eyes from the folder.

"I guess not."

"Why not?"

"I guess I'm not smart enough."

"So, you don't think you're smart? Do you realize that you've scored in the top ten percent for reading skills every year since the first grade?"

I didn't know what he was talking about. He spun the folder around and let me see it.

"The Iowa tests, remember? You took them every year. Your reading comprehension scores are among the best students of your age in the United States. So, don't tell me you're not smart. Not trying is more like it."

This was news. Why were they keeping this a secret? Why couldn't they tell my parents?

"Your history and science scores are average," Mr. Granger went on. "Your math scores are below average. How are you doing in Mr. Stratton's class?"

"Not too good."

"What is it about math that spooks you?"

I took a deep breath.

"I don't know, Mr. Granger. It makes sense when the teachers explain it, but when I try to do the problems, I can't remember what they said, and I get the wrong answers."

"Math's important, Gary. Just because you're good at reading doesn't mean you can ignore math. Now, go back to class, and don't spit off the second floor anymore, or I'll give you a suspension."

I didn't get it. I had spit on Mr. Heywood, and instead of getting a swat, I was sent to my next class, bonehead math with Mr. Stratton. He was yelling at the blackboard, with his back to the class, as I walked in and sat down.

"ANYBODY, WHAT IS THE NAME FOR THE EXPRESSION I JUST WROTE ON THE BLACKBOARD?"

Mr. Stratton yelled a lot because he was hard of hearing from that grenade in Korea. After five seconds of silence, he continued.

"IT'S CALLED A POLYNOMIAL, PEOPLE. PO-LY-NO-MI-AL. IF YOU GUYS THINK POLYNOMIALS ARE TOUGH, WAIT UNTIL YOU GET TO VIETNAM!"

Mr. Stratton walked around the classroom, working his way over toward Connie Swank. Connie wasn't exactly beautiful, but she was sort of tough and sexy. She was a redhead. She smoked cigarettes. She wore miniskirts and had a scoop of green eyeshadow on each eyelid like some old western movie saloon girl. Connie didn't see Mr. Stratton coming toward her because she had her head down. She was busy scribbling something on a piece of paper and showing it to Annabella Caldarella, a pretty Italian girl with long black hair and the biggest bra size of any girl on campus—or any grown woman on the faculty. Connie and Annabella were giggling as Mr. Stratton snatched the paper away from Connie. He held it up for everyone to see. It was a sketch of him, Mr. Stratton, a pretty good likeness, except he had horns coming out of his head, bloodshot eyes, and pointed teeth dripping saliva. A few people laughed.

"THIS IS ALL CONNIE SWANK IS GOOD FOR," Mr. Stratton announced to the class. "AND THIS IS WHY SHE WILL PROBABLY NEVER AMOUNT TO ANYTHING IN LIFE, UNLESS SHE TAKES MY ADVICE AND WAKES UP AND STARTS PAYING ATTENTION."

He was trying to embarrass her, but Connie didn't embarrass.

"Fuck you," she said.

The whole class went silent. Nobody had ever said that to a teacher, especially not to Mr. Stratton. He stared at her for several long seconds.

"YOU'RE WELCOME," he said.

Connie was saved by Mr. Stratton's bad hearing. He thought she said *thank you*. He never understood why the whole class started laughing.

I was reading about the Polynesians crossing long stretches of the Pacific in canoes and reaching tiny islands without instruments. Pinpointing a position in the middle of the ocean seemed like magic. I asked Dad if he knew how they did it.

"If you want to find out, crack the books," he said. "Nobody ever got hit in the ass with a magic wand and woke up smart."

Despite my weak math, I was determined to figure out how it worked. The encyclopedia in the school library explained that dead reckoning was an educated guess based on your course and speed from your last known position. *The Complete Book of Boating* covered navigation within sight of land, which wasn't hard to understand. The only book in the library on celestial navigation, *Navigation the Easy Way* by Lane and Montgomery, was like swimming against the current. I read it and re-read it and couldn't get a grip on it.

I took a mail correspondence course on celestial navigation from the Davis Instrument Company in San Leandro, California. The magic procedure was called sight reduction. You started with an assumed position. Noting the precise time, you used a sextant to measure the angle above the horizon of a celestial body like the sun, the moon, Venus, Mars, Jupiter, Saturn, or one of fifty-eight stars. The *Nautical Almanac* provided you with the earthly position, latitude and longitude, directly below the celestial body at the exact second of your sextant sight. That was the sight part.

The reduction part was using that information to figure out what the sextant angle *should* have been if you really were where you thought you were. Since that was never the case, there was always a difference between what you observed and what you calculated. That difference, known as the intercept, could be plotted on the chart to give one line of position. You were somewhere on that line. Multiple sight reductions gave you several lines of position. If at least three lines crossed at the same point, you had a fix. You knew exactly where you were.

The tricky part was calculating what your angle should have been. To avoid memorizing spherical trigonometry formulas, most sailors looked up pre-computed altitudes and azimuths in tables. The rest of the math was third-grade addition and subtraction for corrections, but there were lots of corrections. One mistake could put you miles off.

The Davis Instrument Company sent me navigation problems to work out. I had some sense for geometry from shooting pool with Nate and Chuck at the bowling alley. I plotted positions on a chart with dividers and parallel rulers. I mailed them back to somebody in San Leandro who would correct my mistakes in pencil and mail them back to me. I slowly learned the steps that led to the right answers, but I didn't see the big picture. I couldn't understand *why* it worked. None of it explained how the Polynesians found their way without any of this stuff. It was still magic.

One Wednesday, our Sea Scout group had a father-son night. All the guys showed up with their dads, except me.

"Where's *your* dad, Thorpe?"

It was Frank Lyle.

"Nigeria," I said.

Lyle's dad was on the far side of the room talking to Mr. Hessler. They were golfing buddies. Mr. Lyle sold insurance. He drove a green '67 Imperial that he bought at Mr. Hessler's dealership.

"I saw that place on a map," Lyle said. "It's spelled like nigger."

"That's Niger," I said. "It's not even the same country."

"Your dad must be a jigaboo," he said.

"Your dad must be the father of a moron."

It took him a few seconds to get the insult, which sort of proved my point. Then, he shoved me, so I gave him a pop in the mouth. Mr. Hessler and Mr. Lyle came running over. All the guys were staring at us.

"Gary, why did you hit Frank?" Mr. Hessler asked.

"What happened, Frank?" Mr. Lyle asked.

"I don't know, Dad," Lyle replied. "I just asked him where his dad was, and he hauled off and belted me."

"I want you to do ten push-ups, Gary," Mr. Hessler said. "Then, apologize to Frank and shake hands."

"You left out the part where you called my dad a jigaboo," I said to Lyle.

"My son knows better than to use words like that," Mr. Lyle said. I could see where Lyle got his ugly mug from.

"Your son is a liar," I said.

"Gary, I gave you an order," Mr. Hessler said. "Do ten push-ups."

Lyle was grinning at me.

"No," I said.

"A scout can't disobey an order from his skipper," Mr. Hessler said.

"I quit," I said, and I walked out.

That was the end of my time in the Sea Scouts.

My parents weren't getting along. Their friends said Dad had a dream job because he travelled to interesting places and ate his meals in nice restaurants. Dad said they didn't understand that travel was work. When he came home from his trips, he wanted my mother's home cooking. Mom loved to go out to restaurants. Dad was sick of restaurants.

That was only one source of friction between them. Mom was alone half the time and cooped up with an overworked husband the other half. When Dad wasn't traveling, he would come home exhausted after a workday and hours on the freeways. I understood Mom's point of view. She was alone when he was gone, and she was alone when he was home. Dad didn't see the problem. As far as he was concerned, he was doing his job and supporting his family. His job happened to be traveling and entertaining clients. Dad wasn't about to have Mom tell him how to live his life. I could see his point of view, too, but I wondered why he got married in the first place if he felt that way. I didn't wonder for long. Dad moved out and got a place closer to his office. Toward the end of my ninth-grade year, they got divorced.

During the final week of ninth grade, Nate, Chuck, Randy, and I were signing each other's yearbooks. Several girls, including Randy's lunchtime harem, had written in his. *To a really bitchin guy. Love ya, Sally. See you next year. Love, Sandra. Have a boss summer. Luv, Nancy.* Girls really liked to throw around that word *love*. They thought it was charming or something to say how much they love everything and everybody, but they overdid it until it lost all meaning. I have heard girls say "I love those shoes" with more enthusiasm than they say "I love my boyfriend."

In Sunday school, they say we should love everybody because we are all brothers and sisters. That sounds good until you give it a little thought. If everyone is a brother or sister, then brothers and sisters are nothing special. Besides that, what kind of weak, watered-down version of love puts family and friends on the same level as some bastard who kicks dogs and drowns cats? Anybody who really cared about every single person on earth would never stop crying.

I wrote in Randy's book. *See you in high school, Gary T.* The bell rang for the end of lunch.

"I'm sick of this place," Randy said.

"Let's ditch school," Chuck replied.

"How about the bowling alley?" Nate suggested.

We left campus separately and met up at the bowling alley. We spent an hour shooting eight ball on this horrible old table with dead cushions and ripples in the surface. We planned to stay there until the normal time to go home so our mothers wouldn't get suspicious. It would have worked if a local cop hadn't walked in and spotted us. He was six feet tall, with a pistol, a big gut, and a jaw like a hatchet. The brass name plate above his badge read: OFFICER BEEBIN.

"Aren't you boys out of school a little early?" he asked.

"The school year's almost over," Randy replied, which was true but didn't answer the question.

"I'll check into it," Officer Beebin said.

The next day, Mr. Granger called the four of us to his office.

"Rydell, Stansfield, Throckmorton, and Thorpe," he said. "You were seen off campus during school hours yesterday without authorization. I could send you to see Mr. Hellfrick for a couple of swats, or you can stay after school with me until 5:00 and pick up trash on campus. What'll it be?"

Chuck spoke up for all of us:

"I always appreciated a clean campus."

The next day, Mr. Hellfrick called me into his office. He wasn't there when I walked in, but his secretary, Mrs. Reifschneider, told me to sit down. Mrs. Reifschneider always kept a pencil or two in her knot of gray hair. Some of the guys called her "Satan's receptionist." Mr. Hellfrick walked in wearing an electric-blue suit.

"Have you contacted his mother, Mrs. Reifschneider?"

"Yes, Mr. Hellfrick. Mrs. Thorpe is on her way down."

"Good. We'll wait for her."

He went into his office and closed the door. I was racking my brain, going over my recent activities. This couldn't be about ditching school the day before, or Randy and Chuck and Nate would have been sitting there with me. Mom showed up in half an hour. She gave me an exasperated look that said: "What now?" I threw up my hands and shrugged. Mr. Hellfrick opened the door and called us into his office.

"Please sit down, Mrs. Thorpe," he said. "I'm sorry to have to bother you, but this is of a very serious nature. I'm sure Gary didn't fully realize what he was doing when he did this."

"Did what, Mr. Hellfrick?"

Hellfrick cleared his throat.

"One of our girls, Jennifer Murray, took her yearbook home last night. She was understandably upset when she found what Gary wrote in it. Her parents were upset, as well. They're thinking of contacting an attorney, although I would think the fact that they erased most of it will hurt their case. It's not easy to read, but I think you can make this out."

Jennifer Murray sat next to me in study hall. She had blonde hair and long legs. She usually wore miniskirts. It was mild torture watching her cross and uncross and recross her legs for the whole class period. Hellfrick handed Jennifer's open yearbook to Mom. I looked over Mom's shoulder. The writing was in pencil, more legible than mine and mostly rubbed out, though the first line was clear enough. *Jennifer, I want to fuck you.* The rest of it was erased, except for my name signed at the bottom.

"Mom, can I see that?"

Mom handed me the yearbook. I knew I was off the hook as soon as Hellfrick finished talking. It was true I signed Jennifer's yearbook. I flipped through the pages and found my sloppy writing that my own mother would and did recognize. *Hi Jennifer. Have fun this summer. Good luck next year in high school. Gary.* When Mom showed it to Hellfrick, he tried to brush it off.

"Well, Mrs. Thorpe, you saw the same thing I saw. Gary turned right to it. Obviously, he's innocent. Somebody else must have done this. Gary, can you think of anyone who would want to get you into this kind of trouble?"

I could think of a dozen guys who would want to get me into that kind of trouble. Mom spoke up before I could say anything. Her eyes took on a hard glitter, an expression of disapproval I knew well, but her anger wasn't directed at me.

"Mr. Hellfrick, I don't think it was necessary for you to have me come all the way down here for something Gary could have cleared up in a few seconds. You pulled him out of class for this, and we both know his grades need work. Frankly, you have me wondering if you don't have something against my son. Can you give me one good reason why I shouldn't lodge a complaint about your handling of this matter with Mr. Granger and the school board?"

Hellfrick looked nervous. I loved it.

"Mrs. Thorpe, you have my sincere apology," Hellfrick said. "You too, Gary."

I could tell he didn't mean that last part. Mom never did lodge a complaint. Still, it was the perfect goodbye to junior high.

CHAPTER 7

Captain Quimp

Stretch was at an all-day working party. Cool was cleaning the bridge windows. I was shining the brass binnacle. Like most binnacles, ours had two iron balls, one attached to each side. The port one was painted red, and the starboard one green. Known as the navigator's balls, their purpose was to counteract the effect of magnetic deviation on the compass and, according to Stretch, "to compensate for our navigator's lack of balls." When Mr. Southcott overheard that joke, he sent Stretch to the working party instead of me.

A new guy showed up on the bridge. He was about five foot six and no more than 130 pounds, with brown hair, a mustache, and new dungarees. Chief Lasko asked him if he kept all his notes from quartermaster school. The new guy took the bait and said yes. The chief told him to shitcan them, and he had his singlehanded laugh. Then, Mendoza told him the bridge was a showplace and handed him a broom.

I was shining the brass turnbuckles and trying to remember why I joined the Navy when I felt something hit my foot. The new guy had his broom up against my boondocker, and it was no accident.

"Don't let me get in your way," I said.

He leaned toward me and whispered:

"Got any pot?"

"No."

"Lookin' for any?"

He was ready for me coming and going. I was in a bad mood. I had to take crap from Southcott, Lasko, and Mendoza, but I wasn't about to take any from some half-pint, sawed-off seaman apprentice with less time in than me.

"I don't know who you think you are, but if you don't get that broom off my boot, we're gonna get acquainted."

He gave me a big grin.

"You got a hair trigger, don'tcha?" he said. "Jeff Hutchinson, Corpus Christi."

"I thought everything was bigger in Texas."

Making fun of a guy's height is a cheap shot, but I was trying to wipe the smirk off his face. It didn't work. Maybe he'd heard that one before. He wasn't moving the broom.

"They call you Shortcut, right? Mind if Ah call you Short, for short?"

The cocky little bastard was either a karate expert or he was letting his mouth overload his ability. I couldn't tell which. Either way, he was calling my bluff. I wasn't about to punch him, but he didn't know that—or maybe he did. He was leaning on that broom handle, grinning. I don't know how long our standoff would have lasted if Mr. Southcott hadn't walked in.

"All right, Thawpe. If you and Hutchinson are finished socializing, let's turn to."

The following week, another new quartermaster arrived on the bridge. He was stocky and squarish, with blond hair and a full beard.

"*Seaman* Peter Brogan?" Chief Lasko said. "Why are you already an E-3?"

"I had a year of college," Brogan replied.

"Did you save all your notes from quartermaster school?"

Brogan's blue eyes got wide.

"Damn it, Chief, I must have left 'em in the bus station."

Chief Lasko wasn't laughing, but Stretch was.

"You don't look like college material to me, Brogan," Mr. Southcott said. "Thawpe, take Mistah College down to the paint lockah and get some red lead and some haze gray. There's nothing worse than running rust undah paint."

Brogan followed me down the ladders to the main deck. As we made our way to the paint locker, we walked past Malolo, overseeing six deck apes as they painted nonskid on part of the deck. Malolo was one of Kickback's payday collectors, a poker-faced Samoan with a green tattoo of an eagle on his right arm over the letters *USA*.

"Does Mr. Southcott always act like such a douchebag?" Brogan asked.

"He's not acting," I said. "Where are you from, Brogan?"

"French Lick, Indiana."

"You said you went to college?"

"I wanted to major in forestry, but college wasn't for me. I like to read, so I thought I could hack it."

"What kind of stuff do you like to read?"

"*The Hobbit*. Ever read it?"

"No."

"It doesn't teach you much, but it was pretty good. At least the part I read."

"Didn't you finish it?"

"I would have, but I lost it somewhere."

As much as I hated to agree with Mr. Southcott on anything, Brogan didn't strike me as college material, either. He seemed a little lost.

The next afternoon, the officers and crew mustered on the fantail for the arrival of our new CO. Mr. Crookshank stood alongside Captain Grant, our departing CO. Captain Grant, was a real captain, a four striper, the commissioning skipper of the *Okmok*. He was getting a promotion to admiral and an assignment to the Great Lakes Naval Station in Illinois. He was built like a wrestler. He had a massive head with short dark hair graying at the temples, deep set eyes, and a nose like an eagle's beak.

"I AM GOING TO MISS THE FINE CREW OF THE *OKMOK*," Captain Grant said into the microphone. "WELL, MOST OF YOU, ANYWAY. NOW I WOULD LIKE TO INTRODUCE YOU ALL TO YOUR NEW CO, COMMANDER LEONARD J. QUIMP."

To say Commander Quimp looked thin was an understatement. He looked like a starved prison camp survivor. He lifted his head slowly, as if the gold embroidered "scrambled eggs" on his hat visor were too heavy for his scrawny neck to support. He had a shiny facial scar on his starboard side that ran from his temple to his jaw like a jagged bolt of lightning. He saluted Captain Grant. Then, they shook hands. Commander, now Captain, Quimp spoke into the microphone.

"UH...THANK YOU, CAPTAIN GRANT...YOU ARE LEAVING A GREAT...LEGACY...I AM SURE THE OFFICERS AND MEN OF THE *OKMOK* WILL NOT LET YOU DOWN AS WE CONTINUE THAT TRADITION OF...SERVICE."

Combined with his cadaverous appearance, Captain Quimp's high-pitched whining voice and hesitant speech patterns did not inspire confidence.

"WE WILL...MAKE READY FOR SEA TRIALS...IN PREPARATION FOR OUR UPCOMING WESTPAC DEPLOYMENT."

When Captain Quimp dismissed the crew, Captain Grant walked to the quarterdeck. He saluted Chief Strickland, the OOD on watch. He saluted aft toward the flag flying on the fantail, and he walked down the brow to the pier. Delgado spoke over the 1MC.

"CAPTAIN GRANT, DEPARTING."

After knockoff, everybody in 02 berthing except for the duty section was getting ready for liberty call. Swampass came out of the head, and Estorga went in. He immediately came back out holding his nose.

"Jesus, Swampass," Estorga said. "You need to see a doctor."

Stretch had the duty. He was playing casino with Cool and Brogan. I was changing into civilian clothes. Hutchinson was all set to go, in a white shirt, jeans, and cowboy boots. He sat at the table, watching the card game.

"Want to play a hand, rookie?" Stretch asked.

"Ah'm not familiar with that game," Hutchinson replied, "but Ah'm willin' to learn."

Hutchinson took the deck in his left hand. He spread the cards face up. He pulled out the ace of spades, put it on top of the deck, shuffled twice, and showed everyone that the ace of spades was still on top. He asked Stretch to cut, took the ace of spades off the top again, showed it to everyone, and put it back on top. He dealt three cards around the table and one to himself.

"High card deals," he said.

Stretch had the jack of clubs. Cool had the ten of hearts. Brogan had the queen of diamonds. Hutchinson flipped over his card—the ace of spades.

"*Damn*," Cool said.

"Forget it," Stretch said.

Hoodwink's voice came over the 1MC.

"NOW, LIBERTY CALL FOR ALL NON-DUTY SECTIONS TO EXPIRE ONBOARD AT 0700 TOMORROW. LIBERTY CALL."

"If you hadn't put on that little show, you could have cleaned us out," Stretch said.

"That'd be bad for morale," Hutchinson replied with a grin. "You ready, Pete?"

"Yep," Brogan said.

"Where are you guys going?" I asked.

"There's a Jack Nicholson double feature, *Easy Rider* and a new one called *The Last Detail*. Want to come with us?"

"Okay."

I was surprised he asked me. After our stalemate on the bridge, I didn't think we were going to get along. Hutchinson had a sky blue '65 Chevy Biscayne in the parking lot on the pier.

"Nice car," Brogan said.

"Ah just bought it from a lieutenant on base," Hutchinson said.

As we drove up to the main gate, the petty officers on watch saluted us. Hutchinson returned their salute and spoke up.

"Carry on, men," he said.

"They think we're officers?" I asked.

"Ah haven't got around to taking the lieutenant's sticker off the front bumper yet. We look just like three ensigns goin' out clubbin', don't we?"

We drove straight to a liquor store. Since Brogan was over twenty-one, we sent him in to get two six-packs. Then, we drove to the Concord Drive-In.

"How come you guys joined the Navy?" I asked.

"I dropped out of college," Brogan replied. "I didn't have a job. My girlfriend broke up with me. She was a babe. Here's her picture."

He opened his wallet.

"Hey! I lost her picture!"

"Seems like you lose things a lot," Hutchinson said.

"That's what my girlfriend used to say. Then, I lost her, too."

"How come you joined up, Hutchinson?" I asked.

"Daddy was in World War Two," Hutchinson replied, "Granddaddy was in the Spanish-American War, and Great-Granddaddy was in the Civil War. They named me after Granddaddy, Jefferson Davis Hutchinson. That gives you a clue which side Great-Granddaddy fought on."

"So, you're carrying on the family military tradition?" Brogan asked.

"Not exactly. Ah got busted in high school for selling pot. Daddy gave me a choice: Straighten up and join the military like all the Hutchinsons, or forget about mah inheritance."

"What inheritance?"

"Great-Granddaddy left us a little piece of land up in Hutchinson County. They struck oil on it."

"What about you?" Brogan asked me.

"What about me?"

"Why'd you join the Navy?"

"I read too many sea stories."

"You guys want to smoke some pot?" Brogan asked, but when he checked his pockets, he realized he didn't have any. Hutchinson had some in the glove compartment.

"Sell me a dime bag, Jeff?" Brogan asked. "I'll catch you next payday."

"Sure, Pete," Hutchinson replied. "You need some, Shortcut?"

"I don't like to put smoke in my lungs," I said.

"You never even *tried* it?"

Hutchinson sounded surprised.

"I tried some last New Year's Eve, but it didn't do anything for me. Maybe because I was already drunk."

"That's how it was for me the first time," Brogan said.

"Which do you guys like better?" I asked. "Pot or booze?"

"Pot," Hutchinson replied.

"How about pot or sex?" I asked.

They looked at me. Then, they looked at each other.

"Pussy," Brogan said.

"Yeah," Hutchinson agreed. "Pussy—but you should try a hit. You got the head for it."

"No thanks," I said.

"Ah can always get some, in case you change your mind."

I realized why Hutchinson invited me. He was looking for customers. Hutchinson seemed to have more on the ball than the stoner burnouts I remembered from high school—I guess a dealer had to be smarter than his buyers—but he evidently hadn't straightened up like his "daddy" wanted.

The movies started. *Easy Rider* was supposed to be good, but I thought Peter Fonda acted like he just got out of bed. Jack Nicholson couldn't save it. We got some laughs out of *The Last Detail*, especially that part when Nicholson picks a fight with some marines in the head at a train station. While Hutchinson drove us back to the base, we kept repeating Nicholson's lines and laughing. A senior chief on watch at the main gate saluted us. Hutchinson saluted back.

"Ah'm going to have to take off that sticker," he said, "one of these days."

CHAPTER 8

One Out of Five

By the time I entered Lincoln High, the school district had made some changes. Swats became taboo. Dress codes were done away with. It was strange to see guys walking around campus with shoulder-length hair and wearing white t-shirts instead of shirts with collars and buttons.

Randy rode the school bus with me, but we didn't have any classes together. There was a guy on the bus from our neighborhood. Randy and I could tell he was a football player the first time we saw him. He had the skinhead haircut and open sores on his forearms from hitting the sleds. He entertained the other kids on the bus with endless football stories. He sounded to me like he had a chip on his shoulder. I probably would have avoided him if he hadn't turned up in my American History class. He was rehashing last week's scrimmage against Western for a group of people. He kept talking in a low voice right through the class period. The young student teacher turned on him.

"Dennis," she said, "since you want to do so much talking, why don't I give you an extra assignment?"

"I give up, why?" he replied.

A few people laughed.

"See me after class."

"Wow," he said to his audience, "I thought the wicked witch was dead."

"WHAT DID YOU SAY?" flared the teacher.

"I said my pen skips. I think I'll switch to lead."

On the bus the next morning, he recognized me.

"Hey," he said, "you're in my history class, right? What's your name? Thorpe, right? I'm Dennis Beck. I want you to read something, okay? I need your opinion."

He handed me some papers that were stapled together.

"What is it?"

"It's a report on the Lewis and Clark expedition. That bitch made me do it for extra homework."

I read it through. It didn't seem to be anything special. I couldn't see what he was after.

"So, what do you think?" he asked. He had an intense look, like he was trying to read my mind.

"Looks okay," I said.

Beck broke into a false-looking grin.

"Lies," he said. "Solid crap from the first word."

"What are you talking about?"

"I made the whole thing up. You know that part about the Indian guide who died on their second week out? Pure bullshit. And the funeral for that stray dog that saved one of the men's lives? I saw that on *Rawhide* when I was seven."

He went on talking while I re-read the report. It seemed hilarious now in places where it hadn't before. All the time, it had the authoritative ring of a textbook. Beck was good with words.

"Do you think she'll go for it?" I asked.

"Most people will believe anything," Beck replied. "I blame television."

"Television?"

"Sure. Why do you think they call 'em 'programs'?"

The next Monday morning, I got aboard the bus as usual. Randy was sitting in back. He didn't always ride the bus because he had a Honda 250 motorcycle. If Randy was riding the bus, it meant he was out of gas money, or his bike was broken down. I sat in the seat across from him as we got rolling.

"Well, I guess we won't be seeing that Beck guy for a while," he said.

"Why not?"

"I thought you knew."

"Knew what?"

"He went to France."

"France?"

"Yeah, France. His grandmother died. He told me Friday that her funeral was going to be in Paris—what's so funny?"

"Come on, Randy, you didn't believe him, did you?"

"Huh? Why not?"

"He was bullshitting you."

"How do you know?" Randy sounded angry. "You weren't even there when he told me."

That was true enough, but I could just picture Beck reeling off this ridiculous story. When we pulled up to the next stop and Beck climbed aboard, Randy's mouth dropped open.

"Hey, Beck," I yelled. "How's the weather in Paris?"

Beck looked back at us. When he saw Randy's face, he gave us a crooked grin and nodded toward Randy.

"Believed every word of it," he said.

The history teacher had done the same thing. Beck got an A-minus for his Lewis and Clark assignment. She even penciled in a comment: *A very interesting report, Dennis. You have told me things even I was unaware of.*

Randy, Nate, Chuck, and I walked to the bowling alley on Saturday night to shoot some eight ball. I had told Beck we would be there, and he showed up. When I beat Randy, Beck picked up a cue stick and broke. The five ball went in.

"Solids. I got a riddle for ya, Thorpe," he said while sinking the one ball in the corner. "One man builds it, but he doesn't keep it. Another man buys it, but he doesn't use it. A third man has it, but he doesn't know it. What is it?"

"Don't know," I said.

"A coffin."

"That's not funny," Nate said.

"I didn't say it was funny," Beck replied, sinking the seven in the side, "I said it was a riddle."

I thought I knew our warped table with the dead cushions, but Beck kept making shots and keeping up a line of chatter until he beat me. After he beat Randy and Chuck and Nate, too, he gave us a ride home in his blue '66 Volkswagen bug. He was a junior, a year ahead of us, so he had his driver's license.

Beck started hanging around with us. Beck was not only good at pool. He was also a brutal chess player, better than all of us. Playing him was frustrating. Whenever I made a bad move, Beck would say: "The eye sees, but the brain does not comprehend." That was usually just before he said checkmate.

We spent a lot of time playing chess, shooting eight ball, playing pinball, throwing the football, or cramming into Beck's Volkswagen and cruising around. To drive was a huge deal. I had my learner's permit, but I didn't have a car. We considered a drive-in movie or a pinball arcade a great time.

Sometimes, we would find a liquor store where they didn't check IDs. One Saturday night, we got a Chinese liquor clerk to sell us a six pack of Colt 45 and a bottle of Boone's Farm apple wine. Beck drove us to the park to drink it. That night, Chuck started our running joke about statistics.

"I heard on the news last night that one out of every five people is insane," he said.

"If you ask me," Beck replied, "Nate looks a little jumpy."

"Nate always looks jumpy," I said.

"Yeah," Randy agreed. "It's got to be Nate."

"I can eat five Big Macs," Nate said.

"Bullshit," Beck replied.

"No way," Chuck agreed.

"No, really," Nate said. "I bet I can eat five Big Macs."

"Did you say *bet?*" Beck asked.

"Five bucks."

"You're on."

"I'll bet five," Chuck said.

"Me, too," Randy added.

If Chuck had claimed he could eat five Big Macs, nobody would have taken the bet because Chuck was a pretty big dude. Nate was the smallest of us—we would sneak him into drive-in movies in the forward trunk of Beck's bug—but I didn't bet against Nate because I had seen him eat before. He could hold a lot. We laid down the ground rules. Nate had to eat five Big Macs with all of us watching and hold them down for one hour. Losers had to pay for the five Big Macs. The date was set for Saturday. We were all yapping and not paying attention to the parking lot behind us, so we didn't see or hear the police car pull up.

"Pour it all out on the ground, boys," Officer Beebin said, appearing out of the darkness. "Don't let me catch you guys again drinking in public.

And five is too many to fit in a Volkswagen. Go home."

Then, he gave Beck a ticket for an expired registration.

On Saturday, we all got into Beck's bug and drove to the McDonald's on the north side of town. I had been pep-talking Nate all week. We each bought a Big Mac and set them down in front of Nate. The first two went down easily. Nate was chewing slower on the third one. The guys started razzing him.

"It's over," Beck said.

"He's finished," Chuck agreed.

"Don't listen to them, Nate," I said.

Nate finished the third Big Mac and started on the fourth.

"You're going to ruin your stomach," Randy said.

"That's right," Beck agreed. "You know what they put in those things?"

"Foul!" I yelled. "No fair psyching him out."

Nate finished the fourth Big Mac. He took a deep breath and just stared at the last one.

"Oh, yeah," Beck said. "Feel the pain."

"I hope you brought some Alka-Seltzer," Randy said.

"Take your time, Nate," I said.

Nate picked up the fifth Big Mac and took a bite. He chewed it for a long time. When he swallowed, it looked like he was trying to choke down sand. The guys kept ragging him, but Nate gradually devoured the fifth Big Mac. They got quiet as Nate swallowed the last bite. Beck drove us home down a back street full of potholes. The frame of the Volkswagen rattled.

"Remember," he said, "he's got to hold it down for an hour."

Randy and Chuck laughed. Nate leaned his head back with his eyes closed.

"Knock it off, Beck," I said. "No fair trying to make him puke."

"Don't say puke," Nate said without opening his eyes.

Nate managed to last the hour. He collected five bucks from Beck and five bucks apiece from Chuck and Randy. They reimbursed us for the two Big Macs we bought. We dropped Nate off, and he walked slowly up his driveway toward his front door.

Everyone at school was talking about the upcoming Fight of the Century between Muhammad Ali and Joe Frazier. They were both undefeated. Ali was popular with people who weren't even boxing fans because he refused to be drafted and go to Vietnam. Others didn't like him for that same reason. I thought Ali's mouthy routine was just a way to psych out challengers. Everyone was sure Ali would win, but I was rooting for Frazier because he was tough and he didn't talk much. He was a fighter, not a political symbol. I didn't think Frazier would let Ali beat him with his mouth.

I would have gone out for boxing, but there was no boxing team at Lincoln High, so I went out for track. I wasn't much for team sports. Boxing and track seemed more practical. With boxing you can defend yourself, and if you couldn't fight, your next best bet was running, but nobody ever settled anything by saying: "Let's step outside and see if you can stop me from running a ball across some damn goal line."

Still, football was the glamour sport. Football players commanded respect around campus. They had pretty girlfriends. So, I stayed after school one night to watch a football practice. I talked to Coach Hammond. He said it was too late in the season for me to go out. He told me to come back next year. I hung around a while feeling disgusted. I had missed the bus, so I would have to hitchhike home. Then, I noticed these guys doing laps around the perimeter of the athletic field—the cross country team. I figured running would get me in shape for football, so I talked to Coach Steinbrink, the cross country coach. He wore sneakers, gray sweatpants, a green nylon jacket, and a ball cap. He had a nickel-plated police whistle around his neck.

"Do you need anyone else for the team?" I asked.

He looked me up and down.

"Have you ever run before?"

"Sure."

I didn't tell him that I used to race the bus home in junior high after the driver threw me off for practicing drum beats on the back of the seat.

"Okay," he said. "Come out tomorrow for practice."

I showed up the next afternoon after sixth period. There were only eight guys on the team. They weren't built like me. They were mostly under six feet, lean light guys, all legs and lungs. Coach Steinbrink drove us in an old Chevy carryall to the hills. He took out a stopwatch.

"We're going to run circuits," he said. "Down the slope here and around the wrecked Pontiac and uphill to the flat spot and back. Two-minute cycle. Ready?"

Coach Steinbrink blew his whistle, and we took off. The idea of the circuit was if you could make it in, say, a minute and forty-five seconds, you could rest for fifteen seconds before Coach blew the whistle again. If you took the whole two minutes or longer to make the circuit, you never stopped running. Going down the slope was easy. As we turned around the wrecked Pontiac and went uphill, people stretched out. The juniors and seniors were out in front. Some of the sprinters from the track team were in the middle. I was dead last. I made it back just under the two-minute time limit. The seniors were taking a breather. At the end of two minutes, Steinbrink blew the whistle, and we all took off again. He gave us ten circuits. I didn't do any more of them under two minutes. I never stopped running. Then, we took a long "cool down" around the perimeter of the hills. I fell in alongside two other sophomores, Bud Doyle and Scott Latham.

"I don't see how you guys do this every day," I said.

"You'll get used to it," Doyle replied. He was skinny, with dark hair. "This is only your first day."

"I hate this fucking hill," Latham said. He was also skinny, with brown hair.

"LATHAM?" Coach Steinbrink called from about half a mile away. He had his hands cupped around his mouth.

"Yeah, Coach?"

"IT'S NOT A FUCKING HILL."

"He's got ears like a rabbit," Latham said to us.

"Your voice carries in these canyons," Doyle said.

"Who are those guys out front?" I asked between breaths.

"Ray Henshaw and Dan Kelly. They're studs."

"Animals," Latham agreed. "Who do you guys think will win the Ali–Frazier fight?"

"Ali," Doyle said.

"Frazier," I said.

"You're shitting me," Latham replied. "HEY, COACH!"

"YEAH!"

"WHO'S GONNA WIN THE ALI–FRAZIER FIGHT?"

"MUHAMMAD!"

"THORPE IS BETTING ON FRAZIER."

Coach Steinbrink shook his head and gave us a thumbs-down.

"I never said I was betting," I said.

"Because you'll lose," Latham replied.

"Okay. Five bucks."

"You're on."

"I'll bet five, too," Doyle said.

They each shook my hand.

After we drove back to the gym and took showers, my legs were so stiff I could hardly walk, and I thought I was in shape. After a week or so, my legs toughened up. My lungs held me back. They were getting better, but I was far behind the studs of the team. Ray Henshaw and Dan Kelly looked like two ordinary skinny guys walking around the campus during the day. At practice, they transformed into tireless endurance machines. They were always the first two to arrive at any destination the coach set for us. They were always the fastest during circuits. They never bragged. They seemed to have no egos. As team co-captains, they encouraged the other team members—John Muldoon, Albert Donato, Roger Framm, Howard Bickler, Doyle, Latham, and me. All of them, though not as talented as Kelly and Henshaw, were better than I was. For me, it was enough to finish, which I always did. I wasn't out to break anyone's record.

Bickler was the geek of the team. He kept his blond hair in a crew-cut, and he wore thick glasses. He was the butt of jokes. When Donato saw Bickler stretching out in the lunch line, he told everyone about it, and they kidded Bickler all the time, even sophomores like Latham.

"Hey, Bickler," Latham said, touching his toes with his ankles crossed, "I'll have a chili dog and a chocolate milk."

"You're a *senior*, Bickler," Muldoon said. "You shouldn't take that kind of crap from him. It makes us all look bad."

Bickler just blinked his eyes. He lived in a world of his own. One time, Framm and Muldoon tackled Bickler and sprayed a can of Tufskin—the stuff we used to cover tender spots on our feet—under Bickler's left arm. They glued his arm to his side. Bickler never complained. He was a great runner. That was all he cared about.

None of these guys were glamour boys like the football players. They didn't have girls after them. Most girls didn't know the cross country team existed. Henshaw and Kelly were the only guys on the team who had girlfriends.

When we ran a cross country meet against Bishop High from across town, there were only six people out there from Lincoln to watch us. We had more people than that on the team—and we were on our home turf. The course was three miles long. Henshaw and Kelly had already won for us in the senior race. Now, I was running with everyone else in the underclassmen's race. The pack spread out quickly with me fading back. I couldn't keep pace with all the lean running machines, but I was determined to finish with a halfway decent time.

"COME ON, FRAMM, DOYLE, THORPE!" Coach yelled.

"Let's go, Thorpe!" Henshaw yelled.

My lungs were on fire. I gave up the idea of a decent time. All I wanted now was to keep from coming in dead last. I managed to beat one guy who just came out for the team that week. He was around five foot seven, with dark hair and sprinter's legs. We had to yell out our names as we came across the finish line. When I exhaled my name, the manager handed me a wooden tongue depressor with a number on it, twenty-five. It was a twenty-six-man race.

"Giovanni," gasped the guy behind me, "Sapienza."

"*Gesundheit!*" someone yelled from the Bishop team. He got a few laughs from his pals.

"How do you spell that?" the manager asked.

Sapienza spelled his name between gulps of air. Coach Steinbrink was shaking hands with the Bishop coach. Doyle had won the underclassmen's race for us.

"Okay, let's hit the showers, people," Steinbrink said. "Thorpe, Sapienza, I can see we're going to have to work on those times."

"Jesus," Sapienza said, still breathing hard. "I'm a sprinter. I just came out for this lousy sport to get in shape for track season."

"Johnny," called a girl coming toward us. "*Johnny!*"

She had dark hair and brown eyes and a big smile. She was wearing a blue blouse, white shorts, and sneakers.

"Hi, Laura," Sapienza said.

"You didn't look too good out there," she said.

"Thanks a lot. Laura, this is Thorpe."

"Gary," I said.

"Gary, Laura Ledezma."

"I haven't seen you around school," I said to her.

"I don't go to school here," she replied. "I go to St. James's. It's an all-girls Catholic school."

"Nice race, guys," Doyle said, slapping me on the back.

"You must be kidding," Sapienza said.

"See you later, Johnny," Laura said. "Do you want a ride home?"

"Yeah. See you in a few minutes."

When we were in the showers, I asked Sapienza:

"Is she your girlfriend?"

"No," he replied. "Why?"

"She seems to like you."

"She's crazy," he said, making circles with his finger beside his ear.

"How do you know her?"

"We go to the same church."

"She's cute," I said.

Latham snapped a towel at me.

"Thorpe's in love," he said.

CHAPTER 9

Sea Trials

Two days after Captain Grant's departure, Captain Quimp got the *Okmok* underway before dawn for sea trials. Chief Lasko had Stretch and me up on the signal bridge taking visual bearings. We cruised down the Carquinez Strait into San Pablo Bay, but it was so dark we couldn't see much. Even the sea birds weren't awake yet.

We passed under the Golden Gate Bridge. The ocean and low clouds were as gray as the *Okmok*, and they swallowed the western horizon as the California landmass receded astern. The soft glow of sunrise filtered through the rain clouds over the Pacific. Rain fell through the cold wind off San Francisco.

Stretch was stationed on the starboard gyroscope repeater, and I was on the port one. We each had a telescopic alidade that fit over each repeater and rotated 360 degrees. We shot bearings to various landmarks and relayed the bearings via sound-powered phones to Chief Lasko on the bridge below, where he plotted them on the chart.

We headed west. The wind picked up, and the rain really started. From up there on the signal bridge, I could see the bow of the *Okmok* cutting through the water, climbing and dropping over the oncoming swells from the northwest that hit our starboard bow diagonally and rolled us thirty degrees to port and thirty degrees to starboard. I felt like a flea riding on the end of a metronome.

I wore the set of phones over my wet wool watch cap. I had my sweater and my pea coat on, but I was cold and shivering. My nose and fingers were going numb. I was torn between my orders and survival instinct. All I could think about was walking off my station.

Skidmore and Hankins were drinking coffee inside the signal shack. Skidmore was playing solitaire. Hankins was looking at a *Playboy* magazine. He always looked pissed off, even while he was staring at the fold-out of the month. I would have traded places with either one of them. I beat my fingers against my thighs to restore circulation, asking myself again what I was doing in the Navy. I'd had reasons for enlisting, but I couldn't remember any of them.

"Stand by," came Chief Lasko's voice through the phones. "Mark."

The drops of water on the eyepiece of the alidade made it tough to see the Golden Gate Bridge.

"South span of the Golden Gate, zero eight one," I said into the mouthpiece. "Sutro tower, one two zero."

"South Farallon, two five three," Stretch said.

I could barely make out his silhouette through the rain. Stretch was wearing a rain slicker. I had forgotten to grab one. Stretch liked giving me a bad time because I was from southern California and couldn't handle cold weather. No matter how cold it was, Stretch always said that it was nothing compared to his hometown, Seattle. The rain was coming down at a high angle, closer to horizontal than vertical. The wind cut through me. My teeth chattered.

"It's freezing up here," I said. "When do we secure the sea detail?"

"Not until Lightning Lenny says," Stretch replied.

The crew had started calling Captain Quimp "Lightning Lenny" because of the lightning-bolt scar on his face, but the name really caught on because his halting speech and general lack of confidence was pretty much the opposite of lightning fast.

"Quit your bitching, Thorpe," Chief Lasko said. "Stand by—Mark."

We had been on station for two hours, since we left the pier at Concord. We were nearly in international waters, not another ship in sight, but Lightning Lenny hadn't secured the sea and anchor detail. Navy regs required that we take fixes every three minutes during sea and anchor detail, which made sense when we were entering or leaving port surrounded by shipping traffic. By now, Stretch and I should have been down on the bridge, taking radar fixes instead of visuals, but Lightning Lenny didn't see it that way. Lightning Lenny wasn't freezing.

Not that I expected sympathy. If the gentry could order non-rates like me to kill or be killed in combat, they could sure as hell order me to lose sleep, peel potatoes, scrub toilets, or freeze my ass off. This was better than slogging through a jungle in Vietnam, but at least there was some dignity in dying in combat. Freezing to death during sea detail would be a stupid death, like slipping on a banana peel.

One level below us, on the bridge wings, Doglike and Bootleg were standing port and starboard lookout. Bootleg always wore his sunglasses, indoors or outdoors, rain or shine. They were wet and cold, or maybe Doglike wasn't so cold since he was covered with all that hair. They couldn't see anything in the rising fog, but they weren't allowed to go inside, either. Never mind that we had a million dollars' worth of radar in the Combat Information Center. Doglike and Bootleg had to stand there—seeing nothing, reporting nothing. The duty boatswain's mate was a bulky blond guy from Minneapolis named Kaczmarek, but everyone called him Crapshoot. He kept coming around to make sure Doglike and Bootleg didn't doze off.

The joke was that CIC picked up every contact long before the two visual lookouts reported it. I thought about Goldbrick and Coatrack nice and warm down there in CIC with their scopes and maneuvering boards, drinking hot coffee and bullshitting about baseball or cars or girls. Thinking about things only made them worse. My fingers were stinging. It hurt to open and close my hands.

"I'm freezing, Chief. Can I come down and grab a rain slicker?"

"Stand by, Thorpe — and don't give me none of your shit — Mark."

I balanced freezing to death against being sent to the brig for abandoning my station. At least the brig was probably heated. Stretch, who could hear everything I said over the phone circuit, was grinning at me. Damn him and his Norwegian Viking anti-freeze blood. How could I claim to be freezing if Stretch wasn't complaining? I'd never hear the end of it, assuming I lived to never hear the end of it.

Finally, the chief sent Hutchinson and Brogan up to relieve Stretch and me. I handed Hutchinson the phones and hurried down the ladder to the 06 level. I walked around the port bridge wing to the watertight door and wrung the water out of my watch cap before entering the bridge. Stretch came through the starboard door. He hung his rain slicker in the locker in the chart house. Doglike and Bootleg stayed outside, the poor bastards.

During special evolutions like sea and anchor detail, a rated quartermaster, Mendoza, steered the ship and a rated snipe, Koslowski, manned the lee helm. Chief Lasko and Mr. Southcott stood at the chart table. Cool was scribbling in the ship's log. All hands were required to stand on station except for Lightning Lenny. He sat in the starboard captain's chair, staring out through the forward row of bridge windows and picking his nose. Mr. Kempton, the first lieutenant, stood beside Lightning Lenny. Mr. Kempton was the deck officer and the OOD for all ship's special evolutions. He looked like some movie actor playing the part of a naval officer. He had shining dark hair and smoked a pipe. He had a different pipe for each ship's evolution.

"CIC reports a contact," Gink said. "Range six thousand yards, relative bearing two zero seven."

Gink wore a set of sound-powered phones plugged into the JL circuit to relay the position of other ships from CIC and the lookouts to Mr. Kempton.

"Very well," Mr. Kempton replied, and Gink marked the position of the contact on the transparent plastic status board with a grease pencil. "Right three degrees rudder, Al."

"Right three degrees rudder, aye, sir," Mendoza answered. "Rudder is right three degrees."

"Very well. All ahead full. Make turns for fifteen."

"All ahead full, aye," Koslowski answered. "Engine room answers all ahead full, sir. Making turns for fifteen knots."

"Very well."

Mr. Southcott was looking at me over the top of his glasses.

"Yaw dripping all ovah the deck, Thawpe," he said.

"Sorry, sir."

I stepped away from him to the coffee area and poured a cup. I didn't drink coffee. I just wanted to hold something hot in my hands. I swallowed some of the bitter crap and regretted it. Stretch poured himself a cup. His wet hair was plastered to his forehead. He was dripping on the deck, too, not as much as me since he had been wearing the rain slicker, but Mr. Southcott didn't say anything to him. What difference did a little water on deck make? They had us swabbing it every half hour. Stretch lit a cigarette and looked at me.

"Your lips are blue," he said.

I could see my warped reflection in the cylindrical coffee maker. He was right. My lips were blue.

"Go change clothes, Thorpe," Chief Lasko said.

Since nobody was around, I ran down the ladder to the 05 level. I usually ran up and down the ladders for practice. During General Quarters, hesitating on a ladder would get you run over by the guys behind you. Going down to the 04 level, I grabbed the horizontal bar above the ladder, swung my feet out, let go, and landed on the deck. I did it two more times until I got to the 02 level. It saved steps. In 02 berthing, I changed into dry dungarees, and I looked in one of the mirrors screwed to the bulkhead. My lips were less blue.

When I got back to the bridge, the rain had stopped.

"Relieve Cooley on the log, Thorpe," Chief Lasko said as soon as he saw me. "It's your watch."

At sea, the quartermasters did the job we were trained for, standing bridge watches, keeping the quartermaster's log, and plotting the ship's position on the chart. We used radar ranges and bearings when out of sight from land. When we were too far out for radar, we maintained dead reckoning positions.

We had enough quartermasters for four rotating sections—Stretch, Hutchinson, Brogan, and me—so the same man didn't always get stuck with the midnight to 0400 mid-watch. Since he hadn't gone to QM school, Cool stood watches with Stretch. Mendoza was there as a backup. Chief Lasko didn't stand watches.

"Let's test the Iron Mike, Al," Mr. Kempton said.

"Aye aye, sir," Mendoza replied.

Iron Mike was Navy slang for autopilot. Mendoza pressed a button on the console that allowed the gyro to steer the ship. Mendoza still had to stand there to make sure we stayed within half a degree of our course. We steamed southwest. After ten minutes, Mr. Kempton went back to manual steering. A blond, baby-faced ensign watched Mendoza steer.

"Who's the new ensign?" I whispered to Estorga. Whenever officers were within earshot, enlisted men communicated in voices barely louder than thoughts.

"Just reported aboard last week," Estorga whispered back. "Fresh out of the academy. Kip Priskett."

"Sounds like a snack cracker."

"It's ten thousand yahds to the operations area," Mr. Southcott said.

"Very well, Tod," Mr. Kempton replied.

"Secure the sea and anchor detail, Jim," Lightning Lenny said.

"Aye, Captain," Mr. Kempton replied. "Pass the word, Boats."

Crapshoot spoke into the 1MC.

"NOW SECURE THE SEA AND ANCHOR DETAIL. THAT IS, SECURE THE SEA AND ANCHOR DETAIL."

"Guzman," Mr. Kempton said, "take my sea detail pipe and get me my regular underway pipe."

"Aye aye, sir," Guzman replied. He was a frail kid with coal-black hair and the voice of a twelve-year-old girl. He had started out in deck force, but he was too weak to do the work of a deck ape, so Mr. Kempton put him in the deck office as a yeoman striker and his personal assistant. Guzman handed him his pipe.

"Guzman, how many times do I have to tell you? My regular underway pipe is the ebony. This one is the cherry wood, my UNREP pipe."

"Let's go to GQ, Jim," Lightning Lenny said.

"Aye aye, Captain," Mr. Kempton answered. "Guzman, scratch the regular underway pipe. Get me my GQ pipe."

"Aye aye, sir. Which one is that again?"

"The briar. General Quarters, Boats. *Let's* go. *Let's* go."

Crapshoot's voice came over the 1MC.

"NOW GENERAL QUARTERS, GENERAL QUARTERS, ALL HANDS, MAN YOUR BATTLE STATIONS. THAT IS, GENERAL QUARTERS,

GENERAL QUARTERS, ALL HANDS, MAN YOUR BATTLE STATIONS."

Every man buttoned the top button on his shirt and tucked his trousers into his socks, as if cotton was protection against flying shrapnel. When the crew was at battle stations in gas masks and helmets, Lightning Lenny looked at his watch.

"Goddammit, Jim. That took six minutes. *Six minutes!* That's unsat. We'll have to do better than that."

"Aye aye, sir."

"Men," Mr. Priskett said as he walked back and forth in front of the console holding a gas mask, "this is the Mark Five gas mask. The Mark Five is the most advanced gas mask available today. To put on the mask, you first grasp the canister with the left hand, pulling the straps over the back of the head with the right."

He sounded like Barney Fife. Everyone on the bridge had put on gas masks before. Mr. Priskett's remarks were garbled as he continued talking with the mask over his face.

"What is that ensign talking about, Jim?" Lightning Lenny asked.

"Kip," Mr. Kempton said, shaking Mr. Priskett's shoulder. "KIP! TAKE OFF THE MASK, KIP."

"Secure from GQ, Jim," Lightning Lenny said.

"Aye aye, Captain. Secure from GQ, Boats. Set the regular underway watch."

"NOW SECURE FROM GENERAL QUARTERS. THAT IS, SECURE FROM GENERAL

QUARTERS. SET THE REGULAR UNDERWAY WATCH."

During regular underway steaming, deck apes took the helm and lee helm. Evans relieved Mendoza, and Salazar relieved Koslowski.

The next morning, we were scheduled to UNREP with an aircraft carrier, the *Midway*. I had the 0400 to 0800 watch with Mr. Kempton and Crapshoot.

"Set the RAS detail, Jim," Lightning Lenny said.

"Aye, Captain. Set the RAS detail, Boats."

"NOW, SET THE REPLENISHMENT AT SEA DETAIL. THAT IS, SET THE REPLENISHMENT AT SEA DETAIL," Crapshoot announced.

Mendoza and Koslowski manned the console.

"Steady as she goes, Al," Mr. Kempton said. "All ahead two thirds. Make turns for ten."

"Steady on two two seven, aye, sir," Mendoza said.

"Engine room answers all ahead two thirds, making turns for ten," Koslowski said.

"Very well," Mr. Kempton replied.

Mr. Priskett stood behind Mendoza, watching the gyro closely. During UNREPS, a junior officer monitored the helmsman to ensure he never varied more than a quarter of a degree from the ship's course. He was supposed to take over the wheel in case the helmsman lost control.

"CIC reports a contact," Estorga said. "Range three thousand yards, relative bearing one nine five."

"Very well," Mr. Kempton replied.

We maintained a steady course for five minutes, with the *Midway* trailing us off our port quarter. Mr. Kempton aimed his binoculars at the huge carrier.

"Goddammit, Jim," Lightning Lenny, now seated in the port captain's chair, said. "Are the RAS stations manned yet?"

"I'll see, Captain," Mr. Kempton replied. "Gink, what's the status?"

"Chief Skinner reports all RAS stations manned," Gink answered.

"Very well. Chief Skinner reports all RAS stations manned."

"Hoist the Romeo pennant, Jim," Lightning Lenny said, referring to the signal for the receiving ship to come alongside us. Since we were in the service fleet, we were always the delivering ship and the other ships were the receiving ships.

"Aye aye, Captain," Mr. Kempton answered, and he pressed the button on the squawk box. "Sigs, hoist the Romeo pennant. *Let's* go. *Let's* go."

"Aye aye, sir," came Skidmore's voice over the squawk box. "Romeo pennant is hoisted."

"Very well. Guzman, get me my UNREP pipe."

"Aye aye, sir," Guzman answered.

"The *Midway* is coming alongside, Captain," Mr. Kempton said, looking through his binoculars.

"Very well," Lightning Lenny replied.

The *Midway* blocked out the sunlight as it came alongside to port.

"Make the announcement, Boats," Mr. Kempton said.

Crapshoot blew his boatswain's pipe through the 1MC. The high-pitched shriek rang throughout the ship.

"GOOD MORNING, USS *MIDWAY*," his voice echoed. "WELCOME ALONGSIDE THE *OKMOK*. STAND BY TO RECEIVE SHOT LINES FORE AND AFT."

Our deck apes fired bright orange shot lines upward to the deck of the *Midway*. I wrote in the log: *0722, Midway received shot lines.* We passed the shot line so we could use it to pass heavier lines for equipment. Both ships hung big manila fenders, known as camels, over the sides to protect the hulls from coming into contact. The suction created by the rush of water between the two ships tended to pull the ships together. Sixty feet of separation supposedly eliminated the suction. To indicate the distance between the ships, we passed a marker line with square pieces of canvas attached, a red piece at twenty feet, yellow at forty, blue at sixty, white at eighty, and green at one hundred. Deck apes had a saying to help them remember the order of the colors, "Rub Your Balls With Grease."

All the lines required constant tending, slacking off and hauling in, as the ships moved apart and closer together. Our crew set up a span wire rig for the fueling hose. The *Midway* crew began hauling the six-inch diameter hose across. I wrote: *0742, Commence transferring fueling hose to Midway.* The hose looked like a 200-foot black snake suspended by three trolleys that rode along the span wire. I wrote: *0755, Nozzle sealed aboard Midway. Commence transferring fuel to Midway.*

Depending on the amount of fuel needed, refueling can take up to an hour for a destroyer and several hours for larger ships. It took an hour and forty-five minutes to complete the refueling job, break away, and secure from RAS detail.

As we steamed toward port, Estorga was fishing on the fantail, where he had set up three trawling lines. Needler and the XO saw him from the hangar bay. Needler wanted to write Estorga up, but Mr. Crookshank decided that the officers' mess could use some fresh fish. He asked Estorga what he would take in trade for his catch. Estorga asked for steak and got it. The officers ate fresh cod and barracuda for supper. The rest of the crew had hot dogs with mac and cheese.

CHAPTER 10

Glamour Sport

The Fight of the Century went the full fifteen rounds. Frazier won by a unanimous decision, handing Ali his first loss. Doyle paid me five bucks the next day. Latham avoided me for a couple of days, but he paid off, too.

In the spring semester, all the guys on the cross country team went out for track in the long distance events. Guys from the football team came out, too, as hurdlers, high jumpers, long jumpers, shot putters, and sprinters. I wasn't much as a distance runner. I was even worse as a sprinter. Those guys had explosive power and thighs like telephone poles. I ran the 1320, a compromise between sprinting and long distance.

I was doing better in high school than I did in junior high. I hadn't had a fight in a long time. I still had trouble with math. My algebra teacher was Mrs. Fernandez, a Filipino four feet ten inches tall. She talked fast, with an accent that made quadratic equations that much more difficult to understand. I took a seat up front so I could hear her better.

Something hit me in the ear and landed on my desk—a spit wad. I turned around. Richard Moss, Eddie Camerino, and Sean Kiernan were grinning at me from the back of the room. Moss was big and ugly and not too bright. We knew each other from junior high. He used to throw pennies out onto the blacktop at lunchtime and yell *"Scrounge"* at anyone who picked them up. The three of them approached me in the hallway after class. Camerino had stringy brown hair and glasses with black plastic frames. Kiernan was a dishwater-blond creep with empty eyes.

"Never thought I'd see you again," Moss said.

"Pleasant thought, isn't it?" I said. "I see you still have no taste in friends, Dick."

Moss didn't like that.

"It's Richard, punk," he said.

"You'll always be a Dick to me."

"This guy's a real dork," Camerino said.

Mrs. Fernandez came outside and looked up at us.

"You boys stop loitering. Go to your next class."

That was the beginning. Every day after that, whenever Mrs. Fernandez wasn't looking, a rain of spit wads hit me. I took the ink cartridge out of a Bic pen and used it as a blowgun to shoot a few back at them, but I was no match for all three of them. Sometimes, Mrs. Fernandez would catch one of them at it and send him to the office, but the other two were still there. When Mrs. Fernandez called Moss to the blackboard to work an equation he couldn't solve, I called out to him.

"Atta boy, Dick!"

Moss stared at me with pure hate. Then, Mrs. Fernandez called him Dick, too.

"Sit down now, Dick," she said.

Everyone laughed, but nobody louder than me.

"It's Richard, Mrs. Fernandez," Moss said. "Richard."

As he walked past my desk, Moss hissed:

"You're dead meat after school, Thorpe."

Almost everyone heard him say it, except Mrs. Fernandez.

"I have track practice," I said.

"We'll wait," he replied.

I knew they had to catch the bus home. I didn't think they would really wait until 5:30 for me to finish my workout. I figured they would cool off and forget it. Coach Steinbrink had us run to Bloomfield Park and back. When I came out of the gym, there was no sign of them. I walked to the phone booth to call for a ride home. When I was almost there, I saw them following about fifty yards behind me. They weren't in any hurry. I dropped a dime in the phone, dialed Mom, and told her I was ready to come home. When I hung up, I felt a hand on my shoulder. It was Moss.

"How's it going, rabbit?" he asked. "Did you have a nice run?"

Dad always said: "If a group of guys ever gangs up on you, pick out the biggest one and hit him in the nose just as hard as you can. The nose always bleeds. Blood makes an impression."

Moss was the biggest. I put a grin on my face, turned around fast, and used the momentum to slam my fist into his nose. He fell backwards. Kiernan and Camerino were on top of me in a second. I took punches and kicks as Moss got back on his feet. The three of them started whaling on me, and all I could do was cover up my head and take it.

"HEY!" came a voice from somewhere. "THREE AGAINST ONE! NO FAIR!"

The punches stopped. I didn't know why. Many hands were pulling them off me. The voice belonged to Sapienza, and he wasn't alone. Doyle and Framm were there, along with Henshaw, Kelly, Donato, Muldoon, and even Bickler. What had been three against one was now nine against three. Camerino and Kiernan tried to run, but running was futile against Henshaw, Kelly, Doyle, Bickler, and Framm. They caught them easily, while Muldoon, Sapienza, and Donato continued working out on Moss. After a minute, Camerino escaped and ran. Kiernan ran after Camerino. Moss ran after Kiernan. We let them go.

When I sat down the next day in algebra class, the people who heard Moss threaten me the day before seemed surprised to see me alive. They looked even more surprised when Moss, Kiernan, and Camerino came dragging in. Moss had a cut on his forehead and a swollen nose that I hoped I was responsible for. Kiernan had twin shiners. Camerino had a fat lip, and his glasses were taped together. I was sore, but the punches I took were mostly in the body, so they didn't show. I looked better than they did. Our classmates were shocked because it appeared that I had singlehandedly wiped these guys out. I said nothing to correct their false impression. I hoped the story would spread so everyone would leave me alone. It was peaceful that day in Mrs. Fernandez's algebra class. No spit wads.

In my junior year, I went out for football as an offensive tackle. I thought football would help me meet girls, but it didn't work out that way. At six three and 195 pounds, I had the size for football, but I didn't have the drive. To be honest, I never liked football, but admitting that was like admitting you were a communist. I enjoyed watching a game while it was happening, the same way most people enjoy music. When a game was over, I never wanted to keep talking about it, like Nate. He was always asking questions like: "Remember that Syracuse game in '69, when that guy from Pitt intercepted that pass on the three-yard line?"

I didn't.

Before the school year started, we had to show up for a week of conditioning known as Hell Week. We lifted weights, ran wind sprints, and hit the sleds. I had no problem with most of it, until we started running plays. Coach Hammond was a stocky guy, with a flat nose and cheerful cruelty in his eyes. He was also the wrestling coach. When Bill Rogers called Coach Hammond a son of a bitch, Hammond picked Rogers up and threw him about five feet, no easy trick, since Rogers weighed over 200 pounds.

"Call me a son of a bitch, and I'll act like one," Hammond said.

When Hammond explained the plays to us, half the time, I didn't know what he was talking about, and I was embarrassed to admit it because everyone around me already seemed to know this stuff, even Vince Hicks, who was flunking out in every class. During a scrimmage, the whistle blew, and I forgot whether to pull and seal the defensive tackle or help double-team the guard. Coach Hammond blew the play to a stop.

"Thorpe, what the hell are you doing? Do I have to light a candle for you, son? What's the end doing on a buttonhook play?"

Everyone was waiting for me to answer.

"I don't know, Coach. I'm not an end. As long as I do my job, why do I have to know what he does?"

The guys laughed. Beck was cracking up the loudest. Hammond shook his head slowly as he slapped the front of my helmet with his beefy hand and spoke in a sad voice.

"Thorpe, you've got the size for this game. You might even have the strength for this game, but you just don't have the right attitude, son."

He was right. Most of these guys had played football in junior high, while I was playing drums. That was why they all knew the plays, and I didn't. Vince Hicks played defensive guard. He took a dislike to me. Whenever I faced him on the line, he ran right over me. I hit him as hard as I could, but I was uncoordinated. Hicks was built like a bank safe. He was already shaving every day. He took delight in knocking me on my ass. Hammond cringed.

"Thorpe, you need work—lots of work. All right, let's hit the sleds."

I couldn't concentrate. My only thought, whenever I took the field in my pads and cleats, was to try not to embarrass myself. I understood nothing about the big picture of the game. Before the season started, I was at practice one afternoon. We would get down in our stances to come off the line and do wind sprints across the width of the field. As I got down in my stance again and again, a pain in my lower back started getting worse. I couldn't bend down anymore to get in a stance. When I told Hammond about it, he was as sympathetic as a hammerhead shark.

"Go see the trainer," he said.

The trainer was an old guy named Mack. He told me to take off my jersey and pads so he could take a look at my back.

"Wow," he said. "Your lower back is all swollen up. What the hell did you do?"

Mack put me in the whirlpool. He told Coach Hammond I couldn't return to the football team until I got a doctor's okay. The next day, Mom drove me to the doctor's office. He took an x-ray.

"You have spondylolisthesis," the doctor said, "a defect of the fourth lumbar vertebra. You probably had it since birth. Your muscles are inflamed. They'll be all right, if you take it easy. No more football, though. Stick to running. You shouldn't be playing contact sports."

That was the end of my football career. My back stopped hurting after two weeks. It has never bothered me since. The football team went on to win the league playoffs that season. Beck lettered on the varsity squad.

We were sitting in Beck's Volkswagen outside a liquor store one night, talking about how to get some beer. A debate came up over which one of us looked the oldest. I was the tallest. Beck had the greatest profusion of peach fuzz on his upper lip. Chuck came up with an idea.

"If we had a black felt pen, maybe we could darken in Beck's moustache a little."

"That would be more convincing," Randy agreed.

"I have a magic marker," Nate said. "I'll do it."

They talked Beck into sitting back and letting Nate go to work on him. Nate had neglected to mention that his magic marker was purple. When Nate was finished, Beck looked like a six-year-old with a grape juice mustache. The inside light in Beck's bug didn't work, and his rear-view mirror was shattered, so he couldn't check himself out. With straight faces, we assured Beck that the transformation in his appearance had exceeded all our expectations.

"Really?" he asked.

"Oh, yeah," I said.

"Amazing," Randy agreed, nodding.

Beck was no sooner inside the liquor store than our bottled-up laughter broke out. We watched Beck walk to the beer cooler. Then, he walked to the cash register and placed two six-packs of Michelob on the counter, confident that he looked impressive, and he did, just not in the way he thought. We were in stitches as the man behind the counter fixed his dull gaze on Beck's purple upper lip. Chuck had tears coming from his eyes when Beck caught a glance of himself in the mirror behind the counter. As Beck came storming out of the store toward us, Nate spoke up:

"Hey, Beck, did you know that one out of every five people gets leprosy of the lip?"

In April, we had a track meet against Western. Sapienza ran the hundred-yard dash. He came in third out of seven guys. Laura was there to watch him. She stayed and watched me run the 1320. I came in third out of four.

The next Saturday, after practice, I picked up the phonebook in the pay phone outside the gym. I found a listing under Ledezma, Joseph. The address was a few blocks away from school. It took me a while to decide what to say. I finally dropped in a dime and dialed. A woman answered.

"Hello," I said. "May I speak to Laura?"

"Who's this?"

"Gary Thorpe. I'm Johnny Sapienza's friend."

"Hold on."

I waited a minute. Then, Laura came on.

"Hello?"

"Laura, hello, this is Gary Thorpe. Remember me? Johnny's friend on the track team?"

"Oh, hi, Gary. How are you?"

She sounded happy, like she was glad I called.

"Fine," I replied, "just fine. How about you?"

"I'm fine, too."

That settled that. Everyone was fine.

"That's good," I said. "Listen. I was wondering if—that is—I thought maybe if you weren't doing anything today...uh...I just got finished with practice, and I thought —"

"Are you at school now?" she asked.

"Yes."

"Why don't you come over for dinner? I'll give you the address."

"I already have the address from the phone book."

"Okay. See you soon, Gary."

That went easier than I expected. In the gym, I showered and changed and went into the bathroom to comb my hair. On the wall next to the mirror, somebody had written: *Why change Dicks in the middle of a screw? Vote for Nixon in '72.* Nearby, in a different scrawl that looked like Beck's, was this: *Vince Hicks sniffs girls bicycle seats.*

Dad let me drive his car sometimes, when he was out of town. I drove to Laura's address. It was a tract house with an iron gate. Two dogs from the house next door barked at me as I came up the walk and knocked on the door. Laura came to the door wearing jeans and a yellow t-shirt. There was a painting on the wall behind her of Jesus on the cross. Next to that was a wooden crucifix. The house smelled of cooking.

"Come in, Gary," she said. "This is my mom, Rita."

"I hope you like Spanish food," Rita said.

"It smells good," I replied.

Rita dished up plates of stewed beef with red bell peppers over rice. Laura's father, Joe, was a manager at a foundry. His conversation ran mostly to the molecular structure of cold-rolled steel. I think he was trying to figure out how smart I was.

"This food is delicious," I said.

"You'll have to come back again," Rita replied.

On Sunday, Chuck and Nate told me about their Saturday night.

"You should have been with us," Chuck said. "Beck flipped out."

We all knew Beck had a crazy streak. He would drive like a maniac and then argue with cops when he got tickets.

"What happened?" I asked.

"We went to the Golden State Lounge," Chuck said.

The Golden State Lounge was a bar with a dance floor. We were too young to buy drinks, but we went there sometimes because they had this Pong game in the lobby. It was the first video game we'd ever seen, a lot more fun than pinball.

"We played Pong until we ran out of quarters," Chuck went on. "When we left, there were these two huge dudes in the parking lot."

"They looked like Soviet weightlifters," Nate said.

"Yeah. Their car wouldn't start. They had the hood up. They asked us for a jump start. Beck told them 'sure.' He can be real friendly when he wants to."

"We got in Beck's bug. Chuck got in back, and I was riding shotgun. Then, Beck gets this weird look on his face. He rolls down his window and starts yelling at them —"

"Yeah," Chuck cut in, "he was screaming: 'You bodybuilders are all FRUITS! I'll bet you wear LIPSTICK on your EYES and MASCARA on your LIPS!'"

"They just stood there like they couldn't believe it," Nate said. "I couldn't believe it myself. Then, they started running toward us."

"All the windows were down, and Beck wasn't starting the car. Me and Nate were yelling at him to get us out of there. He turned the key, but the goddamn Volkswagen wouldn't kick over."

Beck's bug never was super-reliable. Sometimes, we had to push-start it.

"What happened?" I asked.

"We got the windows up," Nate said. "Just in time, too. Those guys climbed on the car and started beating on the windows with their fists. Beck gave them the finger. He finally got it started, and we got out of there. I was really sweating."

"Me, too," Chuck said, "but Beck was laughing."

I started taking Laura out for ice cream and movies. She seemed to like me, but then again, she liked everybody. She was always talking about school or her future career or her future children. She was a serious Catholic, and she said her kids would be Catholics. I was a half-ass Presbyterian, and I wasn't thinking about kids until she mentioned them. She wanted a thousand things. I wanted one thing—sex. One night, we were watching TV in her living room. Her parents had gone to bed. We started making out on the couch.

"We should get married," she said.

My hand inside her blouse froze.

"We're sixteen," I said.

"I mean in a couple of years."

That was the deal—sex in exchange for marriage. I might have done it, except for one thing. The Pope didn't believe in birth control, so neither did Laura. All her talk about having kids made me stop and think. I was too young to have kids. The Pope probably saved my ass.

When the girls at school talked about getting married, they never said: I want to marry John, or I want a guy like Bob. It was always just: I want to get married. That sounded like an unfinished sentence. I never understood how girls could want to get married without mentioning *who* they wanted to marry. They all had real specific ideas of the kind of wedding ring, bridesmaid dresses, and china and crystal they wanted. They could describe the house they wanted, the cabinets they wanted, right down to the sheets and towels they wanted, but I never heard any of them ever say what kind of *man* they wanted. The *state* of marriage was the goal. The husband was a minor detail.

While I was spending time with Laura, Beck had taken control of the group. Our main meeting place switched from the pool table at the bowling alley to Beck's house. Beck lived with his father, his stepmother, and his four-year-old half-sister. Beck's father was an orthopedist. He drove a new Corvette. He was also an audiophile. Whenever Dr. Beck would get a new stereo component, he would give Beck his old gear. Beck was reading about electronics. He kept his stereo in a continual state of modification, always trying to boost its power. Beck had lots of albums — The Stones, The Doors, The Moody Blues. One time, we were sitting around in Beck's room listening to Led Zeppelin. Near the end of "When the Levee Breaks," Dr. Beck suddenly opened the door. He had dark hair like Beck's, and he looked tired and pissed off. We never saw Dr. Beck much. He never seemed interested in any of us.

"TURN DOWN THAT GOD-AWFUL NOISE!" he yelled at Beck.

He started to close the door, but then, he noticed the mess of tools lying around everywhere. An unintelligible maze of wire ran all over the floor. A copy of the *Los Angeles Times* was scattered across Beck's bed. The headline page read: FIVE BURGLARS ARRESTED AT THE WATERGATE. Dr. Beck started yelling again.

"SO, THIS IS HOW YOU TREAT THE STEREO EQUIPMENT I GAVE YOU. IT'S A MESS,

EXACTLY LIKE THAT CAR OF YOURS. I SWEAR, DENNIS, YOU HAVE THE MIDAS TOUCH IN REVERSE. EVERYTHING YOU TOUCH TURNS TO SHIT!"

That was the only time I ever saw Beck look embarrassed.

"YOU GUYS HAD BETTER LEAVE NOW," Dr. Beck yelled. "I NEED TO HAVE A LITTLE TALK WITH DENNIS."

When Beck graduated—a year ahead of the rest of us—he was packed off to Idaho to attend Dr. Beck's alma mater, Boise State. We had our eight ball and Pong finals before he left. We made several last cruises to the liquor store. Finally, Beck packed up the bug and drove off to college.

CHAPTER 11

REFTRA

In March, I got an automatic promotion to E-3. The *Okmok* departed for REFTRA—refresher training—for four days. During every 0400 to 0800 watch, the duty quartermaster woke Chief Lasko and Mr. Southcott so they could shoot morning stars. Celestial navigation wasn't necessary, since we were usually within radar range of land, but sight reduction practice was part of REFTRA, the only part I liked.

At forty-five minutes before each dawn, two non-rate quartermasters went up on the signal bridge with the chief and Mr. Southcott. On the first morning, Stretch and I were up there. The second morning, I was with Cool. I was with Hutchinson on day three. I was always there because I volunteered for it. I wanted to take part in as many sight reductions as possible and get familiar with the procedure.

On the morning of day four, I was with Brogan. We waited, holding stopwatches and clipboards, while the chief and Mr. Southcott sighted through their sextants.

"Stand by, Thorpe," Chief Lasko said. "Mark. Sirius, thirty-six degrees, fifteen point two minutes."

"Stand by, Brogan," Mr. Southcott said. "Mark. Procyon, twenty-four degrees, six point three minutes."

They each took four shots. The chief used a standard Navy Mark III sextant. Mr. Southcott had a beautiful old Plath sextant manufactured in Hamburg, with a bronze frame and black lacquer coating. He never got tired of telling anyone who would listen about the great deal he got it for at a pawn shop in Annapolis. He was so proud of it that he gave it a name: Wildebeest.

Brogan and I wrote down their readings next to the exact times of each shot. Brogan was scribbling and walking at the same time, and he bumped into Mr. Southcott.

"Brogan, you moron," Mr. Southcott said. "If you make me drop Wildebeest, I'll have you polishing the undercarriage of the old man's jeep with a toothbrush."

The chief and Mr. Southcott had their sextants attached to lanyards that they always kept looped around their necks, so Brogan couldn't have made him drop it. Brogan either didn't notice the lanyard, or he saw the wisdom in not mentioning it.

"Sorry, sir," he said.

At the chart table, Mr. Southcott plotted a three-line fix that showed us slightly south of track. Chief

Lasko's lines and two radar ranges confirmed our position.

"Wildebeest nevah fails," Mr. Southcott said.

Every day during daylight hours, we did UNREPS. Mendoza would take the helm for the whole time. Lightning Lenny ordered dinner for the crew to be served on station—dry sandwiches and mealy apples—so we wouldn't have to stop for chow. Dinner was the midday meal. The evening meal was supper. In the Navy, there was no lunch.

On our last morning at sea, Mr. Kempton had the deck and the conn. Mr. Southcott and Chief Lasko stood at the chart table. Koslowski was on the lee helm. Mendoza was on the helm. Mr. Priskett stood behind Mendoza to make sure he stayed on course. Estorga stood beside me as I kept the quartermaster log.

"I was in the wardroom yesterday," Estorga whispered. "The XO was telling Mr. Sforzando that Priskett got carded at a liquor store in San Francisco. Ain't that a damn shame? An officer in the United States Navy, and he can't even buy beer."

"CIC reports two contacts," Stringbean said, "relative bearing three four seven, range six thousand yards and zero one two relative at eight thousand yards."

"Very well," Mr. Kempton replied. "Must be the convoy. Navigator, how far to the op area?"

"Five thousand yahds to the operations area," Mr. Southcott replied.

"Very well, Tod," Mr. Kempton replied, turning to Malolo, the boatswain's mate of the watch. "Pass the word, Boats."

Malolo spoke over the 1MC.

"NOW, SET THE REPLENISHMENT AT SEA DETAIL. THAT IS, SET THE REPLENISHMENT AT SEA DETAIL."

"Steady as she goes, Al," Mr. Kempton said. "All ahead two thirds. Make turns for eight."

"Steady on two five nine, aye, sir," Mendoza said.

"Engine room answers all ahead two thirds, making turns for eight," Koslowski said.

"Very well," Mr. Kempton replied.

Lightning Lenny sat in the starboard captain's chair, as usual, while everybody else stood. Things could have been so much easier with a few chairs. The Navy justified every aggravation by calling it tradition. Their attitude seemed to be: We've done it that way for the last hundred years, and we'll do it that way for the next hundred.

"The convoy's waiting, Captain," Mr. Kempton said, looking through his binoculars.

Destroyers, cruisers, and oilers were lined up to the horizon, waiting their turn to come alongside the *Okmok*.

"Goddammit, Jim," Lightning Lenny said, digging his index finger up his nostril. "The lookouts haven't reported the convoy yet."

"Aye aye, Captain," Mr. Kempton replied. "Boats, ask your lookouts why they haven't reported those ships yet."

"Aye aye, sir," Malolo said, and he went out through the port wing door to rouse Doglike and Bootleg.

Seconds later, Stringbean reported:

"Port and starboard lookouts report contacts ahead at six thousand yards."

"Very well," Mr. Kempton replied.

"Uh, Goddammit, Jim," Lightning Lenny said. "We're going to have to expedite these UNREPS, or we'll never win the Big E."

The Big E stood for efficiency and was awarded each year by fleet command to one ship in each class. Lightning Lenny planned to make the *Okmok* the number one ammo ship by volunteering for more UNREPS than anything else on the water. If the *Okmok* won the Big E, we would get to paint a big white letter E on each side of the stack.

"Aye aye, Captain," Mr. Kempton said. "Stringbean, what's the status?"

"Chief Skinner reports all RAS stations manned," Stringbean replied, his eyelids at half-mast.

"Very well. Guzman, take my sea detail pipe and bring me my UNREP pipe."

"Right away, sir," Guzman replied.

"*Right away, sir,*" Estorga whispered, mocking him. "I'll bet you that *joto* hasn't touched a vagina since he came out of one."

Mr. Kempton pressed the button on the squawk box.

"Sigs, hoist the Romeo pennant."

"Aye aye, sir," came Hankins' Oklahoma drawl over the squawk box. "Romeo pennant is hoisted."

"Very well."

The captain's steward, Lim, set down a tray and took the silver cover off Lightning Lenny's breakfast: four strips of crisp bacon, sunny-side eggs, fried potatoes, buttered toast with marmalade, coffee, and orange juice. Mr. Kempton walked toward the captain's chair.

"The *Davis* is coming alongside, Captain," Mr. Kempton said.

"Goddammit, Jim," Lightning Lenny replied. "We're going to have to expedite these UNREPS, or there won't be time for drills this afternoon."

"There's nothing in the POD about drills, Captain."

"I don't give a rat's ass about the POD, Jim. We're having drills today *vice* the POD. Make it so."

"Aye aye, Captain. I'll have Chief Skinner set up his gear on the port side as soon as we have the *Davis* alongside to starboard. Pass the word, Boats."

The *Davis*, a destroyer, was coming up fast. Malolo blew his boatswain's pipe into the 1MC.

"GOOD MORNING, USS *DAVIS*," Malolo's voice echoed. "WELCOME ALONGSIDE THE *OKMOK*. STAND BY TO RECEIVE SHOT LINES FORE AND AFT."

Our deck apes fired orange shot lines to the deck of the *Davis*. I wrote in the log: *0602, Davis received shot lines.*

"Stringbean," Mr. Kempton said, "tell Chief Skinner to standby to receive the *Racine* to port."

"Aye aye, sir," Stringbean replied. "Chief Skinner reports all hands in first and second division on station."

"Very well."

The *Davis* crew began hauling the fueling hose across. Lim poured more coffee for Lightning Lenny.

"Goddammit, Jim," Lightning Lenny said. "Let's hoist that other Romeo pennant."

"Hoist the Romeo pennant to port, Hankins," Mr. Kempton said into the squawk box.

"Aye aye, sir," Hankins replied. "Hoist the Romeo pennant, aye."

I wrote: *0615, Romeo pennant hoisted to port.*

"*Let's* go, Boats," Mr. Kempton said, walking to the port bridge wing, as the tank landing ship *Racine* came alongside to port.

"Aye aye, sir," Malolo said before blowing his pipe into the 1MC again.

"GOOD MORNING, USS *RACINE*. WELCOME ALONGSIDE *OKMOK*. STAND BY TO RECEIVE SHOT LINES FORE AND AFT."

It was a double UNREP. I wrote in the log: *0621, USS Racine is alongside to port. 0625, Nozzle sealed aboard Davis. Commence transferring fuel to Davis.* Our deck crew fired shot lines to the *Racine* and set up the wire highline to transfer ammunition from our deck to theirs. They attached a skip box filled with projectiles to a trolley on the highline so it could travel back and forth between the two ships. I wrote: *0645, Racine receiving anti-aircraft projectiles by wire highline transfer.*

"Cooley, relieve Thorpe on that log," Chief Lasko said.

"Thawpe, Brogan, Hutchinson," Mr. Southcott said, "get some wiah brushes out of the geah lockah and get moving on the bridge wings."

Mr. Southcott didn't care about the bridge wings. It was a bullshit order to get rid of us, which was okay with me. Every enlisted man learns to tell the difference between a real order that matters and will be checked on and a bullshit order that can be delayed or worked around because it will be forgotten when things get back to business as usual. We went outside to the starboard bridge wing, maximum distance from Chief Lasko and Mr. Southcott, and we began half-assing the scrape job of the haze gray paint we had applied days before.

"Uh, goddammit, Jim, I don't give a rat's ass about the POD," Hutchinson said in a decent impersonation of Lightning Lenny's high voice. "Let's UNREP for the next thirty-six hours. Make it so."

Brogan laughed, exhaling cigarette smoke.

"Pretty good, Jeff," he said, "but Lightning Lenny sounds a little whinier."

Hutchinson looked around in all directions.

"Let me borrow your lighter, Pete."

Brogan handed over his lighter. Hutchinson walked aft of the bridge wing and disappeared through the watertight door on the side of the stack. Brogan and I continued to scrape paint. Minutes later, Hutchinson came out of the stack with red eyes and a drifty grin. The wind quickly blew away the scent of pot.

"NOW THE *DAVIS* IS DEPARTING TO STARBOARD," came Malolo's voice over the 1MC. "STAND BY TO RECEIVE THE *KILAUEA*."

Brogan took the rest of a joint from Hutchinson and stepped inside the stack. The *Davis* pulled away and the *Kilauea* took its place.

By 1530, we had completed UNREPS with five more ships, and we secured from RAS detail. Hutchinson was on watch, keeping the log.

"Hutchinson," Mr. Southcott called from the chart table, "get me anothah set of dividahs."

"Yes, sir," Hutchinson answered, and he got a pair of dividers from the chart house. When he brought them to the chart table, Mr. Southcott stepped backward, and they bumped into each other. Hutchinson dropped the dividers on the deck and picked them up. Mr. Southcott took them from him and looked them over.

"Good thing for you these ahn't broken, Hutchinson. Otherwise, I'd have your pay docked for damaging government property, and rightly so."

"You knocked 'em out of mah hand, sir," Hutchinson replied.

"One maw word, and I'll write you up, Seaman Apprentice. Do you read me? It was yaw negligence. Now get back to the logbook, and try not to break any windows."

"Let's have a man overboard drill, Jim," Lightning Lenny said.

"Man overboard drill, Boats," Mr. Kempton said.

"THIS IS A DRILL. THIS IS A DRILL," said Malolo over the 1MC. "MAN OVERBOARD, STARBOARD SIDE. MAN OVERBOARD, STARBOARD SIDE."

The deck apes threw Oscar, the practice dummy, over the starboard side.

"I'd like to nominate Lightning Lenny for an Oscar," Stretch muttered.

He pulled the tag off a smoke pot and threw it off the starboard bridge wing to mark the spot where Oscar went into the water. After the deck apes fished Oscar out, Lightning Lenny consulted his watch.

"Goddammit, Jim. That took seven minutes. We'll have to do better than that."

"Aye aye, sir."

"Goddammit, Jim, we have not had an abandon ship drill."

"Aye aye, Captain. Abandon ship drill, Boats."

"THIS IS A DRILL. THIS IS A DRILL," said Malolo over the 1MC. "ABANDON SHIP. ABANDON SHIP. ALL HANDS, DON FLOTATION GEAR AND REPORT TO YOUR LIFEBOAT STATIONS."

Everyone on the bridge put on kapok life vests. I kept my own personal survival kit in a plastic bag inside my jacket: a magnetic compass, a Swiss army knife, two Hershey bars, suntan lotion, twenty-five dollars cash, and a pocket-size Spanish-English dictionary. I liked abandon ship drills. I dreamed of abandoning the *Okmok*.

After the drill, REFTRA was over. We were steaming back to port.

"Relieve Hutchinson on the log, Thorpe," Chief Lasko said.

"Okay, Chief."

Hutchinson had filled in a lot of pages in the logbook. I looked back to see what he had written. He had entered the divider-dropping incident as it happened—complete with dialogue. Hutchinson had made Mr. Southcott's remarks part of the ship's official permanent record.

They told us in quartermaster school that you can't write too much in the logbook, but this was asking for trouble. I never could tell whether Hutchinson had more guts than brains, or if he just didn't care. Hutchinson must have been counting on the fact that, like most government documents, nobody ever read the ship's logs. They were filed and forgotten, unless there was a damn good reason to dig them out.

CHAPTER 12

Peace With Honor

Nate, Chuck, Randy, and I were tossing a football around on a Saturday afternoon. Beck pulled up in his Volkswagen bug, got out, and walked toward us.

"What happened to college?" Nate asked.

"College was a drag," Beck replied.

"What are you going to do about all those traffic tickets you ran up before you left?" Randy asked.

"I forgot about that. Beebin—that yo-yo. Any of you guys know where I can get my car repainted?"

Beck had stolen a bunch of Club cocktails in little cans from his dad. We went for a cruise in his Volkswagen. Randy spotted two girls we knew from junior high, Connie Swank and Annabella Caldarella. They were both wearing miniskirts. Annabella wore fishnet stockings. It looked like Connie still put on the green eyeshadow with a putty knife. Randy called out the window to them. Annabella waved.

"Shit, who's that?" Beck asked.

"Annabella," Nate answered. "She's really stacked."

"No, the other one."

"Pull over," Randy said.

Beck pulled to the curb. Connie and Annabella knew Randy, Nate, and me, but they didn't know Chuck or Beck.

"How about a cocktail?" Randy offered.

They smiled and walked over to the car. Randy was the ladies' man of our group. With his blue eyes and long straight hair parted down the middle, Randy looked like every painting of Jesus, or every surfer in Huntington Beach. Randy could always think of something to say, and girls always seemed willing to listen to him. We were happy to use him as bait. Annabella took a rusty nail, and Connie had a brass monkey.

"What are you girls up to tonight?" Randy asked.

"We were over at the bowling alley earlier," Annabella replied.

"You play football?" Connie asked Beck because he was wearing his green and white letterman's jacket.

He didn't answer her right away. He stared at Connie for a few seconds before he finally spoke up.

"Can I lick your legs?"

Connie flipped him off. She turned around and walked away. Annabella shrugged and followed her.

"COME BACK," Randy yelled. "HE WAS JUST KIDDING."

But they kept walking.

"I wasn't kidding," Beck said.

"Real smooth, James Bond," Randy said.

"Yeah, nice work, Beck," Nate added.

We finished off the canned cocktails. When Beck dropped me off at my house later, he was feeling the effects of the booze.

"I gotta take a wizz," he said, walking toward my front yard. He was staggering and trying to unzip his trousers.

"Hey, Beck, don't piss on my yard, man."

He ignored me.

"Beck," I said. "If you piss on my yard, I'll piss on your car."

The next sound I heard was dry leaves crackling, along with Beck's voice:

"AHHHHHHHHH!"

Chuck and Randy started laughing.

"All right, Beck, you son of a bitch," I said, unzipping my fly. I soaked down most of his right rear fender and bumper. Everyone was laughing, except Beck. He couldn't believe his eyes.

"You pissed on my car, Thorpe," he said.

"You pissed on my yard," I replied.

He hit me in the face. It was more of a slap, but it sobered me up. I grabbed his wrist.

"If you want a fight, Beck, I'll oblige you when we're sober."

"You're lucky I'm having that car repainted, Thorpe, or they'd be tracing your body in chalk."

"All right," Chuck said with happy enthusiasm. "A little action."

Chuck was getting out of the car to watch the fight. Beck had his back to Chuck. He flashed me his counterfeit smile and winked. His face turned angry again in an instant. Neither one of us liked the idea of Chuck enjoying potential violence with no desire to participate.

"Ah, screw it, Thorpe," Beck said. "Let's settle this right now."

"Fine with me, shithead," I said.

"DITCH HIM!"

We jumped into the Volkswagen. Nate and Randy were still sitting in the back seat.

"WAIT UP, YOU GUYS!" Chuck yelled as we drove off, leaving him to walk the few miles to his house.

"Did you know that one out of every five people gets mugged in this town after dark?" I said.

"Better him than us," Beck replied.

Laura phoned me the next night.

"You're spending a lot of time with your buddies lately," she said. "You should let your hair grow more."

She changed subjects a lot. She didn't like it if I pointed that out.

"They make us keep it short for track," I said.

"I wish you wouldn't wear t-shirts all the time. Your clothing should make a statement."

"Statement?"

"Yes. What statement are you making with jeans, sneakers, and t-shirts?"

"I'm not naked."

"I'm serious. You should wear nicer shirts."

"Since you brought that up, I don't like that purple blouse of yours."

"We're talking about you, not me."

"I thought we were talking about us. You want me to wear different shirts, and I never liked that purple blouse."

"Are you saying you won't wear nicer shirts unless I get rid of that blouse?"

"No. I'm saying we are telling each other about things we don't like."

"You're selfish."

"Wait a minute. It's okay for you to point out my flaws, but I can't mention yours?"

"*Flaws?* What flaws?"

"Come on. Nobody's perfect."

"My friends say you don't have any goals. How's that for a flaw?"

"You keep changing the subject."

She hung up. Talking to her was frustrating. She was logic-proof. Laura may have been right about me not having goals, but I wasn't about to admit that to her.

Halfway through my senior year, it was obvious that I hadn't saved nearly enough money to get the sailboat I always wanted. I didn't want to go to college, even if my grades were good enough to get in, which they weren't. I had been nowhere but school my whole life, and I was sick of it. A job in an office or a factory didn't sound good either.

When my dad graduated high school in 1945, he joined the Navy. By the time he was out of boot camp and assigned to a minesweeper, World War II was over. Like Dad, I was born at the right time to miss the war. In January 1973, the United States, South Vietnam, the Viet Cong, and North Vietnam signed the Paris Peace Accords. Nixon said it would bring "peace with honor." The war continued, but Nixon stopped sending in new combat troops, and he started withdrawing troops. All Mr. Stratton's threats were for nothing. Nobody in the class of '73 was coming home in a wooden box for flunking algebra.

A Navy recruiting ad on television featured sailors surfing turquoise waves on white sand beaches, sailors riding horseback through tropical jungles, sailors in dress whites sipping margaritas with señoritas at sunset. At the end of the ad, a baritone voiceover said: *"The Navy. It's not just a job. It's an adventure."*

Partly under the influence of that ad, I walked into an armed forces recruiting office. The Navy recruiter saw me coming. He wore dress blues, and he stood up to shake my hand. The brass nameplate on his desk read: BM1 ROOKER.

"Sit down, sit down," he said, grinning like a fisherman who just had a forty-pounder jump into his boat. "I'm Boatswain's Mate First Class Rooker. The Navy's a great life. I've been in for thirteen years and never regretted a day. Have you decided what rate you want?"

"Quartermaster," I said.

"Quartermaster is a seagoing rate, one of the three oldest rates in the Navy. The other two are boatswain's mate and gunner's mate. Sure I can't talk you into boatswain's mate?"

"I'm interested in navigation. That's a quartermaster job, right?"

"That's right, but first, you have to take a little test."

He gave me a general classification test. It had questions on vocabulary words, basic math, and mechanics. There was a tool identification section to see if I could tell the difference between a torque wrench and a ball-peen hammer. The general intelligence questions were multiple-choice, such as: *Which of the following statements is always true about an apple? It is a) red, b) round, c) a fruit, d) Cincinnati.*

"Now, I can't tell you your score," Rooker said after he looked it over, "but you did well enough for any 'A' school. Even electronics or nuclear technology if you sign up for six years."

"I'll stick to quartermaster," I said.

"If you sign up today, I can give you a guarantee for quartermaster 'A' school, no problem."

"I still have a few months of high school to go."

"That's good. The Navy wants high-school graduates. You can still sign up today, though, on the delayed entry program."

I signed up for four years. If someone ever invents a time machine, I will go back to that day and shove my own head down a toilet.

I drove Laura to Burger King. We sat at our usual table. Laura poured ketchup over her French fries until they were completely red. She didn't mention our latest argument, so I didn't bring it up. That was our pattern. We never talked anything out. We took a day or two to cool off, and then, we pretended nothing happened—until it happened again.

"Just think, Gary," she said. "In a year, we could be married, with our own apartment."

"I don't think we should get married," I said.

Laura stopped chewing. Her eyes opened wide. "Why not?"

"I'm joining the Navy."

"The Navy?"

"Yeah. It'll give me time to think, and —"

Tears were running down her cheeks.

"Don't cry, Laura."

"That's easy for you to say," she replied, suddenly angry. "Why don't you just admit that you don't love me?"

"If we really love each other, we'll still love each other when I get out of the Navy."

She blew her nose in a paper napkin.

"Take me home."

"Don't you want to finish your burger?"

"NO! I WANT TO GO HOME!"

She wouldn't speak in the car until we pulled up in front of her house. Then, she turned to me and said:

"You know, you're not the only fish in the ocean, Gary Thorpe."

"And you're not the only bait."

Her mouth dropped open. I shouldn't have said that, but it came out semi-automatically. She got out of the car and ran inside. Sometimes, I felt like I got along better with her parents. If I had been dumb enough to marry her, it would have been a divorce for sure, but I was too green to see it sooner. She was a cute package, full of criticism and disapproval. Maybe it was a good thing she didn't believe in birth control and we never had sex. She probably would have had triplets.

CHAPTER 13

Operation Fairchild

The *Okmok* was tied up to the pier at Port Chicago. At 0600, the shriek of the boatswain's pipe over the 1MC was followed by Crapshoot's voice.

"NOW REVEILLE, REVEILLE, REVEILLE. ALL HANDS, HEAVE OUT AND TRICE UP. ALL REVEILLE POs MAKE THEIR REPORTS TO THE OOD ON THE QUARTERDECK. REVEILLE."

The duty reveille petty officer was Chief Hackburn. As a chief, he didn't have to take that kind of duty, but he loved yelling at us, and he never missed a chance to show off his talent for using the word *fuck* as a verb, adverb, adjective, and noun—often, all in one sentence.

"Let's get the fuck out of the rack, Hutchinson. Billings, wake the fuck up. It's another fucking wonderful Navy day. What the fuck is this, Brogan? Where the *fuck did you get those fucking shoelaces?*"

Brogan's shoelaces were international distress orange.

"It's the shot line we use for UNREPS," Brogan answered.

"And what happened to your regular shoelaces?"

"I lost 'em, Chief."

"Brogan, you drifty motherfucker, how in the fuck does a guy lose his fucking shoelaces but not his fucking shoes? Get to the gedunk and buy some new ones before inspection."

"BREAKFAST FOR THE CREW," said the 1MC.

"What d'ya need?" Sweeny asked.

"Two scrambled," Estorga said. "Man, I thought Hackburn was gonna have a stroke over Brogan's shoelaces."

I took two slices of boiled bacon—not as good as fried, but less complicated for mass cooking—and a slice of white toast with lumpy gravy.

"How can you eat that shit on a shingle, Shortcut?" Estorga asked.

"I don't know why everybody calls it that," I said. "It looks more like dog barf."

"Meet me in after-steering, after Operation Fairchild secures."

"What for?"

"Something good."

"NOW QUARTERS, QUARTERS. ALL HANDS, TO QUARTERS FOR MUSTER, INSPECTION, AND INSTRUCTION. THE CAPTAIN'S PERSONNEL INSPECTION WILL COMMENCE IMMEDIATELY FOLLOWING QUARTERS. THAT IS ALL."

We formed up for muster on the second deck. Skidmore called the roll. It was a typical morning, except, instead of our working dungarees, we wore dress blues and our shiniest shoes. There we stood, over 300 swabbies in our crackerjack suits for the captain's personnel inspection. Brogan had found some black shoelaces.

"*Attention*," Chief Lasko said as the officers' group broke up.

Mr. Southcott and Mr. Sforzando approached us. Chief Lasko and Chief Hackburn saluted Mr. Southcott and Mr. Sforzando, and they returned the salutes.

"At ease," Mr. Southcott said. "Skidmaw, read 'em the POD."

"Item one," Skidmore recited. "All hands are reminded that the captain's ladder is off limits, except during GQ. Any enlisted men found there will be put on report. Item two. Anyone with knowledge of who put Vaseline on the captain's ladder, see the master-at-arms, Petty Officer Needler. Item three. Operation Fairchild will commence at 1300. All hands must remain aboard or ashore until Operation Fairchild is secured."

"X and N division, *attention!*" Mr. Southcott called as Lightning Lenny approached us.

Lightning Lenny walked slowly through the ranks, starting with Chief Lasko and Chief Hackburn and then moving on to Mendoza and Skidmore.

"Very good," Lightning Lenny said. "I like to see squared-away sailors."

Mr. Southcott followed behind with a clipboard, scribbling comments beside each man's name. Lightning Lenny stood in front of me. I stood at attention, staring past his scarred face. Lightning Lenny touched the seaman stripes on my left sleeve.

"A thread," he said. "This man has a thread protruding from his stripes. See that?"

Mr. Southcott looked at me like he had a mouthful of vinegar and no place to spit.

"Yes, Captain," he replied.

Operation Fairchild commenced at 1300. The brow was lifted. The quarterdeck was secured. The smoking lamp was out. No one was allowed to enter or leave the base. Aboard the *Okmok,* everybody on the Special Weapons Team wore an orange plastic badge and carried a .45. Anybody not part of the Special Weapons Team was to stay off the main deck until Operation Fairchild was secured. A freight train approached the *Okmok*. The train came as close to the ship as possible. A squad of marines sat atop the boxcars with machine guns. Inside the boxcars were nuclear weapons.

Sailors assigned to the base unloaded the crated NUCWEAPS with forklifts. They drove the forklifts on to the pier while the marines watched. Our deck crew used the same cargo hoists and booms attached to kingposts that we used during UNREPS to lift the crates from the pier to the freight elevators on deck that went down to the ammo holds. When the last weapon was stowed, the train pulled away. The brow went down, and the smoking lamp was lit. Operation Fairchild was secured, and things got back to abnormal.

I went down to the second deck and headed toward after-steering. Estorga was waiting for me. Sweeny was there, too, holding a plastic trash bag. A voice came over the 1MC.

"THE ROACH COACH IS MAKING ITS APPROACH. THAT IS, THE ROACH COACH IS MAKING ITS APPROACH."

"Somebody's going to captain's mast for that," Sweeny said.

Loophole's voice came over the 1MC next.

"BELAY THAT LAST WORD. THE MOBILE CANTEEN IS ON THE PIER. THAT IS, THE MOBILE CANTEEN IS ON THE PIER."

"Gimme a hand with this, Shortcut," Estorga said, flicking his cigarette over the side. He grabbed two lines that were tied off to a cleat on the deck, and he handed one to me. "We have to haul these in together, so don't get ahead of me."

We hauled on the lines. Slowly, we lifted a rectangular cage out of the water. The cage was about five feet long, three feet wide, and a foot deep. It was covered with dripping seaweed. My line was tied to half of the cage, and Estorga's was tied to the other half. The two halves were wired together at one long end to form a hinge. We got it aboard, and Estorga opened it. Six mud crabs crawled out.

"Look at those beauties," Estorga said.

Sweeny put the crabs in the plastic bag then left.

"Come on, Shortcut. Help me get this thing back in the water."

We pulled the seaweed off the cage and lowered it to the water's surface. When we let go, it sank out of sight. The two halves were designed to fall open like big jaws when it hit bottom.

"Where did you get that thing?" I asked.

"Mr. Wheeler put in a two-kilo for a wire basket for the officers' laundry. I take two-kilos to Mr. Crookshank for his signature all the time. Half the time, he tells me to stamp them myself instead of signing them. Anyway, when I took Wheeler's request to Crookshank, Sweeny was up there serving dinner. Wheeler had a drawing on the form of how he wanted the basket to look, and Sweeny said it reminded him of the crab cages they used in the gulf in Louisiana. So, I made a deal with Sweeny. If I get the crab cage, he cooks 'em."

"How did you get the cage?"

"I gundecked a three on Wheeler's two-kilo after Crookshank signed it," he said.

To gundeck a document is Navy vernacular for falsification or forgery. The term comes from the days when sailors aboard wooden warships painted phony gun ports on the side of the hull to give the false impression of having more guns on their gundeck than they really had.

"The snipes built us two extra baskets. Screwball had 'em welded up in two hours. Sweeny got the wire to tie 'em together. Wheeler got his laundry basket, and we got fresh crab meat."

We met Sweeny in the galley. The three of us ate crab meat with butter and lemon juice and parsley potatoes.

"Beats shit on a shingle, don't it?" Estorga asked.

After knockoff, the radio played over the 1MC in 02 berthing.

"...and that was Al Green singing 'Call Me' on the Bobby Ocean show. In news headlines, the House Judiciary Committee has subpoenaed the White House tapes."

Stretch and Cool were getting ready to go ashore. Hutchinson had the duty. He was playing solitaire. Nobody would play cards with him since his little card trick. Brogan changed clothes fast and took off for a date with some girl he met in Concord. He was in such a hurry that he left the combination lock on his coffin locker hanging open.

"Hey, look," I said. "Brogan went on the beach and left his locker unlocked."

"No wonder he always losin' shit," Cool said.

"That guy would lose his ass if it weren't attached," Stretch said. "What a squirrel."

We opened Brogan's locker. Inside was a Planters peanut can filled with cash.

"160 dollars," Hutchinson said after we counted it. "It's a whole payday."

"Let me hold on to it," I said, and I locked the peanut can inside my locker. "We'll give it back, but first, we'll make him sweat. How long do you think it takes him to notice it's gone?"

"A day," Hutchinson guessed.

"A week," Cool said.

"What a squirrel," Stretch said.

Stretch, Cool, and Estorga were headed for the EM club. I went with them. We ordered beers, and they all lit cigarettes. Estorga blew a smoke ring toward the center of the room. Cool blew three little smoke rings that drifted slowly one after the other. Stretch blew a big smoke ring toward the ceiling followed by a little one that went through the center of the big one.

"Hey, Shortcut," Estorga said, "I'm going home this weekend. Want to help me out with the gas money?"

"I got the duty Saturday."

"I'll stand by for ya," Stretch offered.

"Thanks, Stretch. I'll let you know."

"What's to think about?" Estorga asked. "After that brow goes down Friday, those people out on Interstate Five aren't going to be saying: 'There goes a Plymouth.' They're going to be saying: 'There went a Plymouth.'"

"I need to make a phone call," I said.

I didn't want to mention that getting a standby chit approved would mean getting Mr. Osterkamp's signature. To do that, I would have to tell him I was in his section, which I'd been putting off since I came aboard. I knew there would be trouble when he found out I had never stood an in-port watch, but the longer I delayed, the worse it would get.

I walked across the club to a pay phone, dropped in a dollar forty in change, and dialed

Laura. I took out my wallet and looked at a photo of the two of us.

"Hi, Gary," she said. "Are you coming home soon?"

"Maybe. We're leaving on a six-month cruise in June, and I either have the duty or we're going to be at sea every weekend until then, so I won't be back until next year."

"I guess we'll have to announce our engagement next year."

She always took it for granted that we would get married.

"Laura, I don't think we should get married."

She paused for so long that I thought the line went dead.

"Why not?"

"I don't think it's a good idea."

"Did you meet someone else?"

"No. It isn't that."

"What is it, then?"

"Everything's different since I joined the Navy. I think I made a mistake. I don't think it would be a good idea to make any more big moves right now. My parents got married young, and they're divorced. There's this guy on my ship named Hankins. He's already divorced with a daughter. I wouldn't want —"

I stopped talking because I could hear her sniffling.

"You think we're going to get divorced just because of your parents and some guy?"

"No. That's not what I mean."

"Why don't you just admit that you don't love me?"

"That's not it. It's the whole situation."

"I DON'T WANT TO TALK TO YOU ANYMORE!"

She hung up. I thought about calling her back, but I didn't know what else to say. There was nothing else to say. I handled it wrong, but I didn't know what else to tell her. Maybe I did the right thing, but I felt terrible. It had taken me too long to figure out that she didn't like me for what I was, but for what she thought I ought to be. I didn't know myself what I thought I ought to be. I looked at our photo. I had never noticed how distracted she looked. In the photo, I was looking at her, but she was looking at something beyond the camera in the distance. I put the photo in my wallet and my wallet in my pocket and went back to the table.

"You jus' made it," Cool said. "Estorga almos' drank yo beer."

"Who was on the phone?" Estorga asked.

"Nobody."

"Sounds like a personal problem."

"So, how about that standby chit?" Stretch asked.

"I'll talk to Mr. Osterkamp."

The more I thought about Laura, the more I wanted to talk to her in person. I made out a standby request chit the next day. Stretch signed it, and I took it up the chain of command through Mendoza, Chief Lasko, and Mr. Southcott. After they okayed it, I took it down to the gunnery office. Mr. Osterkamp was at his desk, busy with paperwork. He was over six feet tall, with short blond hair. He had furry eyebrows like two blond caterpillars. A standby request was such a routine thing that he almost signed it without thinking. Then, he took a closer look at me. The caterpillar eyebrows arched high on his forehead.

"I didn't know you were in this section, Thorpe."

"Yes, sir."

"You haven't been standing quarterdeck watches, have you?"

The easiest time to be honest is when the jig is up.

"No, sir."

"I'll have to correct that," he said, handing the chit back to me, "and you can shitcan this chit, Thorpe. You'll be on the watch bill on your next in-port duty day."

"Aye aye, sir," I said, moving away.

It was my own fault for not mentioning his oversight sooner. Now, he knew, and it was over, or so I thought. I wasn't finished paying yet.

CHAPTER 14

Drums and Bugles

In late June, I graduated high school. On the last Friday morning in July, Sapienza drove me downtown to the AFEES, Armed Forces Examining and Entrance Station, on Wilshire near Crenshaw. A group of us stood around all morning shooting pool. Some older guy was re-enlisting in the Air Force. He was king of the table. Nobody could beat him.

They lined us up outside a room and called us in one by one. My turn came. A chief petty officer and a marine sergeant sat behind a table. The chief told me to sit down.

"Are you now or have you ever been a communist?" the sergeant asked me.

"No."

The chief was taking notes.

"Are you a homosexual, or have you engaged in homosexual acts?"

"No."

"Have you ever used illegal drugs?"

"No."

The chief stopped writing. He looked up at me for the first time.

"Never?" he asked.

"No."

"Not even pot?"

"No."

"Oh, come on. You have never even smoked one joint?"

"No."

I could tell they didn't believe me, but I was telling the truth—then, at least. They looked at each other.

"That'll be all," the chief said. "Next."

They gave us physicals and a free lunch. We signed our enlistment contracts. Then, an officer swore us in. We raised our right hands, faced the flag, and I repeated the oath with the others.

"I, Gary Thorpe, do solemnly swear or affirm that I will support and defend the Constitution of the United States against all enemies, foreign and domestic; that I will bear true faith and allegiance to the same; and that I will obey the orders of the President of the United States and the orders of the officers appointed over me, according to regulations and the Uniform Code of Military Justice. So help me God."

Late that afternoon, they loaded us aboard two buses headed for boot camp in San Diego. As we arrived at the Recruit Training Center, guys in blue dungarees cupped their hands around their mouths and yelled at us:

"YOU'LL BE SORRY!"

When we got off the bus, some other guys, in newer dungarees, started screaming at us.

"FORM UP, MAGGOTS! FORM UP!"

They were called adjutants. They had buzz haircuts and wore gold-braided shoulder aiguillettes. They all had hoarse voices from screaming all the time. They marched us to the chow hall and made us line up.

"NUTS TO BUTTS, MAGGOTS! NUTS TO BUTTS!"

They stood over us and hassled us while we ate.

"YOU HAVE FOUR MINUTES TO FINISH THAT CHOW, WORM! FOUR MINUTES!"

Since it was a Friday, we couldn't get our uniforms until the following Monday morning. The adjutants were our babysitters for the weekend. Their job was to wake us up before sunrise and march us around the grinder in our civilian clothes while calling us maggots, worms, squirrels, boots, and pukes at the top of their lungs. On Monday morning, a chief petty officer talked to us.

"Welcome to California," he said, "the queer capitol of the world."

That was news. I lived here my whole life and never met a homo, except for maybe Mr. Trimble, a poetry teacher in high school.

"Some of you guys are going to have family members die while you're here. It's statistics. If that happens, you will be granted thirty-six hours leave. Otherwise, you will not be leaving here until you graduate. To stay out of trouble, here are some things NOT to do: attempt to leave the base without authorization, neglect to show military courtesy to all officers, ignore the chain of command, disobey any orders. Any questions?"

A guy raised his hand.

"Yeah?" the chief asked.

"Is it too late to get married?"

The chief told us the adjutants had only been here a month. They were E-1s, just like us. We marched down to get haircuts down to our scalps and our "full issue" of uniforms. I was surprised to find out that we had to pay for our uniforms. When my dad was in the Navy, they gave him his uniforms. Though our seventy-five-dollar-a-week salaries came from taxpayer funds, we had to file tax returns to pay still more taxes on our taxpayer-provided salaries and use part of what was left of our double-taxed income to buy uniforms that had also already been bought and paid for by the taxpayers. It sounded like a racket to me, a tax on a tax. I thought about asking somebody why they didn't charge us for meals, too, but I didn't want to give them any ideas.

We stenciled our names and social security numbers on every article of clothing, including our skivvies. The chief had us box up our civilian clothes and ship them home. He marched us to the dispensary to get shots. We lined up, rolled up our t-shirt sleeves, and stepped in-between two guys standing on each side of the line. They were holding air guns. As we stepped forward, they gave each of us a shot in both shoulders. The air guns sounded like nail guns—*TFFF! TFFF!* Blood dripped down our arms. They may have charged us for the uniforms, but at least the haircuts and the shots were on the house. The chief told all the guys who graduated from high school to go stand off to one side. They were separating us right off the bat. Two first-class petty officers asked us if we could play any musical instruments. About fifty hands went up.

"*No guitars!*" said one of them. "We're from the drum and bugle corps. We want horn players and drummers."

I almost forgot I was a drummer. I raised my hand with some other guys, not nearly as many now that they excluded guitars. The two first-classes took us off to a separate building. One of them told the horn players to come with him. The other one talked to us dozen or so drummers. He brought us in one at a time. When it was my turn, the guy asked me if I could read music. He looked tired.

"Yes."

He looked me in the eyes and raised his eyebrows.

"You can?"

"Yes."

He put a piece of sheet music on a table next to a practice pad and a pair of sticks. It was the snare drum part for "The Downfall of Paris." He pointed to the top line.

"Play that," he said.

There was doubt in his voice. I played it for him. I made a couple of mistakes because I was rusty. He stopped me when I got to the third line.

"You *can* read," he said. "How would you like to be in Special Company? You won't have to carry a rifle. You get to go off base on weekends for parades and football halftime shows."

So, I was assigned to Special Company 935 with other drummers, horn players, and flag carriers from all over the country. The only thing "special" about us was we were all high-school graduates.

Our company commander was Electrician's Mate Chief Herrera, a tough-looking Filipino, about five foot eight and maybe 140 pounds fully dressed. The creases in his khaki uniform looked sharp enough to slice a pineapple. His eyes looked like hardening concrete.

"All right, you mudderpuckers," he said, "I want eberyone to donate ten dollars to da United Way."

Chief Herrera picked a guy named Don Payne for our RCPO (Recruit Chief Petty Officer) because Payne had ROTC training in high school. Payne was in charge of collecting the United Way money. After finding out I was paying for uniforms that had already been paid for, I was not feeling charitable when Chief Herrera asked us—ordered us, really—to donate. I wanted to say not only no, but hell no, but every other guy in the company came across with ten bucks. If we had a hundred percent compliance, our company would get a worthless pennant that signified absolute groveling submission. This was explained to me, though not in those words, by Dale Bardeen, the recruit master-at-arms and the biggest guy in the outfit.

"Don't be a cheap prick, Thorpe," he said. "You want to be the only guy in the company to fuck over charity?"

Since he put it that way, I caved and gave up the ten bucks.

Boot camp was eight weeks of rifle classes, first aid classes, knot-tying classes, naval history classes, swimming classes, hygiene classes, damage control classes, and fire-fighting classes. We had to memorize eleven general orders and reel them off whenever asked. We had to make our racks so that a quarter would bounce off them. We had to fold our towels, uniforms, and sea bags and stack them "dress edge forward" for inspection.

Whenever anybody made a mistake, Chief Herrera made the whole company do push-ups, but, sometimes, he would single someone out for punishment. A guy named Crawford folded his sea bag wrong and flunked inspection. Chief Herrera made Crawford put the green canvas sea bag on over his head and fast-walk around the long tables in the barracks for twenty laps, blindly feeling his way along while yelling over and over again: "SEA BAG, WHY DID I FOLD YOU WRONG? SEA BAG, WHY DID I FOLD YOU WRONG?"

Aside from Bardeen, who was from Bakersfield, the only other fellow-Californian in the company was a flag carrier from Santa Rosa named Tom Yates. One morning, Chief Herrera asked Yates to recite his second general order, and Yates got it wrong.

"Goddammit, Yates, you stupid mudderpucker," the chief said, and he smacked Yates in the side of the head.

Yates was over six feet tall. He towered over Chief Herrera, but he didn't do anything. He just stood there. I wondered how much self-control I would have if the chief decided to hit me.

The chief took us to a swimming pool and made us prove we could swim. We had some guys from the Midwest who had never gone swimming in their lives. We took positions on a fire hose and put out a fire inside a mockup of a ship's compartment. We put on gas masks and entered a sealed chamber the size of a garage. First, they filled it with tear gas to prove the masks worked. Then, Chief Herrera made us take the masks off to prove the tear gas was real. I would have taken his word for it.

We went to the rifle range. From a prone and sitting position, we fired at targets 200 yards away, using Springfield bolt action .30-06 rifles leftover from World War I. I didn't shoot too well. A guy from Tennessee named Cobb hit the target every time. A lieutenant asked him if he wanted to try out for the SEAL team. We never saw him again.

On Sundays, we had a choice of attending the Catholic, Protestant, or Jewish services, or staying in the barracks and cleaning the heads. Everybody went to church but Yates, a horn player named Barnes, and me. We drilled each other on our general orders while we scrubbed sinks and toilets.

We made a game out of it. When you got one right, it was your turn to ask the next guy.

"Number five," Yates said.

"To talk to no one, except in the line of duty," I answered.

"That's seven."

"What's five?"

"To quit my post only when properly relieved. Number three."

"To report all violations of orders I'm instructed to enforce," Barnes answered.

"Right."

"Number one."

"To take charge of this post and all government property in view," I said.

"Right."

"Number two."

"To walk my beat, beat my meat, and fuck everything within fifteen feet," Yates answered.

"Is that what you told Chief Herrera before he smacked you?" I asked.

"Officers aren't supposed to strike enlisted men."

"Chief Herrera isn't an officer," Barnes pointed out.

"So, what's your story, Thorpe?" Yates asked. "How come you'd rather scrub pissers and shitters then go to church?"

"I don't think a Navy chaplain has anything to tell me I haven't heard before," I replied. "What about you?"

"Easy duty. The chief makes us keep 'em clean all week, anyway, right? So they never get too bad.

The quicker we get it done, the more time we have to skate. What about you, Barnes?"

"I'm from Indianapolis."

"No, I mean how come you'd rather clean the head than go to church?"

"I'm an atheist."

I had never met an atheist.

"You don't believe in God?" Yates asked. He sounded shocked.

Barnes exhaled. Then, he inhaled and said:

"When a guy says he believes in God, and another guy says he does, too, they think they agree because they're both saying the same words, but both guys might not be thinking the same thing. A better question is: Do you agree with my idea of God? That forces people to define their terms, but nobody wants to think that hard. What do you think God is?"

"Mom always said that God was good with one O," Yates answered, "and the devil was evil with a D in the front."

"God is good and all-powerful, right?"

"Right."

"Then, where do war and crime and diseases come from? If God wants to stop all that but can't, that proves God isn't all-powerful. If God can stop it but doesn't, that proves God isn't good."

"You think that up all by yourself?" Yates asked.

"I forget who said it. Some ancient Greek."

"I thought the Greeks had lots of gods," I said.

"Not this guy," Barnes replied.

Yates was right. Cleaning the head was easy

duty. We finished up before the rest of the company got back, so we had plenty of time to shoot the shit. Barnes started writing a letter.

"You going to 'A' school after boot camp?" Yates asked me.

"Yeah. Quartermaster. What about you?"

"Hospital corpsman."

"I hope the real Navy is better than boot camp."

"It will be. The whole purpose of boot camp is to get you to the point where if an officer ever says 'Go get me a bucket of shit,' you won't ask why like a civilian. You'll just go get him a bucket of shit."

The physical challenges of boot camp weren't as tough as high-school football training. Every week, we ran two miles for time. Our time had to improve with each run, or we had to run it again. We ran the obstacle course over and over. More than anything, we marched. We marched to classes. We marched to chow. We marched for punishment, and we marched just to practice marching. Sometimes, I marched in my sleep. The only difference for me was that, instead of marching with a rifle, I marched with a concert snare drum.

If a guy kept screwing up, he was set back to a less advanced company to spend more time in boot camp until he could do whatever it was he couldn't do before. We lost a third of the guys we started with for one reason or another. Some guys couldn't swim. Some guys couldn't execute marching commands. Some guys had such rotten teeth that it took extra weeks for them to undergo dental work. One guy had such bad acne that they discharged him and sent him home. Some guys got in fights and went to the brig. A few guys went over the wall.

None of the other drummers could read drum music, so they made me head of the percussion section. I played the four marching cadences until they all learned them by ear. A black guy from Alabama named Lester Briffit was a hot player with some flashy stick tricks, so I put him front and center on multi-toms, where everyone could see him. A Montana cowboy named Rawlins was second best. I picked him to play snare alongside me. My two tenor players were Rhodes, a black guy from Baltimore, and Metcalf, a freckle-faced farm boy from Iowa. On cymbals, I had Iverson, a redheaded guy from Milwaukee. The worst drummer was Jackson, a black guy from Detroit who was big enough to make the bass drum look small and could just barely keep time on it.

Besides the four marching cadences, we had ten songs. Of course, we played "The Star-Spangled Banner," "Anchors Aweigh," "Bell Bottom Trousers," and "Columbia, the Gem of the Ocean," but we also played pop tunes like "Mercy, Mercy," "Spinning Wheel," and "Proud Mary." Thibodeaux, a horn player from New Orleans, wanted to do a version of "Iko Iko." We worked out a Bo Diddley style marching cadence for it.

We played every Saturday at a parade on the grinder when all the recruit companies passed in review in front of the base commander. One weekend, we marched in a parade through downtown San Diego. When we got to "Iko Iko,"

Thibodeaux forgot he was in the military and started swinging his horn from side to side like he was in a second line band at Mardi Gras. The base commander had Thibodeaux set back to another company. We never saw him again.

We had a horn player from Wichita named Stacy Sweetfellow. I never would have survived school with a name like that. Sweetfellow was about five ten and around 280 pounds. He had a physique resembling a pile of cottage cheese, with a face like a confused bloodhound. He overloaded his tray in the chow line. He was distant last in every two-mile run. He kept tripping and falling on the obstacle course. He couldn't do push-ups. Chief Herrera was constantly on his ass, screaming at him.

"SWEETPELLOW, YOU ASSHOLE, YOU BETTER NOT BE IN LAST PLACE AGAIN! SWEETPELLOW, YOU ASSHOLE, GIB ME TEN PUSH-UPS OR YOUR CANDY ASS IS GOING TO A MARCHING PARTY TONIGHT! SWEETPELLOW, YOU ASSHOLE, STOP EATING SO MUCH GODDAM PEANUT BUTTER!"

The guys in Company 935 were not the most compassionate types, but they took it easier on Sweetfellow than I would have expected. He was too easy a target. Anyone could tell he had probably been getting a bad time his whole life. One morning, Sweetfellow started vomiting. He had a high fever. Chief Herrera sent him to the dispensary. We never saw him again.

Payne messed up one afternoon and marched us across a bridge. Troops aren't supposed to march over bridges because the rhythm of marching, amplified by the weight of all the men, can make a bridge collapse. Payne might have gotten away with it, but an admiral was watching us through his office window. The admiral called somebody, who called somebody else, who called Chief Herrera.

"Payne, you stupid mudderpucker," Chief Herrera said just before he replaced him with another RCPO, a guy from Phoenix named Alvarez.

One night after chow, during letter-writing time, some of the guys were having races from one end of the barracks to the other. I didn't get in on it. I was no sprinter, and we had some fast guys in the company. Briffit was the fastest. A lot of guys challenged him, but Briffit beat them all. I had an upper rack right over the finish line.

"NEXT!" Briffit yelled when he reached the end of the barracks before Crawford.

His cocky attitude infuriated some people. He didn't even take a breather between races. Alvarez challenged him, and Briffit won again.

"NEXT!" Briffit yelled after pausing long enough to do the complicated handshake with Rhodes and Jackson that they called "the dap."

Ryan, the religious petty officer, gave it all he had, but Briffit was first again.

"NEXT!" Briffit yelled.

Ryan forgot to put on the brakes. He shot past Briffit, threw up his hands, and hit the wall—or bulkhead, as we were being trained to call it. Ryan stared at his hands in shock. He went to the dispensary with two broken wrists. We never saw him again.

"MARCHING PARTY TONIGHT, MUDDERPUCKERS," Chief Herrera said when he found out about it. "EBERYONE ON DA DECK! PUSH UP POSITION! DOWN! UP! DOWN! UP!"

We did push-ups until he got tired of yelling. Then, we marched on the grinder for two hours after dark.

Our drum and bugle corps played in a halftime show at a Chargers football game at Jack Murphy Stadium. During the second half, I was sitting in the stands when I heard shoes clomping behind me. Somebody said: "Fascist." I turned around and saw two hippies with long stringy hair. One of them wore a tie-dyed t-shirt and faded jeans. The other one wore newer jeans with a black t-shirt that said *Woodstock* across the chest in yellow letters. They walked away laughing. The smell of pot lingered after them. Yates and Bardeen were headed toward me.

"Hey, Thorpe, what the hell happened to you?" Yates asked.

"Ya got mustard all over your uniform," Bardeen said.

I turned around. Bright yellow stuff was all over the side and the back of my dress blue wool jumper. Empty plastic packets of mustard were on the concrete. The clomping noise I heard was those guys stomping on them.

"THOSE TWO GUYS!" I yelled, pointing. "OVER THERE!"

The hippies started running when they saw me pointing at them. I ran after them with Yates and Bardeen right behind me. By the time we caught up to them, we had drawn the attention of Crawford, Briffit, Alvarez, and two stadium security guards.

"What's going on here?" one of the guards demanded.

"These guys squirted mustard on the back of my uniform," I said, and I turned around to show him.

"We didn't do anything," said Tie-Dye.

"Bullshit," Yates said. "We saw it."

Yates hadn't seen anything. He was just backing me up.

"Look at that," I said, pointing at some yellow mustard on Tie-Dye's shoe.

Bardeen grabbed him by the collar.

"Now, we don't want any trouble here," said the other security guard to Bardeen.

He sounded nervous. Bardeen towered over him.

"BARDEEN, LET GO OF DAT MAN," Chief Herrera yelled, appearing from out of nowhere in his full dress uniform.

Bardeen obeyed orders and let Tie-Dye go.

"ALBAREZ, WHAT HAPPENED HERE?"

"These dudes threw mustard on Thorpe, Chief," Alvarez said.

The chief spoke to the security guards in the same sharp tone he used to give marching orders.

"What are you going to do about dese two punks attacking one of my men?"

"We're not the police," said the first guard.

"Call da police. We will all wait here por da police."

"Okay."

The guard lifted his walkie-talkie.

"Wait a minute," Woodstock said. "Look, we're sorry. Can we pay the cleaning bill?"

"Is dat okay with you, Thorpe?" Chief Herrera asked.

"I don't know if this stuff will come out of my jumper," I said.

"I got seven dollars and fifty cents," Woodstock said. "How much you got, Rupert?"

"Four bucks," Tie-Dye replied.

"Eleven fifty, then. Is that enough to pay for another jumper?"

I nodded. They handed me the cash, and the guards escorted them to the gate. We had settled it without violence. Bardeen looked disappointed.

"Rupert?" Yates said, shaking his head.

Our drum and bugle corps marched and played at our graduation from boot camp. We all received National Service medals for being on active duty during wartime. They didn't mean much, since everybody got one. I never knew they handed out medals to people who never entered a combat zone. It didn't make sense that a guy in Vietnam got the same medal as a cook peeling potatoes at Point Mugu. They sent us home for two-weeks leave. The Yom Kippur War broke out, and the TV news said all active-duty military personnel were on standby.

CHAPTER 15

Captain's Mast

After a day of UNREPS, the *Okmok* was tied up at Mare Island in Vallejo. Brogan and I were off duty, so we went to a bar in town, a place called Hannigan's. The bartender didn't ask for ID.

"I can tell you guys are in the Navy by your haircuts," he said. "I'm Hank. What'll ya have?"

"Two Buds," Brogan replied.

Hank brought the beers and a bowl of pretzels. Brogan picked up a deck of cards from the bar.

"Hutchinson taught me a card trick," he said. "Pick a card and put it back in the deck."

I did. Brogan shuffled the deck, tapped it on the table, and pulled out the seven of hearts.

"Was this your card?"

"No."

He pulled out the three of clubs.

"How about this?

"No."

He pulled out the jack of spades.

"How about this?

"Give it up, Brogan. It was the nine of diamonds."

We finished our beers and had another round. Hank brought the check.

"Twenty dollars?" I said. "That seems high for two Budweisers apiece."

"You're lucky I served you at all," Hank replied. "I don't care if ya are in the Navy. You ain't twenty-one. Try another bar, if you think you can do better."

I had my ten dollars, but Brogan only had five. I would have loaned him five. I knew he was good for it since I still had his cash in my locker, but I didn't have any more on me.

"I'll come back tomorrow and pay you," Brogan told Hank.

"Do I look stupid?" Hank asked.

"Here, you can hold on to my watch. It's worth more than five bucks."

He took the watch off. It was an old Elgin with a rectangular face on a twist-o-flex band. Hank looked it over.

"Just don't lose it," Brogan said.

Hank put it on his wrist.

"Ok, Sailor. See you tomorrow."

The next day at liberty call, I had the duty. Hutchinson and Brogan were getting ready to hit the beach.

"Don't forget to pick up your watch," I said to Brogan.

"What's he talking about, Pete?" Hutchinson asked.

Brogan told Hutchinson why he had left his watch at Hannigan's with Hank. I was hoping Brogan would start searching his locker for the Planters peanut can full of cash and freak out when he didn't find it, but Hutchinson spoke up.

"How much did you pay for that watch?" he asked.

"Twenty bucks at a pawn shop."

"How'd you like to get fifty for it?"

"How?"

"We'll work a play. Just do like Ah tell you."

The next day, Mendoza had Hutchinson and me correcting charts and publications in the chart house. Hutchinson told me he had gone into Hannigan's alone, sat at the bar, and ordered a beer. When Hank brought the beer, Hutchinson said he liked his watch.

"Ah told him mah granddaddy had one just like it. Ah offered him a hundred dollars for it if he could wait two days for me to come back with the cash. Hank agreed, and we shook hands. Ah finished the beer and left. Brogan went in ten minutes later, and Hank offered him twenty bucks for the watch," Hutchinson said with a laugh. "Brogan held out for sixty. Ah believe he's forgotten all about that can of money in your locker. Anyway, we can't ever go back to Hannigan's."

"You're a tricky bastard, Hutchinson," I said.

"Speakin' of bastards, we gotta do something about Southcott."

"Like throwing him overboard, you mean?"

Hutchinson was looking at the shelf where we stowed the sextants.

"He thinks he's such a hot-shot navigator," he said. "What if we messed with his Wildebeest?"

"He'd know it was one of us."

"Sure he would, if we damaged it. We need somethin' more subtle."

"Like what?"

"He's always double checking his sextant correction notes. How about if we gundecked 'em?"

"How are we gonna do that? They're locked up with his sextant."

"Keep a lookout."

I opened the door to the passageway and looked up and down. Nobody was there.

"All clear," I said.

Hutchinson used two paper clips to pick the lock on Wildebeest's mahogany case. Mr. Southcott kept a sheet of paper inside the felt-lined case with his handwritten sextant corrections for perpendicularity, side error, and collimation. Last on the list was IE, for index error. No sextant is perfect. If a bathroom scale showed three pounds with nobody standing on it, you would subtract three pounds to get the correct weight. Index error is the same idea.

Wildebeest had an IE of minus one-point-three minutes of arc. With a vertical stroke of black ink, Hutchinson changed the minus sign to a plus sign. Since a minute of arc is equal to one nautical mile, it would throw off all Mr. Southcott's sights by two point six nautical miles. Hutchinson closed the lid and put the box back on the shelf.

"Let's see him figure that out," he said.

The next time section six had the duty, Mr. Osterkamp put me on the watch bill for my first quarterdeck watch. The POD said I was scheduled for the noon to 1600 watch, with Chief Skinner and Big Time. As the most senior enlisted man aboard, Senior Chief Boatswain's Mate Skinner wasn't required to stand quarterdeck watches, but he was a gung-ho, haze-gray-all-the-way lifer, and he loved it. I put on my dress blues and reported to the quarterdeck at 1145 to relieve Bootleg as messenger of the watch.

"How about some coffee, Thorpe?" Chief Skinner asked.

"No thanks, Chief."

"Goddammit, I want some," he said. His eyes seemed to bulge out, and a mesh of red capillaries on both his cheeks got a little bit redder. "I heard about you, Thorpe. Mr. Osterkamp says you've been sandbagging in this section since December. I don't like sandbaggers, and I don't like skates. That's what's wrong with the Navy today. Twenty years ago, a non-rate like you never would've —"

A police whistle blew from below, on the main deck. Chief Skinner put his hand on his .45.

"Come on, Big Time," he said. "Let's see what's up."

They left me standing there. Graff approached the quarterdeck in his dress blues and white hat. Graff was one of Kickback's debt collectors, a deck ape from Washington D.C. He was black, six foot four, at least 230 pounds, and as strong as a steel bulkhead. He was without a doubt the toughest guy on the ship. The scuttlebutt was that Graff had joined the Navy after being charged with multiple counts of assault and battery. The judge gave him a choice between the military or jail. Graff saluted me and held out his ID card in his other hand.

"Requess' permission to go ashore," he said.

He wasn't smiling, which was good. When Graff smiled, it meant he was about to beat someone into a coma. It was odd that he would be going ashore before liberty call. I remembered one Sunday in the ship's TV lounge. Twenty guys were watching a Bears-Dolphins game. It was fourth and inches when Graff walked in and changed the channel to a Bugs Bunny cartoon and sat down laughing. Nobody objected then, and I wasn't about to question him now.

"Permission granted," I said, returning his salute.

He walked down the brow to the pier parking lot and drove away in a gray Oldsmobile Cutlass. Chief Skinner and Big Time were back in a minute.

"False alarm," Chief Skinner said. "Some maggot with a whistle. Anything happen while we were gone, Thorpe?"

"Negative, Chief. Graff went ashore."

"Graff? He's scheduled for captain's mast. Mr. Kempton wrote him up for slushing."

"They had captain's mast already, Chief," Big Time said. "It's over by now."

"Call Needler," Chief Skinner said.

Big Time picked up the phone and dialed three digits. He spoke into the phone and then turned to Chief Skinner.

"Needler says Graff was on restriction."

"But he had his ID card, Chief," I said. "Don't they take away your ID when you're on restriction?"

"You might find out, Thorpe," Chief Skinner replied.

"The captain just put him on restriction," Big Time said. "He was supposed to be on his way down to turn in his ID to Needler."

"And Thorpe just let him go over the hill."

"How was I supposed to know he was on restriction, Chief?"

"Didn't you think it was unusual that he was leaving during working hours?"

"Yeah, but how could I stop him? You guys have the weapons."

Big Time smiled. Chief Skinner wrote me up for improper watch standing and sent me to see Needler. Master-at-Arms First Class Needler had a pink face, bristly hair, watery gray eyes like shucked oysters, and upturned nostrils that looked like a double-barreled shotgun. The scuttlebutt was that Needler had reenlisted after being rejected from the San Diego police department.

"Tell me who blew that police whistle, Thorpe," Needler said.

"I don't know. It could have been anybody."

"Were you in on it?"

"In on what?"

"What did Graff pay you? A little cumshaw?"

"Nobody paid me."

"You're going to captain's mast, Thorpe, for assisting Seaman Graff to go over the hill."

"Thass heavy, man," Cool said when I told him and Stretch what happened. We were scraping paint on the port bridge wing.

"I went to captain's mast last year in Hawaii," Stretch said. "Southcott wrote me up for getting sunburned. He called it destroying government property. Captain Grant fined me a hundred dollars."

"What do you think Lightning Lenny will do to me?" I asked.

"Don't worry about it. We'll be underway soon. When you're at sea, it's a good time to be restricted."

"You gon' be restricted your own self, Stretch," Cool said.

"Maybe not."

"What are you guys talking about?" I asked.

Stretch lit a cigarette.

"Yesterday," he said, "my name was in the POD to report to the mess decks with twelve other guys. Goddammit Jim told us we had all been chosen for the Special Weapons Team. Kip passed out security clearances for all of us to sign."

The Special Weapons Team was called into action during a security breach or during Operation Fairchild. In case of a security breach, members of the Special Weapons Team run to the armory, break out a .45, and secure the main deck.

"Nobody asked any questions," Stretch continued. "Everybody signed the papers without reading them, but I read mine. It pretty much said that I was supposed to shoot my own mother if she showed up on the main deck without an orange ID tag during Operation Fairchild. So, Kip says: 'Something wrong, Stromsvag? You didn't sign.' 'Yes sir,' I say. 'Well, why not?' he says. So, I told him: 'I think it's a bunch of shit, sir.'"

Cool let out a laugh. Stretch kept talking.

"Then, Goddammit Jim looks up and says to Kip: 'What did he say?' And Kip says: 'He said he thinks it's a bunch of shit, sir.' So, Goddammit Jim sort of smiles and says: 'Okay, Stromsvag, you're dismissed.' All the other guys were staring at me. I'll bet some of them were wishing they didn't sign it."

The brass was gleaming on the port bridge wing for my captain's mast. I had polished it myself. Lightning Lenny stood behind a wooden podium. On the front of the podium was a wooden plaque painted gold with an image in relief of the *Okmok* crashing through carved wooden waves. The ship's motto—*To Serve, and Serve, and Serve*—was engraved at the bottom of the plaque. Needler stood in front of the podium alongside his assistant masters-at-arms, Meech and Snyder. Meech was a second-class storekeeper, pale as a piece of paper, with a sloping forehead and dead eyes in a stone face. Snyder was a second-class engineman, bald, with little eyes set too close together. Apparently, working for Needler was easier than working in their rates. Meech and Snyder were the two goons Needler had sent to shadow Stringbean in search of his drug connection only to find out he was stoned on paint fumes.

Doglike and Thumbs were up first.

"Seaman Bansley and Seaman Ware," Snyder said, and Doglike and Thumbs came to attention.

"Fighting again," Meech said to nobody in particular. "They tore up deck berthing, Captain."

Doglike and Thumbs stared at the deck. Their bad blood was common knowledge, and each one of their retaliations was worse than the previous attack. They had hated each other for so long that no one remembered anymore what started their feud. Doglike and Thumbs might not have remembered themselves what started it.

"What was it this time?" Lightning Lenny asked.

"It was him, Captain," Thumbs said, pointing at Doglike. "He tied my jumper and my bell bottoms in knots before inspection."

"I swear it wasn't me, Captain," Doglike said as he raised his right hand to heaven, a sign that he was probably lying.

"By the time I got the knots out, I was late for inspection. So, Chief Skinner wrote me up."

"Did you see me do it?"

Thumbs lunged for Doglike, knocking some papers off Lightning Lenny's podium. They had each other by the throat before Meech and Snyder pulled them apart.

"Two hundred dollars apiece, goddammit," Lightning Lenny ordered, "plus two weeks extra duty."

"Get those two clowns out of here," Needler said.

"Who's next?"

"Quartermaster Seaman Thorpe," Needler said. "You are charged with allowing a restricted man, Seaman Graff, to depart the ship without authorization."

I stood at attention while Chief Skinner told Lightning Lenny how he and Big Time had been decoyed by the police whistle. He finished up by saying: "I didn't like Thorpe's attitude." Mr. Osterkamp testified next.

"This incident of Graff's unauthorized absence took place during Thorpe's first quarterdeck watch, though, quite obviously, Thorpe has been aboard since last December."

As my division officer, Mr. Southcott was also there, looking at me like he had just sucked on a lemon. Lightning Lenny spoke to me.

"Since you're to blame for Seaman Graff's unauthorized absence, Thorpe, I do not think it's unfair to have you serve the same the two weeks restriction and two weeks extra duty that I awarded him. Petty Officer Needler will supervise you. Mr. Southcott, I want to see you in my stateroom in ten minutes, at which time I expect an answer as to why this man has never stood a quarterdeck watch until today."

"Yes, Captain," Mr. Southcott replied, frowning at me.

That night, I worked after everyone else knocked off. Needler assigned me to a working party of restricted men. We loaded the ammo holds with anti-aircraft projectiles brought from the base. I was second to last in a human chain that included Doglike and Thumbs. Last in the chain was

Kickback. He was on restriction for passing nonstandard phraseology over the 1MC. On the day Estorga and I were catching mud crabs, Kickback was the guy who announced: "The roach coach is making its approach."

I passed projectiles to Kickback, and he loaded them into the chain-driven ammunition elevator that took them below to the ammo holds. The ammunition elevator moved slowly enough to give Kickback time to write on the nose of one shell with a felt-tipped pen: *You'll get a bang out of this!*

"Hey, Needler, how about a cawfee break?" Kickback asked in his New Jersey accent.

"Shut up over there," Needler answered.

I passed Kickback another projectile. He wrote on its nose: *We care enough to send the very best!*

The morning after my two weeks of extra duty ended, Cool, Hutchinson, Brogan, and I reported to the bridge as usual.

"Okay, wheels," Mendoza said. "Let's get a broom and a swab and a foxtail and some Brasso rags, and let's clean up this shithouse up here. The bridge is a showplace."

"Where's Stretch?" Chief Lasko asked.

"Probably in the chart house," Brogan answered.

"He's not in there," Mendoza said. "Was he at muster?"

"No," Chief Lasko replied. "I figured he was up here. Today's his duty day."

Mr. Southcott was sitting at the chart table, lubricating his sextant.

"Have Stromsvag paged," he said.

Chief Lasko called the quarterdeck and had Stretch paged over the 1MC, but Stretch never answered. So, Mr. Southcott called the XO and reported Stretch as UA, unauthorized absence.

"Never thought Stretch'd go over the hill," Cool said.

"Never mind, you guys," Mendoza said. "Let's get busy."

"Not so fast, Thorpe," Chief Lasko said. "You're going to mess cooking. Report to Radford on the mess decks."

"I just got off restriction, Chief," I said.

"All divisions are required to send mess cooks, Thorpe."

Then, he said in a lower voice:

"We were going to send Stretch. It wasn't *my* idea."

The chief nodded toward the chart table.

"Cheer up, Thawpe," Mr. Southcott said with a smirk. "It's only ninety days."

Radford, the petty officer in charge of the mess cooks, was a fat first-class boiler technician. He assigned me to the scullery. After the crew finished eating, they carried their dirty trays and silverware outside the mess decks to a passageway where they dropped them through a slot in a door. I stood on the other side of the slot. I sprayed off the trays and handed them to Carranza, who fed the trays into the sterilizer. Carranza was a deck ape from Denver, half Mexican and half Arapaho. He had straight black hair, a scorpion tattoo on his right hand, and a big smile for the misfortunes of others. According to scuttlebutt, he was dangerous when angry, and he was usually angry. Because he had the most time in the scullery, Carranza was the senior mess cook, so he had the best job. The worst job was the deep sink filled with scalding water, where Mooney, a non-rate snipe striker, was scrubbing pots and utensils in elbow-length rubber gloves.

"That's what you'll be doin' in a few days, Shortcut," Carranza said in a cheerful voice. "So, you watch and see how old Mooney does it. Don't put your arm in too deep. If you fill up a glove, you'll cook your arm. Ain't that right, Mooney?"

Mooney stopped scrubbing a spatula. He looked at Carranza through steamy glasses and blinked. He started scrubbing the spatula again.

"Some guys burn themselves on purpose to get out of mess cooking," Carranza continued, grinning to show he liked the idea. "I've even seen guys cut themselves on purpose."

"Maybe they'd do anything to get away from you, Carranza," I said.

"I got my own plan for getting out of the Navy," Carranza replied, ignoring my insult, or maybe not getting it. "I got the idea when I was walking past this commie bookstore in Frisco. I bought the *Red Book* of Chairman Mao and *The Communist Manifesto*."

"I never figured you for a big reader."

"Don't need to read 'em," he said as he shoved another tray into the machine. "I just put 'em in my locker. Next time Needler has one of his locker searches for drugs, it'll be aloha, *Okmok*. Get it?"

"You think they'll give you a discharge for being a commie?"

"Bingo, gringo."

CHAPTER 16

'A' School

After boot camp, I came home on leave. Beck had repainted his Volkswagen orange. Nate got a job in a grocery store. Chuck had bought himself a hot-rod Camaro, and Randy had picked up a case of the clap.

"One out of every five people gets it," he said.

We had a homecoming celebration that night. We took a ride in Beck's bug. Though we were still underage, we had no trouble getting beer with my military ID.

"Was boot camp tough?" Nate asked.

"Nah," I said. "The whole point of boot camp is to get you so that if an officer says 'Go get me a bucket of shit,' you won't ask why. You'll just go get him a bucket of shit."

"So, I guess you think I can't still kick your ass now that you've been through boot camp and everything," Beck said.

"What do you mean *still*? You never could."

"Want to find out?"

"Pull over somewhere."

Beck drove to a deserted park. We all got out.

"Freestyle?" he asked.

"No holds barred," I said.

The next thing I knew, I was looking at the sky. Beck had knocked me flat on my back. He tried to jump on top of me, but I rolled out from under him, and he landed on the grass. We both jumped up and connected with each other a few times. Chuck, Randy, and Nate were cheering us on. I was bigger, but Beck was quicker. I got tired of taking punches, so I grabbed Beck to throw him on the grass. He must have been thinking the same thing because he tripped me. We both wound up on the ground but not the way either of us planned it. I used my size to pin him and take a rest.

"Oh, take it easy," Beck said, breathing heavily when I was on top of him. "It's my first time, darling."

We all started to laugh. Then, I realized Beck was trying to make me laugh so I wouldn't be able to hold him down. I stopped laughing.

"Okay, you big pig," he said after a while. "Let me up."

I did, and we left, and that was that.

After my boot leave, I returned to San Diego for four weeks of quartermaster 'A' school. There were twenty-three guys in my class. I roomed with two of my classmates, Comstock and Griggs. The quartermaster who taught the course was a first-class named Kelso. We solved navigation problems easier than the ones I worked on from the Davis

Instrument Company of San Leandro. We didn't do sight reductions. We only plotted visual bearings on charts. Kelso taught us how to correct charts and hydrographic office publications, make weather observations, and how to keep the quartermaster's log.

"When you're standing watch, you need to enter every command issued by the OOD along with the time," Kelso said. "That means every change in course and speed, every contact sighted, every single thing that happens. You can't write too much in the quartermaster log."

That night, just for drill but mainly out of boredom, I decided to start keeping my own personal version of a quartermaster's log, just a few sentences in a notebook every day or so about whatever was happening.

While I was in school, Spiro Agnew resigned as Vice President. When the Soviets offered support to Egypt, Nixon went to DEFCON three, and the Yom Kippur War ended after a few weeks. Because of our support for Israel, Arab oil producers launched an oil embargo against the United States.

Kelso said that if we did well enough in school, we would be more likely to get our choices from our "dream sheets" or duty preference requests that we had filled out at the end of the second week of school. There was no guarantee that we would get our choice of duty stations, but we were told that every effort would be made to grant our requests, so long as our requests matched the needs of the Navy. I wanted to see the South Pacific, so I requested any ship based in Pearl Harbor.

There was a double feature one night at the base theater: *American Graffiti* and *The Day of the Jackal*. Comstock and Griggs went to see them. I had the fire watch patrolling the stairwell in the enlisted quarters. The building was made of brick and couldn't burn, but the idea was to get us used to standing watches. I had to phone in every half hour to report all secure. It was boring. Five black guys came climbing up the stairs. They were in civilian clothes, coming back from town. Two of them were laughing. They all wore dark jackets with white embroidered letters across the back that read: BOOSTERS.

"What's the Boosters?" I asked.

Nobody answered me, so I asked louder:

"WHAT'S THE BOOSTERS?"

"Say what?" the smallest guy asked.

"I just asked what the Boosters was."

"None yo business, cracker."

Why is it always the smallest guy who has the biggest mouth?

"My name's Thorpe. Do I know you?"

"*Hell*, no."

"Give me any more crap, and we're gonna get acquainted."

One of the other guys let out a laugh.

"You gon' take us all, Casper?" Mouth asked. "We kick yo honkey ass."

I had been ignoring the other four guys. I had to say something to save face and also to save my face.

"With five guys, sure," I said, "but I'm just talking to you. What if your buddies let it stay between me and you?"

I was staring straight into his eyes, praying his buddies would stay out of it, but if they didn't, Mouth would pay a price before I did. I was all set to nail him as soon as anybody moved. I think he could read my mind.

"Fuck you, Whitey," he said, and they all walked upstairs.

They probably didn't need the hassle that would have followed when the watch PO found my bleeding body on the stairwell. There had to be some Navy regulation against assaulting the fire watch, but I wasn't too sure these dudes cared about regulations. I never found out what the Boosters were about, but Mouth made them seem like a tan Klan.

I came home for a weekend of liberty, and I ran into Chuck.

"Did you hear about Beck?" he asked. "He's talking about joining the Navy."

I thought about letting him go ahead. Then, I could say that two out of five people are idiots. I decided I couldn't do it, not even to Beck.

"I'd better talk to him," I said.

"He went camping this weekend," Chuck replied.

"I have to go back Sunday. You'd better tell him I think he'd be making a big mistake. I kind of wish I hadn't done it."

"He sounded serious."

"Talk him out of it."

A week later, I gave Chuck a phone call.

"Beck went ahead and signed up for six years so he could go to the Navy electronics school," he said.

"What happened, Chuck? I told you to talk him out of it."

"I tried, but he said his dad wanted him out of the house."

My class graduated quartermaster school the same week Nixon gave his "I am not a crook" speech. We all received automatic promotions to E-2. We could now wear the quartermaster wheel on our sleeves. The submarine service in New London, Connecticut needed quartermasters, and Kelso told us we had until the next day to tell him if we wanted to volunteer. I didn't sleep much that night, trying to make up my mind. Sub crews were sort of elite. They got better food and better training. They were always underwater, though, and there was no point in learning celestial navigation if I couldn't see the sky. Besides that, there weren't that many sub bases, so I didn't think I'd get to travel as much. In the morning, I requested the surface fleet.

On the last day of quartermaster school, each of us received an envelope containing our orders. Comstock was sent to a destroyer in the Mediterranean. Griggs was assigned to a cruiser in Hawaii. I tore open my envelope and read my orders.

"USS *Okmok*, AE-73. AE? What's that?"

"An ammo ship," Kelso said. "A floating bomb. Congratulations."

"Where's Port Chicago?"

"Concord. Ever hear about the Port Chicago disaster?"

About three months after I reported aboard the *Okmok,* I got two letters at mail call, one from Nate and one from Beck. I was surprised to see another one so soon from Nate. He had just sent a letter updating me on things back home. Gas prices had doubled to fifty cents a gallon. The gang had loosened up. Randy moved away to get a better job. Chuck got engaged. As I sat down at a table in 02 berthing to read them, Jerry Reed was singing "Amos Moses" on the radio over the 1MC. That was always one of Beck's favorites, so I opened his letter first. He wasn't exactly a ray of sunshine.

> *Dear Asshole,*
>
> *Greetings from Electronics Technician 'A' school in Great Lakes. The weather is fucking cold. I got to be number one in the class by staying on base every night and studying instead of going into town with the other guys and drinking. So, I haven't made any friends. I didn't mind not being Mr. Popular, but now my grades are slipping. I'm not number one, anymore. My old man is going to have a stroke.*
>
> *Chuck said you told him to tell me that joining the Navy was a mistake, but I figured you were trying to keep a good thing to yourself. If you really wanted me not to enlist, you should've told him*

> *to tell me it was great. After all our time*
> *at each other's throats, you should have*
> *known I'd believe the opposite of*
> *whatever you said.*
>
> *At least I know you're as miserable*
> *as I am.*
> *Dennis*

It sounded like I had confused Beck by being honest. We spent so much time bullshitting each other that he would never expect straight advice from me. If I'd told him he should enlist, he wouldn't have done it unless he thought that's what I'd think he'd think. I had to laugh when I thought of the old chess player outsmarting himself. Next time I saw him, I would be sure to say: "The eye sees, but the brain does not comprehend."

I opened Nate's letter. It was short and to the point.

> *Gary,*
> *I've got bad news. Last night, I was*
> *working the cash register at the grocery*
> *store. Beck's stepmother came through*
> *my line. She told me they found Beck*
> *dead in a motel room in a bathtub full*
> *of water. He had stripped one end of an*
> *extension cord, plugged the other end*
> *into the wall. He got into the water,*
> *dropped it in, and electrocuted himself.*
> *Nate*

On the radio, somebody said that twenty percent of people who commit suicide are teenagers. Twenty percent—that's one out of five.

PART TWO

The Navy is a master plan designed by geniuses for execution by idiots. If you are not an idiot, but find yourself in the Navy, you can only operate well by pretending to be one. All the shortcuts and economies and common-sense changes that your native intelligence suggests to you are mistakes. Learn to quash them. Constantly ask yourself: "How would I do this if I were a fool?" Throttle down your mind to a crawl. Then you will never go wrong.

—Herman Wouk,
The Caine Mutiny

CHAPTER 17

Westpac Widows

In June, the *Okmok* pulled away from the pier at Concord. Before we got underway, our shipmates had exchanged goodbye kisses with their wives and girlfriends on the pier. Now, our crew stood on the weather decks, waving to their sweethearts as the ship glided away. Sailors from the *Kilauea*, knowing we wouldn't be back for six months, waved to us as they hit on *Okmok* wives and girlfriends who were now WESTPAC widows and considered fair game. Our crew had done the same thing to the *Kilauea* during its last WESTPAC. The *Kilauea* sailors grinned and waved at us until we were too far out to see what was happening.

Estorga and I stood near the twin gun turret on port side of the 05 level. He lit his cigarette with one snap of his Zippo, despite the wind.

"Never thought I'd say this," he said, "but watching those bastards makes me almost glad I don't have a chick."

"Alaska's hitch is almost up," I replied, "but he has to ship over to pay alimony. I'd never get married while I'm in this Navy. Even if I found the perfect girl."

"The UCMJ says you have to get permission from your CO to get married."

"If Lightning Lenny was for it, I'd be against it. What's with all the paperwork?" I asked because Estorga was carrying a clipboard filled with papers under his arm.

"Nothing," Estorga said. "Makes me look busy, so the officers leave me alone." He looked at his watch. "I better get moving."

"I think I'll head up to the bridge. See what's going on. For old times' sake."

"Don't piss off Mr. Southcott."

"What else can he do to me? I'm already in mess cooking."

I walked up a ladder to the 06 level and passed the stack to the port bridge wing. Hutchinson was above me on the 07 level, shooting bearings on the port gyro repeater as I entered the bridge. Lightning Lenny was sitting in the starboard Captain's chair.

"Guzman," Mr. Kempton said, "what's the status on my regular underway pipe?"

"Here it is, sir."

"Thank you, Guzman. Tod, what kind of ETA do you have for the Golden Gate?"

"Fifty-five minutes, sir," Mr. Southcott answered.

"An hour?" Lightning Lenny moaned. "Goddammit, Jim, we'll have to do better than that.

I don't want to get caught in the middle of shipping traffic."

"I'll increase our speed, Captain."

"I don't give a rat's ass how, Jim. Just make it so."

"Aye aye, Captain. Left three degrees rudder. Steady as she goes."

"Steady as she goes, aye, sir," Mendoza replied.

"All ahead two thirds," Mr. Kempton said. "Make turns for six."

"All ahead two thirds, aye, sir," Koslowski replied. "Making turns for six. Engine room answers making turns for six."

"Very well," Mr. Kempton replied, trailing pipe smoke as he walked along the row of bridge windows.

"Thawpe," Mr. Southcott said. "What are you doing up heah, besides taking up space? Don't you have some trays to scrub?"

"Not yet, sir. It's another hour until supper."

I walked outside on the starboard wing. Brogan was above me, looking through his alidade on the starboard gyro repeater. We passed the C&H Sugar stack at the end of the Carquinez Strait. As we crossed San Pablo Bay, a dozen pelicans glided in formation over the water. Two of them made their clumsy looking dives. I have never seen one fail to come up with a fish.

A strong breeze came off the Pacific as Angel Island drifted by to starboard and Alcatraz to port. When we passed under the Golden Gate, I spotted a tall guy standing on the bridge waving at us. He looked like Stretch, but he was too far away for me to tell for sure. It might have been just some guy waving at ships. I waved to him, anyway.

When we hit international waters, Lightning Lenny secured the sea and anchor detail and set the regular underway watch. I took my last look at California for a while, and we headed west toward the Far East. The boatswain's mate of the watch called supper for the crew, and I went to work. Two hours later, all the trays, silverware, and pots and pans were clean, and Radford secured the scullery.

The horizon off the bow glowed brilliant orange and red. I helped Carranza and Mooney toss a dozen sacks of trash and garbage off the fantail. An albatross with a ten-foot wingspan was following us, flying in a sideways figure-eight pattern. He swooped down on everything we threw overboard. Loophole's voice came over the 1MC.

"NOW SWEEPERS, SWEEPERS, MAN YOUR BROOMS. GIVE THE SHIP A CLEAN SWEEP DOWN FORE AND AFT. SWEEP DOWN ALL DECKS, LADDERS, AND PASSAGEWAYS. EMPTY ALL TRASH CLEAR OF THE FANTAIL. SWEEPERS."

Movie call was at 1930. A Clint Eastwood spaghetti western was on. The mess decks were packed.

"Fucking Eastwood," Estorga said. "He shoots somebody every time he sucks on that little cigar."

"Shut up, Estorga," Swampass said. "I'm trying to watch it."

"Hey, Swampass, I'll bet you ten bucks you can't count how many guys Eastwood kills in the next five minutes."

"Can I get in on that?" Stringbean asked.

"Sure thing."

"Get in on what?" Bootleg asked.

"Estorga bet me ten bucks we can't count how many guys Clint Eastwood wastes in five minutes," Swampass said.

"Put me down for ten," Carranza said.

"You got it," Estorga replied.

They picked Finesse to hold the cash and keep track of time. For the first three minutes, no one had any trouble counting the three Mexican bandits Eastwood shot. In the fourth minute, Eastwood blew away two more guys.

"Five down," Alaska said.

"Kiss your cash goodbye, Estorga," Swampass said.

With thirty seconds to go, Eastwood dynamited the Mexican village. Bodies flew everywhere in rubble and dust—way too many to count.

"Son of a bitch," Carranza said as Eastwood squinted and chewed his cigar. Finesse handed Estorga the cash.

"You didn't make any friends," I told Estorga. He stowed the cash in his wallet, looked around, and whispered:

"Ain't my fault if I've seen this flick before."

I worked in the scullery every day of our Pacific crossing. It was boring and hot, but it had some advantages. The GQ alarm went off around the clock for drills—man overboard, fire, security breach. None of that mattered to me. As a mess cook, I was part of supply, so I didn't have to take part in drills. I may have been in a steamy scullery scrubbing 300 trays and sets of silverware three times a day, but I got a full night's sleep every night, no matter what special evolutions Lightning Lenny ordered. I also didn't have to deal with Southcott. I was beginning to think he did me a favor by sending me to mess cooking—without meaning to, of course.

Every night, after the pots and pans and trays were clean, I carried plastic bags of garbage and trash down to the fantail. In the darkness, the ship left a glowing trail of phosphorescence astern. The same albatross followed us from San Francisco, flying his figure-eight pattern off the fantail. He sure had tremendous endurance. This was his feeding time. I tossed the bags overboard.

On my way back, I would pass Needler's blue Buick Regal tied down on the second deck. Each night, it had a few more dents in it than the night before. The restricted men Needler had put on report would kick his car or hit it with a dogging wrench whenever they got a chance. Needler couldn't assign a full-time watch to it. Since he hadn't caught anyone doing it, the crew started calling him No-Clue Needler.

One night, I climbed into my rack. Hutchinson was in his rack, reading an old newspaper with the headline: NIXON NAMED AS CO-CONSPIRATOR. Brogan opened his locker. He started digging through his dungarees like a dog in a dumpster. Hutchinson looked at me and nodded toward Brogan and winked. I had forgotten all about Brogan's Planters peanut can of cash. I faced the bulkhead to keep from laughing until I heard Brogan slam his locker shut. He had found what he was looking for: his Zippo lighter.

"Okay, guys, let's play cards," he said as he lit a cigarette and sat down with Hoodwink and Hankins.

"Do you believe that?" Hutchinson whispered. "He doesn't even know it's gone."

"He'll figure it out," I said. "Who needs money at sea?"

Everybody knew it was only a matter of time until Thumbs got back at Doglike for tying his uniform in knots and getting him put on restriction. One morning after muster, the guys in 02 berthing got word that Doglike reported to sick bay for burn treatment. They were badgering Finesse for confirmation that this had something to do with Thumbs' long-anticipated revenge.

"Okay, listen up," Finesse said, "because I'm only gonna tell this story once. Doglike was in the head down in deck berthing. He's barely awake, taking his morning dump over the trough shitter."

In the 02 berthing head, we had regular flush toilets. The heads below decks for the snipes and deck apes had World War II-era galvanized troughs installed with saltwater flowing through them. A row of wooden toilet seats above the troughs could accommodate more asses per hour in less space than individual toilets.

"Thumbs comes into the head and spots Doglike sitting there," Finesse continued. "Thumbs wads up a bunch of toilet paper, lights it on fire, and drops it into the saltwater flow directly upstream. Doglike sees it coming, but he's in no position to do anything about it."

A few guys started chuckling.

"Anyway, you guys know how hairy he is—or was. He went up in flames like a field of dry grass. They say you can still smell burnt hair down in deck."

This cheered up everybody in 02 berthing for the rest of the day.

We were about halfway across the Pacific when Finesse got a more serious case. A snipe named Hayes came to sick bay with a toothache. An x-ray showed an impacted wisdom tooth. With an infection that close to the brain, Finesse wanted to medevac Hayes. So, Billings got in touch with a Navy hospital in the Aleutians. We altered course north. A CH-46 chopper landed on the helo deck. After the chopper took off with Hayes, we got back on course. When I got out of the scullery that night, the usual casino game in 02 berthing was underway between Hoodwink, Hayashi, Alaska, and Finesse.

"Heard anything about Hayes?" Hayashi asked.

"The doctor said he'd make it," Finesse replied, lighting a cigarette. "I really didn't know what to do, so I just packed his ass full of penicillin. The duty MD said that's what saved him."

"Thank God," Skidmore said.

"Thank penicillin," Finesse replied.

Skidmore stopped combing his hair.

"What do you mean by that?" he asked.

"I mean penicillin saved Hayes, not God."

"That's sack—sacrilegious. God controls everything."

"If God controls everything, why did Hayes get infected in the first place?"

"That's not for us to know."

"The Lord works in mysterious ways, huh? Tell me, Skidmore, if you got real sick, where would you go: a hospital or a church?"

"I damn sure wouldn't go to some atheist like you. If you don't believe in God and hell, what's to stop you from stealing my wallet?"

"I never said I didn't believe in hell. We all enlisted in it. As for your wallet, I wouldn't steal it because it doesn't belong to me. But you didn't answer my question. Where would you go if you got sick: a hospital or a church?"

"A hospital, of course, but it would be up to God whether I lived or died. If it's my time to go, no doctor could save me."

"If that's how you feel, why go to the hospital?"

"Because maybe it would be God's will to save me."

"So, if the doctor saves you, God gets the credit? I'll bet if you died, your family would blame the doctor, not God."

"Either way, it's God's will."

"Either way," Hoodwink said, "the doctor gets paid."

"Not in the Navy," Finesse replied. "I make the same pay as any E-5, whether I got two men in sick bay or two dozen."

There had to be a better argument for the existence of God than the one Skidmore made, but I couldn't come up with one. There's more to religion than the skeptics think but less than the believers think.

Swampass walked in. Finesse and Hoodwink held their noses.

"Take a shower, Swampass," Alaska said.

"I already took one," Swampass replied.

"He means this year," Finesse said.

"I've had it," Hoodwink announced, standing up. "Let's get him!"

Hoodwink and Alaska dragged Swampass into the head. They held him under a cold shower, sprinkled him with abrasive cleanser, and scrubbed him with the brushes we used to clean toilets. I couldn't sleep with them yelling and Swampass wailing, so I climbed up to the 06 level.

The bridge was covered in the glow of red lights that we put on after dark to cut our nighttime visibility. Mr. Barker was the OOD. Shilgenkrauser was the boatswain's mate of the watch. Chief Lasko and Hutchinson were at the chart table. The phone rang. Crimmons answered it. He spoke briefly, hung up the phone, and turned to Mr. Barker.

"Forward torpedo room reports all secure, sir."

"We don't have any forward torpedo room," Mr. Barker replied. "You've been had, Crimmons.

And for future reference, in case anybody asks you, there's no such thing as a skyhook or relative bearing grease."

"Thorpe, why aren't you in the rack?" Chief Lasko asked.

"Sheer boredom, Chief," I answered.

"Our last fix shows us about thirty miles from the International Date Line," Hutchinson said, circling it in pencil.

"Right," Chief Lasko replied. "We'll enter the Realm of the Golden Dragon sometime after midnight. You better not stay up, though, Thorpe. Morning chow comes early."

Crimmons was listening to us and peeking at the chart.

"How far are we from land, Chief?" he asked.

"About two miles."

"*Two miles?*"

"Yeah, straight down. *AH HA HA HA HA HA!*"

"How long before we'll be able to see it?" Crimmons asked.

"See what?" Hutchinson asked.

"The International Date Line."

Crimmons was looking out the forward bridge windows like a kid waiting for Santa Claus.

"Funny you should mention that," the chief said. "I was about to ask for a volunteer for the International Date Line watch. You interested?"

"You bet, Chief," Crimmons answered.

Hutchinson started laughing, but he turned it into fake coughing. The chief slapped him on the back to make it look good.

"Okay, you're our man, Crimmons," the chief said. "Thorpe, Hutchinson, you guys get the equipment."

"What equipment, Chief?" Hutchinson asked.

"Oh, that's right. This is your first time crossing the line, isn't it? I'd better do this myself. Come with me, Crimmons."

Crimmons followed Chief Lasko into the chart house.

"Chief Lasko's in a great mood," Hutchinson said. "He's been outshooting Mr. Southcott during morning and evening stars. Mr. Kempton took his own sights and confirmed that the chief's fixes were more accurate than Mr. Southcott's," — Hutchinson lowered his voice to a whisper — "*and Southcott hasn't cottoned on.*"

Hutchinson meant that Mr. Southcott had not discovered his gundecked index error correction on Wildebeest. When the chief and Crimmons came back out to the bridge, Crimmons was wearing a lifejacket, a set of sound-powered phones, a helmet, and a pair of binoculars. The chief had also given him a clipboard with paper, a stopwatch, and a flashlight.

"Now listen up, Crimmons," the chief said. "I want you to go up to the signal bridge. Plug these phones into the JL circuit and keep a sharp eye out. When you see the dateline, it'll be covered with blinking lights of various colors — red, green, blue…"

"Like Christmas," Crimmons said.

"Yeah," the chief replied with a straight face, "like Christmas. They help us navigate, but this is very important. You have to write down what color lights you see and time them with the stopwatch so we know how often they blink. Got that?"

Crimmons was trying to concentrate.

"Why do I need the helmet?"

"It'll keep your head warm."

"Okay, Chief."

"We're depending on you."

As soon as Crimmons left the bridge, everybody started cracking up. Shilgenkrauser walked over to the chart table. He was another recruit from the criminal justice system. A former member of a West Virginia biker gang, Shilgenkrauser had been convicted of felony assault. The judge gave him a choice of prison time or a hitch in the military. Shilgenkrauser had taken Graff's spot as the last guy anyone wanted to argue with. He was built like a small bear. He had the Harley Davidson logo tattooed on his right arm and a skull and crossbones on his left arm. He looked like the kind of guy who could—and would—rip your leg off, beat you to death with it, then eat it.

"What happened to my messenger, Chief?" Shilgenkrauser asked.

"He's up on the 07 level," Chief Lasko replied. "I gave him the International Date Line watch. Your boy's a few bricks short of a full load."

Shilgenkrauser grinned, revealing a missing tooth.

"Leave him up there till he figures it out," he said. "It's the only way he'll learn not to listen to you quartermasters."

I went out to the bridge wing and looked up. There was Crimmons, up on the signal bridge, wearing the lifejacket, the phones, and the helmet. The Pacific was as calm as a lake. I never knew an ocean could be so calm. The ocean was a deep black mirror reflecting thousands of stars. Saturn had passed through the Milky Way. There was no moon. The horizon was invisible. I couldn't tell where the sky stopped and the water started. If you didn't look aft at our greenish phosphorescent trail, it looked like the ship was floating through outer space with infinity in every direction. I was alone. Someone else had to see it. Crimmons was up there looking through the binoculars for blinking colored lights that didn't exist. He was missing it.

"HEY, CRIMMONS!" I yelled, but he didn't hear me. The phones covered his ears.

I was about to call out to him again, but a gust of wind rippled the water and ruined the whole thing.

CHAPTER 18

Realm of the Golden Dragon

We crossed the Pacific in seventeen days, arriving in Yokosuka, Japan on the island of Honshu, about twenty-eight miles south of Tokyo. We could have made the crossing in a week, but Lightning Lenny had the crew practicing drills all day, every day. As the *Okmok* approached land, I was on my way up to the bridge for my first look at Japan. Billings was drinking out of the scuttlebutt in the passageway outside of radio.

"What's new, Billy?"

He straightened up and took off his spectacles and wiped them on his dungaree shirt.

"Nixon's in deep shit," he said.

"That's what you said last week."

"Probably still be true next week."

The crew was at sea and anchor detail. Lightning Lenny sat in the starboard captain's chair. Mr. Kempton stood beside Lightning Lenny, looking through his binoculars. Mendoza stood at the wheel. Koslowski stood at the lee helm. Mr. Priskett stood alongside Mendoza. Estorga was messenger of the watch. He wore a set of sound-powered phones. Mr. Southcott stood at the chart table with Chief Lasko. Cool was keeping the log.

Through the bridge windows, I could see a cloudy sky over the hills surrounding Tokyo Bay, or Tokyo *Wan* as the Japanese called it, but there was enough sunlight to see the busy harbor filled with merchant ships at anchor and lots of small craft and fishing boats underway. Land smelled after seventeen days at sea. Japan had a smell I couldn't describe.

"What's our position, Jim?" Lightning Lenny asked.

"We're almost in the center of the channel, Captain," Mr. Kempton answered, still looking through his binoculars.

Lightning Lenny dug a finger in his nose.

"Come right, Jim," he said.

"Aye aye, Captain," Mr. Kempton answered, waving his smoldering pipe toward the console. "Right three degrees rudder, Al."

"Right three degrees rudder, aye, sir," Mendoza answered, giving the wheel a twist to the right. "Rudder is right three degrees."

"Keep your eye on the gyro, Al," Mr. Priskett ordered.

"Roger that, Kip."

"*Shhhh!*" Mr. Priskett hissed.

Mr. Priskett sometimes let senior enlisted men get away with calling him by his first name—

unheard-of behavior for an officer—but only when other officers were not around.

"Navigatah wishes to remind you of the rocks at eight hundred yahds to stahboard," Mr. Southcott said.

"Thank you, Tod," Mr. Kempton replied. "Rudder amidships. Steady as she goes, Al."

"Rudder amidships, aye," Mendoza answered. "Steadying up on zero zero nine, sir."

"Very well."

"What are you doing here, Thorpe?" Chief Lasko asked. He was bent over the chart table, holding a protractor and pencil, a cigarette in his mouth, sweat dripping from his forehead onto the chart.

"Just taking a break from the scullery, Chief," I answered.

"Thawpe," Mr. Southcott snapped, "if yaw going to be up heah, don't be an impediment."

"Aye aye, sir. Nice day for boating."

Mr. Southcott stared at me over the top of his glasses like he was looking at a cockroach on his breakfast.

"Forward lookout reports Japanese fishing vessel converging directly on our bow," Estorga announced.

"Goddammit, Jim," Lightning Lenny said. "That fishing boat is changing course again."

Everyone on the bridge had noticed the Japanese fishing boat heading toward us. I walked out on the starboard wing for a better look.

"Right three degrees rudder," Mr. Kempton said.

"Right three degrees rudder, aye, sir," Mendoza answered. "Rudder is right three degrees."

"Steady as she goes, Al. Make turns for three knots."

"Make turns for three knots, aye," Koslowski answered. "Engine room answers making turns for three knots, sir."

"Very well."

"Steadying up on zero one one, sir."

"Very well."

We came right. The fishing boat came left. It was coming at our bow again.

"Goddammit, Jim," Lightning Lenny said. "What's he doing? I don't give a rat's ass how you lose this fishing boat. Just do it."

"Forward lookout reports —" Estorga began.

"Belay that, Estorga," Mr. Kempton said. "Come right three degrees, Al."

"Right three degrees, aye, sir," Mendoza answered.

"Navigatah wishes to remind you of the rocks six hundred yahds to stahboard," Mr. Southcott said.

"Very well, Tod," Mr. Kempton replied, trailing pipe smoke as he paced along the row of bridge windows. "Koslowski, make turns for two."

"Make turns for two, aye, sir," Koslowski answered. "Engine room answers making turns for two."

"Very well. Steady as she goes, Al."

"Steadying up on zero one four, sir."

Again, we moved from the center of the channel toward the rocks, and again, the Japanese fishing boat altered course for a head-on collision with us.

"Forward lookout reports fishing boat dead ahead," Estorga announced.

The fishing boat disappeared under our bow. Lightning Lenny leaped from his chair and ran out to the starboard wing.

"ALL STOP!" he yelled. "ALL STOP!"

"All stop," Mr. Kempton echoed, following Lightning Lenny outside.

"All stop," Koslowski answered. "Engine room answers all stop."

Lightning Lenny and Mr. Kempton were beside me, leaning over the rail. Below us, the Japanese fishing boat motored between our starboard side and the rocks. Three Japanese fishermen stood on the flying bridge, grinning at us as they headed out to sea. One of them was giving us the finger. Lightning Lenny's face turned purple.

"I'll report that boat to the harbor master," he yelled, waving his fist. "Signalman, I want the name of that boat. SIGNALMAN!"

"Yes, Captain?" Skidmore answered. He was looking down from the 07 level.

"Get on the big eyes. I want the name of that fishing boat before it gets away. Hurry up."

"Aye aye, sir."

"Navigatah wishes to remind you of the rocks four hundred yahds to stahboard," Mr. Southcott said.

"Aye, Tod. All ahead one third," Mr. Kempton said. "Left three degrees rudder."

"Skidmore!" Lightning Lenny yelled. "What's going on up there? Can you see it, Skidmore? SKIDMORE!"

Skidmore was looking at the fishing boat through the starboard big eyes, one of two pairs of gigantic binoculars mounted on each side of the signal shack.

"SKIDMORE?"

Skidmore glanced down at Lightning Lenny. Then, he looked into the big eyes again.

"PETTY OFFICER SKIDMORE, CAN YOU SEE THE NAME OF THAT BOAT, OR CAN'T YOU?"

"Affirmative, sir."

"WELL, WHAT IS ITS NAME?"

Skidmore took his time, hesitating after each word.

"It's…in…Japanese…sir."

Nobody laughed, but everybody wanted to. Every man on the bridge turned his back to Lightning Lenny and stifled his laughter. Hutchinson was grinning up there on the telescopic alidade. Even Mr. Kempton was smiling without showing any teeth. The Japanese fishing boat motored away to stern. Lightning Lenny sat in his chair. He put his finger up his nose.

"Steady as she goes, Al," Mr. Kempton said.

"Steady as she goes, aye, sir," Mendoza answered.

An hour later, Lightning Lenny's facial color had returned to normal. We were tied up at a pier as far as possible from the main gate of the base. As the most junior CO in Yokosuka, Lightning Lenny got last choice of mooring spots. The crew gathered on the fantail for the XO's orientation speech. Mr. Crookshank wore shooting glasses with yellow lenses. He had more campaign ribbons on his khaki-covered chest than Lightning Lenny. He spoke into the microphone.

"I WANT TO INFORM YOU MEN ABOUT THE PROTESTERS ON THE BEACH. THEY OBJECT TO THE PRESENCE OF AMMO SHIPS LIKE THE *OKMOK* BECAUSE THEY FEEL WE MIGHT BRING NUCLEAR WEAPONS INTO JAPAN. THAT'S WHAT THAT FISHING BOAT SKIRMISH WAS ALL ABOUT THIS AFTERNOON."

The United States had made an agreement with Japan after World War II never to bring nuclear weapons into their country. Every crewmember knew we were violating the agreement. You didn't need a top-secret clearance to know there were NUCWEAPS aboard the *Okmok*.

"LOOSE LIPS SINK SHIPS," Mr. Crookshank continued. "STAY TOGETHER. USE THE BUDDY SYSTEM. USE YOUR HEAD, AND USE A CONDOM—AND GET YOUR PLEASURE FROM A JUG. SMOKING MARIJUANA IS A FELONY IN JAPAN."

In 02 berthing, everybody who didn't have the duty was changing clothes and looking forward to liberty. Mendoza was already dressed in civilian clothes, sitting at a table smoking a cigarette.

"What are you doing, Al?" Estorga asked.

"Just waiting for the sun to go down," Mendoza replied.

Brogan was getting dressed slowly. He looked depressed.

"What's the matter, Pete?" I asked.

"Oh, hell," he said, "I think Hutch is playing a trick on me. At least, I hope so. Otherwise, somebody ripped me off."

"What are you talking about?"

"I had some money in my locker, about a hundred bucks."

I took his Planters peanut can of money out of my locker and handed it to him.

"It was 160 bucks," I said.

"You bastard," Brogan replied, but he was smiling. "I was afraid I shitcanned the can."

"Lock your locker, or the next time your money's missing, it won't be us."

After seventeen days at sea, I was looking forward to going ashore. Estorga and I flashed our ID cards to the quarterdeck watch, saluted aft toward the flag, walked down the brow, and headed for the main gate. We saw some Japanese students carrying hand-lettered signs in Japanese. They had some in English that said: NO NUKES. I started across the street.

"Whoa, Shortcut," Estorga said, grabbing the back of my collar. A speeding Toyota shot past from behind us. "They drive on the other side of the road here, man."

We followed the crowd of sailors to the Alliance Club—the club for enlisted men—and exchanged our money for yen. The only place we were allowed to go was called Sailor Town, an area the Japanese had set up to keep American military in one place and away from downtown Yokosuka. Most of the bars in Sailor Town were named after American states. We walked into a place called The Texas Club. I looked at the jukebox.

"What's on it?" Estorga asked.

"It's… in…Japanese…sir," I replied.

He dropped in a coin and pushed a button at random. "Mr. Big Stuff" started playing.

"I hate that song," he said. "We heard it every night in Panama."

We ordered two Kirins from a cute waitress in a yellow and black dress. Two delicate girls approached our table.

"You buy me drink?" they both said at the same time.

"Sure," Estorga replied, smiling. "Sit down."

We bought them each a "lady's drink," which cost 1000 yen compared to 300 yen for a beer. They weren't prostitutes. They were there to dance or hold hands with anyone who would keep on buying lady's drinks, which turned out to be little glasses of tea. The conversation was weaker than the tea. Their English was limited to "What ship you from?" and "You buy me drink?"

It didn't take long to figure out that all the bars in Sailor Town were the same. We decided to try a real bar in town, but at the entrance of each one, there was a sign that said: NO AMERICANS. We walked into one, anyway. The place was crowded. The air was filled with smoke. Conversation stopped as every Japanese head turned to stare at us.

"Think they can tell we're Americans?" Estorga asked.

The bartender jabbered at us in angry Japanese. He wasn't saying welcome to Japan.

"*Piñche pendejo*," Estorga replied. "Sounds like a personal problem."

"Let's get out of here," I said.

We went back to Sailor Town, and we found a huge bar called the Royal Club. A bunch of our shipmates were inside. Brogan, Hutchinson, and Crimmons were down on their knees in front of a bandstand. Crapshoot and Malolo were standing over them. Mendoza, Hoodwink, Finesse, and Alaska were up on the bandstand. Bootleg tried a kung-fu move on Crapshoot, and Crapshoot put him in a half nelson. Hoodwink waved a bottle of beer. He was drunk and yelling and slurring his words.

"OKAY, *OKMOK*, LISHEN UP. WITHOUT DELAY, WE BEGIN THE INI-SHIA-SHUN SHEREMONY INTO THE REALM OF THE GOLDEN DRAGON. I SHAY TO THEESH NEW GREEN MEN ON THEIR FIRSHT WESTPAC— YOU GUYS ALL KNEW IT, SO LET'SH GET TO IT, BUT IF YOU WON'T GO THROUGH IT, YOU'LL BE MADE TO DO IT!"

Our shipmates in the crowd raised their beer bottles while Hoodwink, Finesse, Mendoza, Crapshoot, Alaska, and the other WESTPAC veterans took turns pouring beer all over Hutchinson, Brogan, Crimmons, and Bootleg. Hutchinson was laughing as streams of beer fell on him from every direction. The Japanese owner, who had seemed so happy a minute before when he was selling all that beer, was yelling at us for pouring beer all over his floor. Hoodwink poured a little beer on him, too. The waitresses took cover behind the bar. The owner picked up a telephone.

"Hey," Mendoza said. "It's Estorga and Shortcut. It's their first WESTPAC. GET 'EM!"

"Ain't this a bitch?" Estorga said to me.

Mendoza grabbed Estorga's arm. Alaska grabbed my arm, and they brought us forward to the bandstand. Hoodwink and Finesse laughed as they soaked our hair and shirts with beer.

"More beer," Hoodwink yelled.

"MORE BEER!" echoed the crowd. "MORE BEER!"

The owner and his waitresses were shaking their heads, but our crew helped themselves to beers from the cooler. They threw handfuls of wet beer-soaked yen at the agitated owner, and they passed the beers from hand to hand over to Hoodwink, Mendoza, and Finesse. Then, the door flew open. It was the Shore Patrol, four of them. They wore dress whites with white helmets, and they carried billy sticks and .45s.

"What the hell is going on here?" asked their leader, a first-class.

Everybody froze. No one said a word as the Shore Patrol took in the scene: a bunch of beer-soaked guys on their knees in front of a bandstand, surrounded by a bunch of drunken clowns holding beer bottles. Finesse broke the silence.

"Our Father who art in heaven, hallowed be thy name."

His hair fell into his glasses as he bowed his head. Some of the crew joined in with him.

"*Thy kingdom come. Thy will be done in earth as it is in heaven…*"

The Shore Patrol was held at bay by this unexpected recital of the Lord's Prayer. Hoodwink, Crapshoot, and Malolo bowed their heads and fell to their knees in puddles of beer. I looked down at the wet floorboards as Finesse continued to lead us in prayer.

"*For thine is the kingdom, and the power, and the glory, forever. Amen.*"

"AMEN!" yelled the crew.

The other three members of the Shore Patrol were looking to their leader for guidance.

"Keep it down in here," said the first-class, and they left.

Finesse put his hand on Estorga's head.

"THIS MAN HAS THE CLAP," he yelled. "BUT I SAY UNTO HIM, ARISE AND WALK!"

Estorga stood up, dripping with beer.

"It's a miracle," he said. "I can walk. I CAN WALK!"

"HALLELUJAH!" Alaska yelled.

The jukebox played a Tower of Power tune, "What Is Hip." Estorga started dancing.

"I CAN DANCE!" he said. "I CAN DANCE!"

"MORE BEER!" Hoodwink yelled.

The morning after our Realm of the Golden Dragon initiation and prayer meeting, the shriek of the boatswain's pipe sliced through our heads. Shilgenkrauser spoke over the 1MC.

"NOW REVEILLE, REVEILLE, REVEILLE. ALL HANDS, HEAVE OUT AND TRICE UP. ALL REVEILLE POs MAKE THEIR REPORTS TO THE OOD ON THE QUARTERDECK. REVEILLE."

"Let's go, let's go," Meech yelled. It was his turn for duty reveille PO. "Get your candy asses out of the racks. Let's see those feet hit the deck. Chop chop. It's another wonderful Navy day. Move it, or you're on report. Let's go."

Everyone but Swampass crowded into the head to shave and brush his teeth. After breakfast, we mustered on the second deck. All divisions formed up in dress blues and shiny shoes for another personnel inspection.

"All right, you fuckups and fuckoffs," Chief Hackburn yelled. "Let's straighten up those ranks. Straighten up, Swampass, you fat fuck. Come on, Billings. Get going, Estorga. Let's go, Hankins. Stop scratching your ass, Brogan. Cooley, get your skinny ass in line. That goes for you, too, Thorpe."

Chief Hackburn, Chief Lasko, and Mendoza stood side by side as Skidmore called roll.

"*Attention*," Chief Lasko said.

"At ease," Mr. Southcott said. "Have you read 'em the POD yet, Skidmaw?"

"Negative, sir."

"Well, let's get it."

Skidmore cleared his throat.

"Item one. Anyone with knowledge of who vandalized Petty Officer Needler's vehicle, report same to Petty Officer Needler."

"No clue," Hutchinson said.

A few guys laughed.

"Shaddup," Mr. Southcott said.

"Item two. Gambling is against Navy regs. Anyone caught gambling —"

"Skip on down, Skidmaw."

"Item three. Crewmembers who are not on the watch bill have been eating early chow before the watch. Early chow is for watch standers only. It will now require an early chow pass to be admitted to the mess decks for early chow. These passes will be issued to the leading petty officer in each division —"

"Fahthah down, Skidmaw. Regahding the personnel inspection."

"The crew will prepare for sea and anchor detail immediately following the Captain's personnel inspection. We will be getting underway to UNREP with the *Jouett* and —"

"Belay that, Skidmaw. Okay, you heard it. You quartermastahs, I want every swingin' dick on the bridge right aftah the inspection. And this time, I want *no discrepancies*, got that, Thawpe?"

Some guys choked back laughter. Everybody knew that I had never passed a personnel inspection.

"Yes, sir," I answered.

"X and N division, *attention!*" Mr. Southcott yelled as Lightning Lenny approached us.

Lightning Lenny walked slowly through the ranks. Mr. Southcott followed behind him with a clipboard. Soon, Lightning Lenny was standing in front of me. He scrutinized every detail of my uniform. I had shined my shoes and smoothed a crease out of my jumper. It was beginning to look like I might pass this time. Then, Lightning Lenny reached out and flicked the hair above my left ear.

"This man needs a haircut. See that? The hair makes contact with his ear. That is unsat. And those shoes look a little dull. You'd better work on that, Sailor."

"Aye aye, Captain," I answered.

Lightning Lenny moved on to Brogan. Mr. Southcott stepped up.

"See the bahbah befaw you come up to the bridge, Thawpe," he said.

"Aye aye, sir."

After Lightning Lenny dismissed us, I visited Scully, the ship's barber. It took less than a minute for Scully to run his clippers above my ears and make my head look like a white sidewall tire. When I arrived on the bridge in working dungarees, Cool, Hutchinson, and Brogan were setting up the bridge for sea and anchor detail.

"Thawpe," Mr. Southcott said. "You were the only man in the division with a discrepancy, as usual. Except this time, it was *two* discrepancies." He was reading from the division records. "Last time, it was a protruding thread. The time befaw that, it was a missing button. Yaw ruining the division average. What's it going to take to get you squared away?"

"I'm trying, sir."

"Yaw *very* trying. If we weren't about to get underway, I'd make sure this wouldn't be a pleasant day for you, Thawpe. Now, get out of heah, and get back down to the scullery."

"Aye aye, sir."

I couldn't remember the last pleasant day I had since joining the Navy.

We got underway and steamed out of Tokyo *Wan*. We spent the afternoon doing an UNREP with the cruiser, *Jouett*. I was in the scullery all day with Carranza and Mooney, but we could hear the progress of the UNREP over the 1MC.

"GOOD MORNING, USS *JOUETT*," Shilgenkrauser's voice echoed. "WELCOME ALONGSIDE THE *OKMOK*. STAND BY TO RECEIVE SHOT LINES FORE AND AFT."

It was a routine UNREP. We refueled the *Jouett* and transferred pallets of projectiles from our deck to theirs. After the *Jouett* disengaged and steamed away, we made a turn to port. A swell hit us, and we heeled way over. Brogan told me later that the bubble clinometer on the bridge went past forty-five degrees. Silverware spilled onto the deck in the scullery, and a stack of trays capsized. Two loose pallets of anti-aircraft projectiles slid along the main deck, and thousands of dollars of ordnance went over the side to the bottom of the Pacific.

Lightning Lenny demanded to know who was responsible for securing those pallets. Mr. Kempton asked Chief Skinner. Chief Skinner questioned his boatswain's mates and found that Loophole had assigned Thumbs to secure the pallets. Chief Skinner put Thumbs on report. Shit rolls downhill. That was standard Navy procedure. Finding a real solution to the problem was never the goal. The question was always: Who can we hang?

We could see Mount Fuji to the west as we steamed into port by 1630. After we secured from sea and anchor detail, Mr. Crookshank spoke over the 1MC before liberty call.

"THIS IS THE XO. WE HAD AN INCIDENT LAST NIGHT AT THE ROYAL CLUB. THE OWNER COMPLAINED TO THE SHORE PATROL ABOUT A GROUP OF *OKMOK* SAILORS POURING BEER ALL OVER THE FLOOR OF HIS ESTABLISHMENT. HE WAS UNABLE TO PROVIDE ANY NAMES, BUT I WARN YOU, ANY *OKMOK* SAILORS IDENTIFIED PARTICIPATING IN INCIDENTS LIKE THAT WILL HAVE THEIR LIBERTY SUSPENDED. LOOSE LIPS SINK SHIPS. STAY TOGETHER. USE THE BUDDY SYSTEM. USE YOUR HEAD, AND USE A CONDOM. AND REMEMBER, SMOKING MARIJUANA IS A FELONY IN JAPAN. THAT IS ALL."

Estorga and I headed for the Alliance Club. The band was playing a Creedence tune, "Born on the Bayou." A few couples were on the dance floor. We sat at a table with Hutchinson and Brogan.

"Did you hear Southcott's leavin'?" Brogan asked, lifting a bottle of Kirin.

"Tell me you're not shitting me, Pete," I said.

"No shit. Billy Billings told me he radioed some traffic to BUPERS. Lightning Lenny's sending Southcott stateside. We're getting a replacement navigation officer. Not only that, but I heard Southcott tell Mendoza he wanted to get a good deal on a Jap motorbike before they sent him home."

"Mah prayers have been answered," Hutchinson said. "Now our only enemy is the North Vietnamese."

The place was called the Alliance Club because it was open to all branches of the service, but sailors and marines didn't always mix. Since Admiral Zumwalt became the Chief of Naval Operations, sailors were allowed to have beards, and we didn't have to wear uniforms on liberty. Marines held that against us since they still had to wear buzz haircuts and dress uniforms. Some idiot from another ship yelled.

"JARHEADS AIN'T NOTHIN' BUT ERRAND BOYS WORKIN' FOR THE NAVY!"

There is no quicker way to piss off marines than to remind them that they are a branch of the Navy.

A fight broke out on the far side of the dance floor. A table fell over. Glasses crashed. Girls screamed. The band ran for cover. A chair went flying. Two marines knocked Koslowski down, but he came up from the deck with an uppercut for one of them. Hoodwink broke a chair over the other one. Crapshoot put a marine in a come-along wrist hold and ran him headfirst into a bulkhead. Malolo picked up a small marine by the ankles, swung him around in a circle, and let him fly up on the bandstand into the drums. Bootleg got into a kung-fu horse stance, and a marine knocked off his dark sunglasses when he clobbered him with a bottle.

"Let's get out of here," Estorga said.

We headed for a side door, but a group of marines spotted us.

"YOU SQUIDS TRYING TO SNEAK BACK TO THE WATER?"

Somebody blindsided me, and I caught a fist over my left eye. I threw a return punch that didn't connect with anything. Another guy fell into me and Estorga, knocking us down. The sounds of people getting hurt were all around me. Brogan was grunting and scuffling, and Estorga was cursing in Spanish.

Then, police whistles started blowing from behind us. The Shore Patrol had arrived. The side door was not far away. I crawled toward it, but the marine who hit me wanted to wrestle. He let go when the butt end of a flying gin bottle bounced off his forehead. Estorga was crawling toward the door—only six feet away—with me right behind him. The door flew open in our faces, and more Shore Patrol burst in.

"ON YOUR FEET!"

They put us in handcuffs and loaded us into gray vans. They accidentally put Shilgenkrauser into the wrong van with two marines, and he kept on pounding them.

"All right, Shilgenkrauser," Crapshoot called out, laughing. "Take care of my light work."

It took three of the Shore Patrol to pull Shilgenkrauser out of there and get him into the van with us. As they drove us back to the ship, Shilgenkrauser kept yelling:

"SEND MORE MARINES! SEND MORE MARINES!"

CHAPTER 19

Sayonara, Southcott

The next morning, I looked in the mirror. The skin over my left eyebrow was purple. Estorga had scraped knuckles. Brogan's cheek was bruised. Only Hutchinson came out of the fight clean. There was a long line of guys in the passageway outside sick bay.

"Keep it down out here," Garvey called out, but he was only an E-3, so everybody ignored him.

Finesse poked his head out of his office.

"All you guys with hangovers," he yelled, "get out of here. I can't do anything for hangovers. Go take an aspirin."

"I'm not drunk," Doglike said.

"Yeah, and Nixon's not a crook. Nobody sober ever says: 'I'm not drunk.'"

After morning muster, Needler had a surprise locker search. Meech searched in engineering and supply. Needler searched both deck divisions. Snyder searched in 02 berthing. The only thing he found in my locker was dirty laundry.

When I went back to mess cooking, the scullery was filled with steam and noise. The sterilizer supplied the steam. Carranza supplied the noise.

"What happened to you, Shortcut?" he asked, looking at my forehead. "Somebody say shut up, and you thought he said stand up?"

"Did Needler find your communist books?" I asked.

"The bastard dug right past 'em. He found a marijuana seed and wrote me up. I don't know where that damn seed came from. Now, I'm gonna have to go to captain's mast again."

Two new deck apes were assigned to mess cooking, so I got the weekend off. After knockoff, Hutchinson was changing clothes in 02 berthing. Brogan and Cool were staying aboard. They had weekend duty.

"Ah'm gettin' tired of seein' Japan from the inside of a bar," Hutchinson said. "Let's catch the bullet train to Tokyo."

We walked to the train station and stood on the platform. Hutchinson was looking through a Japanese dictionary. I spoke to a Japanese guy.

"Is this where we get the train to Tokyo?"

"*Hai, hai,*" he said.

"Hi," I replied. "Is this the place for the train to Tokyo?"

"*Hai* means yes, Shortcut," Hutchinson explained.

Within an hour, we had a room at the Imperial Hotel with padded carpet and two double beds for eight thousand yen. After sundown, we drank

Asahi beer and Suntory whiskey in the walnut-paneled bar on the top floor overlooking the city.

"Ah was reading about the Japanese," Hutchinson said. "They do things different."

"Like what?"

"Like what do you do when you get a letter?"

"Open it."

"Me, too. But when the Japs get a letter, they put it aside. They don't just tear into it and read it standing up. They wait for the right time. They look forward to it. They change clothes and sit down and relax, and *then*, they open it like a bottle of good whiskey."

We slept in late the next morning, with no reveille or boatswain's pipes. After breakfast, we flagged down a cab at the taxi stand outside the hotel. The cabby drove the white Datsun like he stole it, squealing rubber around blind corners, crisscrossing lanes, and flying through tight openings.

At the World Trade Center, we took an elevator that traveled at thirty meters per second up forty stories to the top. We could see the Tokyo Tower but not much else because the smog was worse than Los Angeles. We could barely make out Mount Fuji in the distance. Hutchinson took some photos with his thirty-five-millimeter Pentax. We had another wild cab ride back to the vicinity of the hotel.

"Man, these cab drivers really get it on," Hutchinson said.

We spent the afternoon wandering around the bridges and fountains in Hibiya Park and the gardens surrounding the Imperial Palace. For a late lunch, we split the world's smallest pizza.

"Eighteen hundred yen," Hutchinson said when the waitress brought the bill. "That's almost twenty bucks."

We walked through the city. Though most Japanese smoked, there were no cigarette butts on the sidewalks. There was no trash or graffiti. The trashcans in the alleys all had lids and stood in straight rows.

"You'd never see alleys that clean in the States," I said.

After nightfall, we made our way to the Ginza. We entered a narrow bar about forty feet long and just barely wide enough for the bar and the barstools. We ordered seven and sevens at 400 yen each and switched to whiskey when we realized that we were being charged 200 yen for the Seven-Up.

Hutchinson was looking through his Japanese dictionary. I walked upstairs to the bathroom. The height of its ceiling was at my shoulders. I bent at the knees and crouched to get inside. I had to stay hunched over the whole time. When I came back down to the bar, Hutchinson was laughing with two Japanese businessmen wearing suits and ties.

"*Konnichi wa,*" Hutchinson said. "They're laughing because you had to duck to fit inside the head."

The businessmen nodded. They were shorter than Hutchinson, laughing with the bartender about my height. I felt like a carnival attraction.

"Look," Hutchinson continued, "they bought us some hors d'oeuvres. *Arigato*."

On the bar was a plate of salami bits alongside a martini glass full of bite-sized butter chunks filled with raisins. The businessmen finished their drinks, stood up, bowed toward us, and walked outside to the crowded street. Hutchinson called for another round. When the bartender brought the bill, we were charged for our drinks, their drinks, and the hors d'oeuvres.

"Those guys ripped us off," Hutchinson said.

"Your Japanese needs work," I said.

After we paid the bill, the bartender gave Hutchinson a dirty look and grunted.

"What's his problem?" Hutchinson asked.

"He saw you counting your change," I replied.

That wasn't our last financial setback. The next day, we checked out of the Imperial Hotel. The bill was 18,800 yen.

"I thought it was eight thousand a night," I said to the desk clerk.

"Ah, yes," he said with an incongruous smile. "Eight thousand for room, plus fourteen hundred service charge."

"Service charge?" Hutchinson asked.

"For towels and telephone."

"We didn't make any calls," I said.

"Ah, yes," the clerk said with no further explanation.

After we paid him, I stood there looking at my wallet.

"Now I don't have enough money for the train back to Yokosuka. Can you lend me ten bucks until payday, Jeff?"

"Don't worry, Shortcut. Ah got you covered."

Hutchinson took a five thousand yen bill out of his wallet.

"Excuse me," he said to the clerk. "Will you break this for me, *kudasai*?"

The clerk took the bill and gave Hutchinson three one-thousand-yen bills, two five hundreds, and ten one hundreds.

"*Arigato*," Hutchinson said. "What's your name?"

"Yoshida."

"This sure is a beautiful hotel, Yoshida. Ah understand it was designed by Frank Lloyd Wright."

"Yes."

"Ya know, I have too many hundred yen notes here. You can probably use some hundreds, right? Can Ah give you back these ten hundreds for a thousand note?"

Yoshida took the cash and handed over a thousand-yen bill.

"Must be an interesting job, gettin' to meet people from all over the world. How long have you worked here?"

"One year," Yoshida replied, counting the money. "Excuse me, sir. You give me only nine hundred yen."

"Oh, *sumimasen*, Ah must not be awake yet," Hutchinson said, smiling as he handed over another hundred. "There, that makes an even thousand. Tell you what, Yoshida. Here's another thousand." Hutchinson held out two five hundreds. "May Ah please have two one thousand notes, if it's not too much trouble?"

Yoshida took the money and handed over two one-thousand-yen bills, and we walked outside.

"Let's move, Shortcut," Hutchinson said, waving down a cab, "before old Yoshida figures out he just gave me two thousand yen for a thousand. Told you Ah had you covered."

The next morning on the bridge, Mendoza had a big grin on his face.

"Well, wheels," he said, "this is the end of my third hitch. Ten days and a wake up. Skinner tried to talk me into signing up for another four years. He gave me the full sales pitch. You should have heard him: 'The Navy's like an anchor you can depend on, a buddy that won't run out. It's food, clothing, home.' I let him go on until he ran out of steam. Then, I told him: 'As we say in Spanish: No.'"

"What's a lifer like you going to do once you get back to the States?" I asked.

"I'll join the Navy again. Eight more years, and I'll have retirement."

"I don't get it, Al. Why leave just to join up again?"

"So I can get off this ship, buddy. I've been trying to get a transfer since Lasko took over, but Southcott blocked all my requests. Now, they can't stop me. It's *adios, Okmok*."

We got underway to UNREP with a destroyer group. A new officer had reported aboard in Yokosuka. Lieutenant Tobias was Mr. Southcott's replacement. He had a thick neck and wide shoulders that looked like they'd been meant for a taller man. Lightning Lenny kept Mr. Southcott aboard for the UNREPS rather than putting him off in Yokosuka so that he could break in Mr. Tobias as navigator. They stood at the chart table with Chief Lasko.

The final UNREP of the day was with the *Ranger*, which was bound for the States. Our deck apes fired the orange shot lines—now known aboard the *Okmok* as "Brogan's shoelaces"—over to the deck of the *Ranger*. Mendoza and Mr. Southcott got ready to depart as our crew set up the manila highline rig with a special smaller skip box for transferring personnel.

Mendoza had trained us to steer. Without Mendoza, the primary helmsman position would fall to the senior striker, Brogan. When Brogan took the helm, Kip kept an eye on him. I went out on the starboard wing, where Hutchinson and Cool were pretending to shine the brass. Hutchinson had his camera around his neck.

"So, that's the new navigator," I said. "He can't be as bad as Southcott, right?"

"Can't tell yet," Hutchinson replied.

"Leas' we gettin' rid of little Adolf," Cool said.

We looked down on the main deck. Mendoza got into the skip box. It looked like a cage attached to the trolley that rode along the manila highline that ran between the two ships. Because Mendoza was part of the original commissioning crew, he rated a special announcement over the 1MC.

"QUARTERMASTER FIRST-CLASS MENDOZA, PLANK OWNER, DEPARTING," Shilgenkrauser said.

At the signal from Chief Skinner, Loophole and Thumbs released the skip box. The Ranger crew pulled the inhaul line, and our crew tended the outhaul. The trolley glided across the manila highline, carrying Mendoza and his gear above the waves. The skip box landed on the main deck of the *Ranger*. We waved at Mendoza after he got out. Mendoza saluted back. Our deck apes hauled the skip box back, and Mr. Southcott got in with his sea bag and the mahogany case containing Wildebeest.

"First, they test it with an enlisted man to see if it's safe for an officer," Hutchinson said.

Loophole and Thumbs released the skip box, and Mr. Southcott took the same ride over to the deck of the *Ranger*. When Loophole and Thumbs received the skip box again, they disconnected it. They rolled out a motorcycle with shining chrome and a glossy blue paint job.

"That Southcott's bike?" I asked.

"A brand-new Kawasaki 500," Hutchinson replied. "Nice, huh?"

"He be talkin' all mornin' how much money he save, buyin' it in Japan," Cool said.

Loophole and Thumbs wrapped two wide nylon straps around the motorcycle and shackled them to the highline trolley. Hutchinson focused his camera on the motorcycle as they maneuvered it out over the side. It was suspended from the highline, and the *Ranger* crew started pulling the inhaul line. When the motorcycle was about halfway between the two ships, it stopped. The deck apes aboard the *Ranger* kept pulling on the inhaul, but something was snagged. They got it to move a little bit. Then, a shackle broke open. One of the nylon straps was flapping in the wind. The motorcycle dangled at an awkward angle, supported by the other strap. It twirled slowly. Then, it slipped out. Hutchinson snapped rapid-fire motor-drive photos as Mr. Southcott's shiny new Kawasaki splashed down into the ocean and sank like a brick.

We could see Mr. Southcott screaming from the deck of the *Ranger*, but his words were drowned out by the wind. Chief Skinner screamed at the deck apes. Cool was cracking up. We waved at Mr. Southcott. He didn't wave back. Cool and Hutchinson gave each other palm slaps.

"Goddammit, Jim," Lightning Lenny yelled. "What the hell happened?"

"I'll find out, Captain. Stringbean, get Chief Skinner on the phones."

"You had your camera ready," I said to Hutchinson.

"That's the secret of great photography," he replied.

"You knew ahead of time. You had something to do with that."

"Ah don't know what you're talkin' about," he said, but his grin told me he was lying.

"That was *beautiful*," I said. "I'll pay for copies of those photos."

The *Ranger* broke away, heading east. Lightning Lenny had Mr. Kempton secure from replenishment at sea detail and set the regular underway watch. Then, he left the bridge.

"*Captain's departing the bridge,*" Shilgenkrauser yelled.

"Navigator," Mr. Kempton said, "let's steam for Yokosuka. Plot us a course for Tokyo *Wan*."

"Aye aye, sir," Mr. Tobias answered. "Double check that course for me, Chief."

"I get two nine eight, sir," Chief Lasko said.

"Glad we agree. We wouldn't want the wrong *wan*. Navigator recommends course two nine eight."

"Very well, Russ," Mr. Kempton replied. "Right standard rudder, Brogan. Steady up on new course two nine eight."

"Right standard rudder, aye," Brogan answered. "Steadying on new course two nine eight."

When we arrived in port, Japanese shipyard workers were doing calisthenics. Lightning Lenny and Mr. Crookshank mustered the crew on the fantail. Lightning Lenny spoke into the microphone.

"IF ANY CREW MEMBERS GET INVOLVED IN ANY FIGHTING, LIBERTY IN THIS PORT WILL BE CANCELED—REPEAT—CANCELED FOR THE ENTIRE CREW. THAT IS ALL."

Mr. Crookshank took the microphone.

"LOOSE LIPS SINK SHIPS," he said. "STAY TOGETHER, ALWAYS IN PAIRS. USE YOUR

HEAD, AND USE A CONDOM, AND GET YOUR PLEASURE FROM A JUG. SMOKING MARIJUANA IS A FELONY IN JAPAN."

Cool had the duty. Estorga, Hutchinson, Brogan, and I went ashore and headed for Sailor Town. We were drinking Sapporo beers at the Texas club, when Loophole walked in.

"Howdy, partner," Hutchinson said.

"Don't you mean accomplice?" Brogan asked.

Hutchinson lifted his beer and made a toast.

"Here's to the first man in naval history to sink a Japanese motorcycle."

"Can't take all the credit," Loophole said, showing off the gaps between his teeth. "Ain't my fault if Thumbs used the wrong pins in the wrong shackle."

"Is that what happened?" Estorga asked.

"That's what it'll say in the report."

"Yeah, but who gave the job to Thumbs?" Brogan asked.

"Nobody better for that kind of duty," Loophole replied. "He was on restriction, anyway, for losing those ammo pallets, but it'll blow over. Lim said some of the stewards heard the XO laughing about it in the wardroom with Mr. Osterkamp and Raccoon Face. Mr. Southcott wasn't real popular among the gentry."

Estorga and Brogan were grinning like two jack o' lanterns. A waitress brought another round of beers. Hutchinson looked around before passing a plastic bag of pot to Loophole under the table. It looked to me like a payoff. Loophole put it inside his jacket, finished his beer, and took off.

"Ah got a little more," Hutchinson whispered. "If anybody wants to partake."

"Roger that," Brogan replied.

"Not me," Estorga said. "I ain't been stoned since I saw *The Exorcist* on mescaline."

"Suit yourself," Hutchinson replied, and he and Brogan took off.

"Can't believe Loophole took a risk float-testing Southcott's bike," I said. "He's a petty officer."

"He's also a petty criminal," Estorga replied.

After we finished our beers, Estorga and I tried our luck in real Yokosuka again. We avoided the bars with signs that said: NO AMERICANS. We found a bar with a bunch of Australian merchant sailors and got into a drinking contest with them. I'm not sure who won. We staggered up the brow after midnight. Cool was standing messenger of the watch.

"Truly," I said, "is that really, truly Truly Cooley?"

Cool could see we were hammered.

"Better getcho fool asses down to 02 before Hackburn come back out here," he said, nodding toward the quarterdeck shack where two marines were talking with Chief Hackburn. Estorga and I stumbled our way to 02 berthing. Estorga crushed out his smoke in a butt kit and headed for his rack. The lights were on near my rack. Hutchinson and Brogan were packing their sea bags.

"You guys deserting?" I asked.

"We're goin' to the brig," Hutchinson replied.

"Very funny. HA HA."

"The Japanese police caught us smoking pot," Brogan explained. His voice sounded hoarse. "That snipe Crimmons was with us. There's a couple of grunts on the quarterdeck waitin' for us."

"Hang on to mah camera for me, will ya, Shortcut?" Hutchinson said.

They picked up their sea bags and walked out. I locked up Hutchinson's camera. I didn't think I could sleep, but once my head hit the pillow, I was out.

It was tough getting up when Radford came to wake me at 0515. As I sprayed off trays in the scullery, I heard some commotion outside. Chief Lasko was having an argument with Radford.

"Look, Chief," Radford said, "I don't care if you're shorthanded. You can't take Thorpe back to the bridge until your division sends a replacement."

"Listen, fat boy," the chief said back, "there ain't going to be no replacement."

The door to the scullery opened. I could make out Chief Lasko's round silhouette through the steam.

"THORPE, YOU IN HERE?"

"Yeah, Chief."

"Let's go. You've been transferred back to the bridge."

Carranza's mouth fell open. I dropped the stack of trays and walked out. Radford looked angry. I felt better, despite my hangover, as I followed Chief Lasko up to the bridge. I didn't expect this side effect of Hutchinson and Brogan going to the brig. I felt bad for them, but at least I was out of the scullery.

"Well, Thorpe," Chief Lasko said, "are you glad to be back on the bridge?"

"You bet, Chief."

"Good. Get a broom and a swab and a dustpan and a foxtail and some Brasso."

Here was another unforeseen consequence. Cool and I would have to take up the slack for Hutchinson and Brogan. We swept, swabbed, waxed, and buffed the deck of the bridge. Cool shined the brass, and I scrubbed the sink and toilet in the head out in the passageway.

That afternoon, Lightning Lenny set the sea and anchor detail. As we were getting underway, Lightning Lenny passed the word over the 1MC.

"UH, THIS IS THE CAPTAIN SPEAKING. AS YOU ALL KNOW, WE ARE LEAVING BEHIND THREE OF OUR CREW MEMBERS IN THE HANDS OF THE JAPANESE POLICE. THEY WERE CAUGHT SMOKING MARIJUANA OFF BASE, AND THERE'S NOTHING THE NAVY CAN DO ABOUT IT. THEY COULD RECEIVE AS MUCH AS FIVE YEARS IN JAIL. I HOPE THIS IS A LESSON TO ALL OF YOU. THAT IS ALL."

With Stretch over the hill, Mendoza discharged, and Brogan and Hutchinson under arrest, I became the primary helmsman. It wasn't so much a promotion for me as it would have been a disgrace for Chief Lasko to have to take the helm like an ordinary seaman. I was on the helm all day during UNREPS. After the UNREPS, I had the bridge watch, so I went down to the mess decks for early chow. Meech was standing watch on the chow line.

"Where's ya chow pass, Shortcut?"

"Mendoza had 'em. Nobody knows where he put 'em. The whole division is out of chow passes."

"I can't let you in."

"But I have the next watch. My name's on the POD, see?"

I pointed at the POD, posted on the bulkhead beside him.

"That's got nothing to do with it."

"What do you mean, that's got nothing to do with it? That has everything to do with it. The whole reason for the early chow pass was for guys who have the watch."

"All I know is: No pass, no early chow."

"Look, you know Mendoza is gone, and you know I have the next watch."

"No pass, no early chow."

"Meech, talking to you is like talking to a machine."

"DILLIGAF."

"What?"

"Do I Look Like I Give a Fuck?"

I looked into his rodent eyes.

"No, Meech, you don't. I guess that's why you got this big important job."

"My heart pumps purple piss, Shortcut. Get in line and wait."

Of all the petty officers aboard the *Okmok*, Meech was one of the pettiest. Meech knew the reason for the chow pass, but he only cared about compliance with the rules, not what the rules were intended to accomplish. When supper for the crew was called, I was first in line. After chow, I went up to the bridge. Mr. Tobias held a piece of message traffic.

"I put in a request to BUPERS for replacements for Stromsvag, Hutchinson, and Brogan," he said. "They just sent back word that the *Okmok* already has its full complement of quartermasters."

"But we're down to one chief and one striker," Chief Lasko said. "And Cooley can't stand his own watch because he never went to 'A' school."

"I know that. Though they are no longer aboard, Stromsvag, Hutchinson, and Brogan are officially counted as crew members. Therefore, we aren't entitled to any replacement quartermasters. Here's the reply from BUPERS."

He let us read the message.

"Okay, Thorpe," Chief Lasko said. "You and me are going to be standing port and starboard watches. Sleep will be at a premium until further notice. I'll take Cooley for my section and train him as fast as I can. We'll come on after supper, and you can get some rack time until the mid-watch."

"How come I get the mid-watch, Chief?"

"Because you're a seaman, Thorpe, goddammit, and I'm a chief."

So, that was that. Every station in the underway watch bill rotated four sections, except for the quartermasters. Whenever Chief Lasko and Cool were off the bridge, I was on, and vice versa. I would get up at 2330 and stand watch until breakfast when the chief and Cool would come on. I could sleep until noon as long as Lightning Lenny had no UNREPS, drills, or other special evolutions, which he usually did. I would take the watch again until supper. Then, I could sleep until 2330 and repeat the cycle. I was lucky to get three uninterrupted hours of rack time a day. After a week, the scullery didn't seem so bad.

Then, Lightning Lenny ordered us to make a course for Sasebo *Wan*.

CHAPTER 20

The Soviets

Sasebo was in the northwest of the Japanese island of Kyushu, thirty miles north of Nagasaki, according to the chart. It was a smaller, less industrial, better-looking port than Yokosuka. There were dozens of little houses painted different colors on the hills surrounding the harbor. Estorga had the duty, and I was tired, but I wanted to get off the ship. I went ashore on my own.

I found a place called the New Moon Bar. There were no marines, only a few guys from the *Racine* sitting in a booth. The walls were paneled with the same dark varnished wood as the bar. I slid into an empty booth. A few Japanese customers were sitting at the bar, laughing at a Japanese comedian on television. I couldn't understand the jokes. A waitress in a black dress came over. She had an hourglass figure and a heart-shaped face framed in shining black shoulder-length hair. She was gorgeous. I ordered a Kirin. She brought the beer, sat down across from me in the booth, and smiled. A wave of perfume hit me.

"My name Miyoshi," she said. "What you name?"

"Short—I mean, Gary."

"I am very happy to meet you, Gary," she replied, extending her delicate hand. "Where you from?"

"California."

"I would love to go to America someday."

Her voice was soft and hypnotic. She didn't ask me to buy her a drink, like the bar girls in Yokosuka. If she was a prostitute, she was an expensive one. I didn't think she was a prostitute, though.

"Would you like a drink?" I asked.

"Yes," she said, and she got up to get it.

She walked to the bar, with my eyes riveted to her swiveling butt. She brought a glass of something transparent and sparkling for herself.

"Thank you," I said. "I mean, *arigato*."

"*Iie, iie,*" she said.

"What does that mean?"

"It means, no, no. It's nothing. If you want to say, you're welcome, it's, *do itashimashite*."

"Do-ita-shi-ma-shi-tay."

She laughed. The *Racine* sailors in the booth were yelling for more drinks—the rowdy bastards—and she got up to serve them. More customers came in, and she brought them drinks. When I finished my beer, Miyoshi brought me another one and a shot of Suntory whiskey.

"Thank you," I said, pulling out a wad of yen. "Can I buy you another drink? You know how drunken sailors love to spend money."

"No, thank you," she said with a small laugh. "What kind of music you like?"

"Almost all kinds. How about you?"

"Me, too."

She kept getting up to take care of customers, but she always came back. She must have felt like talking to me because she sure wasn't making much money off me.

"Do you like movies?" she asked.

"Yes. Can I take you to see a movie?"

"You understand Japanese?"

"You could translate," I said, imagining her whispering in my ear all night.

"I had American boyfriend before," she said, looking down. "He beat me."

"The rat."

"He was bad man."

"Those kind of guys are lower than whale sh— uh, the lowest."

"You nice guy."

"So, how about a movie?"

"Too late tonight."

"Tomorrow?"

"Yes. Tomorrow."

I was discovering the principle of the universe. We sat there until I ran out of money. It was almost midnight. I stood up to leave, and she walked me to the door. She handed me a business card with the address of the bar on it and her name: Miyoshi Murakami.

"You're very beautiful," I told her.

I never would have said it if I hadn't been drunk. She leaned forward and gave me a peck on the cheek. I got another whiff of her perfume.

"See you tomorrow, Gary," she said.

It started raining on my walk back to the ship, but I didn't care. I felt great, and it wasn't just booze.

When the reveille boatswain's pipe went off the next morning, I wasn't moving fast.

"Morning, Shortcut," Finesse said with a grin. "How big were those tits again?"

"And her ass," Hoodwink added. "Tell us about that ass."

"You woke up half the damn duty section yapping about some Japanese chick you got a date with," Estorga explained.

A partial memory was coming back of me telling everyone in 02 berthing about Miyoshi.

"Never seen you so shitfaced, Shortcut," Cool said.

"I'll say," Billings agreed. "Your breath just about dissolved my dog tags."

"What about that ass?" Hoodwink asked. "Tell us again about that ass."

Lightning Lenny's voice came over the 1MC.

"UH, THIS IS THE CAPTAIN SPEAKING. WE'VE RECEIVED ORDERS FROM FLEET COMMAND TO GET UNDERWAY IMMEDIATELY ON A CLASSIFIED SERVOPS MISSION. THAT IS ALL."

Within an hour, we were underway, steaming out of Sasebo *Wan*. My date with Miyoshi was blown. She would think I stood her up.

"Steady as she goes, Thorpe," Mr. Kempton said with his back to me. He gazed through the bridge windows, his pipe between his teeth.

"Steadying on two one eight, sir," I answered.

"Secure the sea and anchor detail, Jim," Lightning Lenny said.

"Secure the sea and anchor detail, Boats," Mr. Kempton said.

Crapshoot blew his boatswain's pipe into the 1MC.

"NOW SECURE THE SEA AND ANCHOR DETAIL AND SET THE REGULAR UNDERWAY WATCH. SECTION TWO, MUSTER ON THE BRIDGE WITH PETTY OFFICER MALOLO. THAT IS, SECTION TWO, MUSTER ON THE BRIDGE WITH PETTY OFFICER MALOLO. THAT IS ALL."

"*The captain is departing the bridge,*" Crapshoot yelled as Lightning Lenny left.

Section two took the watch. Doglike relieved me on the helm. Mr. Tobias, Mr. Kempton, and Chief Lasko gathered around the chart table. Mr. Tobias was laying down a track. They stopped talking when Cool and I walked over.

"If Thorpe and Cooley are going to stand quartermaster watches, they have to know where we're going," Mr. Tobias said.

Mr. Kempton exhaled a cloud of pipe smoke.

"You two have come up in the ranks since we lost Mendoza, Stromsvag, Hutchinson, and

Brogan," he said. "Quite an attrition rate in the quartermaster gang."

"Fleet command has been monitoring radio transmissions from a group of Soviet vessels," Mr. Tobias said, "a destroyer, an oiler, and two subs operating in the vicinity of Midway Island. We received an urgent dispatch from Admiral Griffin ordering us to get underway with the cruiser *Jouett*, intercept the Soviet ships, follow, and observe them."

"We're observing EMCON," Mr. Kempton said. "Emission control, no sonar, radar, or radio transmissions."

"That means we'll have to use the LORAN for navigation," Mr. Tobias explained, referring to the long-range navigation receiver in the chart house. "The chief and I will take celestial shots of morning and evening stars."

Mr. Tobias had Chief Lasko plot the course to the projected interception point. Mr. Kempton relinquished the deck to Mr. Barker and the conn to Mr. Sforzando. Cool and I got the news of our mission five minutes ahead of the rest of the crew. Lightning Lenny passed the word over the 1MC from his cabin, telling the crew about our pursuit of the Soviet ships.

"...AND SO, I WAS PLEASED TO VOLUNTEER THE *OKMOK* FOR THIS SPECIAL COMMITMENT, AS MORE EVIDENCE OF OUR DESERVEDNESS TO WIN THE BIG E, AND IN KEEPING WITH THE SHIP'S MOTTO: TO SERVE, AND SERVE, AND SERVE. THAT IS ALL."

Mr. Crookshank came over the 1MC next.

"THIS IS THE XO SPEAKING. SINCE WE DON'T KNOW HOW LONG IT WILL BE UNTIL WE REACH PORT AGAIN, WE WILL NEED TO CONSERVE WATER. UNTIL FURTHER NOTICE, THERE WILL BE NO MORE HOLLYWOOD SHOWERS. ALL PERSONNEL WILL TAKE NAVY SHOWERS. THAT IS, GET WET, TURN IT OFF, LATHER UP, TURN IT ON, AND RINSE OFF QUICK. ALL DIVISION PETTY OFFICERS WILL REPORT ANY MEN TAKING HOLLYWOOD SHOWERS. THAT IS ALL."

Chief Lasko and Cool had the evening watch. I wanted a few hours of rack time before relieving them at midnight, but sleep was impossible with everyone in the 02 berthing compartment angry about Lightning Lenny's announcement.

"Lightning Lenny voluntordered us for another lame detail," Hankins said. "Things were better during the war. We got stamps for free, no bullshit inspections, or locker searches."

"War is hell," Alaska said, looking at his cards. "But peace is even worse."

"How come the best command in the Navy is always the one you had before?" Finesse asked, looking up from his cards.

"The Russians are our enemies," Hoodwink said.

"The gentry on this ship are more my enemies than those Russians," Alaska replied.

"Are you some kind of commie or something?" Hoodwink asked.

"It's your play, Hoodwink," Finesse said.

"You sorry bunch of fuckers," Hoodwink said, dropping his cards on the table. "I'm sick of all this candy-ass bitching and moaning. We're supposed to be fighting communism. That's what we're here for."

"We're not fighting communism," Alaska replied. "We're chasing all over the Pacific so Lightning Lenny can curry favor with the higher-ups at fleet command."

"So, what's your beef, Alaska? Are you hungry? Do you have a place to sleep and clothes to wear? Do you get free medical care?"

"That sure sounds like communism to me. I wouldn't run down communists so fast, Hoodwink, because you and me and every other swingin' dick in the armed forces are living just like a bunch of commies."

"You don't know what you're talkin' about."

"The hell I don't. We don't have individual rights. We gave 'em up when we signed up. This ship is as totalitarian as anything in the communist bloc. If a ship's captain isn't a little dictator, I don't know what is. A guy like Lightning Lenny couldn't get a job running a pastry shop in the real world."

"Picking his nose is conduct unbecoming an officer," Finesse said.

I gave up trying to sleep. I got out of my rack and sat near the card game.

"So, what's up, Magellan?" Estorga asked me.

"I'm what's up. I can't sleep. We're chasing Russian ships, and a beautiful woman is sitting back there in Sasebo, thinking I stood her up."

"Shortcut's got a sweetheart," Estorga said in a sing-song voice.

"If you want my medical opinion," Finesse said, "I think Shortcut's a cherry boy."

Estorga looked at me.

"*Are* you a cherry boy, Shortcut?" he asked.

"No," I lied. "Hell, no."

"And Nixon's not a crook," Finesse said, taking a trick. "Don't worry about it. Once we get to the PI, you'll be able to use your dick for something else besides just to piss through."

All the WESTPAC veterans talked about the Philippine Islands, specifically Olongapo City at Subic Bay, as a third-world X-rated paradise, where the streets were filled with hookers and anybody who can't get laid isn't trying.

I got back in my rack and slept for nearly three hours, but it felt like three minutes. I was having a nightmare that Mr. Southcott was back when Cool shined a flashlight in my face.

"You awake, Shortcut?"

"No."

"Come on, man. It's 2330. The chief be in a raggedy-ass mood."

Cool stood there long enough to make sure I didn't go back to sleep. He went back to the bridge when I started getting dressed. I stopped in at the mess decks to see if they had anything good for MIDRATS—midnight rations for the guys standing the mid-watch. They had the same thing they always had: peanut butter and jelly on stale white bread. I passed.

The bridge was bathed in the glow of red lights. Mr. Kempton and Mr. Sforzando were handing the watch over to Mr. Osterkamp and Kip. Ensign Benson was there for some reason. They all stood on the port side of the bridge, talking. Kip wore a pair of sunglasses with mirror lenses. The *Jouett* was steaming a few miles ahead of us.

"Hey, Cool," I whispered. "Why is Kip wearing sunglasses at night?"

"He wear them damn glasses all the time now, since he made lieutenant JG. He tryin' to smoke, too, but watch him. He never inhale."

"This is Mr. Osterkamp. I have the deck," Mr. Osterkamp said, and Cool wrote that in the log.

"This is Mr. Priskett. I have the conn," Kip said, and Cool wrote that in the log. Cool told me how he was getting his fixes.

"We got a LORAN line and a radar range from this morning. We on track now."

Mr. Kempton overheard him as he passed by the chart table. He smiled at us.

"Cooley got his last fix by advancing a radar range with a day-old line of position from a star he didn't know the name of," he said, and he left the bridge.

Chief Lasko came out of the chart house. He was showing signs of wear. He had dark circles under his bloodshot eyes.

"Goddammit, Thorpe, you're five minutes late," he said, lighting a cigarette.

The chief hadn't stood an underway watch in years, much less port and starboard. Losing sleep was hard on all of us, but standing watches with ordinary seamen was a blow to the chief's pride. The other chiefs, mostly Hackburn, were making jokes about him.

"You'll probably have to go to the LORAN machine in another hour or so," Chief Lasko told me. "It won't be a good LORAN area, though. We'll be on the baseline extension."

"How am I supposed to take fixes?"

"Extend an LOP. Dead reckon it. Do the best you can. We're running off the *Jouett*'s course, anyway. Whatever they do, we do. I'm gonna hit the rack."

Chief Lasko and Cool left the bridge. I wrote the midnight entry in the log.

4 August 1974

0005: Steaming with USS Jouett on parallel course 098° at 12 knots. Boilers 1, 2, and 3 are lit off. Generators 1SG, 2SG, and 1SGV are on line. Condition Yoke is set throughout the ship. Observing EMCON in accordance with Captain Quimp's orders. Lt. Osterkamp is the OOD. LTJG Priskett is the JOOD. Ensign Benson is also on the bridge.

"Thorpe," Mr. Osterkamp said. "Mr. Benson will be observing the quartermaster watch."

"Yes, sir," I answered, all military courtesy. Mr. Osterkamp never liked me since he found out I was goldbricking in his section. He and Kip walked out on the bridge wing.

"What do we do first, Thorpe?" Ensign Benson asked. He was somewhere in his early twenties, with kinky red hair and freckles. After Kip's promotion, Ensign Benson was probably motivated to get more time on the bridge so he could also get promoted to Lieutenant JG, and the crew would have to stop calling him Ensign Benson.

"Well, sir, every six hours, we send in a synoptic weather report to fleet command. They're not transmitting tonight because of EMCON, but I'll fill out the report sheet, anyway."

I showed him where to write in the numbers for visibility, barometric pressure, true wind speed and direction, and type and height of clouds.

"How do you know the height of the clouds?"

"I guess."

"What's the guess based on?"

"Experience."

After we filled out the report, I phoned radio.

"Radio, Billings speaking."

"Billy, I've got a synoptic weather report for you to pick up."

In a few minutes, Billings came to the bridge to get the report.

"Aren't weather reports considered confidential, Billings?" Ensign Benson asked.

"By us, yes, sir," Billings answered. "Not by fleet command. They consider our confidential reports unclassified. Our secret reports are their confidential. Our top secret is their secret."

"Time to take a fix, sir," I said.

Ensign Benson followed me into the chart house to the LORAN machine, a gray box about two feet square with a crank on the side that activated a numerical readout like a gasoline pump. It had a little two-inch green screen in the top right corner above the readout. It was state-of-the-art World War II technology. I flipped on the switch and showed Ensign Benson how to take a reading. By turning the crank and adjusting a fine-tuning knob, I aligned the two green waveforms on the little screen and wrote down the numbers from the readout. Then, I tried to pick up another station.

"Chief Lasko was right," I said. "They're not coming in very well."

I wrote down as many readings as I could get. Then, we went to the chart table to plot the lines. I showed him how to use the dividers on the LORAN scale on the chart to interpolate between the lines.

Mr. Osterkamp had the engine room making turns for twelve knots to keep up with the *Jouett*. We could see the Soviet destroyer and oiler on the hazy horizon. Their running lights showed them heading east. The *Jouett* slackened speed.

"All ahead standard," Mr. Osterkamp said. "Make turns for ten."

"All ahead standard, aye," Stringbean answered on the lee helm. "Making turns for ten."

"Forward lookout reports contacts three points off the starboard bow," Bootleg announced.

"Tell him combat identified his contacts twenty minutes ago," Mr. Osterkamp replied, looking through his binoculars.

The Soviet ships split up and took separate courses. The *Jouett* followed the westbound destroyer. Hankins brought a message from the signal bridge of the *Jouett*. Their CO, who outranked Lightning Lenny, ordered us to run a parallel easterly course with the oiler eight thousand yards off their starboard side.

"All ahead standard," Mr. Osterkamp said. "Make turns for fifteen."

"All ahead standard, aye, making turns for fifteen, sir," Stringbean answered.

Mr. Osterkamp got on the phone to notify Lightning Lenny of the course change. Kip walked over to the chart table.

"Thorpe," Kip said. "How is Mr. Benson coming along?"

"Just fine," I answered.

"That's just fine, *sir*, Thorpe. Next time you forget that, you're on report."

I looked into Kip's mirrored sunglasses and saw my own small image reflected twice. Lieutenant JG Priskett was a different animal than Ensign Priskett. Good thing I didn't slip up and call him Kip.

"Aye aye, sir," I said.

"We haven't had one good LORAN fix since we started pursuing the oiler," Ensign Benson said.

"*Say again?*" Kip asked. He inhaled a little smoke from his cigarette and started to cough. He managed to choke out a question. "How did you get your last fix?"

"We're advancing lines of position from evening stars that Chief Lasko shot," I explained. "Our dead reckoning position shows—"

"What's our set and drift?"

"Our set is the distance the currents push us off track, and our drift is the amount of speed we gain or lose depending on—"

"No, damn it, I *know* what it is. What *is* it?"

"If you'll give me a minute, sir, I can figure it out for you."

"Don't get smart with me, Thorpe. You're on thin ice as it is."

Mr. Osterkamp approached the chart table.

"What's the status?" he asked.

"Thorpe hasn't had an accurate LORAN fix since he came on watch. He's uncertain of our set and drift," Kip answered.

"Is that right, Thorpe?"

"Not exactly, sir," I said. "If you'll look at our last—"

"I hear they call you Shortcut, Thorpe," Mr. Osterkamp said, "but you're not taking any shortcuts on my watch. Go wake up Chief Lasko. Right now."

"Aye aye, sir."

I left the bridge and walked down the ladder to the chiefs' quarters. I walked between the racks of snoring bodies until I found the snoring body I was looking for. Even in sleep, the chief looked anxious. He had a tight grip on his pillow. I shook him. His bloodshot eyes snapped open wide.

"Damn it, Thorpe, is it time for morning stars already?"

"No, Chief," I said, half enjoying it. "It's 0130. Mr. Osterkamp wants you to try another LORAN fix."

"*Jesus Christ!* Okay, tell him I'm on my way."

I returned to the bridge. Chief Lasko got there a couple of minutes after me, breathing hard and lighting a cigarette. Drops of sweat fell from his brow as he leaned over the chart. Taking in the information on the chart at a glance, the chief went into the chart house to the LORAN machine with me behind him. I could tell he wasn't getting good lines. I wrote down the numbers that he called out.

"Two nine five four," he said. "Goddamn silver-barred bastards don't impress this LORAN machine one bit. Four three six five. I've passed more lighthouses than these candy asses have traffic lights."

The chief plotted his lines. He advanced one of his earlier lines of position to make his fix. I had already done the same thing. He didn't have any magic tricks.

"Sorry we had to wake you, Chief," Mr. Osterkamp said. "Thorpe had us a little nervous there. You may return to your rack."

The officers walked away from the chart table. Before he left the bridge, the chief spoke in a low voice.

"They should know if *you* can't get anything out of the LORAN, then neither can I," he said.

It was the closest thing to a compliment he'd ever given me.

We continued steaming all night at seven knots, with the helm on the Iron Mike, running a parallel course with the Soviet oiler and keeping her at three miles to port. I went out on the starboard bridge wing for some air. Orion's belt and sword were bright in the southern sky. I walked around to port. There was the Big Dipper and the North Star.

Just for drill, I decided to try my own sight reductions. I started a stopwatch at exactly 0335, according to the chronometers. I grabbed Chief Lasko's sextant and took it up to the signal bridge. It was too early to be taking sights. I could barely make out the horizon, but I took four shots, anyway, Betelgeuse and Rigel to starboard and Arcturus and Spica to port. I wrote down the stopwatch times and worked out the lines of position on the plotting sheet. Spica and Rigel were no good, but I got two LOPs for Arcturus and Betelgeuse. I advanced an earlier LORAN line, and they all three crossed at the same point for a nice running fix. We had followed the oiler almost a third of the way to Hawaii. Now that I was ready for an officer to ask me where we were, nobody asked.

At 0430, I woke Chief Lasko again, along with Mr. Tobias, so they could shoot morning stars. The horizon was clear. I held a stopwatch and a clipboard while the chief and Mr. Tobias sighted through their sextants. They gave me their readings, and I wrote them down next to their times. They shot the same stars I shot plus a couple more. Then, we went down to the bridge to plot the lines. Five of Chief Lasko's lines cut, crossing at a pinpoint for a perfect fix. Mr. Tobias's three-line fix concurred with the chief's fix, but his lines didn't cut as tight.

"I guess practice makes perfect, huh, Chief?" Mr. Tobias said.

The chief shrugged as if to say: "Some of us have it, and some of us don't." Whatever else he was, Chief Lasko was a good navigator. Even with his crossed eyes, he was a better shot with a sextant than Mr. Tobias or Mr. Southcott. I had seen him make six lines cut like a pinwheel, although three were all that was necessary for a fix. Mr. Tobias never got more than four. Mr. Southcott had been lucky to get three, and that was before Hutchinson tweaked the index error correction on Wildebeest.

Mr. Tobias left the bridge to have breakfast. The chief got his camera and tripod from the chart house.

"I'm going to get some photos of the Soviet ships once we get more sunlight," he said. "You're not going to get any good LORAN around sunrise, Thorpe. How about some coffee?"

"No thanks, Chief."

"No, goddammit, Thorpe. *I* want some."

I brought the chief his coffee on the port wing just as the sun was coming up. He had set up his camera on the tripod and fastened a long zoom lens. He squinted through the eyepiece, and he snapped a few shots of the Soviet oiler. A light flashed from the signal bridge of the oiler and stopped. Hankins aimed a signal blinker lamp at them and flipped the shutters up and down. He sent back three flashes—long, short, long. It was Morse code for kilo, the signal to go ahead and transmit. Kip came out to the wing.

"Hankins, did you send something?"

"Just a kilo, sir."

"Who gave you permission to communicate? You don't send anything without permission."

"Sorry, sir. It was a reflex."

"Do it again and you're on report," Kip said, and he went back inside to the bridge.

"You know, Chief," I said, "Kip has really changed into Mr. Sweat Gland himself."

"They all do," he replied. "They're officers."

"How long have you been in the Navy, Chief?"

"I'll have sixteen in six months."

"I thought you'd be closer to twenty by now."

"Well, I was out for a while. I worked for Greyhound—"

He stopped talking and gave me a strange look.

"How old do you think I am, anyway, Thorpe?"

The chief looked every bit of fifty, but I knew he couldn't be that old. I tried to imagine the mileage put on by nearly sixteen years of losing sleep, standing watches, partying in port, living on Navy coffee and Navy chow. I cleared my throat and made what I thought was a safe guess.

"I don't know, Chief, forty?"

His mouth fell open.

"Damn it, Thorpe. I'm *thirty-four!*"

"Sorry, Chief. I'm a terrible judge of age."

"*Captain's on the bridge,*" Shilgenkrauser yelled.

Lightning Lenny, Mr. Crookshank, and Mr. Kempton came out on the wing to stare at the Russian oiler. The oiler had cut its engines and was drifting with the current. They hung scaffolding stages over the side, and their crewmen began to scrub the hull.

"Goddammit, Jim, dammit XO," Lightning Lenny said. "Why are they cleaning their ship in the middle of the Pacific?"

"They must be aware we're following them, Captain," Mr. Kempton replied, staring through his binoculars.

"The oiler is refueling a submarine, Captain," Mr. Crookshank said. "I see a fuel line going down into the water. The hull cleaning job is a cover."

"Let's circle them, Jim."

We circled them for almost an hour. When the oiler finished the refueling job, they hauled up their stages, and they began moving on a northerly track at seven knots. We followed them on a course toward the Sea of Okhotsk for most of the day until radio got a message from Admiral Griffin ordering us to discontinue pursuit.

The next day, we stopped in Okinawa to pick up supplies. We stayed overnight. My section had the duty, so I couldn't go ashore. I sat in 02 berthing, losing another chess game to Billings.

"We got a message from Admiral Griffin at fleet command," Billings said. "The Japanese released Hutchinson, Brogan, and Crimmons as a goodwill gesture. They'll be waiting for us on the base at Subic."

"No kidding?"

"Yeah, but the Japanese government is watching to see what kind of disciplinary action the Navy is going to take with them. Maybe the Japs won't let off future cases so easy if Lightning Lenny doesn't fuck them over good. Checkmate."

The following morning, we got underway. Mr. Crookshank passed the word over the 1MC.

"THE *OKMOK* HAS RECEIVED ORDERS TO PROCEED TO SUBIC BAY, REPUBLIC OF THE PHILIPPINES. THAT IS ALL."

Our crew came to life. Everyone was buzzing. The next stop was Sin City. Standing watch became exciting. Since I knew our course and speed and position, everybody in 02 berthing quizzed me as soon as I got off watch.

"How far we got to go, Shortcut?" Hankins asked.

"What's our ETA?" Estorga asked.

"How fast we goin'?" Swampass asked.

"A couple more days," I answered. "Let me sleep, will ya?"

That night, on my midnight watch, Kip was standing junior officer of the deck, with Mr. Barker as OOD. My latest fix showed us a little to the left of track. I told Kip about it.

"We're being set to the south, sir," I said. "I think we need to come right to two two three to get back on track."

"I can't take the word of a non-rate to Mr. Barker," Kip replied. "Phone Mr. Tobias immediately."

"But he's asleep, sir, and—"

"Belay that, Thorpe. Any more insubordination from you and you're on report. Do you read me?"

"Aye aye, sir."

I phoned Mr. Tobias' cabin.

"Yes?"

Mr. Tobias sounded sleepy. I knew he was tired from reporting to Lightning Lenny around the clock during the oiler chase.

"It's Thorpe, sir. Mr. Priskett asked me to have you double check a course change."

"Tell him whatever you recommend is fine with me."

I liked Mr. Tobias. He showed more confidence in me than Mr. Southcott ever did. Then again, he didn't have much choice since Chief Lasko had to sleep sometime, and Cool wasn't rated. I thought I saw a chance to screw Kip over.

"I don't think Mr. Priskett would like to hear that from me, sir."

"Put him on."

I handed the phone to Kip.

"Good morn—" Kip began. "Yes, sir—yes, sir—it's just that Thorpe—yes, sir—sorry, sir."

Kip hung up and stepped over to the chart table.

"What do you...recommend, Thorpe?"

"I think we're being set to the south, and we need to come right to two two three to get back on track, sir."

Kip's eyes narrowed, but he took my recommendation to Mr. Barker, and Mr. Barker made the course change. My life as a quartermaster had few rewards, but getting over on Kip was one of them.

# CHAPTER 21

Olongapo

It was a clear August morning when the *Okmok* steamed through the Luzon Strait. Mr. Crookshank passed the word over the 1MC.

"PRESIDENT NIXON HAS RESIGNED AS PRESIDENT AND COMMANDER-IN-CHIEF OF THE ARMED FORCES. OUR NEW PRESIDENT AND COMMANDER-IN-CHIEF IS GERALD FORD. THAT IS ALL."

We entered Subic Bay on the island of Luzon at the east end of the South China Sea. As we approached our assigned mooring spot at maximum distance from the main gate, I could see three figures sitting on the pier, leaning back against their sea bags.

"Forward lookout reports Seaman Brogan, Seaman Apprentice Hutchinson, and Seaman Apprentice Crimmons," Stringbean said from the sound-powered phones.

"Well, Chief," Mr. Kempton said to Chief Lasko, "it looks as though your wayward quartermasters are back in the fold."

"Call Needler," Lightning Lenny said. "I want them put on report at once. They're restricted to the ship until further notice."

As soon as the brow went down, Needler hurried down to the pier. He handcuffed Hutchinson, Brogan, and Crimmons before he brought them aboard, which seemed unnecessary to me. If they were planning to go over the hill, they wouldn't have waited around for the ship. Needler took the cuffs off them as soon as they were aboard. When Hutchinson and Brogan arrived on the bridge, Mr. Tobias was not happy to see them.

"We're shorthanded, and we need you," he said. "But don't think I will hesitate to discipline you if there's any more trouble. Understand?"

"Yes, sir," Hutchinson answered.

"Aye aye, sir," Brogan answered.

At mail call, I got an envelope that was delayed over a month. It was a wedding invitation.

> MR. AND MRS. JOSEPH LEDEZMA REQUEST THE HONOR OF YOUR PRESENCE AT THE MARRIAGE OF THEIR DAUGHTER LAURA TO MR. SCOTT LATHAM AT ST. CYPRIAN'S CHURCH SATURDAY THE TWENTY-SECOND OF JUNE, 1974. RECEPTION TO FOLLOW. R.S.V.P.

There was a note inside.

> *Dear Gary,*
> *I'm sure you remember Scott from school. He's an insurance salesman now. I know you can't make it to our wedding, but I sent the invitation, anyway.*
> *Love,*
> *Laura*

Laura got what she wanted. Maybe if she had been less pushy about marriage, I might have chased her until she caught me, but it never would have worked out between us. Sometimes, I wished I'd never met her.

"Somebody gettin' married," Cool said.

He was looking over my shoulder.

"My old girlfriend," I said. "She married a weasel named Latham."

"*Damn!*" Cool said with a happy smile. "Thass some cold shit, man."

"I can tell you're heartbroken."

"Let's quit bullshitting and scrape down those bridge wings," Chief Lasko said.

I shitcanned the invitation. We grabbed wire brushes. Cool and I went out on the port wing with Hutchinson and Brogan.

"How was Japanese jail?" I asked.

"They let us go after two days," Brogan answered. "We've been in Olongapo for almost two weeks."

"Ah talked to a legal officer on base," Hutchinson said. "He said the evidence the Japs used to arrest us wouldn't stand up under American military law. He said to call him if Lightning Lenny gives us even a reprimand." He lowered his voice. "Ah threw that pot in the bushes before the cops got us. They never found anything on us. Needler wanted us to sign confessions admitting we knew there was pot in the area. He knows they don't have a leg to stand on. When we said we wouldn't sign, he asked us to sign another statement that said we refused to sign the first statement."

"They put us in the transient barracks," Brogan added. "We've been hitting the bars, raising money with the lost ring routine."

Hutchinson came up with lost ring scam after Brogan sold his watch to Hank at Hannigan's Bar. Brogan would go into a bar and tell everybody he lost a ring that wasn't valuable but had sentimental value. He would promise a fifty-dollar reward for it and say he'd be back after he checked a few more bars. Then, Hutchinson would come out of the head acting drunk and showing everyone the ring he just "found." Sometimes, they could get twenty bucks for a cheap ring they bought in Japan by the dozen.

"Never mind that," I said, "is everything they say about this place true?"

"This place is crawling with chicks," Brogan answered, "but don't go with street girls. The bars have a better class of hooker."

"Crimmons fell in love," Hutchinson said. "He almost asked the first girl he met to marry him, but Ah talked him out of it."

"You muthafuckas been skatin'," Cool said.

"Not skating," Brogan corrected. "Fucking."

"Me and Brog bought a case of San Miguel beer and took the Perez sisters to the Liberty Hotel just before curfew," Hutchinson said. "They gave us a two-for-one special."

"We pulled the mattress off the bed," Brogan said. "I took the mattress, and Hutch got the box springs."

"Mah girl had a seashell tattooed on the inside of her thigh. When Ah put mah ear up against it, Ah could smell the ocean."

"We were going to swap girls, but we got so drunk I don't remember if we swapped 'em or not. One of 'em was on her period because I had blood all over my dick. The faucet didn't work, so I washed it off with a beer."

"We didn't swap. Ah didn't have blood on mah dick."

"That's a beautiful story," I said.

We spent the rest of the day scraping paint, listening to the cries of birds and chattering monkeys in the jungle. When knockoff went down at 1630, I hurried to 02 berthing. Everyone was changing clothes. Mr. Crookshank's voice came over the 1MC.

"LOOSE LIPS SINK SHIPS. USE YOUR HEAD, AND USE A CONDOM. STAY TOGETHER, ALWAYS IN PAIRS. DO NOT LEAVE TOWN. THERE ARE GUERRILLA CAMPS IN THE JUNGLE OUTSIDE OF TOWN LEFTOVER FROM

THE HUK REBELLION, AND THEY WOULD LOVE TO GET HOLD OF A U.S. SERVICEMAN."

"Lend me twenty bucks, Alaska," Hoodwink said.

"Twenty for thirty," Alaska replied

"Don't be a one-way motherfucker."

"That's a better deal than you'd get from Kickback."

"Your mother," Hoodwink said.

"We ain't gone yet, Shortcut?" Estorga said. "Let's hit the beach. It's oh-beer-thirty."

"Beer, aye," I replied.

"Hurry up, man. We don't want to miss the bus."

I changed clothes fast, and we headed down to the main deck. Snyder had the quarterdeck watch.

"Request permission to go ashore," I said.

"No sneakers on the beach, Shortcut," Snyder said.

"Sneakers are all I've got. They were okay in Japan."

Snyder smirked and shook his head.

"Captain Quimp says no sneakers on the beach."

"Go borrow some shoes, Shortcut," Estorga said, "and hurry up."

I ran back to 02 berthing. Alaska was playing solitaire. He had the duty.

"Let me borrow your boots, Alaska. Snyder won't let me go ashore with sneakers."

"Sure thing, Shortcut. Ten bucks."

I didn't have time to argue. I handed him a ten, pulled the cowboy boots on, and stood up.

"Why do they have to make these damn things so pointy?"

"So you can crush bugs in corners," Alaska replied. "Don't lose 'em, or it'll cost you seventy-five."

Estorga saved me a seat on the bus. It was a bumpy ride through the jungle to the base and then a hike to the main gate. A crowd of sailors were lined up single file. We got in a long line behind Hayashi.

"What's with the line?" Estorga asked.

"The guard is writing down serial numbers of cameras," Hayashi explained. "If you have a camera when you go out, they want to make sure you still have it when you come back so you won't sell it on the black market. It's best to take only your body and your money."

"Hurry up and wait," I said.

When we got to the front of the line, the guard said:

"Any cameras?"

"No," we answered.

We squeezed through the crowd at the gate. We were surrounded by a group of Filipino boys between eight and twelve years old, offering to buy or sell anything.

"Camera? Watch? Stereo?"

"No thanks."

We squeezed past them, repeating "No thanks. No thanks."

We crossed a bridge over a narrow river.

"That's Shit River," Hayashi said.

One whiff explained the name. Filipino boys floated on the brown water in narrow wooden banca boats.

"PESO, PESO," they called out. "PESO, PESO."

Kickback threw a couple of pesos off the bridge, and a bunch of little kids mobbed him asking for more. Two boys dove into the brown water and came up with the pesos. At the other side of the bridge, the money exchange booths were under a concrete arch. Older men hawked cigarettes, gum, and cheap jewelry. We traded dollars for pesos. A jewelry vendor started talking to Hayashi.

"You buy necklace? Berry nice, berry nice. Ring por your girlpriend? Berry cheap price por you."

Estorga and I kept moving. Kids tried to put their hands in our pockets. Estorga grabbed his wallet before a little girl did. She looked around seven. I held my cash in my teeth. They couldn't reach that high.

"PESO, PESO," they cried.

"This is worse than Tijuana," Estorga said.

"Steady as she goes," I replied.

The main thoroughfare was Magsaysay Drive, the only paved road in town. There were no traffic lights or stop signs. Magsaysay Drive was lined on both sides with eating spots and hotels but mostly bars. The locals drove motorcycles with sidecars and old Willys jeeps—called jeepneys—with wild paint jobs and fancy interiors. They taxied sailors from bar to bar. We walked past a place called Pauline's. It had a moat out front with a live crocodile in it and a little footbridge without rails leading toward the entrance.

"I'll bet that keeps down the drunks," Estorga said.

"Want to go inside?" I asked.

"Let's try that place across the street."

He was pointing at a place called the Shamrock Intercontinental Club. We dodged jeepneys, crossed the street, and went inside. As soon as we found a table, two girls headed toward us.

"Two contacts at five yards," Estorga said.

The girls sat down with us. The one closest to me wore a pink blouse with blue shorts.

"What ship you prom?" she asked me.

"You looking por good time?" the other girl asked Estorga. She was wearing a black dress with high heels. "I lub you, no shit."

"Jesus, girls," Estorga said. "The sun isn't even down yet. How about a beer?"

The first girl ran to the bar. She had nice legs.

"You make me horny," the other girl said, grabbing Estorga's crotch. "I puck you silly."

"What's your name?" Estorga asked.

"Burgee."

The first girl returned quickly with two bottles of San Miguel. Estorga lifted his bottle toward the ceiling.

"Here's to Olongapo," he said.

We took a swallow.

"This stuff tastes stronger than Japanese beer," I said.

"What you name?" the first girl asked. She sat next to me with one elbow on the table, smoking a cigarette.

"Gary Thorpe. What's yours?"

"Susie Sadayao."

Burgee and Susie—the names seemed too cutesy to be real.

"You like music?" Susie asked.

"Sure."

"We hab band starting soon," she said. "Rusty Plyingpinger."

She pointed at the amplifiers and instruments on the little stage. The name Rusty Flyingfinger was printed on the front of the bass drum. When we drained our beers, Susie ran to get two more. Estorga leaned toward me.

"Dude, she's warm for your form," he said.

"She's cute," I said. "But I don't want to take the first one I see."

"You want to shop around a little, huh? Yeah, I can dig it. We'll split after a while."

Rusty Flyingfinger and his band were setting up. Susie came back with the beers. Rusty played some rock and roll licks on his guitar to test the sound system.

"Rusty used to hab long hair bepore martial law," Susie said. "Long hair against the law now."

Burgee had her tongue in Estorga's ear. The smoke from his cigarette was crinkling his eyes. After I finished the second beer, I was feeling hungry.

"I think I'll come back later," I said.

"Where you go?" Susie asked.

"Yeah," Estorga said, "where you go?"

"I need some chow," I said. "I'll be back."

"Wait. I'll go with you."

Estorga tried to disengage himself from Burgee. She had her hands under his shirt.

"You come back later," Susie said. It wasn't a question.

"Sure," I said. "See you later."

"I feel like a kid in a candy store," Estorga said when we were outside.

An old man squatted on the sidewalk, grilling shish kebabs on a hibachi between his knees. We bought two.

"Monkey meat," the old man said after I took a bite.

"You think this is really monkey meat?"

"Nah," Estorga replied. "Well, maybe."

Music was pouring out of the bars. We walked up one side of Magsaysay Drive and down the other. The only reminders of President Ferdinand Marcos and martial law were the machine-gun-toting soldiers on the street corners. The sun was going down. We went into a place called the East End.

"ESTORGA! SHORTCUT! OVER HERE!"

Finesse, Billings, Loophole, and Crapshoot were waving beer bottles at us. They all had girls on their laps.

"You're just in time for Penny Poontang," Billings said.

Penny Poontang was onstage doing a strip tease. The guys in the crowd placed empty San Miguel bottles all around the edge of the stage. Each bottle had a peso coin balanced on its mouth. Completely nude, with her hands in the air, Penny Poontang squatted down on top of each bottle.

When she stood up, the bottles were still standing, but the pesos were gone.

"That's one prehensile pussy," Finesse said.

"That ain't nothin'," Crapshoot replied. "Last WESTPAC, they had a split-tail in here named Juicy Lucy. She could pick up a peeled banana and a peeled hard-boiled egg with her snatch, do a belly dance, and then pop 'em out again unbroken in the opposite order."

"Never saw nothing like that in Wisconsin," Loophole said. "Can you imagine the fuck she'd give ya?"

"That's not all she'd give ya," Finesse replied. "You can build up a tolerance to penicillin."

"Lend me a peso, Shortcut," Estorga said.

I handed him a peso, and he hurried to the stage. Estorga was lying on his back with the peso balanced on his tongue. Penny Poontang sat on his face. When she stood up, the peso was gone. She walked off the stage to cheers and applause.

"That can't be sanitary," Finesse said when Estorga came back to the table. "Wipe your mouth, at least."

The show was over. We finished our drinks and went for a walk down Magsaysay Drive. Hankins was walking toward us from the direction of the base. He was bumping into other guys on purpose. He elbowed a guy from another ship.

"Hankins is always picking fights," Finesse said, "ever since he found out his wife is dating the *Morton*. Every time somebody knocks his dick in the dirt, I have to patch him up."

"Who's Morton?" I asked.

"The *Morton*. It's a destroyer."

"She's cheating on him with a destroyer?" Billings asked.

"Better than an aircraft carrier," Loophole said.

Hankins was yelling:

"DON'T GIVE ME A HARD TIME, BOY, OR YOU'LL WAKE UP WITH A CROWD AROUND YA."

Hankins was skinny but wiry. He shifted his weight from foot to foot. He landed two punches on a heavier guy who shook them off like they were nothing. He gave Hankins a hook in the belly that folded him in half and sat him down on the sidewalk. Then, he walked away.

"Let me look at you," Finesse said.

"Getcher hands off me, pecker checker," Hankins replied. "Which way did he go?"

"Ease off, Duane," Billings told Hankins. "Let's get drunk."

Loud music was coming from the Shamrock. It was the Ides of March tune, "Vehicle." I thought it was a jukebox, but when we walked in, we saw it was Rusty Flyingfinger live with a horn section. He was mimicking the vocals perfectly. Burgee latched on to Estorga. Susie spotted me from across the room.

"Where you go?" she demanded. "You butterply on me?"

"What are you talking about?" I asked.

"Butterfly means fool around with another girl," Billings explained. "Not that they're jealous. They just don't want you spending your money on someone else."

"Some of 'em carry butterfly knives," Loophole added.

"GIVE US SOME MOJOS!" Crapshoot yelled toward the bar.

"What the hell is a mojo, anyway?" Estorga asked.

"Forty pesos a pitcher," Loophole replied.

"A mojo," Billings explained, "is rum mixed with pineapple juice and crushed ice, also vodka, bourbon, gin, and beer. They taste great, but they'll take your head off."

When the band finished playing, I went up to the stage and asked Rusty if I could sit in on drums.

"Can you play 'Wipeout'?" Rusty asked me. His Filipino accent sounded nothing like his singing voice.

"Sure."

"How about 'In-A-Gadda-Da-Vida'? You play 'In-A-Gadda-Da-Vida'?"

"By myself?"

"Okay, but don't break 'em," the drummer said.

I squeezed in behind the drums. They played a new Kool and the Gang thing called "Funky Stuff," with Rusty on police whistle.

"Not bad, Shortcut," Billings said when I got back to the table. The guys were hoisting glass mugs of mojos at me.

"You play drums!" Susie said.

She looked happy. She had pretty eyes. She sat on my lap and put her arms around my neck. Billings handed me a glass. The pineapple juice covered the taste of the booze. Mojos were tasty, but I switched back to beer. I didn't want to get drunk. I wanted to get laid.

"YOU BUY OUT PAPER?" Susie asked me. She was yelling over the music.

"WHAT'S THAT?" I asked.

Loophole yelled:

"YOU PAY THE OWNER OF THE BAR TO TAKE YOUR HONEY HOME EARLY. OTHERWISE, SHE HAS TO STAY UNTIL CLOSING TIME AND EARN MONEY SELLING DRINKS. FOR THIRTY-FIVE BUCKS, YOU CAN BUY A STEADY PAPER THAT'S GOOD FOR A MONTH. THEN, SHE DOESN'T HAVE TO WORK AT ALL. SHE'LL WAIT FOR YOU AT THE MAIN GATE EVERY DAY."

Susie was nodding and smiling. Renting a girl for a night was one thing, but I didn't want to hire one for a month. I took Susie out on the dance floor. I wasn't much of a dancer, but neither was anybody else. You just had to rock from side to side with the music and not fall down.

At 2330, The Shamrock Club started to empty out. Billings, Crapshoot, Hankins, Loophole, and Finesse left with girls. Burgee was leaning up against Estorga, breathing in his ear.

"I've got to get out of here, Shortcut," he said.

Rusty and the band were packing up. Susie leaned toward me.

"You wait for me at tea house around the corner," she said. "I meet you there."

Rain started pouring outside, but it was still at least seventy-five degrees. Along both sides of Magsaysay Drive, locals were opening umbrellas.

They looked like dozens of blooming flowers in motion.

I found the Ong Pin Teahouse around the corner on Gordon Avenue. I stood waiting under the blue canopy over the doorway. A dog with three legs hobbled along. It was a quarter to midnight. If Susie stood me up, I'd have to run through the rain to make it to the main gate before midnight curfew. I didn't want to get picked up by the Shore Patrol or, worse, by one of those soldiers with the machine guns. I was about to flag down a jeepney when I saw Susie walking toward me.

"Come with me," she said.

I followed her into the teahouse. She bought cigarettes, a magazine, and some pills.

"What are the pills for?" I asked.

"So I don't catch clap when we make lub," she said.

So much for sweet talk. It was almost midnight when we got aboard a covered motorized trishaw that took us about a mile up Gordon Avenue. Susie paid the driver. She took my hand and led me through a narrow alley between two concrete block buildings to her front door at number ninety-two. Susie's family was inside: an old woman, a ten-year-old boy, and two little kids, a boy and a girl. At one end of the room was a stove. Wall shelves were empty, except for a few cans of food. There was a big canvas sack of rice on the floor. Lizards were skittering along the tops of the interior walls that stopped two feet short of the ceiling. Their toilet was outside. A little white dog sniffed at me, wagging his tail.

"What's your dog's name?" I asked.

"Kip," Susie answered.

I felt nervous and out of place with all these people. They all knew why I was there, even the little kids, but I couldn't go back to the ship now. It was after curfew. I gave up on the idea of sex. I couldn't do it with her whole family watching us.

"Come with me," Susie said.

"Where?"

"My room."

She took me through a door to a separate bedroom, the only other room in the place. The room was taken up almost entirely by a double bed. She turned on an electric fan and picked up an alarm clock.

"What time you hab to be back to ship?"

"Set it for six," I said.

"Take op you shirt and pants. Gib me thirty pesos."

It was cheaper than a pitcher of mojos. I handed her the money. Thirty pesos—about five bucks—would have bought me a hamburger and fries back home, with change back. I took off Alaska's cowboy boots. Susie took the money and the boots to the outer room.

Lying on the bed drunk in my underwear, I could hear Susie and her mother speaking in rapid Tagalog. What were they saying? Let's kill him after he goes to sleep and sell these boots? A lizard crawled up the wall and across a small crucifix over the doorway. The rain was still falling outside. The air was thick, even with the fan on. I was glad she had mosquito netting on the window. In a few minutes, the light went out in the outer room and Susie came in. She took off her clothes and got in the bed. She lit a cigarette and held the pack out to me.

"No thanks," I said.

She turned on a bedside lamp, put on a pair of rimless glasses, and began to read the magazine she bought. She looked younger now that she was naked. She couldn't have been doing this for very long. My conscience started pushing through the booze. It was rotten that Filipinos had to prostitute their daughters to get by. I remembered reading in one of my history classes that the Philippines had been an American "client state" since the Spanish-American War. Being here was different from reading about it. The poverty was worse than Mexico, but I didn't want to go on being a cherry boy. My conscience was overruled. I traced a finger lightly along the contour of her cute butt, trying to get something going. She kept giggling at the damn magazine. I looked at it over her shoulder. It was some kind of comic book, but it was in Tagalog. At last, she put it aside.

"You know I hab many boypriends."

I didn't know what to say.

"I know," I said.

"I do this por money."

"I know."

I wished she'd stop talking. As though reading my mind, she put her glasses on the nightstand, turned out the light, and put her arms around my neck. I kissed her mouth, her throat, her cupcake tits. I was trying to put it in, and I was having trouble. She grabbed it and put it in for me. After that, everything happened on autopilot.

Later, as I was drifting off to sleep, I remember thinking: So, this is what it's all about. I had crossed an ocean, rented a pair of boots, and paid thirty pesos to get laid in a hot room full of lizards, with the girl's family less than ten feet away. Don't get me wrong. It was great while it was happening, and yet, somehow, I expected something more. I wasn't sure what.

CHAPTER 22

Mountain Province

Susie was snoring when the alarm went off the next morning at 0600. I looked around, remembered where I was, got up, and got dressed. In the outer room, the two little kids were holding up Alaska's boots for me, one boot for each kid. When I opened the front door to leave, the morning sun blinded me. A skinny dog was lifting his hind leg on the rear tire of an old motor scooter parked in the alley. I walked to the base and caught the bus to the ship in time for muster.

The chief put Cool and Hutchinson on the port wing and Brogan and me on the starboard wing to scrape paint. First Brogan and then Hutchinson took off to go to sick bay. When Brogan came back, I asked him what was wrong.

"The Perez sisters gave me and Hutchinson a case of crotch crickets."

At liberty call, I rented Alaska's boots again and headed for Magsaysay Drive. I passed the same old man from the night before with the sidewalk hibachi. He waved me into a little restaurant behind him. A woman inside, probably his wife, spoke little English.

"*Pancit*," she said, serving me a noodle dish, "*lumpia, hum bao.*"

She brought over fried spring rolls with some kind of sauce and small buns stuffed with meat.

"*Balut*?" she asked me.

"What's that?"

She brought out a basket of steamy towels with eggs buried inside.

"Duck egg," she said.

She cracked one open. Inside was a duck embryo, including feathers. She picked it up by the beak and ate everything but the beak. It sounded crunchy.

"Berry good," she said.

"No thanks."

After dinner, I made my way to the Shamrock. Rusty and the band were playing "Funky Stuff" again. I didn't see Susie anywhere. I thought some guy had bought her out of the bar. I didn't like that idea, but there was no sense getting jealous. I kept forgetting she was a hooker.

"Where you priend?"

It was Burgee in a blue dress.

"My friend? I don't know. Where's Susie?"

"Sit down. I get her."

The place was crowded. I sat at a table. Susie snuck up behind me.

"Where you go?" she demanded. "You butterply?"

"No," I said.

"You hab another girl."

"If you're gonna get mad, I'll go someplace else."

"Where you go? Stay here. I come right back."

She handed me a San Miguel and left. She was sitting with some sailors from the *Mobile*. She came back to check on me.

"Look," I said, "if one of those guys from the *Mobile* has more money than me, okay. I'm getting out of here."

"Where you go? We go home tonight. We make lub. You wait por me. I come right back."

The pattern was the same as the night before. Around 2330, she told me to meet her at the teahouse. She bought cigarettes and another magazine. We caught a jeepney to her place. I paid the driver this time. I said hello to her mother and brother. The little kids were asleep. We went into her bedroom. She turned on the electric fan and picked up the alarm clock.

"You get up at six?"

"No. Tomorrow's Saturday. Don't set it."

She turned out the light and kissed me. Rain began coming down hard with lightning flashes and thunder crashes. The power went out and the fan stopped.

In the morning, the sun woke us up. Susie made tea. The kids brought me Alaska's boots. I couldn't keep renting them. I told Susie I needed some shoes. She took me shopping. Everything was too small for me except for a pair of white platform jobs.

"These things look ridiculous," I said.

"Like Elton John," Susie replied, and she laughed.

"I guess I'd better get 'em. At least they're not sneakers."

Susie argued with the shoe salesman in Tagalog. She got him to lower the price to fifty pesos, and I bought them. Then, we walked to an outdoor market. She picked out vegetables and fish, and I paid for them. We took everything back to her place. Susie and her mother cooked the fish and vegetables with rice for lunch while I played chess with her brother. He beat me twice in two short games. A kid with no television has plenty of time to conquer chess. After lunch, Susie gave me a small black and white photo of herself.

"You come see me tonight," she said.

It wasn't a question.

I went back to the ship, had a shower, and returned Alaska's cowboy boots. I spent Saturday afternoon wandering around Olongapo. The weather was beautiful, not so humid. In the Cherry Club, I ran into Hoodwink, Finesse, Cool, Loophole, Billings, and Hankins. They pooled their money and bought six girls out of the bar along with two cases of San Miguel in a tub of ice. They rented two jeepneys, and we all drove to White Rock Beach. They took a little boat to Pequeña Island. With all the girls, there wasn't enough room for me, but the island was only half a mile out, so I bought a pair of swim trunks, put my clothes in a locker at the hotel, and swam. I walked up from the beach dripping wet and found Hankins sitting at an outdoor table with his arm around a girl and a cold San Miguel in his hand. Finesse and Billings sat on the sand drinking beer. Hoodwink, Loophole, Cool, and the rest of the girls waded out into the water.

"You swam that, Shortcut?" Billings asked. "There are sharks out there, man."

"Better take the boat back with us," Finesse said. "We'll make room for ya."

Female squeals came from the direction of the beach. Two laughing girls ran out of the water up onto the sand. Hoodwink came stumbling naked after them. They easily outran him and disappeared into the trees.

When we got back to the Cherry Club after dark, Loophole ordered two pitchers of mojos. Sobriety was the first casualty. After drinking beer all afternoon, I was hammered. A dancing girl on stage peeled off her dress. She wore a black bikini underneath. She put her hands behind her back to unfasten the top and pulled it off. I was looking at a flat chest. It was a small guy holding the bikini top in one hand as he pulled off his long-haired wig with the other. He looked bizarre with eye makeup and short hair. He took a bow and said "Thank you, thank you" in a deep voice that sounded like Lee Marvin. That act sobered me up. I threw up in a planter. Many hands gripped me and steered me out to the street.

"You okay?"

It was Finesse.

"Fine," I said, retching into the gutter.

"We're goin' to the Newport Hotel," Billings said.

"Okay," I replied, straightening up.

"Better come with us, Shortcut," Finesse said. "It's getting late."

"I'm goin' to the Shamrock."

When I got there, Estorga was just leaving with Burgee. I went inside and looked around for Susie. She was sitting at a table with some black guy from another ship. I started to leave, but she caught me at the door.

"You must have radar," I said.

"You drunk," she said. "I be right back."

I waited a few minutes, thinking she was going to get rid of the guy. Then, I saw her kissing him, so I left. It was a quarter to midnight. I passed the Ong Pin Teahouse on my way to the main gate. Sailors and girls were hurrying to get off the streets before curfew. Unclaimed girls were offering last-minute discounts. Two girls spotted me. They started talking.

"Come on, come on. I puck you silly."

"I lub you, no shit."

"How much for overnight?" I asked.

"How much you got?" the first girl asked.

I was getting low on pocket personality. All I had was a twenty-peso note. I showed it to them.

"Puck you," the first girl said, and they both took off.

I couldn't remember the name of that hotel where Billings and Finesse went. I would have to run to make the main gate.

"You looking por girlpriend?" came a high voice.

She was walking toward me and smiling. She had a nice shape moving around inside a yellow dress.

"How much?"

"How much you got?"

"Twenty pesos."

She was doing mental calculations. This late in the game, it was me or nothing.

"Okay," she said, grabbing my arm.

We got into a jeepney. She sat up front and gave the driver directions in Tagalog. A rain squall started. We drove for ten minutes. We were going uphill. The road was muddy. I couldn't get my bearings.

"Where are we going?"

"Mountain probince," she said, as if I knew where the hell the mountain province was.

The windshield wipers kept scraping across the glass. We could see Navy ships moored in the harbor below. I could pick out the *Okmok* so far away that it looked like a toy. The jeepney came to a stop. She argued with the driver in Tagalog. I couldn't understand a word.

"He try to obercharge us," she said.

"No," the driver said, "I tell her ten peso."

"You say fibe," she said, and the rapid-fire Tagalog started again.

I didn't know what to do. I could have paid the driver, but then I wouldn't have had enough money for the girl. A man appeared out of the darkness. He was carrying a shotgun. This is it, I thought. They would never find my body. This was why the XO always told us to stay in pairs, but you can't stay in pairs when you go home with a girl.

I couldn't understand their conversation. Mr. Shotgun must have been someone's private security, and he didn't want any problems near his post. The girl and the driver agreed on five pesos. I was still sitting in the back seat of the jeepney when she got out.

"Come on," she said. "We home now."

I got out and sank my new Elton Johns into the mud. She took my hand and led me to her house, a three-room bungalow with big windows. A young girl was in the front room, babysitting a sleeping baby. She paid the girl and sent her home. Then, she took me through the dark outer room to the bedroom, where there was an electric fan, mosquito netting, and a king-size bed. She lit three candles.

"I'm Daisy," she said. "Take op you clothes."

I wondered if all hookers had this same businesslike approach. I got undressed. She slipped her yellow dress off over her head and got on top of me. She was older than me, maybe twenty-three or four. She was softer and more enthusiastic than Susie. Sex with her was way better than Susie. If she was faking, she was a good actress.

In the morning, I didn't know how to get back to town, so Daisy took me down the hill in another jeepney, and she walked with me almost to the main gate.

"You come see me again," she said. "I work at the Kiss Me Club."

"Okay," I said, and I handed her the twenty pesos. She had never asked me for it. She gave me a kiss, and I walked back to the main gate. I got aboard the last bus back to the ship. Screwball and Stringbean were already aboard. I was looking for a place to sit. A pair of legs was stretched across the aisle in back, from one seat to another. They belonged to Estorga. He was sound asleep, barefoot, and covered with dirt.

"Hey, Raul," I said, shaking him. "RAUL!"

He came awake with a jerk and said:

"*Ngahk!*"

"What happened to your shoes?"

His eyes were bloodshot. His hands shook as he inserted a cigarette into his beard.

"That Burgee chick," he said. "We were at her place, goin' at it. She has her bed propped up with bricks because two legs are missing. We have to take it easy to keep the bed from collapsing. So, we were goin' at it, you know, and her fucking brother walks in right in the middle, and the dude was *pissed off!* He had a long knife in his hand like a machete, and here I am, balls-ass naked, on top of his sister!"

He lit his cigarette and kept talking.

"The dude was on the warpath, man, waving that knife around and yelling at her in Tagalog. I didn't wait for no translation. I grabbed my shirt and trousers. He was standing at the foot of the bed, blocking the door and pointing that damn knife at me. He was barefoot, so I kicked the bed, and the whole thing came down on his feet. He screamed, and I took a dive out the window. Thank God, she lives on the ground floor. She screamed, too, the silly bitch. I had to hide all night from that sucker and his friends and those fucking soldiers and the shore patrol. I crawled in under some shack by Shit River and spent the night with a one-eyed cat... What's so damn funny?"

CHAPTER 23

Mooring-Line Watch

Right after morning muster, Lightning Lenny held a surprise personnel inspection. My hair was short, and my shoes were shined, but I had a little smudge on my white hat, so I maintained my record of never passing an inspection. Mr. Southcott would have written me up, but Mr. Tobias didn't. After the inspection, we were changing into working dungarees in 02 berthing.

"Hey, Finesse," Alaska said. "What's this I hear about Swampass getting knifed?"

"Swampass thought it would be funny to throw a handful of washers into Shit River," Finesse replied. "Some kids thought they were coins and dove in, but they came up and yelled to their partners on the bridge. One of them chased after Swampass and slashed the back of his leg."

"NOW TURN TO," said the 1MC, "COMMENCE SHIP'S WORK."

On the bridge, Chief Lasko had us scraping paint.

"I caught the mooring-line watch last night from midnight to four," Brogan said. "Have you guys had it yet?"

"Naw," Cool replied, and Hutchinson and I shook our heads.

Since Navy ships routinely doubled up on mooring lines, thieves could steal up to half the lines without setting a ship adrift. The big hemp hawsers brought money on the black market— enough money to make it worth the risk. After recent incidents of stolen mooring lines on other ships, Lightning Lenny added a mooring line watch to the watch bill.

"It's a roving patrol along both sides of the ship," Brogan continued. "They give you a billy club and a police whistle. In case of unauthorized boarders, you're supposed to blow the whistle and bring the quarterdeck watch on the run. Around 0230, I was patrolling the side of the ship away from the pier. I thought I saw somebody swimming, coming up for air and going back down. I kept watching, but I didn't see him again. Just when I thought I was seeing things, he came up again right at the waterline of the ship. He started swimming around toward the lines on the pier. He didn't make a sound. I was supposed to blow the whistle, but Chief Hackburn was the OOD, and he's such a by-the-book motherfucker I was afraid he'd shoot the guy. I just couldn't blow the whistle. It woulda been like killing him myself. I didn't know what to do. I didn't want to get written up, but I didn't want to give the poor bastard a death sentence, either. I was nervous, and sometimes, when I get nervous, I have to take a leak. So, I aimed it at the guy. It splattered all over his head. The guy never made a sound. He just swam away."

"When that story gets around, Ah bet we don't have any more missing mooring lines," Hutchinson said.

Every morning, I swore I'd stay aboard and get some rest, but by liberty call, I didn't want to miss out on a night on the beach. Estorga and I stopped in at the enlisted men's club on base, the Sampaguita Club. We had a beer and exchanged dollars for pesos. Then, we walked across Shit River and down Magsaysay Drive. As we approached the Shamrock club, Estorga crossed the street.

"I'm not going near that place," he said. "I never want to see that Burgee chick again."

We looked around for the Kiss Me Club, the place where Daisy worked, but we couldn't find it. Where Magsaysay met Rizal Avenue was a place called the Sierra Club. We went in and got a table near the stage. The band was playing Edgar Winter's "Frankenstein." Crapshoot and Shilgenkrauser were sitting at the bar. A man with no legs was on stage, walking on his hands. The crowd threw pesos at him. He stood on one hand, picked them up, and collected them in a cloth bag. The band leader asked the crowd for volunteer talent. They let me sit in on the drums.

Estorga took the microphone and yelled:
"LET'S BOOGIE!"

The guitar player called the tune, "Wooly Bully." Estorga sang the lead.

"UNO, DOS, TRES, QUATRO. WATCH IT, NOW. WATCH IT. WATCH IT."

The guitars came in. I faked it from memory.

"Matty told Hatty about a thing she saw. Had two big horns and a wooly jaw."

The crowd joined in:

"WOOLY BULLYYYYYYYYYY! WOOLY BULLY! WOOLY BULLY, WOOLY BULLY, WOOLY BULLY!"

At the end of the tune, Estorga took a bow and spoke into the microphone.

"Did you hear about the boatswain's mate chief who told the hooker he had no sex since 1957? She felt so sorry for him, she gave him a freebie. Afterwards, she says: 'Not bad for a guy who hasn't done it since 1957.' The chief says: 'Well, it's only 2230.'"

The laughter was weak. I gave him a rim shot. Estorga tapped the microphone.

"Is this thing on? A sailor and a marine were in the head takin' a leak. The sailor finishes first, so he's walking away when the grunt says: 'In the Corps, they teach us to wash our hands after we take a piss.' The sailor says: 'In the Navy, they teach us not to piss on our hands.'"

I gave him a bass drum kick.

"YOU SUCK, SQUID!" yelled a marine.

"I see we have some of our brother marines here tonight," Estorga said. *"Marine—that stands for Muscles Are Required; Intelligence Not Essential."*

I played a cymbal crash. Shilgenkrauser was chuckling. The band played "Wild Thing." The crowd sang along. Estorga was a natural, but he went too far and started to take off his trousers. A bouncer dragged him off the stage. At the back of the room, Shilgenkrauser was choking a marine while Crapshoot gave another one a chin jab with the heel of his hand. Three more marines started trading punches with them. Hankins, Carranza, and Bootleg appeared from out of nowhere to lend a fist. It is a strange fact that guys who don't even like each other aboard ship will jump in to help their shipmates in a fight.

Carranza had this little hop that added snap to the straight jab he planted on a marine's face. Hankins shoved another marine, who knocked over some glasses, slipped on some beer, and hit his jaw on the table on his way down. Bootleg, wearing his dark sunglasses despite the low light, was crouching in a crane stance when another marine knocked him on his ass. The only combat I ever saw in the Navy was between our own troops. Two Shore Patrolmen came running through the main entrance.

"*OKMOK*," I yelled. "GET OUT OF HERE!"

Shilgenkrauser, Crapshoot, Hankins, Carranza, Bootleg and Estorga ran through a side door, with me behind them. Once we were outside, everybody took off running in different directions. Estorga and I crossed the street and slowed down to a fast walk. In front of Pauline's, some kids were selling little ducks to sailors for them to throw to the crocodile. The croc ignored most of the ducks, and the kids would snatch them back and sell them again. As we went inside, a girl grabbed Estorga and started dancing with him. A tall girl in a pink dress was coming toward me on a collision course. She handed me a cold San Miguel.

"You looking por girlpriend?"

"Not anymore," I replied.

She steered me toward a table, and we sat down.

"I'm Kitty," she said. "I lub you, no shit."

Conversation was never on the menu.

When Kitty and I left the bar later, Malolo was wrestling the crocodile, with Big Time, Screwball, and Kickback cheering him on. The poor old croc looked worn out. Kitty took me to her apartment. It had polished wooden floors and interior walls that went all the way to the ceiling. She even had an indoor bathroom. She had a round bed, a stereo playing soft music, and that crucial piece of Olongapo hooker equipment, an electric fan.

"You gib me pipty pesos," she said.

Fifty pesos was higher than the going rate, but it explained how she afforded this nice place. I told her I didn't have fifty. Actually, I had it, but payday was a while away, and I didn't feel like blowing it. She let me sleep there—on the floor. It turned out to be a good thing we didn't have sex. I didn't know it then, but Daisy had given me more than just a good time.

CHAPTER 24

Not A Drill

"UH, FLEET COMMAND HAS AWARDED THE *OKMOK* WITH THE BIG E," Lightning Lenny announced over the 1MC. "IN TWO DAYS, ADMIRAL GRIFFIN IS COMING ABOARD TO PERSONALLY PRESENT US WITH THE BATTLE EFFICIENCY AWARD. THAT MEANS WE HAVE TWO DAYS TO HAVE A FIELD DAY AND TITIVATE AND REPAINT THE ENTIRE SHIP. LET'S TURN TO. THAT IS ALL."

Being a flag officer is as close to royalty as an American can get. Once you make rear admiral or higher, your appearances are announced and prepared for. Everything is clean and polished for your arrival. You have aides to do your bidding, and no one will ever contradict you in public.

The non-rates turned to, and the paint job was done in two days. A smaller, more conscientious group would have done the job just as well in less time—or even better in the same two days. The Navy had taught me several lessons. Nobody works any harder than the people around him. The more people involved in a project, the easier it is to hide out in the crowd. When the reward for work is more work, it doesn't pay to be efficient or effective. When reward is not tied to results, results will be mediocre, at best. You can force grudging compliance but not enthusiastic effort. When motivated by threats, people will do just enough to avoid punishment.

The crew wore dress whites for Admiral Griffin's arrival. He came aboard and presented the award. He didn't inspect the crew or the ship. He didn't notice the colossal paint job that had just been accomplished in his honor. Part of winning the Big E included the crew's choice of an R and R liberty port. Lightning Lenny had requested Guam. Then, we found out that Guam had a curfew, and the crew would have to wear dress whites ashore.

"I was stationed in Guam," Alaska said. "There's no girls there. We used to say Guam stands for Give Up And Masturbate."

"To hell with R and R," Hoodwink said. "We need some I and I: intoxication and intercourse."

Admiral Griffin called a wardroom meeting with the chiefs. He asked if they had any complaints about the command of the *Okmok*. The chiefs told him flat out they didn't think Guam was much of a reward for winning the Big E. Because of that meeting, Admiral Griffin ordered that our crew be given seventy-two hours of liberty at Keelung City in the northeast of Taiwan.

In 02 berthing, I looked through a September copy of *Stars and Stripes*. There were gas lines back home. Gas prices were up to seventy-five cents a gallon, predicted to go over a dollar by the end of the year. President Ford gave Nixon a full pardon.

When I went to the head to take a leak, it burned like alcohol on an open wound. I grabbed the pipes and clenched my teeth. Then, I walked down to sick bay. Finesse looked up from his desk.

"What's up, Shortcut?" he asked.

"When it hurts to piss, does that mean I got the clap?"

"Are ya drippin'?"

"No."

"I need a urine sample to tell for sure."

"It hurts to piss."

"You gotta piss."

He gave me two diuretic pills and some water. I came back later, gritted my teeth, and gave Finesse a urine sample. It felt like I was pissing razor blades. He examined it under a microscope.

"Well, Shortcut, I guess I was wrong about you," he said. "Classic case of clap. Drop your trousers and bend over the table, and don't jump when I stick these needles in your ass."

He gave me four injections of penicillin, two in each cheek.

"You should be good as new in one to five days. I want you to describe the girl you got it from. The civilian medical authorities will try to let her know she's infected. Give me her name."

"Her name was Daisy, but I doubt that's what it says on her birth certificate. I didn't get her last name. She lives somewhere in the mountain province, but I couldn't find the place again to save my life. She said she works at the Kiss Me Club, but I met her on the street."

"That's a beautiful story. Color eyes?"

"Brown. Black hair. About five foot four. Does that narrow it down? Doesn't that describe every girl in Asia?"

"It's just a line on the form," Finesse said, writing it all down. "Close enough for government work. Oh, yeah, and hand over your ID card. When you get the clap, you're restricted to the ship. Be sure to drink lots of water."

"It hurts to piss."

"You gotta piss."

After Needler had talked to Hutchinson's legal officer on base, Lightning Lenny switched the captain's mast date for Hutchinson, Brogan, and Crimmons to our next underway period. There were no legal officers at sea. During the following week of sea time, they went to captain's mast for their pot arrest in Yokosuka. Admiral Griffin wanted an example made of them. He wanted their punishment to satisfy the Japanese, and Lightning Lenny wanted to look good to Admiral Griffin. Shit rolls downhill. Lightning Lenny fined them 500 bucks apiece, and he restricted them to the ship for two weeks, with two weeks extra duty.

When we arrived in Keelung, my infection was cleared up. Finesse returned my ID. Mr. Crookshank gave his orientation speech before liberty call.

"YOU WILL FIND BOOKS, RECORDS, AND TAPES FOR VERY LOW PRICES. THIS IS BECAUSE THEY DO NOT ENFORCE COPYRIGHT LAWS IN TAIWAN. DO NOT BUY THESE ITEMS BECAUSE IT ENCOURAGES PIRACY. ALSO, THE VD RATE IS HIGHER IN TAIWAN THAN ANYWHERE ELSE WE'VE BEEN, SO USE YOUR HEAD, AND USE A CONDOM. STAY TOGETHER, ALWAYS IN PAIRS, AND REMEMBER, LOOSE LIPS SINK SHIPS. IN TAIWAN, DRUG POSSESSION OF ANY KIND CARRIES THE DEATH PENALTY."

Estorga and I went ashore. We exchanged our money at forty New Taiwan dollars per buck and took a bus to Taipei. A room at the Taipei Hilton cost 830 NT. We found another place called the Lucky Hotel, a flophouse where the rooms started at 260 NT. A deluxe suite cost 460 NT. We took the deluxe suite, with two beds, one chair, a shower, and a radio that didn't work.

We got cleaned up and went out. Estorga bought every Beatles album he could find for 200 NT. They were flimsy vinyl inside paper-thin covers. You could play them once and record them on reel to reel. Play them four or five times, and they were shot. He planned to mail them home. We spotted a sign on a door of a place called Uncle Chang's Mongolian Barbecue that said: 160 NT— ALL YOU CAN EAT. I went back for seconds and thirds.

"You got a hollow leg, man?" Estorga said. "I'll bet they're glad you don't live here. You'd break the place."

The next day, we went back to the ship. I was in the chart house with Cool and Brogan when a shock like an earthquake vibrated through the ship. The GQ alarm went off. Mr. Sforzando's voice came over the 1MC.

"THIS IS NOT A DRILL. THIS IS NOT A DRILL. COLLISION, COLLISION. ALL DAMAGE CONTROL PARTIES MUSTER ON STATION. THAT IS, ALL DAMAGE CONTROL PARTIES MUSTER ON STATION."

"Collision?" Brogan said. "At the pier?"

A cargo ship, the *San Jose*, had slipped her anchorage and drifted into our port side. Our crew was delighted. If our ship sustained hull damage, we might have to stay in port for repairs. Unfortunately, the *Okmok* held up. Her hull was not breached, and her frames were not bent. The *San Jose* broke an oil pump and could not proceed according to its schedule to Kaohsiung in the southwest of Taiwan. Lightning Lenny lost no time volunteering us to take their place. Our R and R in Keelung was cut short. The *Okmok* departed the next day for Kaohsiung. Lightning Lenny also volunteered the *Okmok* for a two-week series of UNREPS.

"I'M PROUD OF THIS CREW," he said over the 1MC as we steamed out of Keelung. "I'M ALREADY LOOKING FORWARD TO WINNING THE BIG E AGAIN NEXT YEAR. NOW IS NOT THE TIME TO SLACK OFF ON OUR LAURELS. WE'RE GOING TO WORK TO MAINTAIN THE SUPERIOR STATUS OF THE *OKMOK* AND GO FOR THAT HASH MARK. THAT IS ALL."

If we thought winning the Big E was going to earn us a break, we were wrong. We had UNREPS every day. Lightning Lenny scheduled GQ drills in between. I didn't get more than four hours rack time a day, and that was usually interrupted. Mr. Tobias didn't trust Hutchinson and Brogan to stand watches. We went back to standing port and starboard with Chief Lasko, Hutchinson, and Brogan in one section and Cool and me in the other.

In October, we pulled into Sasebo for one day to take on supplies. The *Ranger* was in port. Aircraft carrier crews were ten times the size of the *Okmok*, so the bars were crowded. Estorga came with me to the New Moon bar, but it had a new name: The Bonne Chance Club.

"So, this is where the perfect woman works?" Estorga asked.

"I'm telling you, man," I replied, looking around, "wait until you see her. She's a babe and a half."

An old man stood behind the varnished wooden bar.

"Do you know Miyoshi Murakami?" I asked him. "Does she still work here?"

"We have many nice girl," he replied, whistling.

A pair of girls walked over.

"You buy me drink?" one asked. "What ship you from?"

"No," I said to the old man. "This girl was taller with longer hair. Very pretty."

"Yes," he replied, nodding. "Velly pletty, velly pletty."

"What happened to the people who used to work here?" I asked, but the old man didn't understand me or didn't want to.

"Forget it, Shortcut," Estorga said when we were outside. "She probably doesn't work there anymore. Hey, I bet that place will take your mind off her."

Estorga pointed at a neon sign down the street that said: ICHIBAN BATH HOUSE. We wound up in a hot tub with two Japanese girls who massaged our necks and backs. My girl had strong hands and fingers. She turned the knots around my shoulder blades into jelly. The girls led us into a steam room, where we stretched out face down on big concrete tables, and they walked barefoot on our backs. Her small feet made my spine sound like a popcorn machine.

The next day, we pulled out of Sasebo and ran straight into tropical storm Della. The thirty-foot seas gave us a rocky roller-coaster ride in 02 berthing. As I tried to get some rack time, I could feel the bow rising way, way up and hesitating before each fall. The hull shuddered as the keel cut down through the water again and again.

Before my next watch, I was brushing my teeth when we heard five short blasts of the ship's whistle. Crapshoot's voice came over the 1MC.

"THIS IS NOT A DRILL. THIS IS NOT A DRILL. MAN OVERBOARD, MAN OVERBOARD. MUSTER THE CREW ON THE SECOND DECK.

THAT IS, MUSTER THE CREW ON THE SECOND DECK."

We took a head count to find out who was missing. I looked out through the hangar bay door. It was too dark to see the huge waves, but we could feel them. Crapshoot spoke over the 1MC.

"SEAMAN STONE, REPORT TO THE BRIDGE AT ONCE. THAT IS, SEAMAN STONE, REPORT TO THE BRIDGE AT ONCE."

Stone was Gink's real name. I'd seen him standing watches and in the chow line, but I didn't really know him. The chances of finding him at night in that storm were zero. There was no moon. A smoke marker would be invisible. The silence on the second deck was spooky.

Then, Gink showed up, rubbing his eyes. A few guys laughed. He had been asleep in one of the engineering spaces. Crapshoot calling his name over the 1MC roused him. With all hands present and accounted for, the crew was dismissed. Crapshoot made another announcement.

"WHOEVER THREW TRASH OR ANY OBJECT OVER THE SIDE IN THE PAST HALF HOUR, REPORT TO THE BRIDGE AT ONCE."

"Sure thing," Estorga said. "Who's dumb enough to volunteer for captain's mast?"

Crimmons, never much for thinking ahead, was the man. He reported to the bridge and fessed up that he had deep-sixed a bundle of magazines and newspapers over the side. Needler wrote him up, along with Gink for sleeping in an unauthorized space, and Stringbean, who had been standing the fantail watch and had reported what he thought was a man falling overboard. By blaming the waste of time and fuel on Stringbean, Lightning Lenny sent a clear message to future fantail watches. When in doubt, report nothing. As usual, the questions were never: How can we improve things; how can we make sure this never happens again? The traditional questions were always: Who had the watch; who can we blame for what? The Navy never separated the problem from the person. Covering your ass was the first priority. The old saying—it didn't happen on my watch—was all that mattered.

During my evening bridge watch, Mr. Kempton had the deck and the conn. A bright star was over the western horizon.

"Is that a planet?" Crapshoot asked.

"It's a new navigation satellite," Mr. Kempton replied. "In a few years, LORAN will be obsolete."

"What about that?" Guzman asked, pointing at a quivering orange light on the horizon. "That's no satellite."

"Boats," Mr. Kempton said. "Call up to the signal bridge. Have Hankins look through the big eyes and identify an irregular flashing orange light at two points off the port bow."

"Aye aye, sir," Crapshoot answered.

He talked to Hankins on the squawk box. It took a minute for Hankins to get back to us.

"It could be a reflection from the mainland, sir," Hankins said. "It's probably nothing."

The words were no sooner out of Hankins' mouth than we saw a red flare shoot straight up from the orange light into the black sky.

"Roger that, Hankins," Mr. Kempton said. "You can go back to sleep now. Come left five degrees. All ahead flank."

"Left five degrees, aye, sir," Smitty answered, altering course toward the glowing orange light.

"All ahead flank," Doglike said from the lee helm. "Engine room answers all ahead flank."

"Boats, set the rescue and assistance detail. *Let's* go. *Let's* go."

"Aye aye, sir," Crapshoot answered.

He sounded five short blasts on the ship's whistle and spoke into the 1MC:

"THIS IS NOT A DRILL. THIS IS NOT A DRILL. SET THE RESCUE AT SEA DETAIL. THAT IS, SET THE RESCUE AT SEA DETAIL. THIS IS NOT A DRILL."

"CIC reports a contact ten thousand yards dead ahead," Gink said, "probably a fishing boat."

"Very well," Mr. Kempton replied. "Steady as she goes."

"Steady as she goes, aye, sir," Smitty answered. "Steadying up on new course two five five."

"Very well. Guzman, get my rescue and assistance pipe."

"Which one is that, sir?"

"The meerschaum, Guzman, the meerschaum."

Lightning Lenny entered through the after door.

"What's the status, Jim?" he asked.

"*Captain's on the bridge,*" Crapshoot yelled.

"Looks like a small boat in distress, Captain," Mr. Kempton answered.

As we got closer, we saw the orange light was a fire on the deck of a disabled wooden Chinese junk about sixty-feet long with two pole masts, no stays, and an elevated poop deck astern. The junk was listing to starboard from taking on water. The Chinese fishermen aboard had lit the fire in a huge iron brazier on deck in a desperate attempt to attract attention. Our deck apes dropped lines to them so they could tie off their boat, but, instead, two of them tried to climb up the lines. Bootleg and Loophole weren't ready for that, and they let go to keep from being pulled overboard. The two Chinese fell into the water between their junk and our port side. They were lucky they weren't crushed between their hull and ours.

My watch ended at midnight, and I was tired, but going to sleep would have been like walking out on a good movie. This was the first time we had done anything that wasn't either a drill or an UNREP. Our crew got all the Chinese aboard just before swells started smashing their wooden junk against our steel hull. Our deck force got the junk in tow. Lightning Lenny had Snyder and Meech place the fishermen under armed guard in sick bay for the night. There were nine of them. They got hot soup, t-shirts, and *Okmok* ball caps. One of them had a gash in his arm. Finesse cleaned it and stitched it up. The last thing I heard as I got into the rack was Shilgenkrauser's voice over the 1MC.

"ANYONE SPEAKING CHINESE OR POSSESSING A CHINESE DICTIONARY, REPORT TO SICKBAY."

When I took the watch in the morning, the junk was gone. There were a couple of jokes that Thumbs must have tied it off, but the truth was we lost it because it got so heavy from taking on water that our towline parted. Somehow, we had determined that the fishermen didn't own the junk. Their engine had broken down, and they'd been pushed out to sea by the storm. They drifted for days. Two of them had a knife fight, which was how the guy's arm got slashed.

Meech brought one of them to the bridge, probably their skipper. He pointed at the chart and then toward the fantail where the towline had been tied off. Mr. Tobias stepped over to the chart table.

"Mr. Tobias, I think this guy is asking me for the position where their junk was lost," I said.

"Go ahead and give it to him," Mr. Tobias replied.

I checked the logbook and found where Brogan had written: *0248, tow line parted.* I worked with dividers backwards along the track from our present position to 0248. I wrote the latitude and longitude on a piece of paper and handed it to him. He bowed toward me.

When Hutchinson relieved me at 1145, Mr. Tobias asked me to help him take a noon sight, an easier way to determine latitude than a full sight reduction, and he would plot it on the chart. I wrote down his sextant reading, and he had me draw the line on the plotting sheet and label it.

"You've learned quite a bit on this WESTPAC, Thorpe," Mr. Tobias said. "You've had a lot of responsibility for a seaman. When we get to port, I am recommending you for the petty officer third-class exam."

"Thank you, sir."

"Do you have all your practical factors?"

"All but weapon competence, sir."

"I'll have the chief get with you after your watch."

Chief Lasko kept a list of practical factors, requirements for promotion to quartermaster third-class. He signed them off as we completed them. Most of them were regular quartermaster duties. I had racked up a bunch of them on this cruise. The only one I lacked was a demonstration of weapon competence, mandatory for petty officers standing quarterdeck watches. That afternoon, while Mr. Tobias was on the bridge, the chief and I went down to the fantail with a Colt .45. He observed as I inserted a full magazine into the weapon and fired seven shots into the Pacific. I showed him the empty magazine.

"Never missed the ocean once," the chief said as he signed off that last requirement.

With the recommendation from Mr. Tobias, all I had to do now was pass the exam. If I made third-class, I wouldn't be a non-rate. No more working parties. No more scraping bulkheads. No more scrubbing toilets. No more lower than whale shit.

CHAPTER 25

Goodwill Ambassadors

From a distance, Kaohsiung appeared to be a city of high-rise buildings. There was no place at the piers for us to moor. Lightning Lenny had to drop anchor out in the harbor and run liberty boats to shore. Mr. Crookshank came over the 1MC before liberty call.

"WELL, MEN, NO GOOD DEED GOES UNPUNISHED. THE OWNER OF THE JUNK WE RESCUED IS ATTEMPTING TO SUE THE NAVY FOR LOSING IT. THAT'S GRATITUDE FOR YOU. BUT NEVER FORGET, MEN, THAT THESE PEOPLE ARE OUR ALLIES. YOU ARE ALL REPRESENTING THE UNITED STATES. WHEN DEALING WITH THE LOCAL CIVILIANS, USE DIPLOMACY. YOU ARE ALL GOODWILL AMBASSADORS. USE YOUR HEAD. USE THE BUDDY SYSTEM, AND USE A CONDOM—AND GET YOUR PLEASURE FROM A JUG. IN TAIWAN, DRUG POSSESSION OF ANY KIND CARRIES THE DEATH PENALTY. THAT IS ALL."

Hutchinson and Brogan had finished their restrictions, but Brogan had the duty, so he couldn't go ashore. Hutchinson, Hankins, Billings, and I got aboard the liberty boat. Shilgenkrauser piloted the boat in to the fleet landing, where pimps on motor scooters dropped off three Chinese girls.

"Welcome, Joe," called one.

"I love you long time," said another.

Hutchinson and Hankins walked off with the two cutest ones. The third one came with Billings and me.

"My name Crystal," she said. "What ship you from?"

"The *Okmok*," Billings replied.

"You heroes. Save fishing boat. Fix man with cut arm. Now, they sue Navy."

"She knows more than fleet command," Billings told me. "Maybe we should ask her where we're going next."

Crystal took us to a bar called the Sea Dragon Club. It had big windows with a view of the street.

"You hungry?" she asked. "We have restaurant upstairs."

"Sure," Billings replied. "Can you go get us a table?"

She nodded, got up, and climbed the stairs.

"Let's get out of here," Billings said, finishing off his beer. "I don't like the way she latched on to us."

We went out the back door because Crystal would have seen us through the big windows if we'd gone out the front. We passed stores selling bootlegged books, records, and tapes. Up the street, we found another place, The Popeye Club. A paper banner hung over the entrance. It said: WELCOME OKMOK. We went inside and got a table. Two pretty girls glided toward us.

"My name Angie," said the closest. "You like me?"

"This is more like it," Billings said. "Who's your friend?"

"Betty," Angie replied. "She no speak English, but she fuck you silly."

A photographer pestered us to let him take our photo with the girls. Angie and Billings were haggling over the price of an out paper. She wanted 660 NT, but Billings talked her down to 475. Angie spoke to Betty in Chinese while Billings gave me semaphore hand signals spelling out the word HOTEL, and I nodded. There was a hotel across the street. We paid for a room.

"I can't make love because I'm sick," Angie said once we were in the room. Angie and Betty went to the bathroom at the end of the hall.

"I think it's her time of the month," Billings explained. "You might as well stay here with the other one. They must make a commission from the hotel owner. I can't figure out why they brought us here."

The girls never came back. Billings realized Angie had picked his pocket and taken his cash.

"Let's find those bitches."

"Forget it, Billy," I said. "I have some money. Let's get another beer."

I was sorry Billings lost his money, but I was glad the girls were gone. The moral arguments against prostitution had not stopped me in Olongapo, but I wasn't interested in getting another case of clap. Besides that, I'd had time to realize that paying hookers for sex was like admitting I was so repulsive that no girl would dream of getting near me without cash compensation.

We went outside and ran into Crystal on the sidewalk. She was angry.

"Where you go? I find you friends, tall guy and cowboy boots."

"Hankins and Hutchinson," Billings said.

"Where are they?" I asked.

"They went to hotel," Crystal replied, holding her fingers to her lips and inhaling on an imaginary joint.

"What hotel?" Billings asked.

Crystal gave us a phone number. I found a pay telephone and dialed it. Hankins answered.

"What are you guys doin'?" I asked.

"We're up here fuckin'," Hankins replied. "It's the Peach Hotel, room 622."

Crystal took us to the hotel. When we got off the elevator on the sixth floor, Bootleg was chasing a girl down the hallway. Crimmons was passed out in a chair. Crystal led us to room 622, and she knocked on the door. A girl opened it. Hutchinson sat on the bed, rolling joints with another girl while Hankins dropped water balloons out the open window.

"Damn, Billy," Hankins said. "Your girl looks like Ho Chi Minh in a dress. I'd sooner fuck a keg of nails."

"She ain't my girl," Billings replied. "How did she know where you guys were?"

"She got us the pot," Hutchinson answered.

Someone pounded on the door. Hutchinson hid the weed under the mattress, and Billings opened the door. There were two cops with white helmets. An angry Chinese guy in a wet business suit stood between them.

"Who is throwing water from this window?" asked one cop.

"I WANT APOLOGY!" yelled the man in the suit.

Hutchinson was on his feet.

"Excuse us, sir," said Hutchinson. "We apologize, don't we, Duane?"

Hankins looked dazed. Hutchinson gave him a little slap to the head.

"Yes, we apologize," Hankins said.

The man in the suit sniffed and nodded at the cops.

"Don't get crazy here," said the other cop.

He glared at each of us before he closed the door. One girl laughed. Hankins lit a cigarette.

"If you guys had been smoking that pot, we'd be on our way to the Taiwanese brig," I said. "Didn't you guys hear what the XO said about the death penalty?"

"Ease off, Shortcut," Hankins replied.

"I think I'll shove off."

"Wait for me," Billings said.

"Those guys sure don't seem worried about getting busted here," I said once we were outside on the sidewalk. "What's wrong with them?"

"Stupidity seems likely," Billings replied.

"Hankins, yeah, but with Hutchinson, it's something else."

"Insanity?"

We had a couple of beers. When my money was almost gone, we headed back toward the fleet landing. Chief Hackburn, Big Time, Screwball, and Finesse were waiting there for the liberty boat. Chief Hackburn was yelling at Big Time.

"You're drunk, Petty Officer Williams. There's an article in the UCMJ about public fucking intoxication."

Big Time stared at Chief Hackburn.

"Just because you're a first-class doesn't mean you can't fucking get written up," Chief Hackburn said.

Big Time twisted at the waist and gave Chief Hackburn a hard right to the chin. The chief's head snapped back, and he collapsed on the planks of the landing. Finesse checked him for a pulse. Big Time sat down and looked across the water. Billings did a little dance around Big Time.

"God, that was beautiful," Billings said. "Name your drink, Big Time. I'm gonna buy you a bottle."

"He's breathing," Finesse announced. "He's out cold."

"When he wakes up, Big Time, you're gonna be in a world of shit," Screwball said.

Big Time looked at Chief Hackburn's motionless body.

"Man oughta know when to shut his mouth," he said.

Shilgenkrauser arrived in the liberty boat. Screwball and Finesse loaded Chief Hackburn into the boat. He regained consciousness on the way back.

"You're on report, Big Time," Chief Hackburn said, rubbing his jaw, "just as soon as we get back."

"Give your jaw a rest, Chief," Finesse said, "at least until I can x-ray it."

The next morning, Hutchinson and Hankins arrived in the last liberty boat. After breakfast, everybody in 02 berthing was waiting for morning muster.

"How's Hackburn?" Billings asked Finesse.

"His jaw wasn't broken," Finesse replied. "Thumbs was worse off."

"What happened to him?"

"While he was sleeping, Doglike tied three feet of nylon fishing line to the rail alongside his rack. He made a slip knot in the other end, dropped it around Thumbs' balls, and sat back and waited for reveille. When Thumbs bailed out of his rack, he almost de-nutted himself. He saw Doglike laughing at him, and the fight was on. Chief Skinner wrote 'em both up."

"Those guys are like the Arabs and the Israelis," Alaska said.

We steamed out of Kaohsiung. During an UNREP with the dock landing ship *Mount Vernon* on our starboard side, a freak swell hit us. Brogan stayed on course, but the helmsman aboard the *Mount Vernon* lost steerageway. As the *Vernon's* bow swung toward the *Okmok*, Mr. Kempton ordered Brogan to come left, keeping the two ships parallel. Then, the *Vernon's* fantail swung in toward us, coming within ten feet of our hull. Hutchinson was on the starboard wing snapping photos. Mr. Kempton ordered Brogan to come right until the ships were parallel again. Brogan got a commendation from Mr. Kempton for his helmsmanship.

Lightning Lenny arranged to have a practice gun shoot. The CO of the aircraft carrier *Kittyhawk* sent up a plane. The plane towed the target, a long red windsock attached to a hundred yards of cable. The idea was to hit just aft of the windsock without destroying it, so it could be used over again for more practice shots. We were expecting a long evolution so that all the gunner's mates could take turns firing the three-inch fiftys. I wondered if I would get even four hours sleep before my next watch.

Gunner's Mate Chief Strickland selected Alaska as the first gunner up. On his first shot, Alaska blew the windsock out of the sky. Lightning Lenny had no choice but to secure from GQ and set the regular underway watch. Alaska became an instant hero in 02 berthing for bringing the gun shoot to a fast finish. Everyone promised to buy him a drink when we got to Hong Kong.

That night, Cool and I stood the mid-watch. Mr. Barker had the deck, and Ensign Benson had the conn. We steamed all night below the Taiwan Strait in the South China Sea approaching mainland China.

To avoid antagonizing the communist Chinese, we had to ensure that the ship stayed inside a narrow corridor.

Just after dawn, I shot visual bearings on a lighthouse and a distant mountain peak. Cool got one radar range from the coastline, and he plotted all the lines on the chart. There is a beauty to watching a fix take shape. Each line of position is like one person's opinion, not worth much by itself, but when they all cross at the same spot, it's like getting confirmation from three different sources. In the unanimous opinion of these three lines, we were right on top of a channel buoy.

Cool and I looked at each other. We ran out to the port wing and looked over the side, and there it was. The buoy was right at the ship's waterline. Any closer and it would have been scraping paint off our hull. We watched as the buoy trailed away astern. None of the lookouts had reported it. If we had run over it, we would have broken our screw, lost steerageway, and drifted out of the corridor, possibly sparking an international incident with the Chinese. That would have been followed by a repair period in the yards and an all-expense-paid trip to my sentence in Portsmouth Naval Prison.

"Leas' we know where we at," Cool said as I erased the fix.

Hong Kong was the most beautiful city I had seen in Asia. If Tokyo reminded me of LA, Hong Kong was more like San Francisco, built on hills with a modern skyline. We dropped anchor in the busy harbor. The crew secured from sea and anchor detail and mustered on the fantail.

"USE YOUR HEAD, AND USE A CONDOM," Mr. Crookshank announced. "DON'T SMOKE POT. STAY TOGETHER, ALWAYS IN PAIRS. STAY OUT OF THE WAN CHAI DISTRICT. WE HAVE REPORTS OF AMERICAN SAILORS GETTING KNOCKOUT DROPS IN THEIR DRINKS. THEY'LL SLIP YOU A MICKEY, AND YOU'LL WAKE UP LATER—MINUS YOUR MONEY."

Hutchinson and I got aboard the third liberty boat. At Fenwick pier, we were surrounded by hawkers handing out flyers for clubs or discount coupons for the tailor shops along Queen's Road. We exchanged our money for Hong Kong dollars at a rate of five HK to one. Swampass was standing in line outside a tattoo parlor.

"I'm gettin' that one," he said. He pointed at a picture in the window—two pigs screwing over the words: *Makin' Bacon*.

"Tasteful," Hutchinson said.

"This time, make sure they spell it right," I said.

"Ever think about gettin' a tattoo?" Hutchinson asked me.

"Scars are free. Why buy one?"

"Scars come with better stories. Who needs identifying marks? First thing they do when you go to jail is take photos of all your tattoos."

"You planning on going to jail?"

"No, but why take chances?"

We went to the Chin Brothers tailor shop on Gloucester Road. Hutchinson got measured for a charcoal gray suit. I ordered a custom-made uniform.

When the tailor asked my rank, I said quartermaster third. With the recommendation from Mr. Tobias, I would have my crow soon enough. We paid in advance. Instead of a cash register, the shopkeeper used an abacus. We got handwritten receipts.

While we were wandering around, Hutchinson spotted an ivory ball in a shop window. It was the size of a grapefruit, carved from one piece, with decorative openings that revealed another smaller freewheeling ball inside the first and an even smaller third ball inside the second. He bought it for 250 HK.

We stopped for a beer in the bar at the Luk Kwok Hotel. Then, we caught a tram to Victoria Peak and spent the late afternoon climbing to the top. Cloud formations filled the sky. Hutchinson had his camera. We got a spectacular view of the city and the harbor with Kowloon and the mainland on the other side. The lights came on at sunset, reflecting on the water.

We had dinner at the China Fleet Club, the serviceman's bar, where drinks were forty cents. It was a big place, with a dance floor and no band. There was hardly anybody there, so we left.

"We're already in the Wan Chai district," Hutchinson said. "Doesn't look so bad."

We went into a place called Club San Francisco Topless. The clientele was all Chinese, except for Loophole and Bootleg at a table close to the stage. We sat with them and ordered drinks from a waitress. A topless girl danced on stage, gyrating to the tinny stereo speakers. When her act ended, Hutchinson noticed his ivory ball was missing.

"GOD DAMN IT!" he said.

He was on his feet, looking under our table and other tables. Customers stared at us. A Chinese guy in a shiny silk suit and yellow tie glided toward us.

"My name is Lou," he said. "I think you leave now, yes?"

"Not without mah ball, man," Hutchinson replied.

Lou said something in Chinese, and four Chinese bouncers came to our table. Bootleg got into a wobbly praying mantis stance.

"You're flirtin' with death, boys," he said.

A bouncer gave him a leg sweep, and Bootleg hit the deck like a sack of sand.

"You leave now," Lou said, "and take Bruce Lee with you."

The bouncers steered us through a back door that led outside to an alley. Lou locked the door behind us.

"Let's find another club," Loophole said. "Come on, Bootleg."

They headed toward the waterfront. Hutchinson and I walked back to the China Fleet Club.

"Buy you a drink, Jeff?" I asked.

"Make it bourbon."

The jukebox was playing an Isley Brothers tune, "Who's That Lady?" Three blue-eyed girls, two blondes and a brunette, sat at a table talking. They had British accents.

"Let's see if they want to dance," I said.

"Nah," Hutchinson replied.

"Look, man, I know you lost money on that ivory ball, but these British babes might cheer you up."

"Ah don't feel like it."

"Come on. It's been a long time since we had a conversation with girls who speak good English. Hell, they *are* English."

Hutchinson shrugged and said:

"Why not?"

The girls stopped talking as we approached the table. None of them smiled.

"Hello," I said, "my name's Gary, and this is Jeff."

"Charmed," said the brunette in a tone of voice that suggested she wasn't.

"How about a dance? They're playing my favorite song."

The brunette looked me up and down.

"Are you asking all three of us?" she asked.

"Oh, Vanessa," said one of the blondes, giggling.

"Sure," I replied. "One at a time."

"Thank you, no," Vanessa said.

"Well, how about you?" Hutchinson said to the closest blonde. "What's your name?"

"Liz."

"Would you like to dance, Liz?"

"Liz," Vanessa said, "remember what mother said."

"Thank you," Liz replied to Hutchinson. "I think not."

We were not exactly Hollywood leading men, but these girls were treating us like two Quasimodos. The booze made me practically insult-proof.

"What about you?" I said to the third one. "Did mother say anything to you?"

"Ignore him, Maggie," Vanessa said before turning back to me. "I think you'd best leave. We're *not* interested."

"It never hurts to ask," I said. "It was a pleasure meeting you ladies."

"Pity I can't say the same," Vanessa replied.

She pronounced *can't* so that it rhymed with *want*.

"You could," I said, "if you were as big a liar as I am."

Her mouth dropped open.

"Ah heard the British can be snobby," Hutchinson said when we got back to our table, "but *damn!*"

"Look," I said, pointing toward the dance floor.

Vanessa and Liz were dancing with each other. The jukebox was playing "Soul Makossa." Hutchinson swallowed the last of his bourbon.

"Let's get out there," he said. "This'll either make 'em laugh or piss 'em off."

We went on the dance floor and danced over to them. Vanessa looked at me with ice-cold blue eyes.

"You had your chance, honey," Hutchinson said to her. "He's all mine now."

Vanessa and Liz went back to their table. They spoke to Maggie, picked up their purses, and left.

"You were right, Shortcut," Hutchinson said. "That did cheer me up. *How about another drink?*"

CHAPTER 26

Third-Class Exam

Fleet command ordered us to leave Hong Kong ahead of schedule. Tropical storm Elaine was coming our way, and ships are safer at sea during storms than in port dragging anchor and banging into each other. A bottle with a cork in it will ride out the wildest storm, so long as it doesn't spring a leak or hit anything harder than water. A lot of guys were angry because they had paid for clothing they couldn't pick up from the Hong Kong tailors.

"Lightning Lenny volunteered us for two weeks of UNREPS," Billings said over his spaghetti supper. "Next thing you know, we'll be getting a message from fleet command telling us to head for Yokosuka instead of Olongapo."

At the next table, Swampass stopped shoveling noodles into his face. He looked at us with wide eyes.

"*Yokosuka*?" he said. His new *Makin' Bacon* tattoo on his left arm looked red and infected, but it was spelled right. Tomato sauce ran down his chin.

"Careful, Swampass," Billings said. "You're getting some of that in your mouth."

"What about Yokosuka?" Bootleg asked, looking up from his tray.

"Goddamn fleet command is sending us to Yokosuka instead of Olongapo," Swampass replied.

"We're not going to Olongapo?" Stringbean asked.

"Olongapo is canceled," Bootleg said. "We're going back to Yokosuka."

"*Son of a bitch!*" Gink said, and they all started jabbering at once.

"Sharp as bowling balls," Billings muttered, shaking his head. "If those clowns ever agreed with me on anything, I'd know I was wrong."

"Aren't you going to tell 'em?" I asked.

"More fun to see how fast they spread the word," Billings said quietly. "You know, like a science experiment."

We did four UNREPS the next day. Brogan and I traded off steering every two hours. After we secured from RAS detail, I went down to 02 berthing. The Yokosuka rumor had spread. Alaska was shouting: *I'll bet Yokosuka was Lightning Lenny's idea!*

Mr. Crookshank's voice came over the 1MC.

"THIS IS THE XO. MOST OF THE TAILORS IN HONG KONG ARE HONEST. THEY WILL SEND

YOUR CLOTHING ORDERS ON TO THE SHIP. BY THE WAY, THERE IS NO TRUTH TO THE SCUTTLEBUTT THAT WE ARE HEADING TO YOKOSUKA. AFTER WE COMPLETE THIS SERIES OF UNREPS, OUR NEXT PORT OF CALL WILL BE SUBIC BAY. THAT IS ALL."

"I knew it was bullshit," Estorga said, "because it came from Bootleg."

We returned to Subic Bay in November. Due to our Big E status, we got a mooring closer to the main gate. The XO was right about the tailors. Everyone received his clothing order—everyone but Hutchinson and me. I held on to my receipt from the Chin Brothers as an expensive souvenir.

The petty officer third exams were to be held on the mess decks at 1400. I stood in line behind Kickback and Mooney and some other E-3s waiting to get in. Kip was sitting at a table looking at the list of recommended seamen.

"Your name is not on the list, Thorpe," he said.

"Mr. Tobias recommended me, sir. He told me himself."

"You'd better go find him, then. The test starts in fifteen minutes."

I ran up the ladders to the operations office on the 06 level. I was afraid Mr. Tobias might be in officer's country, but he was sitting at his desk.

"Excuse me, Mr. Tobias," I said. "The third-class test is about to start, and Mr. Priskett says he doesn't show my recommendation on his list."

"That's impossible," he said. "I gave that recommendation to Chief Lasko to take to the ship's office."

He picked up his phone, called the quarterdeck, and had Chief Lasko paged over the 1MC. The chief reported to Mr. Tobias's office in five minutes.

"Thorpe is under the impression that there has been some finagling with his recommendation," Mr. Tobias said. "Didn't you to deliver it to the ship's office?"

Chief Lasko's crossed eyes shifted from Mr. Tobias to me and back to Mr. Tobias.

"I'm sure if you told me to deliver it, sir, I delivered it," he said.

"Let's go down to the ship's office," Mr. Tobias said.

We walked down to the 01 level. Hayashi and Estorga were on duty.

"We're looking for Thorpe's recommendation for the third-class exam," Mr. Tobias told them.

"We already passed them on to Mr. Priskett, sir," Hayashi answered. "If they were here, they'd be in this file drawer."

He opened the drawer. It was empty. Crapshoot's voice echoed over the 1MC.

"THE PETTY OFFICER THIRD EXAMS ARE NOW COMMENCING ON THE MESS DECKS."

"Sorry, Thorpe," Mr. Tobias said. "It's only six months until the next third-class exam."

I went back to the mess decks to make sure that Kip hadn't overlooked my name. Kip showed me the list. My name wasn't on it. I gave it one last try.

"Mr. Priskett, we both know Mr. Tobias recommended me. Isn't there any way I can take the test now, and we can straighten out the paperwork later?"

"I only know what's on this list, Thorpe," Kip replied.

He might as well have said DILLIGAF. It was Meech and the early chow passes all over again, except instead of a late meal, it was a six-month wait. It was typical Navy bullshit—no connection between goals and actions, apathy camouflaged as procedure. Whether or not I had been recommended or could pass the test was less important than the location of a goddamn piece of paper.

Lightning Lenny decided to throw a ship's party "to improve morale." They rented out the Cherry Club. Officers do not normally fraternize with enlisted men, but all the gentry and the chiefs were there. Estorga and I sat near a window with a view of Magsaysay Drive. Across the street, a sailor and a marine came falling out through the door of New Jolo's, fighting.

"I missed this place," Estorga said.

Everyone was either drunk or getting there, including the gentry. Goddammit Jim, Raccoon Face, Kip, and Ensign Benson sat at a table laughing at something Lightning Lenny said. Chief Lasko and Chief Hackburn wore noisy Hawaiian shirts in a nearby booth, with two girls and a pitcher of mojos.

"Here's to the Navy, Del," Chief Hackburn said, hoisting his glass.

"Roger that, Leo," Chief Lasko replied.

"First girl I ever saw on Hackburn's arm that wasn't a tattoo," Estorga said to me.

"What a pair," I said. "Neither one could make the other seem worse."

"You still pissed off about that recommendation?"

"I could get promoted faster working at McDonald's."

"That's my mojo you're drinking, Bootleg," Thumbs said, seated at the next table.

"You not mess with him," said the girl sitting with Bootleg. "He ship's instructor."

"Ship's instructor?" Doglike asked. "What kind of ship's instructor?"

"Kung-fu. Black belt."

They all laughed. Bootleg's face turned red. Gink snapped a bar girl's bra strap. She pulled a hairbrush out of her purse and used it to beat Thumbs. Thumbs yelled: *'It wasn't me!'* Doglike laughed. Thumbs punched him. Doglike punched back, and the fight was on. Meech and Snyder broke them up, and Needler put them on report. Carranza staggered up to Mr. Sforzando and said: 'How's it goin', Raccoon Face?' Mr. Sforzando put him on report. The party went downhill from there.

When Estorga and I went back to the ship, Radford was drunk and stumbling up the brow ahead of us. Chief Bledsoe was standing quarterdeck watch. Radford could barely request permission to come aboard.

"You forgot to salute me," Chief Bledsoe said.

"I ain't about to salute a coon," Radford replied.

Chief Bledsoe put him on report.

The next day was Chief Lasko's duty day. He had the 0800 to noon quarterdeck watch, but he never reported aboard for morning muster. Meech had to take his watch, and Chief Hackburn reported him UA. We were looking out the forward bridge windows when a gray jeep pulled up on the pier.

"It's the chief," Brogan announced.

"He look bad," Cool said, smiling.

Still wearing his Hawaiian shirt, Chief Lasko moved up the brow as slowly as an eighty-seven-year-old man. He squinted at the sunlight. He could hardly see. He made standing erect at the quarterdeck look like a big effort as he and Meech saluted each other.

"Meech be pissed off," Cool said, laughing.

The chief showed up on the bridge ten minutes later, in a clean uniform. His hair was combed. He was smoking a cigarette and bleeding from a cut on his forehead.

"You're bleeding, Chief," Brogan told him.

"Cut myself shaving," he muttered, handing me a piece of paper. "Found this in my locker, Thorpe."

It was my recommendation for third class with Mr. Tobias's signature.

"Sorry, Thorpe," he said. "I don't know how it got in there."

I had an idea how it got there. He put it there and forgot about it.

"What happened, Chief?" Hutchinson asked.

"I met a girl," he said. "She had beautiful long hair that covered one eye, like Veronica Lake."

"Who's Veronica Lake?" Brogan asked.

"When I left this morning, she was still asleep. I pulled her hair back, and she only had one eye. There was this big empty red socket. I thought '*oh fuck*,' and I tried to get out of there without waking her up. But she heard me, so she asks: 'Are you coming back to the bar tonight?' 'Sure,' I say. 'Okay,' she says, 'I'll keep an eye out for you.' *AH HA HA HA HA HA*!"

Mr. Tobias entered the bridge.

"You're late for your watch, Chief," he said. "Do you think you're setting a good example for the men?"

"Why don'tcha get off my ass, huh?" Chief Lasko replied.

I couldn't believe my ears, and judging by the looks on their faces, neither could Cool, Hutchinson, or Brogan. Mr. Tobias stared at the chief.

"Chief, I want you to relieve Meech on the quarterdeck," Mr. Tobias said. "We'll discuss this later in my office. You quartermasters get this bridge cleaned up for captain's mast this morning."

Cool grabbed a broom. Brogan got a foxtail. Hutchinson cleaned the windows. I shined the brass. Needler was on the port wing, setting up for captain's mast. He had a black eye. The story was all over the ship that three unidentified guys, most likely restricted men with axes to grind, had surrounded Needler's rack before reveille. When they started pissing on him, he tried to crawl out. Then, they started kicking him. Since Needler slept in a lower rack in deck berthing, he couldn't identify anything but six legs in bell bottoms and boondockers.

We could hear most of the captain's mast while we cleaned the bridge. Doglike and Thumbs were each awarded the usual 200-dollar fine plus two weeks of restriction. For striking Chief Hackburn, Big Time was restricted to the ship for a week and fined a hundred bucks. Radford received that same punishment for reporting aboard drunk and addressing the duty OOD, Chief Bledsoe, with a racial slur. Carranza got the worst of it. For referring to Mr. Sforzando as Raccoon Face, Carranza got busted down to seaman apprentice with a two-week restriction and a 300-dollar fine. Though all three were drunk at the time of their offenses, Big Time and Radford got off easier than Carranza because they were both E-6 lifers with over three hitches in, and their injured parties were other enlisted men. Carranza was a lower-than-whale-shit non-rate who insulted an officer.

"It's like the plank owners say," Hutchinson said, "different spanks for different ranks."

"What do you think Mr. Tobias will do to the chief?" Brogan asked.

"Nothing much happened to Big Time and Radford," I said, "and they're not chiefs."

"Naw," Cool replied, shaking his head, "Big Time and Radford wasn' talkin' to no officer. The chief be in a world of shit."

At liberty call, we got the answer. When Estorga and I went to the Sampaguita Club for a beer, we ran into Billings.

"I sent a message to BUPERS," Billings said. "Mr. Tobias and Lightning Lenny are recommending a transfer for Quartermaster Chief Delbert Lasko to an alcoholic rehabilitation program as soon as we get back to the States. Mr. Tobias requested a replacement for him."

"I wonder who they're going to stick us with now," I said. "At least Mr. Tobias will recommend me again for third in six months."

"Tobias is leaving, too. He got his orders for a submarine command in Italy. Kip's taking over as navigator."

"God, no. I'd rather have Southcott back."

"Guess what else?" Estorga said.

"I'm afraid to."

"My enlistment's up next month. Chief Skinner gave me the reenlistment speech. I told him I'd ship over."

"*You* would *ship over?*"

"If BUPERS grants my requests. I asked for yeoman 'A' school and a shore command."

"What shore command?"

"Right here in Subic. If it gets me off the *Okmok*, why not? I like the PI."

"You'll be dead before you're thirty."

"I'll be the corpse with the smile. Seriously, man, the Navy has great retirement benefits."

"They give you those benefits for twenty years because they squeeze thirty years out of you in ten. This shit would make anyone old before his time. Look at Chief Lasko."

"My family has always worked government jobs," Estorga said. "I'm already working for the government, anyway, so why not?"

Mr. Tobias departed the *Okmok* a week later. Kip became the navigator and our division officer.

"Mr. Priskett," I said after muster one morning, "will you recommend me for the next third-class exam? Remember, Mr. Tobias had me down for it, but the paperwork got fouled up. I was thinking, if we got the paperwork to the ship's office ahead of time—"

I stopped talking because Kip was shaking his head.

"Your quartermaster skills are good, Thorpe, but your attitude needs work. I'm not convinced you've shown the leadership ability or the proper level of maturity to be a third-class."

Kip didn't care about the long hours I put in standing port and starboard watches. In his eyes, I was just another non-rate, unfit for any work more challenging than scraping, scrubbing, and swabbing.

"So, you're not recommending me, sir?"

Kip scratched his chin.

"How much do you weigh?"

"About 195."

"That's a heavyweight."

"Sir?"

"Chief Skinner is organizing a smoker for our cruise home. It would look good for X and N division if we had someone to represent us. Have you ever done any boxing?"

"Boxing?"

"If you boxed for our division, I might be able to recommend you for third class. What do you say?"

It might be worth going a few rounds for my third-class crow, but I didn't say so right away.

"Who would I have to box?"

"You'd be matched up with someone in your weight class. Shall I have Chief Skinner put you down for it?"

"I'd like to think about it, sir."

"Don't think about it for too long. We have to get you signed up by the end of the week. Now, get back to scraping that starboard bridge wing."

My next quarterdeck watch was with Crapshoot and Chief Hackburn.

"I hear your steamin' buddy didn't get his request for 'A' school and a shore command," Chief Hackburn said, referring to Estorga. "BUPERS said he could have the shore command without the 'A' school, or the 'A' school without the shore command. One or the other, but not both."

"Which one did he pick?"

"He's getting out. It won't be easy finding another man like him. Estorga is a good yeoman, and he also has common sense."

"Well, Chief. Maybe you can get the same deal BUPERS gave Estorga."

"What the fuck are you talking about, Thorpe?"

"One or the other, but not both."

Hackburn kept me hopping, running errands for the rest of the watch. If BUPERS was willing to give Estorga his choice of school or shore command, it meant they didn't care which one he picked. They just didn't want to give him both his requests, so, now, they were losing him. I was glad Estorga was getting out, but the rest of my time in the Navy was going to be pretty bad under Kip, unless I could make third-class. I went to Kip's office. He was sitting at his desk.

"Sir, I'm willing to box in the smoker if you will recommend me for the next round of third-class exams."

"OK, Thorpe," he said. "You've got a deal."

According to Finesse's scale in sick bay, I weighed 202. My only exercise in the last six months was lifting beer bottles. I started working out in the ship's weight room. I ran laps around the second deck. I went down to the hot boiler room in engineering to skip rope and shadowbox. I stuffed my sea bag with blankets, hung it from the overhead, and threw punches at it.

Estorga and I went to the East End. He had a San Miguel. Since I was trying to get in shape, I ordered pineapple juice.

"So, you're not shipping over," I said.

"After BUPERS turned me down, Skinner tried to talk me into it. He can hang it in his ass."

"Going back to the world."

"Yeah, man. Take showers as long as I want."

"Sleep in a real bed."

"Without ninety snoring roommates."

"Eat when you want to. Change jobs if you want to."

"Go to the beach."

"Stay at the beach."

"Live at the beach."

"I lub you, no shit," said a bar girl.

"Sit down, sweetheart," Estorga said.

I left him there and stopped in at the Shamrock. Susie was standing at the bar. She didn't smile when she saw me.

"How's your brother? Is he still playing chess?"

"I hab a new boypriend," she said. "Hello, Albin."

Crimmons stepped up from behind me.

"Hey, Shortcut," he said, and he put his arm around Susie. "Have you met my fiancée? Susie, this is Gary. We're getting married. Lightning Lenny approved my request chit today."

Susie's eyes opened wide. She looked frightened. Maybe she thought I would talk Crimmons out of marrying her and ruin her chance to go to the States.

"Congratulations, Crim—I mean, Alvin."

"Thanks, man. Grab a girl, and let's celebrate. Come back to the table, honey."

"I come right back, Albin," Susie said.

"Okay. Join us, Shortcut. I'm sitting over there, with Mooney and Stringbean and Swampass. They're all engaged to Filipino girls, too."

Crimmons walked back to the table. The bartender handed Susie four bottles of San Miguel.

"I hab to go now," she said.

Susie took the beers to the table. She sat down beside Crimmons and held his hand. Another girl spoke to me.

"You looking por girlpriend? I lub you, no shit."

CHAPTER 27

Smoker

WESTPAC was over. We received orders from fleet command to get underway for California. Mr. Kempton conned the *Okmok* through the Mindoro Strait at night. We steamed through the Sibuyan Sea, heading east to the Pacific. The crew remained at sea and anchor detail for fifteen hours. Brogan and I traded places on the helm the whole time. Lightning Lenny set the regular underway watch as we entered international waters. He got out of his captain's chair to leave the bridge, stopping at the console to speak to me.

"You've come a long way in your helmsman skills," he said. "You responded well to some fast commands back there. I'm going to write a letter of commendation for your service record."

"Thank you, Captain," I said.

"Think nothing of it, Brogan."

I almost told him I wasn't Brogan, but I stopped when I saw Mr. Kempton standing behind him, looking at me and shaking his head. Goddammit

Jim would make sure that the right commendation letter got into the right service jacket, and I would make sure Goddammit Jim made sure.

We were in the middle of the Pacific on December 7th, the day the smoker was scheduled, Pearl Harbor Day. I was down to 195 pounds for the weigh-in the day before. Lightning Lenny declared holiday routine, which meant that, except for the normal underway watch, the crew had the day off. There was no work and no drills, and the crew was allowed to wear t-shirts. The POD came out with the names, weights, and hometowns of the smoker participants. It was the first time any of us had seen who we were going to be matched with. Estorga woke me up.

"Hey, Shortcut, wake up, man. Have you seen the POD?"

"What are you waking me up for? It's holiday routine."

"Look at this," he said, shaking the POD at me.

There it was in black and white. The name next to mine was Malolo. For a second, I thought Estorga gundecked a phony POD for laughs.

"Is this a joke?" I asked.

"If it is, you're the punchline," Estorga replied. "Remember what Malolo did to that marine in the Alliance Club that night?"

"But Malolo's a mauler, and this is a boxing match. There are rules, you know? Besides, we're shipmates, Malolo and me. He doesn't have anything against me. He'll probably fight fair, right?"

"Yeah," Estorga said with no enthusiasm, "sure."

At morning chow, everyone stared at me like I was on death row. Only Cool had something to say.

"Got twenty bucks on you, Shortcut."

"Thanks, Cool,"

"Swampass give me five to one odds. Couldn' resis'."

I talked to Kip after muster.

"Mr. Priskett, how did I get matched up with Malolo?"

"He was the only volunteer in your weight class, Thorpe."

"He has thirty-five pounds on me, sir,"

"But you have the height advantage, so you have the reach. I know you're going to make X and N division proud."

I kept picturing Malolo wrestling that crocodile at Pauline's. To clear my mind, I ran laps around the second deck. Lightning Lenny had a morning swim call. We turned off the engines, and anybody who wanted to could take a swim in the Pacific. I went in with about thirty guys. I thought a shark might get me, but no such luck. I skipped afternoon chow. I put on my high-school gym trunks, a sweatshirt, and sneakers, and went up to the hangar bay. The deck apes had set up a regulation-size boxing ring on the fantail.

The boatswain's pipe came over the 1MC followed by the announcement.

"THE SMOKER WILL COMMENCE ON THE FANTAIL AT 1300. THAT IS, THE SMOKER WILL COMMENCE ON THE FANTAIL AT 1300."

Except for the underway watch, the whole crew was seated around the boxing ring. Snyder was acting as second in the blue corner. Sweeny was the second in the red corner. Mr. Sforzando was the referee and ring announcer. Chief Lasko was the timekeeper. Finesse was the ring physician. Mr. Crookshank, Mr. Kempton, and Chief Skinner were the judges. They had seats closest to the ring, next to Lightning Lenny.

I watched the early bouts from a distance. First came the flyweights. Lim knocked out Deglado in the second round. Next were the welterweights. Loophole beat Screwball on points. Bootleg lost the middleweight match to Crapshoot despite his martial arts skills. The next contest was the light-heavyweight match between Doglike and Thumbs. They glared at each other from their corners with mutual hatred.

"Okay," Raccoon Face said from the center of the ring. "We have three rounds at three minutes each. In case of a knockdown, go to a neutral corner. There is a mandatory eight count. No hitting below the belt. No rabbit punches. No slaps with the open glove. Rounds will be judged on the number of punches and the velocity of punches landed."

Chief Lasko rang the bell. In no time, Doglike and Thumbs turned it into a brawl, kicking and biting. Needler helped Snyder and Sweeny break them up. Doglike was yelling as they dragged him away.

"WHAT'S THE MATTER? I DIDN'T THROW NO RABBIT PUNCHES. LEMME GO, GODDAMMIT."

The crew hooted and laughed. It was time for the heavyweights. I felt like a gladiator about to be thrown to the lions. I walked out to the red corner and took off my sweatshirt. Finesse handed me a plastic mouth protector, and Sweeny helped me lace on the gloves. Malolo stepped into the ring wearing a t-shirt and black trunks, his deadpan face as lifeless as one of those gigantic stone heads on Easter Island. Raccoon Face spoke into the microphone.

"In the blue corner, weighing 230 pounds, from Si' Ufaga, American Samoa, Boatswain's Mate Third Class Nuli Malolo."

The deck apes went wild.

"KILL HIM, MALOLO!" Carranza yelled.

"RIP HIS HEAD OFF!" Swampass screamed.

"And in the red corner, weighing 195 pounds, from Seal Beach, California, Quartermaster Seaman Gary 'Shortcut' Thorpe."

Estorga, Cool, Billings, and Brogan yelled for me—not much of a cheering section. They couldn't drown out the rest of the crew howling and laying last-minute bets against me. Malolo and I stepped into the center of the ring, and we tapped gloves. I smiled. Malolo wasn't smiling. I really wanted to be somewhere else.

Raccoon Face repeated the rules for us. We returned to our corners. Chief Lasko rang the bell for the first round, and Malolo and I moved toward each other. I danced around, keeping my hands up and my elbows in. Malolo moved slowly, sizing me up, reacting rather than attacking. I figured he was saving himself for the later rounds. I threw out my left, measuring him, trying to eat up the clock.

The crew didn't like that. Loophole, Stringbean, and Chief Bledsoe were shouting, goading us on. They wanted blood—my blood. Then, Malolo caught me in the nose with a fast left jab, and I saw colors. He followed up with a right hook to my ribs. Blood was streaming out of my nose down my chest. I pushed him off and danced away, holding my hands high. Malolo came at me with his guard down, so I gave him a left jab in the nose and a right cross to the head. It didn't faze him, but he stopped coming forward, giving me a chance to catch my breath. Chief Lasko rang the bell, signaling the end of round one.

"Straighten out your legs while you're sitting," Sweeny said, sponging the blood off me. "He's strong, but you've got the stamina. You gotta keep moving, and you gotta keep *him* moving."

In round two, I kept moving—backwards. I threw jabs at Malolo's face, but they didn't take anything out of him. I caught glimpses of Hoodwink and Alaska, laughing and pointing. Malolo missed me with a swing, and that gave me confidence. It shouldn't have. I gave him a right hook to the head. He came back with an uppercut to my chin that almost put my lights out. If he had followed through with another wallop, he could have finished me off right then.

Sweeny was right. Malolo didn't have a lot of stamina. He smoked a lot on watch. He had some flab on him. He was older than me, too, at least twenty-three. He was running short of wind. So far, this was saving me. Malolo threw a hard right hook that would have hurt if it hadn't glanced off my left arm. I popped him in the head twice with a left and a right, but Malolo had a head like cement. I didn't have the strength to knock him out. I hoped I was scoring points. Then, Malolo caught me with a stiff left. I could hear Chief Hackburn's wicked cackle.

"*YEAH!*" he yelled. "NOW HOOK HIM! *HOOK HIM!*"

He hooked me. I threw up my hands and tucked in my chin. Was this round ever going to end? It felt like we had been out there for half an hour. I recognized the voices of Radford, Needler, and Mr. Osterkamp, all rooting for Malolo. We exchanged a couple more worthless blows before the bell finally rang. As I went back to my corner, I caught a glimpse of Lightning Lenny picking his nose. Finesse came over and peered into my eyes.

"You're not moving around enough," Sweeny said, squirting water from a plastic bottle into my mouth. "You can't overpower him. You gotta out-maneuver him. He's dropping his guard. *That's* when you have to hit him. Keep your eye on his right. He's killing you with his right."

In the third round, my advantage was that Malolo was tiring, so it was becoming harder for him to throw punches upward to hit me in the head. His corner must have advised him to work on giving me body shots to take the wind out of me. I kept dancing around, making him move and tiring him out. Malolo was slowing up, not following me. There were moments when we were both waiting for each other to do something. We were breathing hard. The crowd booed. Malolo came at me with his guard down, and I remembered the old punchiments technique. I tagged him in the face with a flam.

"THAT'S IT," Estorga yelled. "NAIL HIM!"

I gave him a right-left-right triplet on his jaw. He stumbled.

"GET DOWN, SHORTCUT," Cool yelled.

Malolo was out of wind. His punches were losing force. His legs were loose, and he left himself open. That was when I should have moved in on him, but I was slowing down, too. Booing voices were all around us as we circled each other. I had fleeting impressions of faces—Skidmore, Kickback, Goldbrick, Coatrack, Loophole, Screwball, Crimmons, Gink, Big Time, Chief Graves, Koslowski, Carranza, Crapshoot, Kip, and Ensign Benson. I ducked and moved, but I never took my eyes off Malolo. I kept my hands high and my elbows in, jabbing him with my left whenever I got a chance. Malolo wasn't so scary anymore.

Then, the final bell rang.

I sat down in my corner. Mr. Crookshank, Mr. Kempton, and Chief Skinner deliberated with Raccoon Face. Billings sent me a hand semaphore message: NICE FIGHT. Raccoon Face came to my corner with the microphone and told me to stand up.

"The winner and heavyweight champ of the *Okmok*," Raccoon Face announced, holding up my right glove, "Quartermaster Gary 'Shortcut' Thorpe."

Cool was laughing, and Swampass was frowning. I went to the 02 berthing head for a shower. I looked in the mirror. My nose was swollen. It didn't hurt, though. My reflection grinned back at me. I felt great.

In the evening chow line, my shipmates stepped aside and let me cut ahead of them. Some of them wanted to shake hands. I didn't expect all this respect. Cool had collected a hundred bucks from Swampass. He thanked me for winning it for him, but he didn't offer to share any. I sat with Finesse and Estorga.

"I didn't know you had it in you, Shortcut," Finesse said. "Malolo passed out after the fight from sheer exhaustion."

"How ya feel, Champ?" Estorga asked.

"Three three-minute rounds make nine minutes," I replied. "But it felt more like ninety."

"Now that you mention it," Finesse said, "Chief Lasko got so caught up watching you guys, he let the second round go on almost an extra minute before he rang the bell."

After chow, I went to the bridge to relieve Hutchinson. He missed the fight because he had the watch. Mr. Kempton walked to the chart table.

"Congratulations, Thorpe," he said, shaking my hand. "You obviously refrained from demolishing Malolo."

That didn't seem obvious to me, but I didn't contradict him.

"Thank you, sir."

Since Malolo collapsed after the fight, the crew saw me as some kind of honorable good sport for holding back on him when he was open during that final round. They didn't see me for what I really was—a guy after his third-class crow, too tired to take advantage of the situation and just trying to keep himself from getting creamed. That's how false reputations get made.

The *Okmok* arrived in Concord a week before Christmas. Chief Lasko was detached from the crew and shipped off to the alcoholic rehab unit of Oakland Naval Hospital. His replacement was Quartermaster First Class Barlow, a twelve-year lifer out of Charleston, South Carolina. He was thin, with a butch haircut and a blank face on a bucket head. Barlow hadn't seen a ship in six years. He treated the quartermaster gang like we were a bunch of raw boots just out of 'A' school.

"I don't care if you guys have a WESTPAC under your belts," he said on the day we met him. "You're just a bunch of non-rates. Now, let's turn to and get a field day going on this bridge."

Hutchinson and Brogan went outside to scrape paint on the bridge wings. Cool shined brass, and I swabbed the deck.

"This just keeps getting worse," I said to Cool.

"Anotha one-way muthafucka," he replied.

When Barlow left the bridge, we met up in the chart house. Brogan threw a paper airplane he made from a piece of classified message traffic. Hutchinson sang the final verse of his own version of "The Twelve Days of Christmas:"

> *On my twelfth captain's mast,*
> *Lightning Lenny gave to me:*
> *Twelve midnight watches,*
> *Eleven decks a'swabbing,*
> *Ten heads a'scrubbing,*
> *Nine foxtails dusting,*
> *Eight bulkheads scraping,*
> *Seven days restriction,*
> *Six weeks mess cooking,*
> *Five Brasso rags!*
> *Four days in the brig,*
> *Three UNREPS,*
> *Two paygrade busts,*
> *And an all-day working party.*

Hutchinson handed me an envelope with the words *Merry Christmas to Shortcut* written on it. Inside was a photo of Mr. Southcott's motorcycle captured in midair, just before splashdown. On the back of the photo, Hutchinson had written: *Kawasaki Float Test, 1974. Photo by J.D. Hutchinson.*

"Thanks, Jeff," I said. "Merry Christmas."

The next morning, on the bridge, Kip handed me a Zippo lighter with the image of the *Okmok* crashing through the waves above the ship's motto, *To Serve, and Serve, and Serve.* My name was engraved on it along with the words: HEAVYWEIGHT CHAMP—1974 *OKMOK* SMOKER. As usual, every silver lining had a cloud.

"Thank you, Mr. Priskett," I said. "I was wondering if you had time to type up my recommendation for third-class?"

"No, Thorpe, I haven't."

"Well, sir, I sure would like to get that taken care of as soon as possible. I'd hate to miss the next test because of another paperwork foul up."

"I have more important things to think about."

I didn't give up so easily.

"We had an agreement, sir. If I fought in the smoker, you were going to —"

"Don't you presume to speak to me that way, Seaman. Start scraping that starboard bridge wing."

After knockoff in 02 berthing, Hoodwink, Finesse, Alaska, and Billings were playing casino and talking politics.

"Nixon fucked up on Watergate," Alaska said, "but Vietnam was mostly LBJ's fault. Remember the '64 election? Goldwater wanted to either take the war to the North Vietnamese or withdraw."

"Goldwater wanted to use nuclear weapons to clear the jungle supply routes," Finesse replied.

"Right. The Democrats called him a warmonger. They said he would nuke Hanoi. Remember that campaign ad with the little girl picking daisies and the mushroom cloud? LBJ was the goddamn *peace candidate!* He won by a landslide, and look what happened. Every move he made escalated the war. We were barely in it when JFK was killed."

"At least LBJ had enough sense not to run again," Finesse said. "What politician today would refuse to run again just because he didn't deliver on a campaign promise?"

"Back then, when the President said something, people *believed* him," Alaska said. "Those days are gone."

"Are you guys going to play cards or not?" Hoodwink asked.

"If the real truth ever came out about the Kennedy assassination," Billings said, "probably nobody would believe it. Kennedy gave those generals the green light to overthrow the Diem regime *three weeks before he died*. Nobody ever talks about that."

"He had bigger enemies than the Diem brothers," Alaska replied. "The mob, the Cubans, the KGB, the CIA, even LBJ."

"A guy dies and goes to heaven," Finesse said. "God grants him one wish, any wish. So, the guy says: 'I only want to know one thing, who killed Kennedy?' God says: 'It was Oswald.' So, the guy says to himself: 'This conspiracy goes higher than I thought.'"

"Knock off the conspiracy bullshit," Hoodwink said. "Oswald shot him."

"You *buy* that story?" Alaska asked. "You think he was shot by a lone nut, who was shot two days later by another lone nut, who died in prison?"

"Why not? If Oswald was innocent, why did he shoot that cop?" Hoodwink asked.

"I admit Oswald shot Kennedy, but there was another shooter, too, and that makes it a conspiracy." Alaska said.

"Maybe not," Billings said. "Remember, Kennedy had all those enemies. Why couldn't two independent killers, with no connection to each other, show up same time, same day?"

"If it wasn't a conspiracy," Alaska said, "why did Ruby kill Oswald?"

"He said he did it for Jackie," Hoodwink replied.

"*That's it*," Finesse said. "It was Jackie!"

"What was Jackie?" Alaska asked.

"The second shooter."

"WHAT?" Alaska and Hoodwink said simultaneously.

"Sure. She was pissed off because Jack was screwing Marilyn Monroe. Oldest reason in the world."

"Yeah," Billings said. "She could have had a pistol hidden in her pillbox hat. Who would have searched her?"

"It all fits."

"Fuck you guys," Alaska said.

"THE MOBILE CANTEEN IS ON THE PIER."

"Get us two Cokes, Alaska," Hoodwink said. "You fly. I'll buy."

"Get it yourself."

"Your mother."

Loophole, Crapshoot, and Hankins rented an old three-bedroom house on Kentucky Street in Vallejo. They called it the Dilligaf Yacht Club. Since they were all in different duty sections, two of them were there most nights. A lot of the crew hung out there when we were tied up at Mare Island, but it was a short drive from Concord. One day, after liberty call, Estorga and I drove over there in his Plymouth Satellite. Estorga was getting short. He sold Loophole his pea coat on credit, and he wanted his cash before he got discharged.

"Kip backed out of our deal," I said as we went down the road. "All I got was a damn lighter, and I don't even smoke."

"Why do you think they say officers *and* men?" Estorga asked, pulling out a cigarette. "Say, let me see that lighter, man."

I took the Zippo out of my shirt pocket and handed it to him. Estorga lit his cigarette and looked at it.

"This is kind of cool, like a little trophy."

"I wish I had Kip in that ring for three rounds, instead of Malolo."

"Kip'll get his. Hang in there."

"I'm going to put in a chit for a transfer to another ship. Any ship."

When we got to Kentucky Street, Hankins was riding a motorcycle around the front yard in his boxers, boondockers, and goggles. He was digging a circle of dirt into what was left of the dead lawn. A Moody Blues tune, "Question," was booming out through the windows from inside the house. We walked in on Loophole, Bootleg, Crimmons, and Billings playing poker in the center of the living room. They were surrounded by empty booze bottles, overflowing ashtrays, and old pizza boxes.

Hutchinson and Brogan were sitting on the couch, smoking a joint.

"Later, guys. Gotta meet Ultra for dinner," Brogan said, and he left.

"Who's Ultra?" I asked.

"Some hippie fortune teller chick Brogan met in Concord," Hutchinson replied. "Calls herself Ultra Enigmata. Her real name is Joan Sneed. Smells like patchouli oil."

"She saw him coming," Bootleg said. "Brogan's a sucker."

"Have a beer, Shortcut," Billings offered. "They're in the kitchen, and get me one, too, will ya?"

"Sure, Billy. Hey, Crimmons, how are the wedding plans coming?"

"Slow," Crimmons replied. "You wouldn't believe how much bullshit Navy paperwork it takes to get her over here. At first, she said she wouldn't come without her mother. The XO says it'll take another three months to approve that. Now, she says she won't leave without her little brothers and her sister. I've been sending her half my pay."

"You're too good for your own good, Crim," Billings said.

"She saw you coming," Bootleg added. "You're a sucker, Crimmons."

I got beers for myself and Billings and Estorga. We had to wait for Loophole to win two hands before Estorga got his cash. Estorga gave me a nod toward the door, and we left. Hankins was still outside, digging the circle deeper into the dirt. Estorga shook his head.

"This place is going to get raided," he said.

We drove to the EM club on base, got a table, and ordered two beers. Estorga raised his beer mug. "Here's to civilian life. Seven days and a wake up. I'm a one-digit midget."

"You remember Susie from the Shamrock?" I asked.

"Yeah."

"That's who Crimmons is engaged to."

"Sounds like a personal problem."

The next week, Estorga got his discharge and went home.

CHAPTER 28

Aloha, Okmok

When I was seven, my dad took me to one of those rinky-dink traveling carnivals with a Ferris wheel, a rickety roller-coaster, and shooting galleries. I threw three darts and popped three balloons, winning my choice of any of the cheap trinkets on display. I picked out a three-inch tin sailor painted white. A blue anchor was painted on the chest of his tin sweater. His hands were in the pockets of his tin bell bottoms. His tin sailor hat was cocked on a jaunty angle.

On our way home, we got stuck in a traffic jam. Every car came to a standstill. Some guy behind us was honking his horn. Nobody could go anywhere, but this guy kept honking. Dad turned off the engine, got out of the car, and walked back there. Dad had a few words with the guy through his open window. Then, he came back and sat behind the wheel. There was no more honking.

"What did you say to him?" I asked.

"I said: 'My name's Roy Thorpe. Do I know you?' He said: 'No.' So, I said: 'You lean on that horn one more time, and we're gonna get acquainted.'"

For the first two months of 1975, the *Okmok* had a refit period at the Bethlehem shipyard in San Francisco. Life was boring and routine. We scraped, and we painted. One morning in March, I was having breakfast with Billings.

"The Navy picked up Graff in Washington D.C. and Stretch in Seattle," he told me. "They went to their hometowns. You can't go to your hometown. That's the first place the feds look. They never stop looking for you. It might take a year or five years, but they never quit. It's worse for us radiomen because we have secret clearances. The rest of you guys at least get thirty days UA before you're considered AWOL. With us, it's twenty-four hours. There's no future in going over the hill. You have to spend the rest of your life looking over your shoulder."

"What happens to them now?" I asked.

"The brig. And when they get out, their enlistment picks up right where it left off. Stretch might get a hardship discharge because his mom's sick and his dad's dead."

Cool sat down with his tray. He was grinning.

"What are you so happy about?" I asked.

"I axed Kip to recommen' me for 'A' school. Told him Al and Mr. Tobias was gon' send me, but Kip say my hitch be up in eleven months. Wouldn' make no sense to send me to 'A' school unless I ship over. Ship over, my ass. I put in for a swap with some dude aboard the *Kilauea*, and Kip signed off on it. I'ma be gone tomorrow."

That afternoon, I put in a request chit for a transfer to any duty station, but Kip shot it down.

"You're not going anywhere for the rest of your hitch, Thorpe," he said.

The next morning at muster, Cool was gone. Hutchinson and Hankins weren't there, either. Kip told us they had been arrested for drug possession. Barlow had taken Skidmore's position as senior division petty officer, so he read the POD. My name was in it, along with Carranza, Bootleg, and Kickback. We were to report to the mess decks at 1300. When I got there, Mr. Kempton and Kip were sitting at a table. Needler was passing out papers.

"You men have all been selected for the Special Weapons Team," Needler told us. "Go ahead and sign these."

While most of them signed the documents, I read mine. It was a security clearance. Among other things, it said: *…as a member of the Special Weapons Team, the undersigned will be responsible for a Colt .45 during all security breaches. During Operation Fairchild, the undersigned will engage and neutralize any person or persons without an orange authorization badge.*

"Engage and neutralize" were government euphemisms for shoot and kill. The last thing I signed was my enlistment contract. I knew too well how many rights I had signed away. If I had any rights left, I wasn't eager to sign those away, too.

All the rest of the guys passed in their papers. I passed mine forward unsigned. Needler collected them. Kip looked through them.

"Thorpe," he said, "you didn't sign yours."

"No, sir."

Every head on the mess decks turned toward me.

"Why didn't you sign it?"

I took in a breath.

"I think it's a bunch of shit, sir."

Kickback stifled a laugh. Needler glared at me.

"What did he say, Kip?" Mr. Kempton asked.

"He said he thinks it's a bunch of shit, sir."

Mr. Kempton looked at me. His head was surrounded by a haze of pipe smoke.

"Very well, Thorpe," he said. "You're dismissed."

I headed for the bridge. Barlow was there, so I ducked into the chart house through the passageway door. Hutchinson was inside, sitting at the table. He looked depressed. My troubles were nothing compared to his.

"Me and Hankins were at the Dilligaf Yacht Club," he said in a low voice. "The door came off its hinges, followed by six boys in blue."

"Estorga said that place would get raided," I said.

"Hankins had the stereo cranked up, so we couldn't hear them knocking. There was mescaline and pot in plain sight on the coffee table. When the Vallejo cops searched us, they found heroin on Hankins. They charged us both with heroin possession. Ah've never done heroin. Lightnin'

Lenny thinks Hankins and me were in cahoots. Needler called me an incorrigible dope-dealing con artist."

"They could put that on your tombstone, Jeff."

"You want to hear this, or you want to make jokes? They charged Hankins with possession with intent to distribute and released us to Needler. Hankins backed me up when Ah told 'em Ah didn't know about the heroin, so Lightnin' Lenny said he'd lower the charge to facilitating black marketeering. He scheduled us for separate captain's masts. Ah need to call Daddy, but Ah can't leave the ship. They took mah ID. Ah need your help, Shortcut."

"What can I do?"

Hutchinson took a notepad from his shirt pocket.

"Ah'm going to write down Daddy's phone number. Ah want you to call him and tell him Ah need a military lawyer. You're the only person Ah can depend on. Brogan would probably lose the damn thing."

Through the bulkhead, we could hear Kip arrive on the bridge.

"*Where's that goddamn Thorpe?*" he asked Barlow.

"Haven't seen him, sir," Barlow answered.

"Will you make that call for me, Shortcut?" Hutchinson whispered. "You gotta help me unfuck this situation."

"I'll go to the phone on the pier after knockoff."

"Can't you do it now?"

"I need to stay invisible for a while. Kip and Barlow would hear me if I left now."

"Let me try somethin'."

He picked up the phone and dialed three digits. We could hear the phone on the bridge ringing through the bulkhead and Barlow's voice answering it.

"Bridge, Barlow speaking."

Hutchinson cleared his throat.

"Uh, this is the captain speaking," he said, imitating Lightning Lenny's voice. "Get me Mr. Priskett at once."

Hutchinson put his hand over the mouthpiece. Barlow's voice came through the bulkhead:

"Mr. Priskett, the Captain is on the phone."

Kip's voice didn't come through the bulkhead as clearly as Barlow's. Hutchinson took his hand off the mouthpiece.

"Uh, goddammit, Kip, I can't make heads or tails out of these deck logs you approved... I don't give a rat's ass whose responsibility it was. I want you and Barlow down in my cabin on the double with the originals of these logs, is that clear, Ensign?...What's that?... Well, you may not be a lieutenant JG for long if this kind of sloppy work comes across my desk again. Do you read me? You and Barlow get down to my cabin now, Mister, and bring those originals."

Hutchinson hung up the phone quietly. Kip's voice came through the bulkhead loud and clear.

"Barlow, we need to find the original deck log sheets NOW!"

They slammed and banged a few drawers before we heard them leave the bridge. Hutchinson gave me two bucks in quarters and a handful of nickels and dimes for the long-distance call, and I went down to the pier and dialed his old man's number.

"Jack speakin'," said a voice.

"Mr. Hutchinson?"

"Who's this?"

"My name's Thorpe, sir. I'm a quartermaster aboard the USS *Okmok* with your son Jeff."

He paused for so long that I thought we lost the connection.

"What's that boy done now?"

"He's under arrest for drug possession and black marketeering. He says he needs you to get him a military lawyer."

He took another long pause.

"Did mah son say he'd give you somethin' for callin' me?"

"No, sir."

"Why'd you do it, then?"

"To help him out, I guess. He asked me to call you because they've restricted him to the ship."

"Well, now you've called me. Ah'll take it from here. You seem like a decent fella — Thorpe, was it? Let me give you a little free advice. Stay away from mah son if you don't want trouble. He's just like his mother, contumacious since the day he was born."

"Yes, sir," I said, and we hung up.

I made a mental note to look up contumacious.

Mr. Kempton was reassigned to a diplomatic post in London. The crew was sorry to see him go. Enlisted men are required to show respect for officers, but the crew really did respect Goddammit Jim. I never heard anyone say anything bad about him. He did his job, and he got respect without demanding it. People who demand respect, like Kip and Southcott, don't deserve it and never really get it.

I sat at a table in 02 berthing, looking through *Stars and Stripes*. North Vietnam had taken South Vietnam. President Thieu resigned and accused the United States of betrayal. I turned to the classified section, looking for a swap. Though Kip was sure to shoot it down, I thought some quartermaster at another command might want a San Francisco Bay area duty station bad enough to want to find out why a swap that I requested was being disapproved from my end. If the approving officer on the other end outranked Kip, he might be able to force the swap through. It was a slim hope, but short of going over the hill, it was the only hope I had of getting off the *Okmok*.

Screwball's voice came over the 1MC.

"NOW ALL HANDS TO QUARTERS FOR MUSTER, INSPECTION, AND INSTRUCTION."

We formed up on the second deck. Barlow called the roll and read the POD.

"*Attention*," Chief Hackburn called as Kip walked toward us.

Kip was wearing his mirrored sunglasses, though it was gloomy outside. Chief Hackburn saluted Kip and said:

"X and N division present and accounted for, sir."

"Very well. At ease, men. Have you read the POD yet?"

"That's affirmative, sir," Barlow answered.

"Okay, dismissed. I want to see you, Thorpe."

The division broke up. Hutchinson and Brogan glanced back at me as they walked off.

"I'm recommending you for the Special Weapons Team again, Thorpe. This time, I don't want to hear any more shit about not signing your security clearance."

Now that Mr. Kempton was gone, I knew Kip wouldn't give up trying to get me on the Special Weapons Team.

"I'm not interested in signing anything, sir."

"When you get an order, you obey it, Seaman."

"I won't disobey an order, sir. If you order me to be on the Special Weapons Team, I'll be on it."

"Don't get smart with me, Thorpe. You have to sign that document in order to be on the Special Weapons Team. By refusing to sign it, you *are* disobeying an order."

"I signed my enlistment contract, sir. It says I have to obey orders from an officer. I'm not refusing to carry out an order, sir. I'm only refusing to sign another piece of paper."

"I'm going to give you a chance to think about that, Quartermaster. Either you sign that document, or I'll put you in the brig. Now, get your ass up to the bridge."

"Aye aye, sir."

I didn't want to go to the brig. If Kip had been holding that security clearance in his hand right then, I might have signed it. Kip made a mistake when he gave me time to think. On my way up to the bridge, I remembered the time in boot camp when Bardeen pressured me into donating ten dollars to the United Way for a stupid compliance pennant that nobody cared about—then or now. I remembered how ashamed I felt for caving in to pressure. If Kip needed my signature to put me on the Special Weapons Team, then he must not be able to order me to do it without my consent. That's probably why Goddammit Jim didn't push Stretch or me to sign it when we refused. I didn't think Kip could force me to sign something.

"Okay, Brogan," Barlow said. "Get out to the starboard wing and start scraping. Thorpe and Hutchinson, you two take the port wing."

When we were outside, I told Hutchinson what Kip told me.

"Kip is a one-way motherfucker," he said.

"Do you think he can make me sign it? Legally, I mean."

"Do Ah look like a lawyer?"

"*Thorpe!*" Barlow was leaning out the door from the bridge. "Mr. Priskett wants to see you."

I put down the wire brush and went inside. Kip was sitting at the chart table. Barlow stood next to him. The security clearance was lying on the chart table. Kip had a pen in his hand and a smirk on his face.

"Here you go, Thorpe," he said, holding the pen out toward me. "Sign here."

"Mr. Priskett, I will join the Special Weapons Team if you order me to, sir, but I'm not signing anything."

Kip's mouth fell open. Then, it closed. The smirk was replaced by an agitated look, like a man fighting an involuntary bowel movement.

"Barlow, you're a witness," he said.

"Yes, sir," Barlow answered. "Witness what?"

"You're on report, Thorpe. You're restricted to the ship until further notice. I'm going to report this to the XO. You're going to spend some time in the crossbar hotel. Now, get back out there on that wing."

Hankins got a year in Portsmouth and a dishonorable discharge. For Hutchinson's captain's mast, Daddy Hutchinson brought in a military lawyer, a commander with more seniority than Lightning Lenny. After the legal maneuvers were finished, Hutchinson got a dishonorable discharge instead of a stretch in the brig. He was going home.

After knockoff, I was feeling lower than whale shit. I waited in 02 berthing for Needler to come put the cuffs on me, but nothing happened. I was beginning to think Kip's threat was a bluff. This wasn't East Germany or North Korea, where they could force you to sign papers. The 1MC called supper for the crew. I went to the mess decks and sat with Brogan.

"Hutchinson's dad must have had some pull to get him sent home," I said.

"Hutchinson's dad had nothing to do with it," Brogan replied. "Hutchinson was working for Needler."

"What are you talking about?"

"Needler made a deal with Hutchinson after we got busted for pot in Japan. If Hutchinson helped him bust some of the druggies aboard ship, Needler promised to go easy on him."

"Hutchinson agreed to that?"

"Sure, he agreed, but you know Jeff. The slippery bastard played both sides. Needler wanted him to set up Hankins. Remember the time those three guys surrounded Needler's rack and pissed all over him? That was Hankins and Carranza and Hutchinson."

"Why would Hutchinson do that if he was working for Needler?"

"So Hankins would trust him. Besides, why pass up a chance to piss on Needler?"

"How do you know all this?"

"Because Needler tried to recruit me the same time he recruited Hutchinson."

"Why didn't you tell me this sooner?"

"Why should I? They weren't after you. You never bought any pot."

I thought about it. Maybe that explained why Hutchinson was so buddy-buddy with Hankins at the Peach Hotel in Kaohsiung.

"Hutchinson was something else," I said.

"He sure was. Hey, guess what? Kip recommended me for third-class."

"*What?!*"

"I've got the paperwork right here," he said, patting his empty shirt pocket. "Oh, hell."

After chow, I went to the TV lounge. The guys were watching a documentary on Swedish prisons. The reporter said that the inmates were allowed to have jobs, and they were even paid a small amount of money. They were allowed conjugal visits, and they could go to their homes on weekends, so long as they reported back to the prison by the following Monday morning.

"Hey," Crapshoot said, "that's the same deal we got."

"Except we didn't commit a crime," Doglike replied.

"See if something else is on," Alaska said.

"CHANNEL CHECK!" cried many voices at once.

Bootleg got up and turned the dial. He found a sports show that was replaying Super Bowl highlights.

"Kick ass, Miami," Hookwink said.

"I used to play tailback in high school," Crapshoot said. "A few college teams were looking at me, but then, my knee went out. Now, I'm a fuckin' boatswain's mate. You ever play ball, Shortcut?"

"I went out in high school, but—"

I couldn't speak. I was trying to remember something.

"But what?"

"Nothing. I forgot what I was going to say."

"Fuckin' drifty quartermasters."

I left the TV lounge and stood in the passageway, thinking. I climbed down the ladder and went to sick bay. Finesse was at his desk.

"What's up, Shortcut?"

"My back hurts," I lied.

"Can you touch your toes?"

"No," I said, bending forward a little.

"When did this start?"

"It's been off and on. Just now, I got a pain like a needle."

Finesse scratched his head.

"Back pain is pretty common," he said. "We can put some heat on it. Tomorrow, I'll send you to the base dispensary."

The next morning after muster, Finesse must have told Kip that I needed to go to the dispensary. I was halfway down the brow when Kip called to me from above. He was leaning over the rail by the quarterdeck.

"I don't know what you think you're trying to pull here, Thorpe," Kip yelled, using his hands as a megaphone, "but when the base doctor tells us there's nothing wrong with you, you can add malingering to the trouble you're already in. I'll have you scrubbing shitters for the rest of your hitch."

A low-flying seagull scored a bullseye all over Kip's head and shoulders with a long stream of white shit. I took it as a good sign.

The doctor at the dispensary was a lieutenant. He examined me, and he asked a few questions about the pain. He ordered an x-ray of my lower back. Then, he called me in to his office. The x-ray was clipped to a luminous panel.

"You have spondylolisthesis of the fourth lumbar vertebra," he said. "You never should have been allowed in the Navy to begin with. I'm recommending you for an honorable discharge. You should be processed out of the Navy in two weeks."

He detached me from the ship, and there wasn't a damn thing Kip could do about it. I departed the *Okmok* after muster the next morning. I carried my sea bag down to the quarterdeck. Chief Graves, Screwball, and Crimmons had the watch.

"I'm heading home, Crimmons."

"Good luck, man."

"Good luck to you, too, with Susie."

"She sent me a letter. She got married to some E-4 off the *Pyro*. She said he made more money than me, and he could take care of her family better."

"I'm sorry, Alvin."

"I sent her half my pay for three months. I guess Bootleg was right. I'm a chump."

"Do me a favor, will ya?"

"What?"

I wanted to tell him to smarten up, but I didn't know a nice way to say it.

"Don't be too good for your own good," was all I could come up with.

"Sure thing," he said, but I don't think he knew what I was talking about. I wasn't sure I knew myself. "Nice knowing you, Shortcut."

We shook hands. I saluted my way off the quarterdeck and walked down the brow for the last time. I felt happy, angry, and a little sad all at once.

I was scheduled to spend two weeks at the transient barracks at Treasure Island. Navy red tape being what it was, it took more like seven weeks for my discharge to be processed. We kept the barracks swept and swabbed. We stood armory watches and fire watches. We ate chow three times a day, and we watched television news.

At the end of April, American military forces departed from South Vietnam. The Khmer Rouge had taken control of Cambodia. American military involvement in Southeast Asia had officially ended, but not quite. In May, Cambodian gunboats seized the American merchant ship *Mayaguez* and captured its crew. President Ford sent in an aircraft carrier, the *Coral Sea*, a destroyer escort, the *Harold E. Holt*, and a guided missile destroyer, the *Henry B. Wilson*, and he airlifted the Marine Corps in from Subic Bay and Okinawa. The *Mayaguez* crew was rescued, but not before eleven marines, two Navy corpsmen, and two airmen were killed in the assault on Koh Tang in Cambodia. Three more marines were missing in action. Twenty-three more airmen were killed in a CH-53 helicopter crash en route from Nakhon Phanom to U-Tapao in Thailand. Officially or unofficially, it was the final battle of the Vietnam War.

On June 19th, I was released from Treasure Island, holding my discharge certificate like a shield. I caught a bus to San Francisco Airport, and

I bought a one-way ticket to LA. The fifty-minute flight was leaving in an hour. I went to a pay telephone and called Dad. There was no answer. I tried Estorga's number. He didn't answer, either. I carried my sea bag into the terminal bar and took an empty stool. At one end of the bar, three loud-talking guys in business suits were drinking cocktails, smoking, and laughing. One of them was shaking the ice in his empty glass. A bartender in a white shirt walked toward him.

"Yes, sir?"

"BART-NENDER—*hic!*—I'LL   THIS GENTLEMAN—*hup!*—HAVING   HAS   WHAT HE'S HAVE."

The digital clock on the wall said fifty-five minutes until flight time. I picked up a discarded newspaper with a story about the aftermath of the fall of Saigon. Khmer Rouge death squads in Phnom Penh were slaughtering Cambodians. South Vietnamese and Cambodian refugees were coming to the United States.

"Can I help you?" the bartender asked me.

"Do you have San Miguel beer?"

"Afraid not."

"Whatever's on tap, then."

"Got any ID?"

"I'm a veteran."

"NOTHING'S TOO GOOD FOR OUR BOYS IN THE SERVICE," yelled the guy at the end of the bar.

"Sorry, kid," the bartender said.

I picked up my sea bag and started toward the departure gate. A rear admiral in full dress blues entered the bar. I almost came to attention and saluted before I remembered that I didn't have to do that anymore. I was a civilian.

Further Reading
from the Good People at
Falling Marbles Press

FATAL FRIENDSHIP
by Stephen Paul Foster

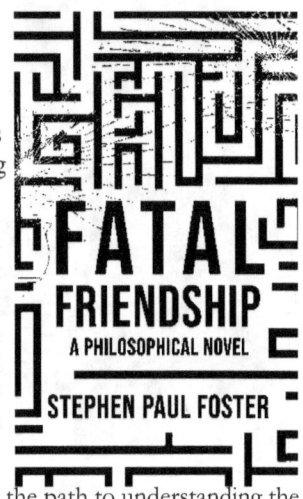

The age-old Rousseau-Hobbes debate solved, merely requiring a grisly murder (or two)

The novel begins when Frank Bradley learns that his best friend, Rich Wahnfried, has brutally murdered his girlfriend. The ghastly news that his friend was a closeted monster detonates Frank's confidence that he knows anyone, starting with himself.

This philosophical novel follows the path to understanding the darkness in the human condition.

RAVENS ON A WIRE
by Andrew Bacevich

Vietnam's dark legacy, as faced on the West German border

The first novel from noted historian and author of over a dozen books, Andrew Bacevich, *Ravens on a Wire* chronicles a routine border incident and its subsequent investigation, during which the wounds of Vietnam find themselves on the verge of being reopened. For some, the regiment's motto—"Duty, with Honor"—would seem to demand this reopening, however painful the results.

Further Reading
from the Good People at
Falling Marbles Press

The Catty-
Corner
Conversations

Fifty
Dialogues
With The
Diagonally
Opposed

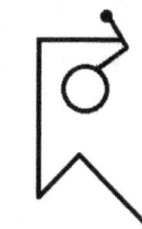

Mike Cole's Catty-Corner Conversations is a launched attack against assumptions. Covering existence to the infinite, these arguments between neighbors address all issues, both the age-old and the new. The Final Edition covers all fifty Conversations as well the Third Edition's Introduction and a new Afterword. Recorded, edited, and designed by Michael H. Cole, this knowledge of all available for $9.99.

F⊙lling
M⊙rbles

Check out the Falling Marbles website for
all current and upcoming titles

www.fallingmarbles.com

www.ingramcontent.com/pod-product-compliance
Lightning Source LLC
Chambersburg PA
CBHW071641260626
47170CB00001B/192